The Scottish Isle of Cairnmor is a place of great beauty and undisturbed wilderness, a haven for wildlife, a land of white sandy beaches and inland fertile plains, a land where awe-inspiring mountains connect precipitously with the sea.

To this remote island comes a stranger, Alexander Stewart, on a quest to solve the mysterious disappearance of two people and their unborn child; a missing family who are now heirs to a vast fortune. He enlists the help of local schoolteacher, Katherine MacDonald, and together they seek the answers to this enigma: a deeply personal journey that takes them from Cairnmor to the historic splendour of London and the industrial heartland of Glasgow.

Covering the years 1936-1937 and infused with period colour and detail, The Call of Cairnmor is about unexpected discovery and profound attachment which, from its gentle opening, gradually gathers momentum and complexity until all the strands come together to give life-changing revelations.

Sally Aviss

The Call of Cairnmor

The Call of Cairnmor
by Sally Aviss

Text © Sally Aviss, 2014
Front cover image courtesy of Kate Philp (www.katephilp.co.uk), © 2014
Rear map source image courtesy of the University of Texas Libraries.

Published by Ōzaru Books, an imprint of BJ Translations Ltd
Street Acre, Shuart Lane, St Nicholas-at-Wade,
BIRCHINGTON, CT7 0NG, U.K.
www.ozaru.net

First edition published 5 February 2014
Printed by Lightning Source
ISBN: 978-0-9559219-9-5

For my daughter Elizabeth,
who needed another book to read

Acknowledgements

I am indebted to my family – Peter, Timothy and Elizabeth Aviss – for their unfailing encouragement and support; to Christine Lord, Annette Vidler and Katie Boughton, my 'reading panel', for their enthusiasm and erudite observations; to Carol Dodd, at my local library, for her ability to conjure up even the most obscure research material; and finally to Ben Jones, of Ozaru Books, for his skilful editorial suggestions, attention to detail and willingness to publish my books.

Note on pronunciation of Gaelic names

For readers unfamiliar with Gaelic, its spelling and pronunciation may appear daunting. In this book, only one such word appears regularly enough to warrant special mention: the name Mhairi is normally pronounced "Vah-ree". Fictional names such as Cairnmor, Lochaberdale, Lochfoyle etc. are anglicized and may safely be pronounced as they appear to an English speaker.

Contents

PROLOGUE

Diary entries:

22nd April, 1909

Mhairi has written to me about the Isle of Cairnmor and how it would be a wonderful place for us to live and bring up our baby after it is born. So today, I went to Hatchards and ordered two books – one on the history of Scotland and the other by the author George Fergus Mayhew, all about his travels around Cairnmor and Cairnbeg.

I shall look forward to reading these; it will help me feel closer to my Mhairi. But any hope of us being together anywhere at the moment seems impossible and I am filled with frustration and despair because of it.

2nd September, 1909

I received another letter this morning... Mhairi sounds desperate... her time is so near. I must go to her. But how?

4th September, 1909

It is all arranged! I am going to go to Mhairi. Maybe if I am there, I can prevent our baby being taken away after it is born. I have written to Mama and explained why I am going.

Thomas got me the train tickets yesterday and has given me money. I said I would pay him back but he said no, he was glad to help, that Sir Charles was being unreasonable and cruel. I have never heard Thomas be so outspoken before.

He and Cook have been true friends to me these past months, especially in making sure that I receive all of Mhairi's letters.

With Thomas's help, I shall make my escape tonight. I have been a virtual prisoner here since February. I cannot stay any longer. I must go to Mhairi. I love her and she needs me...

CHAPTER 1

Cairnmor
October, 1936

The day dawned quietly, just like any other day, but it was destined to be a day unlike any other.

The sun emerged over distant mountains, casting deep shadows across the valley below. Light filtered slowly into the bedroom of a thatched-roof stone cottage set high upon a hillside, gently awakening a young woman as she lay sleeping peacefully. She stirred and turned to face the morning sun; sensing its warmth on her face through the uncurtained windows.

Gathering her thoughts, she remembered that today was Saturday and she had promised herself the morning to do with exactly as she pleased. In the afternoon, she would go down to the quayside at Lochaberdale to see the Royal Mail steamer arrive on its weekly journey from the mainland.

Her reflection turned to the times when the steamer was unable to make the journey to the Isle of Cairnmor – times when the sea was too rough, or the forecast too stormy. Then, the islanders could be on their own for weeks at a time, cut off from civilization; forced to rely upon their own ingenuity and resourcefulness.

However, today was not one of those days. Today the sun was shining, there was little wind and *Lochfoyle*, a veteran of the one hundred and sixty mile round trip from Oban, would arrive and after some hours depart, thus providing the sole incoming and outgoing delivery service for the islanders of post, provisions, produce for market, and any passengers who wished to travel.

Katherine stretched luxuriously in her bed, revelling in its warmth and comfort. However, once she had left the protective layers of blankets and eiderdown, she dressed quickly – for sunshine or not, it was late October and the morning seemed cold. She went into her kitchen, stoking up the range with fresh peat before making porridge for her breakfast, which she ate while reading a book.

She replenished the fire in the tiny sitting-room from the small stack of peat on the hearth, put on her coat and shawl and once outside, followed the steeply sloping path that led downwards to the sea shore.

Sun-lit white sand stretched out before her, clean-washed by the waves. In the hazy distance, majestic mountains soared, dominating the skyline; spacious, uplifting. She loved her part of the island, the southernmost part, and this was her favourite place of all.

Along the curve of the beach, Katherine could see an old tarred wooden shack in the distance and beside this the seated, stooped figure of a man dressed in deep blue, protected from an off-shore breeze by the coarse marram grass of the sand dunes. He looked up in greeting as she approached, pausing from the skilled task of mending the fishing net spread before him; a large needle poised in his work-roughened hands.

"Och, 'tis a fine day, Katherine, especially for the time of year."

3

"Aye, Robbie, it is." She surveyed the view out to sea. "*Lochfoyle* will be along this afternoon, then?"

"Oh aye, though the weather 'tis set to change in the next day or so."

Katherine knew that Robbie was one of the most knowledgeable and well-respected people on the island in his interpretation of meteorological conditions but even he could not always gauge the unpredictable weather on Cairnmor, where huge storms could erupt as if out of nowhere, borne on the westerly winds that blew in regularly from the Atlantic. His standard reply when people ventured to ask him for a forecast was, "Aye, see what it looks like when ye get up in the mornin'!" However, on this day, the accumulation of cirrus clouds in the sky made a prediction straightforward.

"Are ye off for a wee stroll?"

"I thought I'd go up by Flora's cottage."

"The 'family' mansion?" A rare smile crossed his face, but far less rare was the humour that twinkled in the bright blue eyes of his weather-beaten face.

Katherine laughed at this, a gentle expression of acknowledgement. "I wish it was, Robbie, that I do. She and I have the same surname, but I expect that's as far as it goes. 'twould be a good thought if it were true now, wouldn't it?"

"Aye, she would make a bonny ancestor!"

"Well, that's as may be, but our MacDonald cottage is nothing but a sad ruin with the roof caved in and the inside all exposed to the elements – not much of an heirloom there, I think! And especially so as we cannot prove Flora was born here. Other islands can claim that distinction with far greater historical accuracy than we can."

Robbie nodded his head in agreement. "Aye, 'tis true enough."

Katherine turned back towards the old fisherman before continuing on her walk.

"See you at the quay this afternoon?" she called by way of farewell.

The old man replied with a wave of his hand and said, "Aye, lass. I wouldna' miss it!"

Approximately half-way along the six mile stretch of sand, there lay a rocky outcrop and here, Katherine took the path away from the beach; a stony, uneven path that led gradually upwards to a vantage point where she stood for a long time, taking in deep breaths of pure, clear air; absorbed by the spectacular vistas that unfolded before her.

To the west of the island, the magnificent broad sweep of the bay with its white-gold sandy fringe dominated. Further south, a cluster of cottages, tiny in the distance, nestled peacefully by the startlingly blue, sky-reflected water of the tidal sea loch that gave Lochaberdale both its name and the large sheltered natural harbour that enabled commercial contact with the outside world. To the east, in the far distance, rising to over two thousand feet at their summits, were the awe-inspiring peaks of the high mountains.

Finally, although not immediately visible from her viewpoint, beside and beyond these summits and all along the eastern seaboard, sheer cliffs connected precipitously with the sea. Few people lived there, for it was a most inhospitable terrain.

Katherine pulled her shawl closer around her head as imperceptibly, the wind began to rise – in little wisps and fingers at first before gradually becoming more persistent. It had a keen north-westerly edge to it and she decided that Flora's cottage would have to wait for another day.

It was time to go home; time to prepare a meal before commencing her long walk around the bay to Lochaberdale in order to witness the arrival of *Lochfoyle*.

By the time Katherine reached the harbour that afternoon, the quayside was crowded, not only with people and suitcases, but also with barrels, wooden crates and impatient livestock tethered and penned.

Although the ship would stay in the harbour for some hours, the local inhabitants were anxious to book their position in the hold for whatever they wished to transport. All prospective travellers had tickets, of course, but the position in the hold was a matter of local pride and the first in the queue managed to obtain the best places.

At this time of the year, the steamer was always busy, as people took what could be their last opportunity to visit relatives and conduct business on the mainland before the winter storms set in.

On this day, the appointed time for *Lochfoyle*'s arrival came and went. It was late. This caused a great deal of consternation among the island folk as they waited.

What could have happened to it? they asked, turning to each other. Was there bad weather over on the mainland or had it not sailed at all? Worst of all, had it met with some terrible misfortune on the way? But, of course, there was no need to worry – the boat was often late; the crossing from the mainland could take anything from eight to ten hours depending upon the weather.

Speculation about *Lochfoyle*'s late arrival was a regular occurrence and usually cheerful in its delivery. It was just part of the anticipation of a very important weekly event in the lives of the islanders. It also masked an innate respect and fear of the sea, born of long experience, among those who lived on this remote archipelago.

Katherine listened quietly, sitting on the harbour wall, observing the chattering blue-clad women close by, shawls drawn tightly over their heads as protection against the wind.

She waved to Robbie over on the quayside and he returned her greeting. She smiled to herself contentedly; secure within the community she loved and to whom she owed so much; at peace on an island that had nurtured and sustained her throughout her life.

On the horizon, a tiny plume of black smoke became visible and the minuscule dot of a ship gradually became larger and more real as it steamed its way towards Lochaberdale. The pace of activity on the quayside slowed until everyone stood motionless; watching, waiting, anticipating the boat's arrival.

As *Lochfoyle* carefully approached the pier, there was an immediate flurry of activity as ropes were thrown and the steamer moored securely to the bollards that lined the quay.

The gangplank was lowered and the arriving passengers were the first to disembark. There were many hugs and kisses with excited chatter of imparted news that could not wait another moment as relatives, not seen for a while, arrived on shore. Then, having gathered their luggage, they set off in the direction of home.

Last to leave *Lochfoyle* was a smartly dressed man carrying a briefcase and a medium-sized suitcase. This aroused considerable interest among the womenfolk who had come to see the steamer arrive – *a stranger*, they exclaimed to each other, *and one so attractive-looking*! *He must be from the city.*

The children on the quayside smiled shyly at him and he returned their smiles, traces of laughter lines showing round his eyes; his manner conveying vitality and intelligence as he surveyed his surroundings.

He addressed a group of young women nearby who merely giggled and hid all but their eyes with their shawls. Slightly disconcerted by this response, he then spoke to several of the men sitting on the harbour wall. None answered, but there was no hostility in their manner; they merely smiled and nodded.

Feeling somewhat exasperated and his equanimity disturbed, he paused at the start of an upwards-leading path and for a moment his gaze met and held Katherine's as she sat on the wall observing him. She did not blush or look away, but merely continued to regard him steadily, yet not discourteously.

He approached her cautiously and said, "Excuse me, I wonder if you could help me?"

"That depends on what it is you need help with," she replied noncommittally, but very politely.

"I'm looking for the Lochaberdale Hotel."

"You are almost already on the path to it at the moment. If you continue away up the hill, it's the white painted building just there," and Katherine indicated a large, imposing Victorian building that held a commanding view of the loch and the surrounding headlands. "You can't miss it."

"Ah, thank you." The stranger moved to go, but paused and turned back to her, a puzzled expression on his face. "Tell me, no one on the quayside seems to want to talk to me. I'm curious as to why that should be."

"Och, the girls are just shy of strangers and the men sitting on the wall speak only Gaelic." She smiled at him, gently amused. "I presume you addressed them in English?" The man nodded and Katherine continued, "Ah, then that would account for it, would it not?"

He smiled back at her – a very charming and attractive smile. "It would indeed," he said and turned to leave in the direction she had indicated. "Goodbye, and… thank you."

"You're welcome," she said.

For a moment, their eyes met and held and then he was gone. She watched him as he walked slowly up the hill towards the hotel, turning to wave to her before continuing on his way. She raised her hand in acknowledgement and regarded him thoughtfully for a while.

CHAPTER 2

As he approached the hotel, the stranger noticed that its apparent grandeur when viewed from the harbour became slightly tarnished as he grew closer. Signs of wear and tear, together with gently peeling paintwork on the window frames and walls, lent an air of pleasant neglect and homeliness. However, the large front door possessed a shiny well-polished brass handle and elaborate door knocker which he used, firmly and decisively.

When there was no reply, he repeated the action. As this also evoked no response, he tried the door. It was unlocked and opened easily at his touch. Once inside, he found the lobby to be deserted.

A mahogany reception desk with a rank of wooden pigeon holes behind stood to the right of the door. Two large ledger-type books rested on the counter, together with a few smaller ones, hard-backed, with the binding in three different colours – red, green and blue. Next to these was a bell with a notice saying 'Ring for Service', which he duly did.

Nothing. There was no sign of anyone.

He rang the bell again and waited. No one.

So he sat on one of the large sofas that lined the wall opposite the desk, found a newspaper, which turned out to be several days old, and began reading the previous week's news.

Once again, as with his arrival on the quayside, he had the feeling of a somewhat inauspicious start to his assignment. However, he was prepared to make the best of it and became so absorbed in his reading that he jumped involuntarily when a voice, coming from the direction of the corridor leading away from the lobby, called out, "Och, ye must be Alexander Stewart. I received the letter ye sent all right. Welcome to Lochaberdale and the Isle of Cairnmor!"

Alex stood up as the man who had spoken approached him, and they shook hands.

"I'm John Fraser, the manager. I'm sorry to have kept ye waiting – big problem with the hot water boiler. It's the only one on the island and Jimmy Gillies and I have been trying to mend it. One of the pipes sprang a leak, fortunately in the cellar where the boiler is, so the damage is not too drastic – nothing that a mop and bucket won't fix. Needs a new pipe though – we've cobbled it together for now, but I'll have to order another from the mainland. Could take weeks." John smiled, friendly and welcoming, before saying, "Anyway, enough of my problems."

Alex took to him immediately and began to feel more at home in what had seemed, up to that moment, a somewhat alien environment.

"Now, I expect ye'll be needing a hot bath and a meal after yere journey. Was it too unpleasant? *Lochfoyle* is not renowned for her smooth sailing abilities, even when the seas are relatively calm."

"No, it was fine on the whole – just very long," replied Alex.

As he spoke, John moved round behind the desk and opened one of the books next to the large ledgers. He turned it round and placed it in front of his guest, together with an ink pen and pot of ink. "Please could ye put yere name and address and signature, there. Ye're in room eight on the first floor – it's at the front – wonderful views over the harbour."

Having completed his task, Alex asked, "How many rooms do you have?"

John turned the ledger round and added his own signature and the date before replying. "We've sixteen rooms and one private suite for the proprietor."

"The proprietor?"

"Oh aye. The owner of the hotel and most of the island."

"Most of the island?" Alex was surprised. "Forgive me, I seem to be asking a lot of questions."

"Och, that's all right. Ask away, Mr Stewart. Ye see, the crofters and most of the people who live on the island are tenants and pay rent to the proprietor for their property and the right to farm here. Aye, the Laird owns most of this island as well as Cairnbeg, Cairnmor's 'little sister' a few miles to the south of here, and all the smaller outlying ones as well."

Alex's curiosity had been aroused and he asked if the proprietor was a good landlord.

John smiled. "Well let's put it this way, he barely visits the island but once a year when he stays for a couple of months, and that's mainly for the hunting and fishing with his cronies. The rest of the time, the owner leaves his Factor to manage things on his behalf. Ross Muir is a fair man and doesn't interfere, so we're left to run things pretty much as we like. Which suits us independent-minded islanders just fine!" he remarked cheerfully. "No, the Laird's content so long as his rent is paid on time, his tenants are doing well and he doesn't have to make too much effort to look after things!" As he spoke, John collected the keys for room number eight from the row of hooks beside the pigeon holes.

"Shall we go up now?" he said, this being more of a statement than a question, and Alex followed, picking up his luggage, mulling over their conversation.

John led him along the corridor and up some stairs covered in a somewhat threadbare, though still richly red-coloured carpet. The wooden stairs beneath the carpet had a friendly creak to the tread and having reached the top, John turned to the right and opened the door of Alex's room.

"The nearest bathroom is just down the corridor there and dinner is at six o'clock in the dining room. There's no rush, there's only yourself and two other guests – both friends of the proprietor staying at the moment. Take the time to make yourself at home. I must go now and sort out the cellar. Goodness knows what Jimmy has been up to!"

After thanking his host, Alex shut the door and surveyed the room. The bed looked comfortable and warm, with a substantial eiderdown. The furniture was large and Victorian, mostly mahogany, but it was the magnificent view, just as John had said, that attracted Alex's attention. He was immediately drawn to the large floor-to-ceiling bay window and stood admiring the truly wonderful sight before him – the deep blue of the loch, the golden-white sand of the beach, the rocky coves and isolated inlets.

Although here purely on business, Alex found himself irresistibly drawn to this place; an occurrence he had not anticipated, especially given the unpromising reception he had received on his arrival.

Reluctant to leave the vicinity of the harbour, Katherine made her way to the post office to see if she had received any letters even though she knew it was very unlikely that the mail would have been sorted as yet. However, if it had been, then she would save the postman a trip up to her croft.

Katherine's encounter with the stranger stayed with her and she replayed their meeting in her mind several times over as she walked towards the line of single-storey cottages where the post office was situated.

Inside, the bulging hessian bags of post took up most of the floor by the counter, while Donald MacCreggan, the postman, and his wife Annie, who ran the little shop, transferred them to the back room for sorting. Katherine could see it would be some time before the letters and parcels would be available for individual people so, after a brief conversation, she bid the busy couple a cheery goodbye and decided to make her way home.

As she passed the quayside, Katherine suppressed her curiosity and desire to go up to the hotel and find out who the stranger was and why he had come to the island. He had not come for the hunting, that much was certain, because he was neither dressed in the manner of, nor did he look like, one of the crowd who regularly visited the island during the season for fishing and shooting.

Therefore, having resisted the temptation to go to the hotel, Katherine paused to watch the men skilfully operating the hoists on *Lochfoyle*, lowering sacks and crates, farm implements and building materials onto the quayside, from where it was taken away in carts and barrows before being collated for distribution to the crofts and farms. Other men stood by the harbour wall, chatting and smoking, waiting patiently until their livestock and goods could be loaded or lifted into the hold.

Katherine knew only too well that this was the commercial lifeblood of the islanders; of real significance in their ability to survive in their chosen way of life.

As the shadows lengthened and the sun's warmth no longer counteracted the strength of the wind, people began to drift away and Katherine turned for home, ascending the sloping pathway that led around the bay and up into the village of South Lochaberdale where she lived.

"Katie, Katie – fuirich mionaid!"

Because of the direction of the wind, Katherine did not immediately hear anyone call out for her to wait and she only became aware of someone's presence when a very out of breath, attractive young woman of her own age caught up with her.

"Stay a moment, Katie MacDonald, and I'll walk with you. Let me get my breath back first!" Katherine waited obediently, pleased to see her friend.

Few people called her 'Katie' now – she preferred 'Katherine' – but she and Mary had always been close, dating from the time when they were very little, and the childhood name remained.

"I didn't see you earlier. Were you at the pier?" she asked of her rapidly recovering companion.

"Och no, I was seeing Adam and his parents. I've only just come away." With Mary having recovered her breath, the two women resumed their walk up the steep slope.

"Did they want to talk about the wedding?"

"That they did!" Mary's eyes sparkled and she blushed. "Oh, Katie, I'm so excited. It's only two weeks away and I can't wait! Do you really like your bridesmaid's dress?"

"You know I do. You've done marvellous work on it – I could never do such intricate stitching. You're a wonderful seamstress. One day someone from the mainland will come and offer you a job and tempt you away from us!" Katherine smiled.

"Och no, that could never happen, especially as Adam's work is here. He's his own master now that he's got the majority share in the boat. When he's away fishing, I'll be tending the croft and doing my dressmaking. And when he's not at sea, he'll be able to help with the chores. I know it'll be hard work but it's what I would like – that and lots of children!"

"I know you would." Katherine paused before saying, as gently as she could, "Adam has been drinking again recently, hasn't he?"

It had to be brought out into the open; it needed to be discussed. They had few secrets from each other.

Mary was suddenly downcast, her eyes focussed on the path. "Yes, I know he has. He goes out with his friends and can't seem to help himself."

"I'm afraid that they are a bad influence on him. They do nothing to help him curb his addiction."

"It's worse than that. They egg him on. 'twould be better if he never saw them." Mary sighed. "The problem is, that because the three of them own the boat together, when they get back to harbour with the catch, Adam feels obliged to spend time socializing with his mates."

"He doesn't have to."

"I know. But I'm sure that once we're married, I'll be able to help him control his craving. We love each other and that has to be enough to make the difference. He'll be spending his time with me, not them." She hesitated for a moment before adding, "I know you have doubts about him, but I don't. So, please can we leave it at that?"

A look of pleading in Mary's eyes betrayed her mounting anxiety so Katherine, good friend that she was, let the subject drop, not wishing to upset her companion further.

They walked on in silence for a while and then talked of other things, but especially the dance that was happening in Lochaberdale that very evening.

"Robert Campbell and his son will do us proud, don't you think so, Katie?"

"Aye, he's a fine piper and Andrew is a real expert on the accordion. The MacLennan brothers are all set to bring their fiddles too, so it'll be the real event we all hoped for, I think."

"Will you be playing the piano tonight, Katie?"

Katherine smiled. "Only if someone asks. I was quite hoping to have the evening off just to dance and let someone else provide the music for a change! I'll sing though, if that's what's needed."

The sun had begun to set on the distant horizon; a horizon visible between the two headlands at the entrance to Loch Aberdale. Katherine and Mary paused, enjoying the spectacle as the sun lit up the sky in a last red-gold flowering of light before gently sinking below the horizon, leaving the land to darken towards night.

From the window of his room, Alex was startled out of his passive observation of the dwindling activity on the pier by seeing the woman he had met earlier by the harbour wall. She was making her way along the quayside and onto the path that led around the sea loch and up the other side, towards a distant village, not much more than a cluster of cottages, nestling in the hillside. He assumed that this was where she lived.

He saw her friend running to join her and continued to watch as they ascended the steep path arm in arm, pausing to admire the view and the wonderful colours of the setting sun. He watched until he could no longer see them; until twilight had enclosed them in obscurity.

He wondered who she was and knew that he would like to meet her again. It had been a day of surprises and this trip was not going at all as he had imagined it would.

Alex unpacked his suitcase and laid out his wash things. He felt jaded after his long journey, having left home some thirty hours previously.

He had taken the night sleeper from London Euston station, finding the experience most enjoyable, especially as the express train had been hauled by the Royal Scot class *Princess Elizabeth*, one of his favourite engines. Having embarked on his journey to Cairnmor with a feeling of great anticipation, he had slept but fitfully on the train. As a consequence, he was awake and already dressed when the steward had knocked on his compartment door announcing breakfast.

On arrival in Glasgow, Alex had changed stations, taken another train, this time to Oban, and finally, the steam ship to Lochaberdale.

Yes, he was tired. It had been exciting, but now he needed a long, hot relaxing bath.

He took one of the large, white, thickly piled towels from the towel rail that stood beside the wash basin in his room and made his way along the corridor to the bathroom. It was spacious, warm and clean. The mahogany cupboards and panelling on the wall behind the bath and amply proportioned sink lent an air of old-fashioned elegance to the surroundings.

An open fire burned in the grate, not laid with coal or wood, as Alex would have expected, but with what he presumed to be peat. There was a very distinctive smell to the room; not unpleasant, but one he found strange as he was unfamiliar with its smoky, somewhat elusive aroma. The bath was large and Victorian, with plenty of hot water (despite the boiler problems) and for a very pleasant half hour, he gave himself up to the warmth of the water and atmosphere within the bathroom.

When at last Alex returned to his bedroom feeling refreshed and revived, someone (John, the manager?) had replenished the fire in his room and had also lit the ornate oil lamps – one on his bedside table and one on the large chest of drawers. The room seemed cosier, but still quite formal in its style. The décor was functional rather than artistic, but Alex appreciated its practicalities.

Once dressed, he stood at the window again, reflective and relaxed. The steamer was still in the harbour, silhouetted against the last vestiges of light on the western horizon. Only a few people remained on the quayside; their lamps moving purposefully as they completed their tasks, the activity winding down.

Alex drew the heavy brocade curtains, shutting out the night-darkened world, and made his way downstairs to the dining room.

As they reached Katherine's cottage, Mary said, "See you at the crossroads at seven – don't be late! We're on the last run and Donald says if anyone's not waiting for him, the post-bus will leave without them!"

"Aye, but he's a fine person to do the pick up at all – especially after a day's work! See you later!"

Katherine was looking forward to the ceilidh that evening. The villagers, both north and south of Loch Aberdale, had worked hard together over a long period of time to raise funds for the construction of a new hall. Once the necessary finance had been collected, with a generous contribution from the Laird, they had seen the project through from beginning to end – planning, construction, building, decorating.

There was deep pride that the hall had been built by them all; each person's contribution something special, no matter how large or small; each addition appreciated and accepted gratefully. It was a very practical example of community spirit in a very close-knit and supportive community and the dance that night was a celebration of their achievement and the first event to be held in the newly completed hall.

Katherine went into her warm, fire-lit kitchen and as she did so, spied the pile of school books on the table waiting to be marked. She had promised herself a day off and she would keep to that promise; they would still be there in the morning and could be completed then.

Feeling carefree, she busied herself in preparing something to eat. There was time to sit and relax by the fire with her book before getting ready for the evening's exertions. She settled herself, comfortable and cosy. But her attention kept wandering; she found herself starting to read the same words over and over again.

Her mind kept returning to her brief encounter with the stranger earlier that afternoon; the recollection of his words, the sound of his voice but above all, his presence permeated her thoughts. Katherine realized, with some surprise, that he had made a profound impression upon her. She wondered whether they might meet again. Perhaps he would be at the ceilidh.

Her heart quickened at the thought.

CHAPTER 3

When Alex reached the dining room, he found that each table was laid precisely with a crisp, white damask table cloth, cutlery, glasses and napkins. He chose a table near the window and very shortly afterwards, two other guests, both male, ruddy complexioned and laughing loudly at some shared joke, entered the room. They sat at a table by the door and for this Alex was grateful, feeling the need for solitude rather than enforced socializing.

Soon, a tasty vegetable soup was served, to be followed by the rest of a surprisingly good three-course meal. Alex declined the offer of whisky, preferring water to drink, but his fellow diners accepted with alacrity and soon their laughter became even more raucous.

As he finished his dessert, the two men came over to his table and, with jocular coercion, tried their best to persuade Alex to join them at the bar, where they were now heading, to have a convivial drink.

Firmly, but as politely as he could, Alex refused, preferring his own company, but also because their particular personalities were not to his taste.

Disappointed, the two men left the dining room and after emptying his glass, Alex also departed. As he walked through the lobby, he espied John standing behind the desk working at one of the large ledgers.

Alex approached him and said, "That was an excellent meal, thank you. I enjoyed it very much."

"I'm glad to hear it! I'll pass that on to my wife, Marion, who's the cook. She'll be delighted. Not too many of our guests say anything, they just take everything for granted. It's always nice if someone does take the trouble."

"Well, I certainly appreciated it!" Alex paused, wondering whether this was a good opportunity to ask some questions.

This man was certainly an established part of the community; he obviously knew the island and its people well and could possibly provide some information that would help Alex in his quest, the very reason for his journey to Cairnmor.

However, before he could ask anything, John said, "Will ye be joining the other guests in the bar a little later?"

"I don't... think so," said Alex carefully, not wishing to sound impolite.

John smiled, showing a measure of understanding. "Aye, I appreciate what ye mean. Well, if ye're looking for something to do this evening, there's a dance at the new hall just down the road, if that interests ye. Everyone's celebrating its opening and it's the first event to be held there. Marion and I will go a bit later if we can get away. Jimmy's not one for the dances, so he can see to things here. Otherwise, there's not much else to do of an evening for our visitors; plenty for a local person though and ye know everyone. Sometimes we have whist drives and dinner dances for the guests here at the hotel, but that's usually from April onwards once the winter storms have abated and there are more visitors. The islanders come too and we get the pipers in from the mainland – grand occasions they are, indeed. The proprietor usually brings people with him for the summer and sometimes they join in, but usually they spend most of their time with the hunting and fishing." John lowered his voice and leaned forwards across the desk confidentially towards Alex. "Not to my taste personally," he said.

"Nor mine, I have to say," replied Alex, with a smile.

"However, it's my job to make sure they're well looked after and it takes all sorts to make the world go round."

"It does indeed," agreed Alex, liking this man's friendly, fair manner.

He sensed that John wished to return to the task in hand, although he was too polite and hospitable to say so. There would be no time for any enquiries that evening.

"I can see you're busy, so I won't keep you from your work any longer. I think I may go for a walk and then maybe try the dance."

"Aye, that sounds good. Well, take care if ye walk. Away from the main street, it is very dark and there are many places to catch out the unwary, but especially so if ye're new to the island!"

Alex thanked him and assured him that he would be careful. After collecting his overcoat, scarf and hat from his room, he made his way out of the hotel and down the path towards the harbour.

The steamer was about to leave and quite a crowd had gathered to witness its departure. Once it was safely away from the pier and the ship's lights a mere twinkle in the near distance, everyone turned away from the harbour and happily laughing and talking, began to walk along the track towards the line of thatched cottages that comprised the main road of the township of Lochaberdale.

Alex decided to follow them. A walk on his own in the dark had lost its appeal, and these people would presumably lead him to the new hall.

Would she be there at the dance, the woman he had met at the quayside?

He recalled their brief conversation in vivid detail and imperceptibly, his pace quickened.

As Alex entered the hall, having hung his coat, scarf and hat in the entrance vestibule, he was met with a feeling of energy and excitement. Many people wished him a pleasant evening and he felt welcomed by their words and smiles.

He stood just inside the doorway, soaking up the atmosphere and observing the interior of the hall. Although he was no architect, Alex appreciated the thought and care that had gone into the design of this building so that it could serve whatever purpose was needed.

Inside, the hall was spacious in its construction. Wooden beams, arched and high, supported the roof and the walls were stone, whitewashed and pristine, while on the ground were suspended wooden floorboards.

Along one wall there was a pair of open glass-panelled doors and beyond that, down a few steps, Alex could see a second room, smaller than the first, with trestle tables – on this special occasion laden with food.

The larger hall was lit with Tilley lamps supported by brackets attached to the wall as well as hanging from the beams overhead, with a cleverly disguised pulley system for lowering and raising, thus enabling them to be primed and pressurized.

Bathed in their atmospheric light, Alex sat on one of the benches that lined the walls of the main room and waited for what might happen next.

Almost immediately, with a dramatic entrance and a swirl of the pipes, the piper entered the room. Without hesitation, all around him, people stood up forming a large circle and after the musical introduction, proceeded to dance.

Alex recognized it as one of the many he had learned while taking part in Scottish country dancing at university. He had disliked the sessions at first, having gone along merely to support his best friend who needed a distraction at the time but, proving to be rather good at it, had found himself in great demand by the female students, whose attentions he had afterwards increasingly enjoyed.

Alex watched with interest as the dance progressed; the man behind his lady partner, now going forwards, then backwards, turning, the lady going round in a circle and then both of them dancing in a waltz hold until the whole sequence was repeated over and over again.

It was a simple dance in its construction, but there was an expertise here, a natural sense of rhythm and adherence to the beat of the music which the piper played with great panache, mesmerizing in his phrasing and variety of ornamentation.

Alex had never particularly liked bagpipes, the drone and the sometimes variable pitch offended his musicality, but he had never before heard them played like this. They were so right for the setting; so appropriate for the country he was in; so perfect for the island.

He felt moved, an inexplicable stirring deep within him and he wanted to be on the floor, joining in with the dance.

At that exact moment, he saw her, the attractive young lady he had met earlier. She came close to him before moving away almost immediately with the next steps, partnered temporarily by a burly and thickset man who danced surprisingly well for his size and build.

Alex experienced a moment of concern – a boyfriend? – no, there was nothing in her demeanour that gave any suggestion of this. Relieved, he continued to watch the dance. On the next turn she saw him and smiled, a wonderful smile, and then she was gone, away with the next sequence of the dance.

Alex's breath caught in his throat and he knew he had to dance with her.

The sequence ended and without any hesitation, the piper took up a different tune; a slower, introductory melody, and the girls and women immediately took up positions on the benches around the edge of the room. The men formed a long line while the man at the head of the line went over to the benches, bowed and extended his hand to the girl of his choice. She, modestly, with eyes cast down, but with the hint of a smile came onto the dance floor as his partner.

Alex was persuaded to join the men and found himself fifth in line to make a choice. Heart thumping, he watched while the first and second, then the third and fourth made their choices, and when it was his turn, as though in a dream, he went across to the one person with whom he wanted to dance. He bowed and Katherine, after accepting his offered hand, blushed and followed him onto the dance floor in the manner of the other girls.

Glad to have survived the ordeal, Alex, charmingly, placed his hand on his chest with an expression of relief. Katherine smiled at him, understanding at once what he meant. After that, she studied him covertly each time his attention was drawn into watching the proceedings.

Interesting these proved to be, as some girls refused the offer of a particular partner, and needed a lot of persuasion to overcome their reluctance. This caused great amusement among everyone on the dance floor and also among those just watching, because some strong physical tactics were employed in several cases. However, it was all carried out good-naturedly and appeared to be just part of the fun.

When the piper could see that everyone had a partner, he immediately changed the tune and struck up a lively melody for the next dance. Alex recognized the steps and knew that he would be able to participate without fear of embarrassing himself.

His partner was as fluent in the dance as he and they stayed together for the next one and several more after that – all of which followed on without a pause from the piper, who, at the end of the present dance, would play a few linking bars before proceeding onto the next. Eventually, even the prodigious energy of the dancers and piper came to a temporary halt, and welcome liquid refreshments were served.

They walked together to the long table where the drinks were being dispensed, neither wishing to leave the other's company. They both chose lemonade as being the most refreshing beverage available and smiled at each other before moving away from the crowd to sit down across the other side of the room where there were fewer people.

"I think we ought to introduce ourselves – I'm Alex Stewart," and he held out his hand, which she took. It felt warm and familiar after all the dances they had shared.

"And I'm Katherine MacDonald. Hello."

"Hello." A moment's pause, then he said, "You dance very well."

"Thank you. So do you."

Suddenly, there were many questions Katherine wanted to ask, so much she wanted to say, but she was unable to find the words.

They both started to speak at once. "What brings you… ?" "How long have you… ?"

Alex smiled again. "You first."

"What brings you to the island?" she asked.

"I'm here at the request of my father, Alastair," he replied simply.

"Your father?"

"Yes. He's a solicitor." He smiled at her.

"A solicitor?"

"Yes."

"And you are… ?"

"I'm a barrister."

"Oh." Katherine was taken aback slightly. Prior to this conversation, she had assumed he was a tourist; a late-season holiday-maker. She had not expected him to be a barrister. "Are you here professionally?"

"Yes… and no."

16

"Now what's that supposed to mean?!" she exclaimed good-naturedly.

"I'm not here to represent anyone on the island, but I am here acting unofficially on behalf of my father, who was prevented from coming, to try and solve a mystery. You may be able to help me."

"If I can. What kind of mystery is it?" asked Katherine intrigued, wanting to know more.

"The Mystery of the Missing Heir," replied Alex, with suitable dramatic emphasis.

"You make it sound like the title of a Sherlock Holmes detective story or a sensational newspaper report!"

Alex laughed. "I can just see the headline now: Murder! Mystery! Suspense! Remote Scottish Island Reveals All!"

"I sincerely hope it's nothing like that!" Katherine was shocked.

"So do I," agreed Alex. "But it is a very important matter and has to be resolved, and soon."

"So tell me…"

"I'm searching for the missing heir to a vast fortune. My father has, or rather had, a very important client called Sir Charles Mathieson, who recently passed away…"

"Sir Charles Mathieson? The owner of Mathieson's Shipbuilding and Engineering Firm on the River Clyde?"

"The very same."

"Goodness me. A *very* important client!"

"You've heard of him?"

"Of course. Who hasn't?! He's only one of the most famous shipbuilders in Scotland. I used to pass by the firm's head office every day while I was at college in Glasgow."

"You were at college in Glasgow?"

"Aye, I was."

"I should like to hear about that."

"And I shall tell you, but first, if you don't mind, I want to know more about your missing heir."

Pleased by her obvious interest, Alex continued. "Well, twenty-seven years ago, his only son and heir went missing and was never found. My father and I have evidence to show that there may be a connection to Cairnmor…" but before Alex could elaborate further, Mary and Adam came over to them and introduced themselves.

"Isn't the hall looking grand!" said Mary. "I'd so like our wedding dance to be held here."

"It's Donald you'll need to speak to." Katherine turned to Alex and explained, "Donald MacCreggan – he's away over there with his wife Annie – is our postmaster and he's responsible for the bookings for the hall. Mary and Adam are going to be married in two weeks."

"Congratulations," he said warmly, shaking hands with both of them.

"Thank you," responded Mary, before looking up anxiously at her fiancé. "Why don't we talk to Donald – now, while he's free then we'll know it's all settled?"

Adam, who had said not a word and had spent the time looking round the room and fidgeting as though he was anxious to be elsewhere, merely nodded his head.

Mary smiled up at him with such a look of love that Katherine and Alex were caught in its radiance but her glance was returned absent-mindedly by her fiancé, who cooled the atmosphere by his lack of responsiveness. Mary seemed not to notice or, if she did, she closed her mind to it.

Katherine watched them go across the room towards Donald and his wife before saying softly, almost to herself, "I hope she's made the right choice."

Alex took this in, but discreetly chose not to remark upon it. "You're very close to Mary, aren't you?" he observed thoughtfully, also left with a feeling of unease by Adam's manner and his attitude towards Mary.

"Aye. She's my dearest friend, and has been since we were little. In fact, I can't remember a time when we were not close. We've rarely quarrelled, we've always supported each other and I can't imagine being without her. She's like the sister I never had, but without the competition for parental attention."

"Do you not have any brothers?" he asked.

"No, I'm an only child. My parents were much older when I came along and never had any more. Mary has two older brothers and one younger, so I'm something of a sister for her too."

"I can imagine!" said Alex, with understanding. "I have a much younger sister and an older brother who's in the Royal Navy. He's a lieutenant aboard the cruiser H.M.S. *Exeter*."

"Very distinguished. Are you close to him?"

"Not really. I'm closer to my sister Lily and my best friend Michael than I am to Edward. In many ways, he's always been the odd one out in the family. My mother dotes on him."

Katherine was not slow to discern a subtle hint of resentment in his voice.

However, before either of them could pursue any further conversation, the room gradually fell silent, and someone began to sing, spontaneously, unaccompanied; soft Gaelic words blending perfectly with the lilting, haunting melody.

Alex, taken completely by surprise, was moved by its simplicity, its plaintiveness, its beauty. Just as the dancers had focussed on their dancing, they now listened with rapt attention to the singer. There was a stillness in the room such as Alex had not encountered before. He watched the transformation on the faces around him and felt the wonder as, after a while, everyone took up the melody together, voices blending in perfect harmony.

He sat there vulnerable, absorbed and next to him, Katherine's voice rang out, clear and true as she sang the next verse on her own. Admiring the beauty of her singing, Alex knew that to him, she was the most desirable woman he had ever met.

The silence that followed the ending of the song was as special as anyone, even the islanders, had experienced. And that silence was held for a long time, until there was a communal sense in the room that it was time for the dancing to begin again. However, this time, it was the fiddlers and the accordion player who took up the tuneful task.

Alex held out his hand to Katherine, which she took as though it was the most natural thing in the world. Together, they took to the floor to join in with the complex, kaleidoscopic patterns of the dances as they evolved.

Supper was served at ten o'clock, by which time neither the dancers nor the musicians could play or dance any more. The stamina of the islanders was remarkable, but even they had their limits. The benches were carried into the room with the tables and everyone sat down to enjoy a home-made feast, to which all the islanders involved with building the hall had contributed.

Katherine listened and joined in with the general conversation, with Alex sitting by her side as though he belonged there. He was attentive and solicitous towards her and Katherine recognized and acknowledged the deepening attraction between them.

Out of courtesy towards their guest, those that could speak English did so and those that were unable to, spoke in Gaelic, with Katherine acting as interpreter. Alex was regaled with funny stories, mishaps, tales of near disasters and there was so much laughter that many people were in danger of severe indigestion. It was indeed a very good evening for everyone, just as the islanders had hoped that it would be.

Once the used plates, cups and cutlery were stacked and an army of helpers had washed, dried and tidied away in record time, the men formed two lines on the dance floor, facing each other. The piper took up his stance on the raised platform at the end of the hall and Alex whispered to Katherine, before she joined the ladies standing at the side of the room, "I don't think I can dance another step!"

"Wait and see!" was all she replied, producing a white handkerchief from the pocket of her dress.

The ceilidh that evening had begun with the men choosing their partners. So it ended with the girls selecting theirs – dancing individually in turn, firstly down the centre of the two lines and then back up on the outside, placing her handkerchief on the shoulder of her favourite partner. Then the two of them waltzed out of the door together. This continued until the hall was empty and the piper ceased his piping, thus bringing the ceilidh to a definite but attractive conclusion.

Katherine had no hesitation in choosing Alex and together they waltzed out of the door of the hall, out of the vestibule and into the surprisingly mild, but very windy, night air outside. Reluctantly, they let go of their dance hold and as they did so, Alex lightly brushed Katherine's hand with his fingertips. He smiled as she reacted to his caress.

"Shall I see you tomorrow?" he asked softly.

"Yes." She hesitated, her hand still tingling from his touch, before saying quietly, "It's Sunday tomorrow, well, today, and everyone goes to church. Will that suit you?"

Imperceptibly, he paused before replying. "That suits me fine. And afterwards, will you have lunch with me at the hotel?"

"Thank you. I'd like that very much."

"How are you getting home tonight?" he asked.

"I'll be walking up the hill with Mary, as we always do after a dance. But we'll be fine – this is the Isle of Cairnmor, after all, and not an impersonal city where danger lurks round every dark corner!" she replied with a smile.

Alex moved to kiss her but resisted the impulse, very aware that this was not the sophisticated circle in which he habitually moved nor, for her sake, would it be appropriate with so many people around that she knew.

Having collected their coats and located Mary, who had been saying goodnight to Adam, the three of them made their way back towards the quayside, with Katherine and Mary leaving Alex at the footpath to return to the hotel.

He said, as they turned to go, "See you tomorrow."

"Yes," replied Katherine.

The two women continued on and up the long, winding path to their village, treading their way carefully in the darkness.

Mary, good friend that she was, tucked her hand into her companion's arm and after a long silence, the only thing she said, very gently, was, "He is a stranger to us, Katie. And he lives far, far away in London. In a different world."

"I know."

However, nothing could disturb Katherine's sense of happiness and well-being; nothing could detract from the way that she felt. She was walking on air and for the moment at least, practicality played no part in her thought processes.

CHAPTER 4

The next morning was slightly overcast, with a stiff breeze blowing in from the sea. The people of Lochaberdale arrived at their church, which was set high above the small town on the hill overlooking the harbour, in a continuous stream of twos and threes; mostly on foot, some on horseback or a few by pony and trap.

For many, this necessitated a very early start and a late arrival home after the service, but such was their devotion to their faith, they did this every week without complaint and with a genuine piety and humility.

Some of the women were dressed traditionally in warm, thick shawls and long woollen skirts; their hair hidden underneath a headscarf tied tightly at the back. They went in to the building first, while the men remained outside, chatting in small groups, conducting business and making arrangements for deliveries during the forthcoming working week.

At eleven o'clock, the priest, Father Aidan McPhee, Scots-born but of Irish extraction, came out of the church door to check for any late arrivals; waiting for those who had furthest to come. The service never began until Father McPhee was sure everyone had arrived. He was made aware, by their friends or family, of anyone who was ill or incapacitated in some way and could not attend. The good priest would make a mental note to visit the next day, if he did not already know of their infirmity.

His emergence from the church at this time was also the signal for the men to enter. Alex, who had arrived with John Fraser from the hotel, entered the building with his companion and was surprised to find all the women seated on one side of the church and the men on the other.

"An ancient custom," whispered John, as they took their places on the benches on the men's side of the church.

Alex looked for Katherine and saw her near the front, seated with Mary and her mother. From his position he could watch her unobserved, and he smiled with secret pleasure at the thought.

Eventually, the last few remaining stragglers came into the church and Father McPhee, satisfied that all his parishioners were present, came down the aisle and the service began.

The Mass was conducted in Latin (with which, having been raised as a Catholic, Alex was very familiar) interspersed with many long pauses for silent reflection, while the sermon and concluding prayers were in Gaelic. Unable to understand a word of what was being said in both of these (although Father McPhee was obviously striking a chord with his congregation as there were many murmurs of assent and wise nodding of heads at his pronouncements from the pulpit) Alex took the opportunity to look around the building as well as studying Katherine.

Like many island churches, the interior was spartan but not austere – there was a grace and simplicity which Alex found peaceful, yet uplifting. Architecture was obviously very important to these people, as he had witnessed in the new hall, and revealed a tradition of care and attention to detail that must have been handed down through the generations.

The windows of the church were quite high but strategically placed to let in the maximum amount of light, essential for the dark days of winter, while giving the best possible protection from the worst ravages of the weather. The thick whitewashed stone walls gave a feeling of solidity and continuity, as well as light and space.

This was a building of full of spirituality; rich in history and prayer. The décor was not ostentatious – small pictures around the walls illustrated events from the life of Christ – and both the service and the building were devoid of the severe formality that always left Alex with a sense of unease.

It had been several years since he had attended a church service of any kind and as this one progressed, he found himself much affected by the simplicity of the building and the quiet devotion of the people that surrounded him.

At the end of the proceedings, Father McPhee bid farewell to his parishioners with a warm handshake, pausing to talk to anyone who desired his attention. He was welcoming to Alex, whom John introduced.

"'tis always good to greet a visitor," he said, giving him a very firm handshake. "Will ye be staying long?"

"I only have a week and I plan to catch the steamer back to the mainland next Saturday. I have to be in court the following Wednesday, but…" and Alex paused, aware of Katherine waiting for him at a discreet distance, "… that depends, I suppose, on the weather."

Alex gave the sky a meaningful look which, during the time they had been in church, had filled with dark brooding clouds. Even to his untutored eye for island weather, this did not seem to bode well.

"Oh, aye, ye're right. If it's as bad as it looks at the moment, this one could be set in for a while." Seeing other people patiently waiting to greet him, the priest concluded their conversation by saying, "Aye, but it's good to meet ye." Then he chuckled to himself. "Ye danced very well last night with yon lassie over there!"

So, the priest misses nothing, thought Alex.

The two men shook hands, and Alex thanked him, not quite knowing what else to say after Father McPhee's last remark.

"Don't worry, lad, it's fine – she's a grand girl – and if I'm not much mistaken, ye're a grand lad as well!"

Alex smiled pleasantly and they parted amicably. John, who had come out of the church with him, went on his way with a cheery wave of his hand, saying, "See ye shortly – lunch is at one!"

Alex returned his wave and walked over to Katherine.

"Hello," he said simply.

"Hello," she replied with equal simplicity.

They turned and walked together along the stony track across the hill towards the hotel, rather than going down to the harbour and up again.

Katherine glanced at her companion every so often and Alex smiled each time she did so, until they both laughed and he said, "Have you recovered from the exertions of last night?"

22

"Aye, but I have to confess that I ache in places I had forgotten existed but it's not too bad. On Cairnmor, we are used to physical exercise. We tend to walk everywhere if the distance is not too great, otherwise we ask Donald for a ride in the post bus if there's an event or business to conduct on other more remote parts of the island. And then there's John, who will give a lift in his pony and trap if he's free. Many people have bicycles, so we do get around! How about you?" she asked.

"Well, I have to confess that I nearly nodded off once or twice during the sermon, especially as I couldn't understand any of it."

"You'll just have to learn Gaelic!" said Katherine, half hoping and half joking.

"Is it a difficult language to learn? It has a particular syntax with a distinctive rise and fall. The songs last night were incredible." Alex turned directly to face her. "So was your voice."

Katherine blushed. "Thank you," she said. "Do you sing? You certainly seem to appreciate music."

"Ah, well, for my sins I was a choral scholar at Magdalen College, Oxford."

Katherine was impressed. "Goodness! But I thought you were a barrister; surely you would have had to study law?"

"I did. Scholars read a variety of academic subjects, not just music."

"Did it help towards paying your fees?"

As money had not been a consideration for either for himself or his family, Alex smiled at her question.

"It did, and I received an allowance as part of the scholarship. Also, accommodation is provided within the College precincts for all undergraduate scholars. Which is fortunate because Academical Clerks, as choral scholars are known, are required to sing at five of the seven weekly services held at the chapel, as well as attend choir practices and concerts. Our duties took up about twelve hours a week, so I was grateful not to have to find digs in the City and travel into College every day."

"How did you get the scholarship?"

"By competitive audition. I'd been a chorister since the age of eight at Westminster Cathedral Choir School and later at Eton, where I sang in the Chapel Choir once my voice had settled. So, it was a natural progression for me, if you like. But there was no guarantee that I would win a scholarship to Oxford, I just thought that it was worth a try." Alex turned to Katherine once again and smiled.

"Did you have music lessons as part of the scholarship?" she asked thoughtfully.

"Yes. We all had singing lessons as a matter of course, but I also was lucky enough to be able to continue studying the piano as well."

Katherine liked the unassuming, matter of fact way that he had disclosed the information; simple statements in response to her questions. Very lawyer-like, in fact, but with an element of enthusiasm and pride which she found endearing.

Once they had reached the hotel, after hanging up their coats on the coat stand in the corner of the room, they sat down at a table by the window. Terrific storm clouds were building out to sea and beyond the shelter of the harbour, waves were pounding the shore line, throwing up white-capped spumes of spray.

"We could be in for a nasty storm," observed Katherine. She wondered what her companion might think if it should turn into a really violent one.

But Alex seemed unconcerned and once their dinner had been served, he asked, "What about you? I remember you told me at the dance you went to college in Glasgow?"

Education and academic experience were very important to him and with regard to Katherine, it had become a vital piece of information in the jig-saw of her character. But the detail with which she furnished him was better than anything he could have anticipated.

"Yes, but before that, I did a history degree at Edinburgh University. I too was awarded a scholarship but it was an academic one and paid all of my fees, excluding books. I'd had singing and piano lessons while I was at boarding school on the mainland and continued with those at University. I sang in the Edinburgh Choral Society, as well as all the usual college choirs and concerts." She watched the amazement on Alex's face. "It would seem we have a lot in common," she added, touched by his expression of delight and surprise.

"I never expected..." For a moment, he was lost for words, an unusual occurrence.

"To find anyone here on Cairnmor with my background?" said Katherine, finishing his sentence. "We're not backward illiterates, you know!" she added, reprimanding him gently.

Alex was immediate in his response. "Oh no, I wasn't meaning that, not at all."

"I know, I was just teasing."

"I meant that the chances of finding anyone anywhere with that much in common is pretty unlikely but to travel all this way and find someone... someone... like you, here on this remote island... well, the odds against that happening must be... astronomical."

He regarded her with such open admiration that Katherine felt herself blushing and growing warm under his scrutiny.

"What did you get in your degree?" he asked presently. This woman was obviously intelligent, but exactly how clever was she? Again, he was not to be disappointed with her answer.

She smiled modestly, yet she was proud of her achievement. "First Class Honours. Though as I'm a woman, it has yet to be recognized as a degree." She shrugged. "Who knows – maybe the law will change one day and it will be. What about you?"

"The same. Though mine is recognized."

"Perhaps you could move for the law to be changed on behalf of deprived, university-educated females everywhere!"

When he didn't respond in the way she had hoped, they sat in silence for a while; Katherine studying him covertly, just as she had at the dance, wondering about him.

A discreet cough from John awoke her from her reverie, as he waited by the table to remove their plates, both of them having finished the meal.

Slightly embarrassed, she thanked John for providing them with such delicious food and accepted his suggestion of coffee in the lounge.

Once there, Katherine said to Alex, "I still haven't found out what brings you to Cairnmor. We kept getting interrupted last night and of course, there wasn't a lot of time for talking!"

"The dancing got in the way rather, didn't it?!" said Alex, his eyes mischievous.

Katherine laughed. "Just a bit! Though I loved every moment." She stopped, afraid that she had revealed too much.

However, Alex seemed to take it in his stride and she assumed from this that he felt the same.

It gave her the confidence to say, "I really would like to know."

"Wait a minute and I'll show you!"

Alex disappeared upstairs, returning quickly, just as John was serving the coffee, placing a tray containing the coffee-pot, extra hot milk, two cups, saucers and spoons and a small china pot containing lumps of sugar on the low table in front of Katherine, before leaving discreetly.

Like Father McPhee, he too had missed nothing in this rapidly developing friendship between Katherine and Alex Stewart, the very pleasant stranger. It was of great interest to everyone in Lochaberdale but in a protective way, as their schoolteacher was very special to all of them.

Alex sat down on the sofa beside Katherine and extracted from his briefcase a large, manila envelope. It contained three documents. An official looking letter, a photo, very much crumpled round the edges, and a smaller, hand-written envelope, which Katherine presumed contained a more personal message of some kind.

She poured out the coffee and milk – neither of them took sugar – and Alex began.

"My father, Alastair…"

"A solicitor."

"Yes. He's the senior partner in the law firm which he runs, along with two colleagues, and which is situated in London, just off Chancery Lane. He and I frequently work together as it's something we both enjoy; our outlook and approach are very similar. It makes for a very good partnership and as my Chambers are not too far away, near Middle Temple Lane, there is easy communication between us." Alex paused to take a sip of coffee.

"Your Chambers?" asked Katherine.

"Yes. Rather like your Scottish equivalent of advocates, barristers are essentially self-employed, but in England, they work in a building where they share costs and clerical staff, which are called Chambers. It's a system that works very well." Alex paused for a moment. "Now where was I?"

"Sorry," apologized Katherine, anxious that he might not like to be interrupted.

"Please, don't apologize; ask me anything you like at any time! But do stop me if I get carried away with my own enthusiasm!"

"Oh no, I love your enthusiasm!"

Once again, the words had slipped out before she realized what she was saying. For his part, all he wanted to do was to take her in his arms and kiss her, and it was with some difficulty that he prepared to speak again.

After clearing his throat, he said, "One of my father's specialisms is in drafting wills, handling probate and so on, as well as being an executor and finding missing beneficiaries named in a will. Those don't come up too often but on this occasion, he's asked me to help as he's particularly busy and can't be released to do the research himself."

"So that's why you're here in an unofficial capacity to look for the missing heir to Sir Charles Mathieson's fortune."

"Correct." Alex took another sip of coffee. "How much do you know about Sir Charles?"

"Well," replied Katherine, "seeing Mathieson's head office every day made me curious, so I decided to do some research on him in the public library. If I remember correctly, he started out as a surveyor for Lloyds or something and then became chief designer and general manager of a small engineering firm on the Clyde. It prospered through the success of his designs and he became a partner and eventually took it over."

"At which time, he renamed it Mathieson's and his company eventually became a world leader in ship design and marine engineering." Alex was impressed. "You obviously have a mind for detail."

"Aye, I hold a great store of useless information!" she replied self-deprecatingly. "Though in this case not quite so useless, it would seem!" she added, with a smile.

"It's a remarkable firm, actually," continued Alex, "constructing many of the most famous cruise ships and warships in Britain. I believe I'm right in saying that Sir Charles Mathieson designed the majority of those and built up a fantastic design team to assist him."

"Why did he choose a solicitor in London, rather than Glasgow?" asked Katherine.

"That's a very good question," replied Alex. "It would seem that he kept his private and business lives very separate. Sir Charles owned a house in Park Lane, as well as one in Glasgow and once he could leave the day to day running of the shipyard to his highly-trained managers and designers, he spent more and more of his time in London, entrusting his English affairs to a London solicitor. This turned out to be my father, who had been recommended to Sir Charles by a friend.

"Having been made a Baronet, Sir Charles felt he needed to spend more time in the capital. But he still maintained a very close connection with the shipyard, making frequent journeys to Scotland overseeing orders and contracts, as well as being Chairman of the Board."

Alex paused and after offering Katherine more coffee, who declined, he refilled his own cup and took a sip.

"However, before all of this took place, he and his wife, Emily, and their only child, a son called Rupert, divided their time between living at their Park Lane mansion and another very grand establishment called Minton House in Govan.

"When his son was seventeen, Sir Charles decided, against his wife's wishes, so my father tells me, that Rupert should learn the shipping business from the bottom upwards, familiarizing himself with all the many trades that go with building ships, so that when the time came to take over the family firm, he would be in a very good position to do so."

"How did Rupert feel about this?"

"I have no idea. I asked my father the same question when he told me the story and he doesn't know either."

"This is fascinating, please go on. I really want to hear what happens next!"

Alex smiled, finding her enthusiasm refreshing after the affected world-weariness of his accustomed social set.

"Well, Rupert had spent only a few weeks at the shipyard when he met the daughter of one of the foremen working there."

"Let me guess," said Katherine, "they fell in love but with parental disapproval on both sides."

"Well, one assumes so as it would certainly be consistent with the time. Anyway, the romance, for whatever reason, was allowed to continue. However, Mhairi, that was the girl's name, fell pregnant and was sent away in disgrace to an aunt's farm somewhere in the Lake District until she had had the child. Rupert was hauled back to London and he and Lady Mathieson then remained permanently based in the house in Park Lane. However, Rupert and Mhairi must have written to each other, because the evidence is here in this letter. And here's a photo of the two of them."

Katherine and Alex studied the photo together; a very crumpled picture of two young people, clearly absorbed in each other, their lunch spread out on a chequered cloth precariously balanced on the young man's lap, and she sitting on a stool, her face upturned towards him. Behind them both was the half-built structure of a ship, cocooned in wooden scaffolding with long steel cables supporting enormous metal plates.

"You can see how much they are in love, just by looking at them or am I simply being fanciful, putting my own interpretation onto them after the story you've just told me?" said Katherine.

"That's exactly what my father said. He also thought that it looks like the photo has been screwed up and then smoothed out again."

They sat in silence for a while, studying the picture once again. Then Katherine asked, "So what happened, did she have the baby?"

"Well, this is where the mystery begins and the reason for the investigation. Both Mhairi's father, the foreman, whose name was Jock Hamilton, and Rupert's father were insistent that…"

The door to the lounge opened and two people came into the room. Unfortunately, it was the rather unpleasant diners that Alex had avoided on his first evening in Lochaberdale.

Katherine said, in a low quiet voice, "We can't talk here. I've seen these men before and they're not the most pleasant of people."

"That's an understatement!" replied Alex, with equal discretion. "Where can we go? Any suggestions?" He began gathering cups and saucers and stacking them on the tray.

"Not driving you out surely?!" called out the larger of the two men, never one to miss the opportunity of socializing with an attractive-looking woman. "Thought we might all have a cosy chat, what?!"

"Thank you very much, but we were just leaving."

Alex and Katherine made a hasty retreat out of the door with Katherine carrying the briefcase and Alex the tray. She closed the door quickly.

"A narrow escape, *what*?!" said Alex, once they were safely out of earshot, with an excellent imitation of the man's exaggerated English drawl.

"*Oh, quite right*," said Katherine, displaying equally good mimicry skills. "*Tally ho!*"

The two of them were laughing so much that Alex almost upset the tray and had to be rescued by Katherine. Their hands met; their fingers interlocking as they held onto the edge of the tray.

It was a significant moment and they looked at each in acknowledgement. The contact had been made and nothing could change that now.

Taking a deep breath, Alex said, "Shall we take the tray into the lobby and see if we can find John to give it to?"

"That sounds like a very good idea," replied Katherine. "I'm just wondering where we can go to continue our conversation."

"I suppose that my room is out of the question?" It was more of a statement than an enquiry, yet there was more than a little hope contained in the words.

"I'm afraid so." She was definite about this.

Acknowledging her reply, Alex said, "They care for you very much here. I wouldn't do anything in public to harm your reputation."

"Thank you," replied Katherine. "You didn't have to say it, but I'm glad that you did. Look, the storm hasn't broken yet," she added, going over to the window, "and I think we have some time before it does. Why don't we walk round the bay, the wind's not *too* strong? I've enough layers with me for a hurricane and you've got a thick coat. Shall we?"

"Sounds good to me!"

They put the tray down on the desk at reception and Alex quickly went up to his room once again, leaving Katherine to put on her coat and scarf.

Soon he was down again, and the two of them went out of the door into the invigorating air of Lochaberdale.

28

CHAPTER 5

The door swung behind them with a discreetly satisfying 'swish', something that Alex had not noticed the previous day when he had first arrived.

Was it only yesterday? His other life seemed something distant, something remote.

Holding his briefcase in one hand, Alex took Katherine's hand with the other and together they walked down the hill towards the harbour, turning left and up the winding track that led towards Katherine's croft instead of going towards the pier.

The storm was rumbling ominously some miles out at sea; flashes of sheet lightning illuminating the black clouds. Then, unexpectedly, the sun came out over Lochaberdale, drawing out the brilliant green and gold colours of the hillsides and highlighting the darkly foreboding skies across the bay.

With the village and harbour bathed in golden sunshine, Alex and Katherine paused and smiled at each other. Neither broke the moment by speaking but both knew what the other was thinking. Why shouldn't they both feel that the sun had come out especially for them?

Katherine led them along a narrow stone-embedded path which meandered round the hillside for some little while before descending into a small valley, completely sheltered from every direction of the wind. Alex stood still, amazed by the contrast of this scenery with all he had seen so far of the island.

There were trees.

His face must have been a picture because Katherine laughed and said, "Yes, trees! The only ones on the island. It's too windy and exposed in most places or else the soil is too rocky and poor to support the roots."

"There's willow and elder and maple, I can't quite believe it!"

"I know, it's amazing isn't it? I have no idea who planted them, because we're too far away from the mainland for them to be wind-blown or self-seeded originally. They're not very tall, about ten feet or so – in fact they haven't grown that much since I was little – but there are more of them, so they must be seeding themselves."

The sunshine was very warm in the sheltered copse and they both discarded their coats. Then Katherine said, "Come on, I haven't shown you the best bit yet."

This time, she took Alex's hand and they walked round a small rocky outcrop protruding from the hillside and there, in all their ruby reds and deep pinks, thriving in their secluded, sunny home were roses. Alex laughed and shook his head.

"Aren't they wonderful?" said Katherine. "I discovered them as two tiny bushes when I was about ten years old and I used to bring sea-weed from the beach to fertilize them. I even ordered a gardening book from the mainland catalogue on how to look after roses. But the other amazing thing is, the thorns are just soft and bendy, they don't prick you. It's incredible."

"Roses in October?" mused Alex, coming close to her, entranced by her tale but most of all by her.

This time he didn't hesitate as he had done after the ceilidh; this time he kissed her, exploring her lips with his, tentatively at first then with more depth and strength, encouraged by her responsiveness to him. After a few moments, Katherine drew back; her spontaneous reaction to his embrace having caught her off-guard.

"You really love this island, don't you?" said Alex as they sat down together on a large, flat, smooth stone set against a mossy bank.

"Yes, I do. Sometimes I feel as though I'm part of its very fabric, that it's part of me. It's difficult to describe."

Alex considered her words before replying. "I think I understand what you're saying. I've only been here two days but there's something about the island that goes straight to your soul; something deep and elemental. No hiding place."

"Aye, that's very true."

"But of course, how I feel might have something to do with my present company…" He smiled at her disarmingly and pulled her closer to him.

Katherine made no move to resist him, though she knew she should. He kissed her once again; confidently, passionately, until she was lost in his embrace. He laid her back against the bank, his expression full of admiration as he traced a line around her face. Then, filled with desire, he kissed her lips, her cheeks, her neck; his hands moving down over her body.

Closing her eyes, Katherine responded to his caresses not giving a thought as to how fast things were progressing, how rapidly she was falling in love with this man, a virtual stranger; how she wanted this ecstasy to go on forever.

However, when his fingers began to seek out the top buttons of her blouse, she wisely lifted her hand to his and called a halt. He smiled, understanding her action and respecting her wishes, but it took a while for his heart to stop pounding; for his ardour to cool.

After some moments, to distract himself, he said, "Tell me something about you and your life on the island."

Trying to still her own rapidly beating heart, Katherine said, "Where do I start? I suppose Cairnmor is the only home I've ever known and I've always been able to explore it to my heart's content – finding this oasis for example. If I'd lived in a town or city, I couldn't have roamed so far afield, although I love discovering new places." Ingenuously, she smiled up at him.

"So do I," he said, raising an eyebrow and lifting a stray strand of her hair back in place.

He took her face between his hands, feeling her cheeks become warm with his touch and kissed her again. Then, unable to resist the temptation, he undid the top buttons of her blouse, his fingers gently exploring the softness of her skin beneath.

With great presence of mind, she removed his hand and kissed it, holding onto it firmly. She felt no anger at his persistence, as some women might have done, but realized that with this man, she needed to be very strong-minded when they were on their own if she was not to find herself in a compromising situation.

Thus distracted, it was with some difficulty that she managed to bring her mind back to the innocent conversation they had begun earlier. Alex made himself comfortable by laying his head in her lap and Katherine rested her hands lightly on his shirt, occasionally stroking his hair.

Presently, he asked, "Didn't you miss not having any brothers or sisters? I know I would have done."

"Not really. As an only child, I've always been happy in my own company; you learn to make your own amusement. Not that I was ever short of friends, but I never minded having time to myself."

"Didn't your parents mind you going off by yourself?"

"Here, anyone is perfectly safe if you know the terrain and are home before dark. Besides which, there are any number of cottages where you can drop into on your way. And I did when I was younger – island people are very hospitable and rarely turn anyone away, particularly a child; their safety and well-being is always paramount. Local families will always look after someone in distress or who is genuinely lost. Not that I ever did get lost but in that situation especially, any child is cared for and then taken back home to their parents.

"Through my wanderings, I made many friends. If the person was elderly and lived alone, I would help out in some way around the croft and was usually rewarded with milk and biscuits or cake – bliss for a small hungry child. I had quite a collection of people on my 'rounds'!"

"Did you miss the island when you went away to boarding school?"

"Yes, I did, very much. But I suppose we all grow up accepting the education system here. You go to an island school until you are fourteen then you either leave or go onto board at a secondary school on the mainland until sixteen or eighteen. I went to the girls' boarding school in Oban and carried on to University."

"What about your parents? Did you miss them?" Alex was curious, Katherine had not mentioned her mother and father at all. Neither did they seem to have been at the ceilidh.

A shadow seemed to pass across her face, and her eyes filled with tears. She wiped them away hastily. "Sorry," she apologized.

"What is it, darling? Please tell me." Alex sat up and turned to her, concerned that his question had obviously caused her pain.

After a few moments, Katherine spoke again. "I'd only been away for a couple of months at boarding school when there was an outbreak of diphtheria on the island and many people died, including my parents. They were quite elderly by then and I suppose more vulnerable."

"Were they not vaccinated?"

"There had been no vaccinations on the island until that outbreak. Then everyone was given one after that. Those of us who were at school avoided the outbreak and also, we'd been inoculated as a matter of course when we first went to school in Oban. The authorities just hadn't got around to vaccinating the island populations, especially as the immunization programme was quite new. But it was too late to help my parents and all the others."

"I'm so sorry," said Alex, tenderly wiping away a few remaining tears.

31

"Oh, I'm over it now. It's more than twelve years since they went, but it still gets to me sometimes. Perhaps I'm more vulnerable at the moment," she said shyly, hardly daring to look at him.

Alex smiled and said reassuringly, "Well, I'm here now."

"Yes, I know…" she replied, wondering at the implication of his words.

"How did you manage after your parents passed away? Who looked after you? Wouldn't you have had to leave school?"

"No, I was able to stay on. A couple of the other girls in school had lost relatives and friends too, so we were a comfort to each other. And the islanders were wonderful to us when we came home. I was adamant that I wanted to continue living in my parent's croft; I needed to know that my home was still there whenever I came back for the holidays. It was the only way I could cope at the time.

"Understanding this, Mary's parents and brothers took over tending my parent's animals and Mary herself kept the place clean. Father McPhee and Robbie, you haven't met him yet, but you will, together with a few other islanders, raised money for travel and books so I could continue my education. So, you see, once I had qualified, I wanted to come back here and give something to the community that had supported me for so many years. I never even considered looking for a job elsewhere. I was, and still am, deeply involved with island life."

"You don't have any lingering doubts?" He was curious about this.

"No. I suppose intellectually, I would love to have stayed on at Edinburgh and continued by doing a post-graduate course. But I couldn't justify the extra expense. I really enjoy teaching and working with children, so it's no sacrifice."

By now, Katherine had regained her composure and something of her cheerfulness. She looked up at the sky as the sun disappeared completely behind the gathering clouds and she knew it was time for them to make a move. They put their coats back on – Alex helping Katherine into hers – and as they left the shelter of their idyll, rounding the corner and resuming their climb up the hill, they were buffeted by the full force of the wind.

The sky was darkening rapidly, flashes of lightning were visible over the bay; the resultant thunder rumbling loudly. Before they had gone much further, huge drops of rain began to fall, gaining momentum quickly.

"Come on," said Katherine. "My croft is only just a few hundred yards away, round this corner."

They ran as best they could up the steep incline and had just reached the shelter of the cottage when the rain came sheeting down and the storm broke overhead with a ferocity that surprised both of them. Quickly, they went inside, together having to push the door closed against the powerful buffeting of the gale.

"That is some storm!" said Alex with genuine feeling.

"Isn't it just?!" replied Katherine. "When we get them, we get them! This one could go on for days. It has all the hallmarks of being a long one."

"What does everyone do in those situations?" asked Alex.

"We all sit tight and ride it out as best as we can! The children love the extra day or two off school."

"Even if the parents don't!" added Alex.

Katherine laughed. "You're quite right there. But a storm like this is very difficult for tending the animals and making sure they are all safe. And miserable for those who have to go out and see to them. Dangerous too, sometimes." She paused for a moment and then said, "Would you like a cup of tea and something to eat?"

"I thought you were never going to ask!" said Alex. Lunch seemed a very long time ago.

While Katherine busied herself, stoking up the small black-leaded range with peat from a wicker basket in the corner of the room and filling the kettle from the pump at the sink, Alex sat down on one of the chairs at the table in the centre of the room and asked, "Where does the water supply come from?"

"From the burn that flows down the hill. My mother got fed up with having to go out in all weathers and walk half a mile to collect the water every day, so Dad put in underground pipes to the cottage. It made her life so much easier. He did it very well, actually, and it works very efficiently."

"So I see," replied Alex. He looked about him with interest, as well as observing her as she went about her tasks. He could see that she was obviously very capable and practical.

They had come directly into the kitchen which was quite large, yet very warm and welcoming. On the mantelpiece above the range were a couple of oil lamps, which Katherine now lit, and hanging from the ceiling above the table was a Tilley lamp.

Either side of the range were two large wooden chairs with arms, and home-made cushions attached to the back and seat with ties made from the same material. On the wall opposite the range and next to the door was a long wooden settee, scattered with numerous cushions which made it look homely and comfortable. The two windows were small, curtained and revealed the thickness of the walls, the latter providing welcome protection from the violent storm raging outside.

Alex was very aware that whoever designed and built these cottages knew exactly what they were doing. No planners or architects were needed here, just local knowledge and experience.

There was a door to the left of the sink, set at a right angle, and from here Katherine emerged after several minutes holding a plate with sandwiches, cakes and biscuits.

"My pantry," she said and Alex got up to take a look. "Cool all year round, set in the north wall and with marble slabs to keep things chilled," she indicated the shelves that lined the walls, "with enough space to keep plenty of food for the whole village. My grandfather built this cottage hoping for a large family I think, then procured and signed the tenancy agreement and my dad inherited it."

As he had spotted a point of law, Alex asked, "What happens to a tenancy agreement when someone dies?"

"On Cairnmor, the tenancy is generally passed down from father to son, never through the female line. If there are no sons, then it goes to the eldest son-in-law."

"Seems pretty harsh on the daughter. What about you?"

"I have a special tenancy agreement…"

"You mean a Dispensationary Agreement?"

"That's the one. Father McPhee found a good solicitor and persuaded the proprietor to allow me to stay under those terms. However, if I marry, the tenancy reverts to the usual pattern and the croft will go to my husband and then the male heirs if I have any children."

Katherine filled the teapot with boiling water from the kettle and put the plates with the food on the table. Then she returned to the pantry for some milk and sat down at the table next to Alex.

There were many things she wanted to say but first she felt she ought to warn him that it was unlikely he would be able to return to the hotel that night, the storm showed no sign of abating; if anything it was increasing in strength and ferocity.

Alex said mischievously, "What about your reputation then, if I have to stay here overnight?!"

Katherine looked at him meaningfully, "Given what happened just now in the rose garden and the way we were heading, it would be completely in tatters!"

Alex had the grace to look slightly shamefaced but Katherine reassured him. "It's all right," she said. "It was both of us, but it does tell me that we're going to have to be careful when we're on our own."

"Yes."

Alex was grateful to her. There were not many unsophisticated women who would have accepted his behaviour with such equanimity, especially as they had known each other only for such a short while.

He regarded her thoughtfully once again. She had emotional as well as academic intelligence and was rising rapidly in his estimation. He wondered how old she was; about her experiences with other men. He came to the conclusion that there had not been too many of those and that she was probably a similar age to him.

Perfect.

He was roused from his reverie by Katherine wagging her finger at him in a humorous fashion: "Actually, we on the island have our own ways to ensure someone's reputation remains intact..." She looked at him meaningfully. "As soon as my neighbours realize that I'm at home and that you're with me because of the storm, there will be knocks at the door every fifteen minutes or so. People will stay for a while and expect a cup of tea, until quite a crowd will have gathered. At any moment, someone will produce a pack of cards and that will be it for the evening. I hope you can play whist?" Alex nodded. "Good. Then, someone else will offer you a bed for the night in their cottage and that's my reputation sorted and preserved!"

"Now you're teasing me...?" said Alex, not quite sure whether to believe her or not.

Katherine smiled. "You wait and see! I ought to add that I speak not from experience, well, not much anyway" (Alex was glad to have his speculation confirmed) "but from Mary's when she was going out with Adam, before they became engaged. I'm afraid I'm as guilty as the rest for keeping her reputation safe." And Katherine finished with a nod of the head, folded her arms and put a very prim expression on her face.

Alex chuckled. "So what happens when a couple become engaged?"

"That's even worse. They're not allowed to see each other at all!"

Katherine really was teasing him now and Alex spotted it immediately and pulled her onto the settee and tickled her. She tickled him back and just as they were breathless with laughter and he was about to kiss her, there was what sounded like a thump on the door.

"See, I told you!" said Katherine.

"Shall we pretend we're not in?" said Alex hopefully.

"Unfortunately, we can't. I want all my friends to like you."

"That's a nice thing to say," and he smiled at her. "Come on then, let's open the door together, otherwise the wind will blow it off its hinges."

They took hold of the door, supporting it to stop it opening with a bang and breaking. A bedraggled and frightened looking cat blew into the kitchen. It gave a pitiful meow.

Alex and Katherine were so surprised that they almost let go of the door, recovering themselves just in time and managing to shut it only with great difficulty. This time Katherine bolted it top and bottom with metal bolts that had been designed and fitted for this very purpose; certainly not for security as no one locked their doors on Cairnmor.

"My goodness, it must have been blown against the door by the wind," said Katherine.

The cat was, not surprisingly, in a state of shock and just sat on the flagstones shivering and dripping, looking up at them with pleading eyes.

Katherine sighed. "Poor thing. I'll find something to dry it with. I hope it's not injured. I don't think it's feral."

"Why, do they exist on the island?" asked Alex, somewhat taken aback by this. He had no wish to be unexpectedly attacked by some wild beast.

"There are a few stray domestic animals that have decided to become completely … .independent … .and that have turned wild. But this is not one of them. In a state like this, a feral cat would be hissing and spitting at us, so I think it must be a domestic one." And she disappeared out of the kitchen.

Alex slowly and gently approached the cat, which remained in the middle of the floor trembling and mewing pitifully. When he knelt down beside its shaking form, it made no effort to run away.

Katherine was back quickly, with a couple of towels.

"I'm not sure how many we're going to need," she said. "These will do to start with."

She knelt down beside Alex and together they carefully put one of the towels around the cat. It offered no resistance and encouraged by this, he gathered up the animal into his arms and sat down by the range. Katherine spread another towel across his lap and he placed the cat on this.

Gently, Alex rubbed its fur and together with this and the warmth of the fire, the cat gradually became drier. It even managed the occasional purr. Meanwhile, Katherine put some milk in a saucepan and heated it up. When it was warm, she put the milk in a saucer and knelt beside Alex, placing the saucer close to the cat's mouth. It drank daintily until all the milk had disappeared, whereupon, it promptly fell asleep.

"Well," said Katherine, washing up the empty saucer, "looking at its ribs, I'd say that this cat hasn't eaten for a long time. I suppose it must be a stray, although it hasn't been away from civilisation long enough to turn wild."

"That seems to be true."

"When the weather calms down, we'll try to find out if it belongs to anyone in the village."

They waited until the cat had been asleep for a little while and then placed its somnolent form carefully in front of the fire, on a couple of the cushions from the settee. It awoke briefly, stretched luxuriously and then curled up into a ball and fell asleep once more.

Satisfied they could do no more, Alex and Katherine sat on the chairs either side of the fireplace and began to talk about the quest that had prompted Alex's visit to the island, going over the facts they had discussed earlier in the day.

"So, Sir Charles Mathieson, who owns Mathieson's shipyard on the Clyde, has left his entire fortune to his only son and heir, Rupert. How much is the inheritance, by the way?" asked Katherine.

"Huge, enormous! One and a half million pounds plus the shipyard plus the mansion in Park Lane and the house in Govan..." and Alex paused for effect. He was not to be disappointed.

"My goodness!" Katherine was dumbfounded. "I suppose people really are that rich?"

"Oh yes," said Alex, enjoying her reaction.

"You said that his girlfriend Mhairi was pregnant. Did she have the baby?" asked Katherine.

"Well, we assume so. Both Sir Charles and Jock Hamilton, Mhairi's father, were insistent that the baby was given up for adoption immediately after it was born. There is very little evidence to support that this actually took place or to suggest otherwise."

"Do you know what happened to Mhairi?"

"No, or Rupert. Sir Charles, in conversation with my father when the will was drawn up, was all too aware that he was responsible for his son's disappearance. However, he didn't believe there to be a connection between this and Mhairi's, which is rather odd. I'm convinced there was and that he was probably closing his mind to that fact. He also seemed to be full of remorse for his actions."

"What about Jock Hamilton?"

"We haven't managed to trace him so far. Dad wrote to his last known address, but hasn't got a reply as yet. This really is only the beginning of the search."

"You said yesterday that there was evidence to suggest a connection to Cairnmor? So what was it that prompted you to come here and begin your search?"

"Because of this letter." Alex opened his briefcase and handed the smaller of the two envelopes to Katherine.

She pulled two flimsy pages from inside the envelope and began to read:

Dearest Rupert,

Things continue to be good here at Aunt Flora's. She's so very kind and the baby grows daily. I can feel it kicking now as I write and my Aunt says that I have not got too long before the baby comes. I am very big now, but Aunt Flora lets me rest a great deal. She says I will need all the strength I can get in the next few weeks.

I am reading many books and my writing is coming on well now, is it not? I practice while I wait for the baby to be born and Aunt Flora is helping me as she thinks books and learning are important. I never had much chance at home with Ma being poorly a lot of the time and Pa and my brothers needing me to do things for them. There was always so much cooking and cleaning and mending and sewing that I never really had a chance, though I could always answer all the questions when I was at school.

Pa wants me to give our baby up for adoption, but I do not want to. I am frightened that he will take the baby away as soon as it is born. Aunt Flora says that she will help me even if it makes her brother-in-law angry because she thinks that what he wants to make me do is wrong.

What I want to do is to go to the Isle of Cairnmor. Aunt Flora was born there and she has been telling me all about it. It sounds lovely. Her family moved to the mainland soon after her brother, my uncle, was born. Ma is the youngest and was born in Glasgow. I have been reading about Cairnmor in a book Aunt Flora lent me. I'd like to live there with our baby. Will you come to me there after the baby is born?

I know we still love each other. I feel it and your last letter was so much comfort (I have kept it in a safe place).

Please write soon.

Your loving,

Mhairi.

P.S If the baby is a girl shall we call her Anna? I haven't thought up a boy's name yet.

Katherine put the pages down into her lap, moved by the simple, loving language of the words.

"Oh Alex," she said quietly.

"I know," he murmured.

"Where was the letter found?"

"In Rupert's bedroom by Sir Charles. He thought it might be helpful in the search for his son. Perhaps by not destroying the letter, as you would have expected him to do, he was in some small way atoning for his insensitivity in the past. But there's more. After ensuring adequate financial provision for his wife Emily, Sir Charles left his entire fortune to Rupert as his sole heir and in the event of his son's death being proven absolutely, to Rupert's child."

"Do you think that Mhairi did bring the baby to Cairnmor all those years ago?"

"I have no idea, but that is what I'm here to find out."

"Can I help?"

"Of course," said Alex, leaning towards her and taking both her hands in his. "I was hoping you'd say that."

At which point there *was* a knock at the door – and that was the end of Alex and Katherine's privacy.

The evening then unfolded exactly as Katherine had predicted. But it was fun, and as they said goodnight, before Alex went to spend the night in the spare room of the cottage belonging to Mary's parents, Katherine was filled with the joy of certainty, knowing that she would be able to be with him the next day.

The cat, whom Alex christened 'Mistral' (which was promptly shortened to 'Misty' by Mary's youngest brother, Iain) because of the wet and wind-blown nature of its arrival, slept through the whole evening's festivities and only woke up when Katherine went to bed. Whereupon, after drinking another huge saucer full of milk, it followed her into the bedroom and after an extensive wash, settled itself to sleep on the eiderdown.

"You know where your best interests lie, don't you little one?" she told it meaningfully, before climbing into bed herself.

Not that she slept very well of course, and neither did Alex.

CHAPTER 6

The storm continued unabated throughout that night and during the whole of Monday and Tuesday. Every school on the island was closed and normal life put on hold. Alex battled his way through the driving rain to see Katherine, needing all his physical strength to make any forward progress, clinging on to the slippery, wet stone walls of both crofts; the wind determinedly pressing him back the way he had come. It took a great deal of effort to prevent the gale loosening his grip and flinging him onto the ground if he should lose concentration even for a second.

Alex did not particularly enjoy the experience and frequently wondered why he was enduring such discomfort on this undoubtedly beautiful but weather-flawed island. Katherine made the reverse journey under the same conditions but as she was more accustomed to coping with the inclement weather, she thought more about seeing Alex than her own physical comfort.

The MacKinnons, in common with every crofter in weather like this, were concerned for their animals. The cows were safe in the animal shed and the chickens shut in the hen house beside the cottage but there was absolutely no question of being able to check on the sheep grazing the machair, totally exposed to the elements with little or no shelter. The wind was too strong, the rain too torrential to venture far. The sheep would have to manage as best they could and the family would go to them when there was some let-up in the storm.

When Alex and Katherine were able to spend time alone together, they developed a relaxed companionship which for Alex was very different from any relationship he had previously experienced.

Ensconced in cosy arm chairs, bathed in the warm glow from the fire in her tiny sitting room that was filled with the aromatic fragrance of the peat and safe from the storm raging outside, they talked at great length of many things – about their lives, their work, their dreams and aspirations – all the while growing closer.

At other times, they read, selecting a book from one of the many on the well-lined bookshelf that spanned almost the whole of one wall; sometimes individually, sometimes reading aloud to each other.

Katherine loved Alex's voice – its rich sonority and clarity – while he delighted in the expressiveness and variety with which she made each page come to life.

On the Tuesday evening, everyone in Mary's family, including her two older brothers, came round to Katherine's cottage, leaving dripping waterproofs and Wellington boots in the kitchen, standing around the piano while she and Alex took it in turns to accompany the singing.

All Mary's family were fine vocalists – music being an instinctive form of expression for most people on the island – and musical evenings like this were the norm rather than the exception. They sang traditional Gaelic songs, as well as more contemporary numbers such as those by George and Ira Gershwin, Cole Porter and Jerome Kern using Katherine's large supply of sheet music.

When Alex wasn't quick enough to hide his surprise when these were produced, Katherine retorted with a well-expressed, "Huh," and pretended to be highly offended, saying, "We know more than you think we do. Us simple island folk might be isolated, but we don't half know a lot of stuff!"

There was no reply to that of course, so Alex simply put his arm round her and kissed her on the cheek.

"Now, now, children," said Mary, wagging her finger at them. "Behave!"

"Well, ye're a fine one to talk, Mary MacKinnon," said her youngest brother, Iain. "I've seen ye with Adam," he added knowingly.

However, before a family argument could ensue, Fiona, Mary's mother arrived at the doorway to say that the vegetable soup Katherine had prepared earlier was now sitting in bowls on the table, that it looked and smelt delicious and if they didn't want it to get cold and spoil, "Ye'd all better come away and eat it this very moment!" something that everyone did with great appreciation, using home-made bread to wipe the last of the soup from the dishes.

After supper, they cleared away the remains of the meal and Mary, Fiona and Katherine washed, dried and put the crockery and utensils away. The inevitable cards then came out and they played several games of whist, rummy and snap. Alex had forgotten just how enjoyable these simple activities could be and that an evening could be so full of genuine laughter and good humour.

During a lull in the conversation, everyone noticed the silence. The storm had ended as suddenly as it had begun.

"Do ye think there'll be school in the mornin'?" asked Iain, wishing for a reply in the negative.

"I think that's a fair possibility," replied his teacher. "Sorry to disappoint you!"

"Och, that's all right Miss Katherine, I've had an extra two days at any rate."

"You keep to yer learnin', son," said Gordon, his big frame almost filling the tiny sitting-room. "I want ye to have as much schoolin' as ye can. Our Katherine here is a fine teacher and ye've a good brain in that young head of yorn. Make sure ye listen to her and take in what she tells ye to learn."

"I do, Dad, ye know I do!"

"I know, son."

Gordon turned to Alex. "What are ye plannin' for tomorrow? Would ye like to come with Neill, Alain and I up to the machair tomorrow and see how our sheep have fared? That is if we have any left and they haven't been drowned, stranded or blown off the island!" he added dourly.

"Please don't be offended if I say no. But I must get on with my research," replied Alex, secretly glad, but hoping that these people who had been so hospitable towards him would not be upset by his refusal.

"Och, no, of course we're not offended! I'd forgotten that ye have a job to do." Gordon stopped talking and placed his hand on Alex's shoulder before continuing. "Both Fiona and I are truly sorry that we've not been any help. We've talked about it a lot, but neither of us can think that there's anyone livin' on the island called Mhairi and Rupert, nor any couple, strangers to Cairnmor, arriving here all that time ago from the mainland with a babe. Ye need to ask Father McPhee or Robbie McKenzie. Ah, but he'll be away fishing now that the weather's cleared up. But he'll be back in a couple of days, ye can talk to him then. Yes, I'd start with Father McPhee," added Gordon.

"I will do that, and thank you. Katherine suggested them as well. We also talked about asking Donald the postman if he'll take me with him when he goes on his rounds. I presume he won't have delivered the letters from the steamer yet?"

"That's an excellent idea, and no, the weather will have kept him indoors, like everyone else."

Bidding Katherine goodnight, Gordon ushered his family out into the calm night air and they strolled home in a leisurely fashion, leaving Alex to say his farewells to Katherine.

Shutting the door, he took her in his arms, kissing her thoroughly and once again, Katherine couldn't help herself as she melted into his embrace. It was with great reluctance that they eventually drew apart.

She said, somewhat breathlessly and a certain amount of ironic humour, "I think it's just as well you're going back with Mary's family tonight!"

Alex was suddenly serious. "Yes. But we do need to talk."

"I know we do," she replied. "I've been trying not to think about what happens when you have to go home. It's too painful."

"I know," said Alex, although that wasn't exactly what he had been thinking. Becoming gently business-like, he added, "But not now. Tomorrow." He then paused before asking, "What time do you leave for school in the morning?"

"About seven o'clock. School begins at nine."

"I'll walk with you, if I may."

"I was hoping you'd want to do that!"

"I'd better say hello to John and re-occupy my room at the hotel. He'll think I've disappeared for good in the storm."

Katherine laughed and said, "No, he will know that you're with me and that you'll be safe!"

Alex, humorously, twisted her words, giving them a different connotation, "Ah, but am I?!"

Katherine's response – equally humorous – was to raise her arm dramatically and point to the door, saying, "Go! Away with you, impertinent young man. How dare you insinuate such things!" But then seriously, not acting any more, she said, "Oh, my love, I don't want you to go!"

"Nor do I," he murmured into her hair, gathering it into his hands. "But I must."

Alex took a deep breath, beginning to realize that here on the island, he really did have to behave honourably towards her.

Opening the door, he gathered up his waterproof coat, before turning back to her and saying, gently and tenderly, "See you in the morning."

"Yes," and Katherine smiled bravely, knowing that their idyll would come to an end in the next few days; trying not to allow the realization of their inevitably lengthy separation intrude on her present happiness.

The next morning was fine and fresh, all signs of the storm having disappeared completely. It was as if it had never happened.

The walk down to Lochaberdale was very beautiful. Although dark at first when they set out, before long, an imperceptibly grey dawn metamorphosed into a blue sky while the sun, hidden at first by the hill beyond, lit the land with a sudden burst of golden light, illuminating all before it. The air was so pure that even the smallest detail of the landscape was crystal clear and each breath invigorating.

Alex and Katherine were mesmerized by its loveliness and stood close together, unwilling to move and lose the moment. Eventually, though, they had to continue on their way – he to the hotel, she to her school after speaking to Donald and Annie at the Post Office about Alex's request – with plans to meet at the school-house on his return.

"Well now, ye're a sight for sore eyes!" said John by way of greeting, when Alex came through the door.

"I've been staying with the MacKinnon's."

"Oh aye, I've no doubt ye have. Grand family. I knew ye'd be safe with our Katherine to look after ye as well! It's all right, don't look so embarrassed!" (Alex had blushed, something not normally part of his mode of expression). "We all like ye and think it's a great match. But there's some difficult decisions ahead, I think."

"Aye," said Alex tetchily, employing a very proficient Scottish accent to express his irritation. "But reet now I'm in need of a wee warm bath!"

"Touché!" said John. It was his turn to look slightly discomfited. "Sorry lad, that was rude of me; 'tis none of my business."

"Apology accepted. But I really do need that bath!" and Alex went up to his room, glad to escape and be by himself for a while. He knew he had been a bit hard on John, but Alex, for all his sociability, was a deeply private man when it came to his own feelings and he was not about to discuss them with anyone unless he had made the decision to do so.

He bathed quickly, as he did not wish to delay Donald on his rounds. He assumed that it would be acceptable once Katherine had spoken on his behalf; everyone seemed to think it was not a problem, so Alex took them at their word. And that was indeed the case because when he presented himself some half an hour later at the post office, Donald was obviously expecting him.

"Well, we'll be off now shall we?" he said cheerfully, without preamble. "Bye lass," he said to his wife.

"Be careful now, and mind ye look after our guest," she replied.

"Aye I shall." Then to Alex he said, "Climb up, lad, into the seat, and be prepared to hold on – it gets bumpy sometimes. The tracks round here haven't caught up with motor vehicles yet! This one's the first on the island," he added proudly, patting the dashboard. "It used to take me all week to get round the island delivering and collecting the post on foot. I'd just get finished when the next steamer would arrive and I'd have to start all over again! It still takes a fair old time, as some paths can only be walked, so I have to work out my route carefully and Annie worries if I'm not home before dark. Stray off the road in some parts of the island and ye'll end up in a bog that'll swallow ye up completely."

Alex recalled John's warning on his first evening about places to 'catch out the unwary'. Perhaps that was what he had meant.

As they proceeded on their journey, Alex recounted the reason for his coming to the island and, as with everyone else to whom he had talked so far, he drew a blank. The postman, who travelled all over the island, could not recall anyone called Mhairi and Rupert ever having lived on Cairnmor.

"There's certainly no one here answering those names now. Could they have changed their names?" he asked.

"It's perfectly possible," replied Alex, who had considered this very likely, given the circumstances.

Donald thought for a moment. "Twenty-seven years ago, ye say?" Alex waited, giving his companion time to think. "Let's see if I can recall newcomers... Och, folks have left, and come back, bringing spouses with them from the mainland, but there are very few who've come here without family connections or an agreed tenancy or a job to go to. The schoolmaster and his wife over at Balnaguisich came about that time and the priest at Ardross; oh, and Doctor Armstrong, he's been here about twenty-seven years. He was a young man straight out of medical school when he first arrived and within a year had married a local girl. He's been here ever since. Three children; lovely couple. The priest on our little sister island Cairnbeg has been there fifteen years and the schoolmistress ten, but they wouldn't be who ye're looking for."

Alex couldn't help making the observation that people who came, tended to stay. Donald agreed. "Oh, aye, ye're right there, laddie. There's something that gets ye right here about Cairnmor," and Donald thumped his chest in the region of his heart.

Reflectively, Alex stared at the track ahead. Donald glanced sideways at his passenger but discreet man that he was, said nothing. Alex was grateful for this as he was trying to cope with some unexpected emotional turbulence concerning Katherine and Cairnmor of a kind he was not used to.

His work necessitated absolute clarity of mind and the ability to analyse situations critically and objectively. He had always prided himself on being able to call on those skills regardless of what he might be thinking or feeling in his private life, and he had to admit there had certainly been some very unfortunate moments in that direction. But this? This was different and he wondered about its implication for the future.

Their first stop was at a large farm. Alex was distracted from his thoughts by the imposing stone-built house and obvious acres of land. He said, "I was under the impression that everyone who farmed here did so by crofting."

"Aye that's true in most cases, but there are about a half-dozen large farms, complete with ancestral stone farmhouses, who hold leases from the estate rather than being tenants on the proprietor's land. A few of the leases go back a long way, sometimes hundreds of years, where generations of the same family have worked the land. There's a couple of farms that can trace their origins back to the clans who owned the island, before the clan families lost their wealth and had to sell up. And before the clearances, of course."

"The clearances?"

"Aye, lad." Donald got out of the van and said, "I'll be back in a minute. I'll ask the farmer for ye about Rupert and Mhairi," and, having delivered his letters and parcels and made enquiries on Alex's behalf, to no avail, he returned to the van.

As most of the farmyard had been turned into mud by the recent storm, it was with some difficulty that he turned the van around in the narrow available hard surface and after much crunching of gears, they proceeded on their way.

"No luck, I'm afraid. Now, to answer your question. The clearances. It'll be a bit of a history lesson. Do ye mind?" Donald turned to his passenger.

"Not at all." Alex liked the postmaster's enthusiasm. "It sounds like a particular interest of yours."

"Aye, it's become that. Yon lassie of yours held some evening classes on the history of Cairnmor a while back and we all went. She's a fine teacher, lad, and we're all very proud of her, with her university education and everything."

Alex smiled, pleased at the compliment for Katherine, but particularly pleased at what seemed to be the islanders' ready acceptance that she was 'his lassie'; that they were seen as a couple.

Yes, he liked that. He liked that very much.

"So tell me about the clearances," he said.

"A dark period in Scottish history, lad, verra dark. There's still a lot of resentment amongst certain Highland and Island folk with long memories. They see it as yet another example of English cruelty towards the Scots, even though many of the landlords who carried out the dastardly deeds were in fact Scottish. No offence meant to yourself, being English and all."

"None taken," said Alex. "If it's any help, my grandfather came from Skye."

"Och, that's grand then, lad. Ye're almost one of us!" Donald chuckled before continuing. "In the late seventeen hundreds, James VII of Scotland – I think I've remembered correctly – who was also James II of England, lost his throne and was replaced by William of Orange. Cairnmor was one of several islands, along with the Highlanders on the mainland, whose people supported James in what became known as the Jacobite Risings."

"The Jacobite Risings," considered Alex. "Weren't they a series of uprisings and rebellions by the clans against the British government to try and have the House of Stuart restored to the throne? I remember something about it from history at school."

"Aye, that's correct, lad. Well, it led to the Battle of Culloden in 1746 where the Scots armies were heavily defeated and which brought an end to the rebellion."

"Ah, Bonnie Prince Charlie and Flora MacDonald, who helped him escape to Skye after the battle."

"Aye lad, she was reputedly born here on the island. At least we like to think so."

"Really?" Alex was sceptical.

"Oh, aye," continued Donald. "A bonny lass, she was. Very brave. Anyway, the British Government were ruthless in their repression of the clans as punishment for their part in the rebellion. The chieftains were stripped of their right to rule and, in the general population, all swords had to be surrendered to the Government and kilts, tartans and the playing of bagpipes were banned.

"The British were determined to wipe out the culture which had nurtured such rebelliousness. Katherine will tell you, the schools are still affected by it. It's only in the last ten years that some Gaelic has been allowed to be taught in schools once more. But exams and tests still have to be taken in English.

"Now, to make matters worse, there were clan chiefs who accepted the new laws and abandoned their roles as representatives of their people. Instead, along with the absentee English landlords, they ruthlessly forced their people off the land and replaced them with the sheep, which were considered more profitable." Here Donald stopped to draw breath, and he also stopped the van and switched off the engine. "I'm afraid we have to walk for a bit now – the track's too narrow for a while and there are several crofts that I need to deliver letters to."

So both men climbed out of the van and into the bright sunlight.

They found themselves on a narrow path that wound itself along and gradually up the hillside. As they turned a steep corner, they were rewarded with the most stunning view across the dramatic valleys of Gleann Aoibhneach and Gleann Cuineas, with the mountains rising up spectacularly all around.

After a while, Donald spoke again and with obvious pride in his voice, said, "Yon mountains are the highest peaks on Cairnmor, over two thousand feet in height. Breath-taking aren't they?"

"They're magnificent. You can't fail to be uplifted."

"Aye, that's so true. It makes the heart sing."

They walked on in silence and after some while, came to a group of crofts that must have had one of the best outlooks in the whole area.

"Mrs Gilgarry and her son Hamish live here, though Hamish is not home much these days as he's away with the fishing fleet out of Glasgow," said Donald, stopping at the first one. "She might be able to help ye, though she can be a feisty old biddy when the mood takes her."

They were invited into the cottage, a simple two room dwelling with a small black stove set in the hearth for cooking. There was a kettle on one side, from which rose wisps of steam, and a cooking pot on the other, from which exuded delicious smells of a stew.

They were offered tea and Donald and Mrs Gilgarry held a rapid conversation in Gaelic which, when completed, caused the old lady to shake her head, and looking at Alex, spread out her hands apologetically.

Charmed by her good manners and apparent gentleness, despite all that Donald had told him about her character, Alex said, "It's all right. I'm beginning to think I'm onto a lost cause."

Donald interpreted and the old lady replied in Gaelic, "Don't you give up, now. Something will happen to make your search worthwhile."

By way of conversation while they drank their tea, Donald explained that he had been telling Alex about the clearances. The old lady's expression changed and darkened and she said, *"Have you told him of Colonel Rowan Clancy?"*

Once again, Donald interpreted and explained, "Mrs Gilgarry has relatives who suffered at the hands of the notorious Colonel."

"Ah," acknowledged Alex, not quite knowing what else to say.

The old lady continued to speak, with Donald interpreting for her as she uttered her words, her manner becoming more excitable as the tale progressed and quite belying her former quietness.

"This man, a ruthless, heartless villain, bought Cairnmor in 1846 and one of his first acts as landlord was to call a public meeting. And do you know what he did? His henchmen grabbed over a thousand people from the crowd and forced them onto a ship that was anchored in Loch Aberdale. The ship then set sail for Canada.

"For the remainder who clung to their island way of life, they were persecuted and tormented, their crofts burned and their crops destroyed. It was terrible, terrible. And all because of wanting to put the sheep on the best land." The old lady paused, shaking her head, before continuing. "To add to the misery, there was a potato famine like the one that took place way back in 1746 soon after the Battle of Culloden. Everyone was near to starvation and Colonel Clancy took advantage of this, forcing even more poor hungry souls to emigrate. All this so he could make more profit for himself. Bah!"

She thumped her fist on the table to emphasize her disapproval.

"The population of Cairnmor now is nothing in comparison to what it was then. His persecution went on for years. My grandmother and several aunts and uncles were burnt off their land and taken on a ship bound for Nova Scotia in Canada. And that's where all my relatives are today. Nova Scotia. There are a great number of Scots there – they came from all over the Highlands on the mainland as well as the islands. The name means 'New Scotland'. Did ye know that, young Donald?"

Donald, very amused, looked at Alex and interpreted literally. Alex tried very hard not to smile, but was not very successful. So he asked, politely, "How did your parents manage to remain here?"

"My parents escaped when the first people were forced off their land. They had sense because they fled across the sea to Skye," replied Mrs Gilgarry via Donald. Here she chuckled to herself. "A bit like Bonnie Prince Charlie – God rest his soul – and his Flora MacDonald who rescued him. Though my parents didn't dress up as Irish maids in order to escape from Colonel Clancy!" She gave a hearty laugh which ended in a coughing fit before taking another sip of tea while she recovered her composure. "They only returned when it was safe to do so."

When Mrs Gilgarry had finished talking and he could see that she needed to rest, Donald said, "Well, we must be away. Lots of letters to deliver."

"Mine are up there on the mantelpiece. To my relatives across the sea in Canada. Mind they get there safely. Here's money for the postage. Ye can bring me the change next time you come."

Donald collected the letters, replacing them with the new ones and promised to bring the change. Alex and Donald both thanked the old lady for her hospitality and left.

"She's quite a character isn't she?" said Alex.

"Yes, she is."

"How old is she?"

"Well she must be eighty if she's a day."

The two men visited all the other crofts in the village and then took the sloping path that led down to the sea shore. No one seemed to know anything about Mhairi or Rupert and Alex was resigned to the fact that he might not discover anything that day.

"If it's any consolation," said Donald, as they sat in a sheltered part of the beach eating the lunch that Annie had prepared for them, "it'll be all round the island within a couple of days and if anyone does remember or know anything, then they'll tell us soon enough. I'll keep askin' on my way tomorrow and the next day. Now lad, if ye've finished eating, we've a way to go before this day's work is done."

And they set off back the way they had come, returning to the van, and completed delivering and collecting from as many people of the island as they could, arriving back in Lochaberdale at about four o'clock, just in time for Alex to meet Katherine at school.

He discovered his way into her classroom, only to find her deep in conversation with a little boy and his mother. The child seemed very upset and Katherine and his mother were talking to him, trying to reassure him.

Alex kept a discreet distance and wandered round the classroom, looking at the excellent standard of art work on display and the neat compositions pinned up on the wall.

The building itself was Victorian, with high windows and solid walls and the classroom was large, light and airy. He counted the desks and chairs: a class of forty-five children and judging by the variety of sizes of the desks and chairs, a mixed age group too.

The larger ones were at the back, ranged against a hinged partition, set with glass windows, which could be folded back when extra space was needed. The desks and chairs in this other section of the room were tiny – presumably the infant department, thought Alex. He wondered if Katherine had any other staff to help her. It would be an impossible task for one teacher to cope with about eighty children, forty-five was enough in itself.

He thought of his classes of fifteen at Westminster.

Once the conversation had ended, Katherine came over to Alex and he kissed her on the cheek.

"Have you had a good day?" he asked, smiling at her, genuinely pleased to see her.

"Yes, but that poor little lad has been in tears most of the day. He only arrived on the steamer last Saturday and today is his first day at school. He's a 'homer'. It must seem very daunting."

"A 'homer'?" asked Alex. There seemed to be no end to the things he was learning about life on Cairnmor.

"Yes, every so often the authorities in Glasgow decide, in their wisdom, that some children would benefit from a taste of island life – they could be from the slum areas of the city like the Gorbals, where life is cramped and very unpleasant because of the overcrowding in the tenement blocks. Do you know, often there are buildings where you might have a family with as many as eight children living in terrible conditions in one room. I saw quite a lot of that on teaching practice.

Other 'homers' are children from the orphanages in Glasgow who need to experience a better quality of life, with fresh air and good food. So the council sends them here, officially temporarily, but unofficially they seem to forget them. They are never collected and just continue to live with their foster parents. No adult on this island would let a child go without shelter or food, so these children are just absorbed into island life."

"Do they ever send babies?" asked Alex, thinking that this might be a possible avenue of exploration.

"I know what you're thinking, but I've never known it to happen. They're usually two or three years old at the youngest," said Katherine. "It's a good thought though and could be worth following up."

She turned to her desk and began gathering her books. "I'll leave these here and mark them first thing in the morning. I don't want to take them home with me tonight because they're heavy, but most of all because I want to spend my evening with you. I want to hear all about your day!"

They went out of the building and closed the big wooden door behind them.

"Don't you lock the door?" asked Alex.

"No, we never lock any of our doors. Even the children from the roughest slums get trained in the island way of doing things that 'all property is to be respected and left untouched either for the benefit of the community or the individual to whom it belongs'. We reinforce that at school. It's never been a problem."

"Shangri-La, huh?"

"I wish it was! It's a hard life generally, but there are compensations. So you've read *Lost Horizon*?"

"Yes, it's a very good book. Completely improbable though!"

"My favourite James Hilton is *Goodbye, Mr Chips*."

"It had to be, didn't it?!" said Alex, laughing. "Now, will you have supper with me at the hotel? I know it'll be dark by the time we've finished, but I'll walk you home afterwards. No 'buts' now," as Katherine moved to object to the last suggestion. "I can find my way back down again. There aren't too many bogs between the hotel and your croft!"

"Unless you stray off the beaten path." She smiled at him. "Actually I'd like to accept your offer of both very much."

So they made their way to the hotel and over dinner, talked about their respective days. John was very circumspect and discreet throughout the meal and Katherine was amused by this. She asked Alex what had gone on and he explained John's remark when he had returned to the hotel.

"He's right of course," she said, as they began their walk back to her cottage.

"Yes, but it's our business and I wasn't prepared to answer him at that moment."

"Quite right too!" declared Katherine robustly.

Alex put his arm round her as they walked in contemplative silence. Eventually he said, "I have to catch the steamer on Saturday. Please believe me when I say I wish I could stay longer, but I have to be back in London on Wednesday for a trial at the Royal Courts of Justice. Unfortunately, it's a very important case that I can't give to anyone else. I'm just hoping that the weather holds for the weekend."

"I hope so for your sake. Though I'd rather you stayed." She paused and stopped walking. "What are we going to do, Alex?"

"I don't know, my darling. There is no easy answer. All I could come up with was that we keep in touch and sort out the rest as we go. Distance and our working lives make things very complicated."

If Katherine was disappointed with his reply, she didn't show it. They'd met less than a week previously but to her, it seemed as though there had never been a time when they hadn't known each other. Feeling subdued, she began to entertain doubts as to whether he felt the same.

He looked at her and smiled. "Don't worry, we'll work something out. We have to, dear Katherine, for both our sakes."

She was happier with that and they continued their walk until they had reached her cottage. Katherine thought it best not to invite him inside and they kissed circumspectly by the door and said goodnight, both of them feeling bereft as Alex returned to the hotel.

CHAPTER 7

Saturday was to be their last day together.

The weather was fair and clear, very mild with no wind. The calm sea reflected the blue of the sky and both Katherine and Alex were able to undo their coats as they walked along the white-gold stretch of sand. They spoke little, holding hands, enjoying the morning sunshine as best they could, not wishing to spoil these last few precious hours before the inevitable separation.

They had come to the beach to find Robbie, following much the same route as Katherine's walk the previous Saturday. They had tried to contact Father McPhee in Lochaberdale, but to no avail as he was visiting his colleague on Cairnbeg and was unlikely to return until that evening. Katherine had promised Alex that she would talk to him during the coming week about Mhairi and Rupert. Alex expressed his gratitude and then remarked on how warm it was.

"A gift from the Gulf Stream," replied Katherine. "It passes very close to the two islands and keeps the climate temperate for much of the year. But we get many storms, being so exposed to the weather fronts coming off the Atlantic."

"And my one experience was quite something! Are they usually so ferocious?"

"Oh yes, quite often, and they can come up without any warning too. The front reaches us and that's it for a few days."

Alex was curious. "If the island receives such a regular battering, how is it that the sand dunes don't get blown or washed away?"

"I've never known that to happen. They're pretty large as you can see and well bedded down with marram grass, but I've no doubt that some of the old-timers could tell you about violent storms where the sea has broken through the dunes in the long distant past. Anything like that would be devastating for the machair behind."

"People keep talking about the machair. What is it exactly?"

"I'll show you," and Katherine led them through the dunes, a route Alex found to be quite difficult as the sand was deep and high and the grass coarse and spiky, offering no possibility of hand-holds to help them on their way.

After a while they came to a vast, flat plain, very green in places but with many strips of bare earth where the soil had been turned ready for crop planting in the spring. Away to the right, sheep and cows grazed on the lush meadows, loosely contained by fences.

"The machair is just the name given to this very fertile area between the dunes and the mountains. Each crofter has his own designated strip of land that he farms under the tenancy agreement. We grow all our crops here, but I have to say that the soil produces particularly wonderful potatoes. Like no other variety that I've ever tasted. They have a distinctive flavour all of their own. The soil is fertilized by seaweed from the beach, so perhaps that has something to do with it. The older people say that the seaweed also makes the soil heavier in consistency and stops it from blowing away in the wind, which is quite possible as it is very sandy."

As they stood close together, surveying the terrain, Alex said, "This is a truly wonderful place, but it's not an easy life."

"No it's not. Each person is dependent upon their own efforts for survival, each family has to be self-sufficient, though no one would let his neighbour go without food if he himself had any to give."

"Can't people buy in food from the mainland?"

"That's perfectly possible if they are in a profession and are paid a salary, but otherwise there is very little extra money around, except what can be earned by selling animals to the markets on the mainland. There is no industry to speak of and certainly very few employment opportunities. I'm paid a salary so I can afford to buy in food, but I choose not to. I have a financial arrangement with Mary's parents – they farm my land and I pay them for what I need, the rest they can have for themselves. I had a very hard time persuading them to allow me to pay them. If they'd had their way, they would do it all for nothing. How could I live with myself if I allowed that to happen?"

Alex agreed, having had personal experience of their generous hospitality and their adamant refusal to accept any recompense. "And, I suppose," he added, "if the steamer can't get here for a few weeks, everyone has to have enough food put by to survive."

"Yes," said Katherine simply. "That's exactly how it is."

They continued on their way across the machair.

Suddenly, Alex asked, "When Donald and I were out yesterday, we talked a bit about Flora MacDonald. Wasn't she born here, on this island?"

Katherine hesitated. "Well, there are many people who would like to think that. But I'm not so sure. All the historical evidence would seem to point to South Uist as being her birthplace. However, we're not too far away from the cottage where she is reputed to have spent part of her early life."

They walked there and Alex seemed fascinated by both the ruin and its location, with extensive views across flattish landscape to the mountains beyond. He stood still; silent and contemplative.

Katherine said, "Well, wherever she was born, can you imagine it, saving a prince? She was incredibly brave and patriotic. And then having the courage and the strength to row him across to the Isle of Skye. Seems incredible, somehow. She's always been something of a heroine of mine and I've been drawn to this place for as long as I can remember. My father used to bring me here and pretend that she was an ancestor because we have the same surname. He used to try and convince me that this was the remains of our family mansion. I never knew whether to believe him or not!"

"Do you think that she and Bonny Prince Charlie were ever in love?"

Katherine laughed. "Romantic legend would have us believe so but unfortunately, I suspect that the reality was very different. Apparently, after she had taken him safely to Skye and he had said farewell, she never saw him again and what's worse in some people's eyes, he never even wrote to thank her! She also spent a year in the Tower of London for her trouble. Then she married someone from Skye called Allan MacDonald and had nine children, emigrated to America, got mixed up in the American War of Independence, before coming home again to Skye, where they stayed."

"Oh, don't disillusion me!" said Alex, laughing. "I've always wanted to believe in the romantic notion of this brave young woman saving her lover from the wicked soldiers. And I've always loved the *Skye Boat Song*, it has such a simple, lilting melody."

Without preamble, Alex began to sing, his voice deep and mellifluous. Katherine joined in, perfect harmony blending both their voices together, the sound carrying across the beautiful landscape of Cairnmor.

They stood in silence at the end of the song, holding each other, sharing a moment of pure magic that affected Alex profoundly.

Here at last was a woman who lived up to his expectations: intelligent, sensuous, musical, practical – a woman who would make him an ideal wife and bear his children. It was time he settled down.

He breathed in deeply and proprietorially placed Katherine's hand in his own.

They made their way back towards the beach to see if Robbie, the original reason for their outing, was there, hoping that he would be able to shed some light on the mystery that they seemed no nearer to solving. They were not to be disappointed in finding him, for there he was, seated by the black painted shack where he kept his nets and oars and other equipment necessary for his profession.

Robbie waved his hand in greeting and said in English, "Och, there ye are. I've been hoping ye would both come today. Now, Katie MacDonald, introduce me to this young man of yours that I saw ye dancing with last Saturday and that I hear ye've been seeing a lot of."

Alex was introduced and they shook hands. Robbie regarded him for a few moments; his gaze penetrating. He smiled, obviously approving of what he saw.

"Aye, ye'll do, ye'll do. Look after the lass now, she's very special to us all."

Alex was becoming accustomed to this and as Robbie was obviously not the type of man to be deceived, he replied, with total honesty, "I shall do my very best."

Satisfied, Robbie turned and began to whittle away at the piece of wood in his hand. "I hear ye're looking to find some people who may or may not have come to the island some years ago?"

"That's correct. About twenty-six or twenty-seven years ago, so we think. A client of my father's who died recently, left his entire inheritance to his son and offspring, neither of whom can be found, nor the mother of his child."

"And your father's a solicitor, yes?"

"That's correct."

"What do you do?"

"I'm a barrister."

"Where?"

"In London."

"I see." Robbie fell silent.

Alex felt as though he was being cross-examined in court; a novel experience, he thought.

The old man continued, "And what were their names, these two that had a babe out of wedlock?"

"Mhairi and Rupert."

52

The old man's eyes flickered for a moment but that was all. It could have been an involuntary action, or it could have been a small act of recognition – Alex could not be certain which. Katherine's attention had been momentarily drawn out to sea by a boat on the horizon, so she had not shared his observation.

Alex produced the photo from the inside pocket of his coat and showed it to Robbie. The old man's face remained passive but Alex sensed something deeper; a moment of consternation, of confusion, perhaps, or was it just his imagination? Robbie handed the photo back to Alex.

"I canna help ye, I'm afraid."

Alex said, trying to search beyond the man's reserve, "Are you sure you can't help us at all?"

Robbie straightened his back in a manner that emphasized his words. "No, I said that I couldna' and I mean it." He spoke with a finality that ended the conversation.

They bade him farewell, and as they walked away, Alex turned back to see Robbie staring out to sea, a faraway expression on his face.

Katherine saw this too and said, "He was rather brusque, which is unusual if I'm around."

"Perhaps it's me?"

"No, that's not the case. He would have expressed his disapproval when you were introduced. He's been known to do that before."

Alex said thoughtfully, "I think he's hiding something."

"But why would he do that?"

"I don't know. But I think he knows more than he's letting on."

"Lawyer's instinct?"

"Perhaps. But there's nothing that will persuade him to tell, whatever it is." Alex sighed. "Shall we go for lunch?"

"That sounds like a good idea."

They walked back to Lochaberdale, arms round each other, leaving Robbie behind and trying not to think about what was to come later.

Robbie watched them as they receded into the distance. He sighed, remembering a young girl many years ago, who had told him of her story and who had gone away again, making him promise not to tell a living soul. Being a man of his word, he had kept that promise even though it had caused him pain and distress later on.

Even now, it was better that Katherine and her friend go on their way, he thought. If they find out from somewhere else, then that was fine… or was it? And once again, here was the essence of Robbie's dilemma – what should he do? Speak or stay silent?

Unaware of Robbie's inner conflict, Katherine and Alex arrived at the hotel just in time for lunch, finding, as expected, that the steamer had already docked. Once they had finished eating, he collected his belongings from his room and they walked down to the quayside to wait for the signal that loading had finished, enabling Alex and the other passengers to go on board.

The people of Lochaberdale whom he had met came to wish Alex well on his journey – John and Marion from the hotel; Donald and Annie from the post office; all of Mary's family.

Fiona MacKinnon, Mary's mother, had brought him food for his journey. "In case the cook isn't up to much," she said, as she handed him a pie wrapped in muslin and gave him a maternal hug.

"You'll come back and see us, won't you?" said Mary, glancing at Katherine.

"Oh yes, you can count on that," he replied, also looking at Katherine. He felt warmed by their attention and their gifts, very aware of the contrast this made with his solitary arrival.

Suddenly, people were boarding; the purser was checking tickets at the foot of the gangplank and it was time for Alex to leave. Discreetly, the islanders moved away from the pier, leaving Katherine and Alex alone together.

They embraced, holding each other for as long as they could before Alex, the last passenger to embark, had to go.

"Write to me, won't you?" said Katherine.

"Of course I will. And you to me."

"Oh, yes."

"We shall see each other again," said Alex, looking at her.

"I know." And with that he was gone, leaving Katherine alone on the quayside with tears trickling down her face.

Wiping them away with the back of her hand, she waved as the boat drew away, as did Alex, standing against the ship's rail and leaning out as far as he could. Katherine stayed at the end of the pier until the steamer was just a tiny dot on the horizon before it finally disappeared from view.

Mary came and stood by her, offering silent comfort until her friend was ready to leave, and Katherine was grateful for her support and consolation.

CHAPTER 8

Letters

17 Cornwallis Gardens
Kensington
London

Sunday evening.

Dearest Katherine,

Saying goodbye to you was one of the hardest things I have ever done. I stayed watching as you stood at the end of the pier until the boat had travelled so far that I could see you no more. Only then did I go inside, feeling very alone.

The journey wasn't too bad; quite long – about nine hours to Oban, or is this average? Despite the calm sea in the bay at Lochaberdale, once we had sailed out of the shelter of the harbour, it became decidedly choppy, and this was on a supposedly calm day! At supper, the Captain and First Officer regaled us with some horrendous tales of stormy weather; even their matter-of-fact delivery couldn't disguise the dramas they described. I really admire these men for their skill and daring, I couldn't do it. I'm afraid I'm very much a fair weather sailor.

The sea calmed down once we had gone past the lighthouse on Ardnamurchan Point and after that it was really beautiful sailing (or should I say steaming?) as we glided past the dark shapes of islands in the gathering gloom. The occasional light twinkled at us as we passed by, sometimes so close you could make out the individual houses on shore.

Soon we had reached our destination and were mooring in Oban harbour. There was a train waiting in the station when we arrived and I managed to catch it. I'm not sure, but I think they hold that connection? Three and a half hours later at three o'clock in the morning, I arrived at Glasgow's Queen Street Station. I decided to book into the nearby Railway Hotel for the night – not the most salubrious of places, but at least it was somewhere to stay.

I was so tired, I fell asleep as soon as my head touched the pillow. I was up again at 7.00 and caught the 10.00 from Glasgow Central to Euston, arriving home earlier this evening.

It felt very strange to be back in London – the whole journey felt crowded with people and noise after the peace and spaciousness of Cairnmor. However, our house was very quiet after the incessant roar of London traffic outside; like an oasis in the centre of town.

Perhaps here, I should explain that I share this house with my father, Alastair, but we each have our own space and lead independent lives – I occupy downstairs and he upstairs. It's an arrangement that suits us very well. It's also useful if we're both working on a case together and means we can discuss business in the comfort of our own home, rather than having to stay late at my Chambers. This has proved its worth time and again for us.

There is also our housekeeper, Mrs Thringle, who lives in the basement flat with her husband and who have both looked after the family for many years.

My mother prefers to spend her time at the house in Oxfordshire and my father goes there at weekends, unless he has pressing work commitments and needs to stay on in London. That's how it has always been for as long as I can remember.

My father and I have always got on well, although when I was growing up, I didn't see too much of him, except in the holidays when I was home from boarding school. We've always looked upon this present arrangement of house sharing as a bonus, allowing us to spend the time together that we missed out on for many years.

Well, my love, I can hardly keep my eyes open, so I shall finish this letter now. I shall post each one separately but I expect you will get them all in a bundle when the steamer brings the post next week. I'll number each envelope as I write so you'll know in which order to open them. (How's that for a lawyer's organized mind!).

I think of you all the time and keep replaying in my mind the wonderful days we spent together on Cairnmor.

Love from Alex xxx

South Lochaberdale,
Cairnmor

10th November, 1936.

Dearest Alex,
Thank you so much for your letters, which arrived by Lochfoyle *this afternoon. I couldn't wait until they were delivered to the croft, so I plagued Donald to let me have mine straightaway. He was a bit reluctant at first, but Annie made him do it. I had to help them sort the post, but it didn't take too long as some kind person at the sorting office in Oban had gathered together all my letters from you and put an elastic band round them. He must have spotted the numbers, for not only were they all together, but they were in numerical order! He must have a tidy mind, or perhaps he's very good at his job, or it was a quiet day and he didn't have anything better to do! Either way, I was very grateful to him as I'm now sitting by the fire with my feet up on the footstool reading your wonderful letters.*

In answer to your question in your second letter, oh, yes please, I would love to come and spend Christmas with you and your family. I so want to see where you live in London and the house in Oxfordshire and the River Thames, but most of all I want to see you. I miss you so much, Alex, and when I'm not working, I go for long solitary walks in all the places we went to together, reliving everything we said and imagining you walking beside me. It seems incredible that we have only known each other for a week, and yet it feels as though it is a lifetime.

Our little cat – I do think the name 'Mistral' suits her so well – must have been pregnant when she blew (literally) into our lives through the door, because she has had a kitten! Well, she had three but unfortunately only one survived. The trauma of her arrival must have been too much for her poor little half-starved body to deal with.

However, she's recovered now and spends an inordinate amount of time washing her offspring. It must be the cleanest new born kitten on record! Misty is certainly proving to be an excellent mum, and the little one is growing daily. I've named the kitten 'Breeze' (no, don't groan – I can hear you from here!) for two reasons: firstly, that it breezed into our lives just as unexpectedly but much more gently; secondly, it's a smaller version of its mum. What do you think?!

Mary and Adam were married yesterday in the church. She looked radiant. Gordon, resplendent in his kilt and full regalia, was as proud as anything as he walked his daughter down the aisle. The service was held in Gaelic, of course, and afterwards we all walked down to the new hall for the traditional dancing and refreshments. Mary's dress was beautifully made (she's an excellent seamstress) and duly admired by everyone, as was mine, which she had also made. The dancing was very energetic, and several people, who shall be nameless, imbibed a little too much good cheer and were firmly removed from the premises by their wives or family, much to everybody's amusement!

At the end of the evening's festivities, Adam and Mary disappeared off to their cottage to change clothes, amid many good wishes and much good-natured teasing. Adam has taken over the tenancy from his great-uncle, who has no children of his own and who has become too frail to cope with the physical demands of running the croft.

Mary offered to let him stay in the cottage, which has been his home for over fifty years and although he appreciated the gesture, he refused, saying he was going to live with his sister on Cairnbeg (we must go there sometime – it's a lovely little island). I think that Mary and Adam are going to have their work cut out with running the croft, he with his fishing and she with her sewing. But they're young and strong and the little farm has been well managed.

Anyway, they're spending their first few days together in what is commonly known as the 'honeymoon cottage', a wonderful little place in Craigruie set in the middle of nowhere with stunning views and easy access to the beach. The weather has been unseasonably mild and sunny and Robbie thinks it will stay that way for the newly-weds! (He said he had ordered it!). He seems to be his usual cheerful self again, but there was definitely something stirred up when we went to see him.

Well, my love, it's getting late and I have to be up early in the morning. So I'll write some more tomorrow. Goodnight, dearest Alex, pleasant dreams.

All my love, Katherine xxxx

Royal Court Chambers,
Middle Temple,
London.

20th November.

Dearest Katherine,

I have an hour or so before meeting with a solicitor who is coming to brief me on a potential case that the Head Clerk would like me to take on. I'm not too sure if I want to accept it, because from what I've heard, it appears to be a particularly messy scenario. So, I thought I'd use this opportunity to write to you.

All your latest batch of letters have arrived now – the last one came this morning.

I'm so glad that you are able to come to London for Christmas and New Year. That knowledge has made me happier than I have been for these past weeks since we parted, knowing that we shall be together again in about a month's time.

I can't wait! How long can you stay? Would you like me to set up your travel arrangements? It's probably easier for me to do so at this end than it is for you on Cairnmor. Or would you prefer to do it yourself? Let me know.

During Christmas itself, we shall be at our house in Maybury. My mother holds a few 'soirées' as she calls them. Rather tedious, I'm afraid, but all the family is expected to attend. If it's an afternoon social gathering, Dad and I tend to creep away as soon as it's polite to do so, and take Sam, the dog, for long walks by the Thames or out onto the Downs. You'll find the scenery very English, with gentle rolling hills, nothing like the majesty of the mountains on Cairnmor, but lovely just the same. There's so much I want to show you!

There's also the Christmas banquet at Middle Temple. It's a charity fund-raising event and very formal – white tie and evening dress obligatory. It's usually quite an occasion, but not as much fun as our ceilidh in Lochaberdale.

Lady Mathieson requested an appointment to see Dad and came to his office the other day. She's very anxious about progress and that we keep searching for Rupert. She's given us permission to spend time in the Park Lane mansion, looking through Rupert's things to see if we can find any clues. Apparently his room has been left exactly as it was on the day he disappeared; his mother refusing to throw anything away or to go through his things, even after all this time, finding it too difficult. Knowing that, Dad asked her how she had come by the photo and the letter from Mhairi. Apparently, she found them in the pocket of Rupert's favourite coat that he had left hanging in the cloakroom closet. It was the one he always wore and the fact that he didn't take it with him seems, I think, indicative that he must have left in quite a hurry. I wonder why?

Lady Mathieson won't be there. She's staying with friends in Devon over the festive season, so we'll have free rein. She's given us the date of her departure and we can go to the house any time after that. Dad suggested that you and I should go. I've told him you are just as hooked as I am on this mystery! He's looking forward to meeting you very much, especially as I haven't been able to stop talking about you and our week together since I got home.

The clerk has just come in to tell me that the solicitor is here, so I'll finish this letter for now. Keep sending me Misty and Breeze stories and let me know how Mary and Adam are enjoying their new life together.

Love from Alex xxx

South Lochaberdale,
Cairnmor

28th November, 1936.

Dearest Alex,

Please do go ahead and book my train tickets – I can sort out the steamer from here. School ends on 15th December (Friday) and we go back on 12th January (Tuesday), which gives us almost three weeks together. I'll catch the steamer on Saturday 16th, stay in Oban overnight and travel on from there. I can't believe that this is actually going to happen. I expect it will be a rough crossing – it usually is at this time of year, as I remember only too well when coming home from boarding school and university for the Christmas holidays. I really hope the steamer sails that weekend; I can cope with waves if I'm going to see you again. I miss you so much.

Anyway, as soon as I told Mary I was going to a formal banquet, she got very excited and started ordering fashion catalogues from the mainland because she wants to make me an evening dress. These arrived yesterday and we spent the afternoon choosing a design so that she can copy it. We sent the order for the material back the same day – Captain MacTaggart was amazed, especially as Mary made him take the envelope and post it himself in Oban! She said it was a very important letter and didn't want to trust it to just anybody. Well, naturally the Captain was flattered, and couldn't resist Mary's request. She can be very persuasive and charming when she puts her mind to it!

So, it's all ordered and Mary's going to start making the dress as soon as the material arrives. She's insistent that I go in the latest fashion and that I'm not to buy anything in London as it will be too expensive and she can do better – both of which are probably very true! So, when we go to the banquet, I shall be wearing an haute-couture dress courtesy of Mary's 'Fashion House of Cairnmor' and be the envy of smart ladies everywhere who've spent a fortune on clothes they could have ordered from her for half the price!

Misty and Breeze are doing well. The two of them are very close and the kitten follows her mother everywhere. They've been coming to school with me, much to the children's delight, and curling up by the stove where it's warm.

A couple of days after this happened the first time, one of the children came into school with two hand-woven cat-sized blankets, which their mother had made on her loom, and a few days later, someone's father brought in a home-made reed basket for the cats to sleep in. So, the children put the blankets in the basket and the cats now sleep there during the day, or just wander round the classroom. The children are very good with them on the whole; Misty doesn't stand any nonsense from them – or Breeze!

Do you remember that little boy, the homer, who was very upset that day you arrived to collect me from school? Well, he's been the kindest of all and the cats have helped him settle in as nothing else seems to have done. He's very protective of them and it would appear that he has a deep love of animals and seems quite knowledgeable, so I set him the task of telling the class how to look after pets, with special reference to cats. He rose magnificently to the occasion and impressed everyone. It was a real boost to his confidence and his reading and writing are developing very quickly now.

Well, I must go now... I'm counting the days...

Ever your loving,

K. xxxx

17 Cornwallis Gardens
London

6th December.

Dearest Katherine,

Your train tickets are booked and collected and I enclose them with this letter. I can't wait! I'll meet you on the platform at Euston Station on Monday morning. I think you are very wise to stay overnight in Oban, travelling to Glasgow on Sunday and then down to London on the sleeper that night. Everything is arranged, including the hotel.

How is the dress? I'm looking forward to seeing it – but most of all, the beautiful lady wearing it!

I won't stay for more now. In a few days' time we'll be together again.

Travel safely, my love, and I'll see you on Monday the 18th at Euston.

Yours, Alex.

CHAPTER 9

London
December, 1936

Alex arrived at Euston Station to meet Katherine's train half an hour early – he wanted to leave enough time to make sure he was there should the train itself arrive ahead of schedule. It was more than that, though. He couldn't wait at home any longer, given the thoughts that had been going through his mind since he had left Cairnmor and the momentous decision he had made. He was anxious to see her again.

He bought a newspaper from the news stand but could not settle to read it. Instead, he nervously paced up and down the concourse in the Great Hall of Euston station aware of, but not seeing, the crowds of people hurrying to and from the trains. Loudspeaker announcements of arrivals and departures permeated his consciousness but none matched the one that would have made him instantly alert.

From the arrivals board, he located the platform where the Royal Scot was expected and found out from the ticket collector at the barrier that the train was on time. Alex decided to buy a platform ticket and having done so, felt marginally better as he passed through the barrier and onto the platform. At least here, he would be ready.

He walked right to the very end, away from the protection of the glass and metal domed station roof overhead and out into the gusting wind, waiting impatiently for the glimpse of steam that would herald Katherine's arrival.

However, it was the whistle that first alerted him to the Royal Scot's imminent arrival. Vaguely at the back of his mind, Alex wondered which engine was hauling the train but the thought was soon lost in his excitement, knowing that the moment for which he had spent the past couple of months waiting was almost here.

The magnificent maroon livery of the engine slowly rounded the bend before the station and Alex had just enough time to retrace his steps back towards the interior, all the while watching the carriages as they glided slowly into the platform, hoping for a glimpse of Katherine.

When he couldn't see her, he had a heart-stopping moment of anxiety that she had not come or had missed the train, but suddenly, there she was, opening the door of the carriage right where he was standing. He went over to her and took her into his arms and kissed her, oblivious to the people whose path they were blocking or those who disapproved of such a public display of affection.

"Oh, Alex," said Katherine, not wanting to let him go. "I've missed you so!"

"And I've missed you, darling," he replied, holding her equally close. "I can't begin to tell you how much."

They stood with their arms round each other, holding on tightly and smiling at one another, until a discreet cough behind them brought them back to reality as a porter with a heavily laden luggage trolley tried to pass by.

Both of them wished to savour and prolong this special moment after so many weeks of waiting but they needed to be practical as well. Reluctantly, they drew apart and Alex found a porter, who located Katherine's two large suitcases in the luggage van and trundled them up to the ticket barrier, where they relinquished their tickets and emerged into the wonderful elegance and spaciousness of the Great Hall.

Katherine stood still, speechless for a moment, looking up in wonder at the ornate staircases and the equally elaborate decoration of the high ceiling.

"I've never seen any building quite as amazing as this," she said. "And it's only a station! I hope this is indicative of what's to come?!"

Alex, who had been silent, watching her, just smiled somewhat enigmatically and said, "Well, not all the architecture of London is quite as splendid as this, but I think it's a very special place and even more so now that you're here."

Katherine said nothing but her expression held all the eloquence of love. They embraced once more and when they had reached the entrance to the station, Alex tipped the porter and took her suitcases from the luggage trolley.

They went outside and Katherine waited underneath the extravagant elegance of Euston Arch, with its Portland stone pillars and Grecian-style portico, while Alex hailed a taxi. They sank gratefully into its slightly worn leather seats after he had given his address to the driver.

The taxi took its place in the slow-moving traffic of Euston Road, where trams, taxis, private cars, motor-buses, steam lorries and delivery vans – some motorized, some horse-drawn – all jostled for road space. For a while, they didn't speak but just held hands.

Then Alex said, "You look wonderful by the way – I don't think I quite expected to see you looking so... so..."

"Fashionable?" interrupted Katherine, raising an eyebrow.

"Yes... no... I mean, I don't think I'd thought anything..."

"Go on, keep digging yourself in deeper." Katherine laughed, teasing him. "Now see here, Alexander Stewart, you don't think I'd arrive in a metropolis like London in my ankle-length woollen skirt and shawl do you? We're not that primitive or unaware on Cairnmor!"

Alex was suitably chastised and took it all in good part.

"You see," continued Katherine, "Mary and I didn't just order the material for my evening dress, I also chose some outfits from one of the mail order catalogues. Fortunately, they arrived in time and Mary just altered the clothes to fit me better. We had great fun." She grinned at him. "Everyone sends best wishes by the way and hopes you are well and that it won't be too long before they see you again. They mean it, too."

Alex smiled, warmed by their thoughts. "I know that. I think that's one of the things I like very much about Cairnmor. You know exactly where you stand and I found it most refreshing. I felt I made new friends during my time there. It's that sort of place. And I shall come back and see you," he added.

The taxi driver watched them in his rear-view mirror and although he was usually a sociable man and liked to chat with his passengers, he decided on this occasion that his conversation would not be welcomed. This couple only had eyes and ears for each other and, happy for them, he left them to it.

Soon the taxi was making its way along Knightsbridge, turning left into the Brompton Road, past Harrods and onwards to South Kensington. As with all taxi drivers, he knew London streets like the proverbial back of his hand and delivered his passengers efficiently to an impressive three-story, white-fronted house, set back from the pavement in a quietly gracious residential road. Alex paid the driver and carried Katherine's suitcases to the house.

They were met at the glossy blue front door by a plumpish lady in her early fifties, wearing a large, white apron and wiping clean, floury hands onto a tea towel. She greeted them expansively. "Come in, come in," she said, standing aside for them to enter. Before Alex could say anything by way of introduction, she said, "I'm Mrs Thringle, the housekeeper, but Mr Alex here calls me Mrs 'Thing' most of the time, so I'd take it as a big compliment if you'd do the same. You must be Miss Katherine." She paused briefly in her flow of conversation and shook Katherine's hand. "We've heard so much about you, I feel as though I know you already and all about that island where you live. Mr Alex hasn't been able to stop talking about it since he got back."

Alex looked slightly embarrassed at this but Katherine smiled at him, gratified. She took an immediate liking to the housekeeper and said, "Well, I'll have to let you in on a little secret. I'm afraid that I haven't been able to stop talking about Alex either! I'm very pleased to meet you. Alex wrote all about you in his letters."

Mrs Thringle looked at Alex. "Nothing bad, I hope."

Katherine was quick to reassure her. "Not at all. He said that he and his father couldn't manage without you, that you're a real treasure. And your husband, too!" she added.

The housekeeper was suitably pleased and said to Alex, "I definitely approve of *this* one!"

Katherine was somewhat taken aback by this remark and seeing her reaction, Alex discreetly gave the housekeeper a warning glance.

"I didn't mean it to sound quite like that, dear," added Mrs Thringle hastily. "What I meant to say is that Mr Alex here is a very particular man – we were beginning to fear he'd never find anyone who would meet with his exacting standards!"

Reassured to a certain extent, Katherine was nonetheless left with a feeling of insecurity. She had been so happy and so wrapped up in her feelings for Alex, that she hadn't given a thought to any previous relationships he might have had.

It made her aware of just how little she really knew him.

"Leave your suitcases in the hall, my dear, and Mr Thing will take them up for you. Would you mind finding him, dearie, he's in the garden?" she said, addressing Alex, who dutifully went towards the back of the house and into the garden, visible through the French doors at the rear of the property.

Mrs Thringle mounted the stairs. "Let me show you to your room. You're on the top floor, I'm afraid. A bit of a trek, but I always reckon that stairs keep us all fit. We live in the basement and Bob does the garden and any maintenance that's needed around the house. There is a maid who comes in every day and does the cleaning. She's called Hannah and is engaged to Joseph who is a delivery boy for Hamble's the Grocers in High Street Ken."

As Katherine had no idea where or what 'High Street Ken' was, she merely nodded in acknowledgement of the information being imparted.

Her room, when they reached it, was light and sunny and looked out onto the road at the front of the house. Opposite was a large square with grass, bushes and trees, enclosed by black painted railings; a park in miniature, in fact. Mr Thringle appeared at that moment, bearing her luggage and, having been introduced, disappeared downstairs again.

The housekeeper showed Katherine where the bathroom was and suggested that she might like to settle herself in before coming down to Mr Alex's sitting room for a cup of tea, after which it would be time for lunch.

"You must be gasping for a cuppa after all that travelling," she said kindly.

Katherine thanked the housekeeper as she left, grateful for a few moments to gather her thoughts and try to unravel some of the innumerable sights and sounds that she had encountered since her arrival in London.

She unpacked her suitcases, putting her clothes and other items away in the chest of drawers and the wardrobe and stood by the window looking out over an unfamiliar urban landscape, trying not to dwell on anything about Alex's past which might, by definition, affect his future reliability. Quickly, she put that particular thought out of her mind and distracted herself by studying the trees, a part of nature she had always loved. Paradoxically, there were more trees in this city than there were on the whole of Cairnmor and Katherine found this to be an unexpected bonus.

Once downstairs, she found Alex sitting on the cream-coloured sofa, briefcase by his feet sifting through a bundle of papers. He stood up as Katherine came into the room.

"All sorted?" he asked.

"Yes, it's a lovely room," she said brightly, not revealing any of her inner concerns. "Mrs Thing is quite a character, isn't she?"

Having heard herself say it, Katherine decided she would use the housekeeper's proper name in future. Mrs *Thing* didn't feel quite right.

Alex agreed with Katherine's observation of Mrs Thringle's personality. "Yes, she came into our lives when I was very tiny and has organized us ever since – in the nicest possible way of course!"

"How did she get her nickname?"

Alex laughed. "I couldn't pronounce Thringle when I was little, I could only say 'Thing' so I suppose the name stuck and she and her husband have been known to me as Mr and Mrs Thing ever since!" Alex, hesitated, before saying, "I'm afraid I have to go into Chambers this afternoon. I've got a pre-trial conference with my father, who's the briefing solicitor for this particular case, and the client. We have the preliminary hearing in court tomorrow morning, which should only take a couple of hours. After that the trial begins in earnest. I had hoped it wouldn't take place until after Christmas so that we would have more time together, but another trial finished early and a court became available, so they moved our date forward. I have no control over that, I'm afraid."

Alex stopped talking, distracted by Katherine, who was regarding him so lovingly that he could do nothing else but pull her down onto the sofa beside him, kissing her with such eagerness and intensity that it needed gentle firmness and tact from Katherine, breathless and somewhat dishevelled, to end the embrace before they became too carried away. She was also mindful that Mrs Thringle or Hannah could at any moment come through the door.

Having gathered together both themselves and the scattered papers, removing the latter out of harm's way, they sat on the settee sedately holding hands.

"Can I come and watch the trial once it starts?" she asked, her composure restored. "I'd be really interested to see what you do."

"Of course," said Alex. "I'll get you a special pass. Even though members of the public are allowed in to watch, with a pass you'll be able to have a more privileged view of the proceedings."

At that moment, Hannah the maid came into the room carrying a tray with all things necessary for afternoon tea. She smiled shyly at Katherine, who said, "Hello." The girl just smiled again and withdrew.

Alex remarked, "Very hard-working, but doesn't say an awful lot!"

"I can see that," Katherine replied. "Honestly, don't worry about this afternoon. I'm feeling tired, actually, and wouldn't mind a rest."

Alex was immediately solicitous, feeling guilty that he hadn't considered that before. Katherine reassured him that she was fine. "So, what time will you be back?" she said.

"Probably about six o'clock." And then, as casually as he was able to make his voice sound, he said, "I thought we could go out for dinner this evening. I've booked a table at a lovely place that I know of in South Ken, not too far away from here. It's very much like a country house hotel. In fact it reminded me of the hotel in Lochaberdale. The restaurant is open to non-residents. Would you like that?"

"I'd love it!" she said without hesitation. "But please do explain to me – what is all this 'Ken' business? South Ken, High Street Ken and so on."

"Oh, Ken is just a shortened form of Kensington."

"Ah, I see. And Kensington is… ?"

"The district of London in which this house sits."

"I see," said Katherine. "Is this restaurant *very* smart, or just *smart*? So that I know what to wear." She was a little anxious about this and didn't want to let Alex down.

He smiled reassuringly. "Oh, just *smart*! Perfect for you and me. And don't worry, just be you. You'll look lovely in whatever you choose to wear!"

"Aye, lad, so I'll bring out the woollen skirt and shawl then!" she said, teasing him.

"That's fine by me," he said boldly, before suffering a moment of acute anxiety in case she actually meant it.

Katherine, however, took him at his word and hugged him for his answer. Then she said, "Will your father be home at the same time as you"

"Yes, he should be. I think he was intending to come straight from my Chambers to here. He's looking forward to meeting you."

"As I am him."

At that moment, the dulcet tones of a gong sounded, heralding lunch and Katherine and Alex went into the dining room downstairs, another very light room, the one with the double French doors visible from the front door.

Katherine slept deeply that afternoon, more tired than she had realized after her travels, and awoke at about four o'clock feeling slightly disorientated. She bathed in the black and white tiled bathroom – a luxury after her tin bath in front of the range at home – and felt refreshed and recovered.

Afterwards, having dressed ready for the evening, she sat for a while on the cushioned window seat in Alex's sitting room, a book on her lap, open but unread, her head resting against the glass, reflecting upon this new world into which she had come.

It was in this position that Alastair first saw Katherine as he and Alex walked along the pavement towards the house from the Underground station.

Looking up at her as she sat framed by the window, a picture of quiet contemplation, he wondered about this latest young woman that Alex had invited to stay. He hoped that she was as lovely as her appearance seemed to suggest and that she would be right for his son, whose love life to date had not been particularly noteworthy. Alastair could not help but be anxious that Alex was embarking upon yet another new relationship. More than anything, his son needed to find someone who would bring him lasting happiness and stability.

Perhaps, finally, she would be the one to provide this.

Alex waved and Katherine returned his greeting. She felt slightly nervous at the prospect of meeting Alastair but any worries or concerns either of them may have entertained about the other were dispelled from the moment they were introduced for they took to each other immediately.

Katherine found Alastair Stewart to be a kind man, not quite as tall as Alex, and very much younger than she had imagined. He was attractive in appearance and yet modest in his manner, possessing a gentle charm and natural courtesy which she found most endearing.

For his part, being a perceptive man, it took Alastair only a matter of seconds to discern her character and decide that she was exactly the sort of young lady he had hoped his son would find.

He smiled and all at once, Katherine felt at home.

"I'm glad to meet you at last," he said, his handshake firm yet warm and welcoming. "Alex has told me a great deal about you, my dear, and I've been looking forward to seeing the real version very much!"

"I've been looking forward to meeting you, as well," she replied, experiencing a huge sense of relief that this particular hurdle had proved to be such an easy one.

With the formalities over, they sat down while Mrs Thringle brought in the inevitable pot of tea on a tray with all the usual accompaniments.

Presently, Katherine said to Alastair, by way of conversation, but also out of genuine interest, "Alex has told me that you're a solicitor but I have no idea as to the difference between what you do and what a barrister does."

"A lot of people ask that question," he replied. "A solicitor is someone to whom a member of the public goes when they need help with a legal matter, such as the drafting of a will or buying property. But if a dispute arises between two parties and the case has to go to court, or an expert legal opinion is needed on a particular point of law, then the services of a barrister are called upon. A barrister doesn't deal directly with a client in the first instance, that is for the solicitor to do, but the solicitor will instruct the barrister on the case. The barrister reviews the evidence, assessing whether it is viable or not to take it to court. If it is, then the barrister drafts the pleadings and they meet together with the client to discuss procedure and the detailed legal arguments ready for the court hearing."

"I see. So that's what you meant when you said that your father was the 'briefing solicitor' on your case at the moment," said Katherine to Alex.

"That's right," he replied. "Only barristers have what are called 'rights of audience' in the higher courts, like the Royal Courts of Justice or the Old Bailey, and are allowed to present a case before judge and jury. Barristers have to be expert in the particular dispute procedure that they are acting upon. In court, it is their job to present the facts in an effective and convincing manner in order to win the case."

"Presumably, the solicitor is present in court at the trial?"

"Yes, they have to be so that they continue to be part of the whole process," said Alastair, "and instruct the barrister on the client's wishes and advise the client as to the barrister's opinion on any further legal matters as the trial progresses. Alex and I are fortunate in that my main area as a solicitor within my firm is in the drafting and execution of wills and dealing with probate and, as he is a member of the Chancery Division, which deals with Civil as opposed to Criminal Law, that among other things is also one of Alex's specialisms. It is an interest and expertise we have in common."

"Hence the two of you coming together to try to solve the mystery of Mhairi and Rupert."

"Exactly – and fortunately, unlike the case we are about to embark on, there is no dispute about the terms of the will, it's just that the heir or heirs cannot be found."

"A bit critical, really!" said Katherine.

"Definitely," replied Alastair, smiling. "Talking of which, I had a letter from Lady Mathieson today to say that she has, as of yesterday, vacated the London house for Christmas and the New Year and that we are free to go through Rupert's things whenever it is convenient. We can also take anything away that may be helpful, as long as it is properly documented and returned when we have finished with it. I'm not able to be present, but I wondered whether you and Katherine would like to go?"

"We'd love to!" said Alex, confident that he could speak for Katherine.

She nodded her agreement, happy to be able to continue the project that had brought Alex to Cairnmor, but which seemed to have drawn a blank on the island.

"Let's see," considered Alex. "We have the preliminary hearing in the morning, what if we go tomorrow afternoon for a first visit?"

"Aye, that sounds fine to me," said Katherine.

"Now if we're to go out this evening, I need to get changed, otherwise I shall look like a disgrace next to this lovely lady here!" Alex got up from the sofa and kissed Katherine on top of her head, before leaving the room.

Once his son was out of ear-shot, Alastair said, "I do believe you've captured his heart."

It was a simple statement; unaffected, caring.

Katherine smiled. "I certainly hope so," she said, "because he has captured mine."

"I can see that!" said Alastair, smiling with genuine warmth and pleasure.

He said nothing further, nor did Katherine – there was no need – but from that moment on, there was an affinity, a natural understanding between them.

They sat in companionable silence – Alastair with the newspaper and Katherine her book, although she read very little, waiting for Alex to reappear, which he did very shortly.

After putting on their coats and bidding goodbye to Alastair, they went out into the square and as it was a mild night, even for December, walked the relatively short distance to the Prince's Hotel. It was indeed similar in feel to the hotel in Lochaberdale and Katherine felt as though she was on familiar territory within its Victorian interior.

The tables were candlelit and the electric lighting on the walls was discreet and low level. They were shown to their table, hidden away by the window, and the menu produced. The food was delicious and they talked of many things during the meal, glad to be sharing each other's company once again and rekindling the closeness discovered during their evenings in Katherine's cottage while the storm raged outside on Cairnmor.

As they lingered over their coffee, both reluctant for the evening to end, Alex leant across the table and took both of Katherine's hands in his. His heart was beating so loudly, he was sure she could hear it; his mouth was dry and he was more nervous than at any time during a court case. He cleared his throat, all the while not taking his eyes off Katherine.

"There's something I'd like to ask you," he began.

"Yes?" said Katherine, her heart also beating very fast.

He paused for what seemed like an eternity before he asked, "Will you marry me?"

"Oh, yes," she responded immediately; joy and pure happiness flowing through her.

Alex let out a sigh of relief. Katherine smiled and he leaned across the table and kissed her gently on the lips before saying, "Close your eyes and hold out your hands," which Katherine duly did, and into them he placed a small box. Surprised, she opened her eyes and carefully lifted the lid. Inside was the most exquisite sapphire and diamond ring.

"Oh, Alex!" she exclaimed, her eyes filling with tears. "It's so beautiful!"

Carefully, he took the ring out of the box and placed it on the third finger of her left hand. It fitted perfectly. Katherine held up her hand to look. "How did you know whether it was the right size?"

"I couldn't be sure, but when we were on the island, I put my finger round yours and measured it up."

Katherine smiled. "I think I can remember when you did that. It was when we were talking about Rupert and Mhairi at my cottage. You knew you were going to ask me even back then?" she added in amazement.

"I had an idea. But the real moment came when we sang *Skye Boat Song* together. It was then I knew that I wanted to make you mine." And Alex kissed the ring on her finger, sealing their engagement with a gesture of genuine charm.

They walked home in silence, both very aware of the life-changing decisions that would have to be made, both reluctant to disturb the romance and joy of this special moment in their lives. However, after a moment or two, Katherine chuckled.

"What is it, dear?" asked Alex.

"Oh, I was just thinking about what Father McPhee said to me at the quayside before I left home."

"Please tell me"

Katherine hesitated before she said, "He hoped that you were going to look after my virtue while I was in the big city full of wicked temptations. I replied in jest, telling him to mind his own business and that I'm over twenty-one. I think I shocked him somewhat, because unfortunately, he took me literally. He probably thinks I'm doomed already!"

Alex was quiet again, but when he did speak it was in all seriousness. "I think if it is at all possible, we should wait. Not because of what the Father McPhees of this world might think, but because we think it's the best thing for us. But, having said that, I won't find it easy and we should be married as soon as possible because I don't know how long I can last without making love to you."

"I understand," she replied, appreciating his honesty and grateful to him for his forbearance, remembering his physical attentions in the rose garden on Cairnmor and earlier that afternoon; realizing the sacrifice this would entail on his part.

After a while, she said, "As ever, there are things to work out, big things, important issues, like where we're going to live. But, putting those aside for now, what if we got married in the spring, in April? I'd really like to be married on the island if that's possible. It's beautiful at that time of the year and Cairnmor weddings are very special."

Alex smiled. "That would be wonderful," he said. "I can think of no other place where I would prefer us to be married."

They stopped and Alex kissed her tenderly and for the first time, told her that he loved her. Then, putting their arms round each other, in blissful silence, they continued to walk the short distance back to Cornwallis Gardens.

CHAPTER 10

They were up early the next day. Alex and Alastair had case notes to go through before that morning's preliminary hearing and wanted to be at Alex's Chambers in good time. They ate breakfast together, Katherine wanting to see Alex before he left for work, and arranged to meet at lunchtime. Alex gave Katherine directions for Royal Court Chambers in Middle Temple Lane and asked what she had planned to do that morning.

"Well, I thought I'd write to Mary and then explore some of London."

"I have just the map for you!" said Alex, going to the bookcase in the dining room. "An A to Z of London, just published. It's brilliant. Apparently, the lady who compiled it was fed up with trying to navigate her way round London using maps that were twenty years old and out of date, so she spent a year or so making this. A real labour of love, I'd say. It's self-published too. That's dedication for you!" He gave the map to Katherine, who opened it up.

"This is perfect, thank you!" she said, smiling at Alex's enthusiasm.

After breakfast, as he and Alastair gathered their things together and prepared to leave, Alex said, "You'll be all right, won't you? Don't get lost, it's a big city."

"I'll be fine. I like exploring. And don't forget, I have lived in both Edinburgh and Glasgow and survived, so I'm no stranger to cities. Cairnmor may seem like the end of the world, but some of us who live there have travelled a bit, you know!" she added mischievously.

He kissed her briefly on her cheek and Katherine stood at the door and waved to father and son as they left. Before they turned the corner, Alex turned round and blew her a kiss, which she returned.

Feeling very cheerful and anticipating the day to come, she sat down at the large desk in Alex's sitting room and composed a letter to Mary. While she was writing, she thought about her friend, wondering how she was faring. Although Adam was a likeable man, he had some serious flaws which Mary, totally in love, had chosen not to see. Somewhat naïvely, because her parents had a good marriage, Mary believed absolutely in the redemptive powers of love.

Katherine was not so sure. She was worried on two counts – firstly, that Adam would be so involved with his fishing, which was his passion, an obsession almost, that he would be of little help around the croft and, secondly, that he would not be able to control his craving for alcohol.

She knew that Adam had not relinquished it after his marriage as he had promised, nor had Mary been able to stop him drinking with his friends. Katherine was also aware of her friend's growing anxiety and that so far, she had steadfastly refused to confide in her parents, saying that it was her problem and she should be the one to deal with it.

However, Katherine expressed none of these concerns in her letter and wrote cheerfully, describing her journey, the house, the luxury of having electricity, hot water and someone to prepare all your meals and do the housework. But most importantly, she wrote of her engagement and concluded:

*Alex is wonderful (of course) and his father, Alastair, and Mr and Mrs
Thringle are kind and good people. I like it here but do I want to live in
London? I don't know yet. It all seems very new and very strange. And despite
my present happiness, I do miss Cairnmor and seeing all the familiar faces.*
Anyway, give my love to everyone and I'll write again soon.

Katherine signed her letter and addressed the envelope. She went upstairs to get
her coat and put her comfortable walking shoes on – reasoning that pavements
were just as hard on the feet as the stony paths at home – but in her bag, she
carried her more 'elegant' shoes, not being sure where they would be going for
lunch.

She bid farewell to Mrs Thringle and set off on her exploration. She found a
post-box, having previously obtained a stamp from the ever-helpful housekeeper,
and posted the letter. After consulting her map, she walked in the direction of
South Kensington Underground Station, her first point of reference. She decided
not to go in, preferring to wait for Alex before attempting the complexities of the
Underground system alone until she understood how it operated.

Instead, Katherine crossed the road, passing small art galleries and bookshops
and a café until she came to a busy main intersection which she crossed with
other pedestrians, aided by a friendly, but business-like policeman, resplendent in
his characteristic uniform complete with large white cuffs, thus enabling his arms
to be highly visible when directing the traffic.

On her left was the magnificent Natural History Museum and then further up
Exhibition Road, she passed the Geological Museum and the Science Museum.
Those she decided to save for another day. After passing Imperial College, she
turned left into Prince Consort Road and paused a couple of hundred yards later,
looking across the road and up wide shallow steps towards the magnificently
rotund Albert Hall.

These were all places of which she had read, knowing she was coming to
London, from books she had ordered and borrowed from the travelling library
that came to the island every fortnight on the steamer. The architecture was just as
elegant as she had imagined it to be and it was amazing to see the buildings in
real life rather than as pictures in a book.

Katherine's gaze was drawn to individuals and small groups of young people
entering a building just behind her; some carrying cello cases, others violin cases
and some just briefcases. Tantalizing sounds of classical music wafted onto the
street every time the door opened and she looked up at the doorway to read the
words 'Royal College of Music' above. She knew that if it were at all possible,
she would like to go inside.

Along with history, music was her other great love and she had always wanted
to visit a conservatoire such as this, having wondered early on in her life whether
or not to pursue a musical career. So, taking advantage of this opportunity, she
followed the students into the building and asked the porter as he sat in his wood
and glass 'lodge' just inside the door if it would be possible for her to have a look
round. He said that was permissible and asked her to sign the visitors book, which

she duly did, taking great delight in writing '17 Cornwallis Gardens' as her address.

She walked up the few steps straight ahead of her towards the concert hall. Quietly, she opened the door, looked inside and descended into the main auditorium. There was an orchestral rehearsal taking place and for half an hour, Katherine sat and listened, absorbed by the music and fascinated by the rehearsal process unfolding before her. At its conclusion, Katherine left the hall and spent a pleasant and instructive time wandering around the building, discreetly eavesdropping outside the teaching rooms on the lessons taking place within.

She thanked the porter as she left, signed out and emerged once more into Prince Consort Road, this time crossing over the road and up the steps to the Royal Albert Hall. She walked all the way round the building just for the fun of it before heading in the direction of Kensington Gardens. Here, she explored a few of the paths, watching the squirrels as they darted about, up and down the bare-branched trees, not afraid to take food if it was offered them by passing human beings.

Carefully keeping watch as to the time, Katherine made her way back to Kensington Road to the bus stop and waited for the number nine bus which Alex had told her to catch. She didn't have long to wait and decided to sit upstairs. The front seat was vacant, so Katherine had an excellent view of London as it unfolded before her – the wrought-iron gates of Hyde Park; the elegant shops of Knightsbridge; the busy thoroughfare of Park Lane off to her left; Piccadilly, with its centre-piece statue of Eros; Trafalgar Square with Nelson's Column soaring high above the city; the Strand – so many of the famous landmarks about which she had read.

There was an elegance and grandeur to the buildings of central London which she found she liked and admired, together with an energy which she felt she could adjust and tune into. But where was the peace and quiet, the sense of repose? Even in the park, with all its trees and grass, she had felt surrounded by the bustling city.

Perhaps tranquillity was to be found outside of the capital, in the English countryside. Therefore, she would look forward to exploring that with Alex and seeing if it was indeed the case.

Katherine alighted in the Aldwych and walked past St Clement Danes Church on her right and the Gothic splendour of the Royal Courts of Justice on her left. She stopped to admire the magnificence of the building; the intricate stonework and overwhelming grandeur, before turning and crossing the road at Temple Bar. She located the narrow Middle Temple Lane and walked down to the square on her right, past the fountain and onto Royal Court Chambers which were directly ahead.

There she came across Alex's name listed with all the other barristers, each with their own individual brass name plate and, after fondly running her fingers over his, she entered the building. She was shown to Alex's room by the receptionist, where she sat down and waited for him.

There was a large desk in front of the window and branches of trees were just visible through the glass. Books lined the walls – large volumes of case law – and bundles of paper, tied with pink ribbon, were piled on the desk. Katherine sat in one of the chairs opposite, enjoying the feeling of being where Alex worked while he was in Chambers.

The door opened and she turned round expectantly but it was a stranger who entered the room. Her face must have reflected her disappointment because he said, "Sorry. I'm not Alex."

Katherine smiled and said, "That's all right."

He came into the room and introduced himself. "I'm Michael Granger, Alex's best friend. He said that if you arrived before he had finished in court, then I was to entertain you. So, here I am! I'm glad to meet you, by the way. Alex has plagued us, well particularly me, non-stop, talking about you and his time on Cairnmor."

Katherine laughed and said, "Yes, he appears to have done that with his family as well! It would seem I have a lot to live up to. I can only hope I'm up to the task!"

Unexpectedly, Michael asked, "I don't mean to pry, but has he asked you to marry him yet?"

Surprised by the personal nature of the question from someone she had only just met, Katherine replied cautiously, "Er, yes, actually he has."

"Did you say yes?"

"I did."

Michael was relieved. "Thank goodness for that – I couldn't have coped with the emotional upheaval if you'd said no! When he told me that he'd even consider giving all this up for you, I couldn't believe it. If he means what he says, that really is something because Alex is one of the most dedicated men that I know. I never thought he would ever find a woman who... er... suited him. Over the years, he's been a difficult man to please."

On one level Katherine was heartened and reassured by Michael's honesty, while on another, after his last sentence, she experienced yet another bout of insecurity concerning Alex's past. .

Trying to quell her doubts, she said, "Well, neither of us is very sure what we're going to do at the moment. We've rather skirted round the issue, because deciding where to live is going to be a very difficult decision for both of us. One of us will have to make a huge sacrifice but I'm ever the optimist and I'm sure something will persuade us one way or the other."

Michael nodded his head in agreement, appreciating Katherine's approach and understanding her perspective.

"How long have you and Alex known each other?" she asked, presently.

"For our sins, we were at Oxford together. But Alex was the conscientious one. Head down, strong work ethic. Got a First, lucky devil."

Katherine laughed. "How about you?"

"Oh, a Two-One. Respectable, but my father was disappointed, said I'd got more brains than that. But I had a broken romance just before Finals and I let it get to me. Affected the result, unfortunately. Alex was brilliant though, pulled me through. Without his help, I wouldn't have passed at all. He's the very best friend anyone could have."

Katherine was gratified to hear this and liked Michael's loyalty to her future husband. "Do you enjoy your work?"

"Yes, I do. But it's just a job to me, unlike Alex for whom the law is a vocation and means everything to him. I'm good at it, but my heart isn't here I'm afraid. It's on the land." Michael paused, his expression wistful. "I grew up on a farm in Shropshire, you see, and my father wanted me to have something more than he's got, so he made huge sacrifices to enable me to have the best education possible. I did well at boarding school, won a scholarship to Oxford, got a pupillage and then a tenancy with Royal Court Chambers and here I am! But I'd give it all up in an instant and live on one of the crofts on your island – it appeals to my romantic nature, you see, and my need to be close to the great outdoors!"

"It's very hard work."

"Oh, I'm not afraid of that. As it is, I spend every moment that I can on the family farm. Love the land, you see, much more than the law. Hey, marry me instead, and then there'd be no dilemma!"

"Thank you for the offer, but I'll take my chances with Alex."

They both laughed, then Michael said, "What do you do? Alex did say, but tell me again anyway."

"I'm a teacher at the school in Lochaberdale, though history and music remain my passions. It's a job which I love, but I also want to give something back to the community because I owe the islanders a lot as they paid for my education."

"Moral obligation is something of a burden, isn't it?" replied Michael, thinking of his parents. "I can identify with that totally".

"Of course, but it's more than that. I love Cairnmor, it's a very profound part of me as a person. Like all this is a part of Alex," and Katherine indicated the room with all its books and documents and obvious links to his profession.

Michael was thoughtful, aware of her change of mood. Not wishing to let the conversation become too serious and resuming his usual lively manner, he asked, "So, before teaching, did you go to university?"

"Yes, to Edinburgh."

"Reading what?"

"History."

"What did you get?"

"A First," said Katherine apologetically.

Michael clapped his hands to his forehead and gave a mock groan. "Oh dear, another conscientious clever-clogs! I'm surrounded by them!"

"Surrounded by what?!" said Alex, as he came into the room.

"Horrible intelligent people like you. Unlike poor me, of course, who is destined for the scrap heap." And Michael, in a very effective manner, went to make a dramatic exit, but not before he had paused in the door-way and said to Katherine, "It was very nice to meet you, I'm sure we'll meet again soon."

Katherine, highly amused, said that she was sure that would be the case.

"Oh no, not more cases, can't get away from them… !" he said, as he exited the room.

"Idiot!" said Alex affectionately. "Now, let's go and have some lunch as I'm starving after all that depositioning in Court."

74

And, taking Katherine's elbow with his hand, they left Royal Court Chambers and had lunch at a small restaurant in the Strand, catching up on the morning's events. After this, they took a taxi to Park Lane where the Mathieson mansion was located.

"Phew," whistled Alex, as they alighted from the taxi in front of the building. "Even after some of the country piles I've been to, this really is some residence!"

Katherine's eyes opened wide, as she surveyed the impressive façade. "My goodness. Rupert and Mhairi and their offspring are going to have something of a shock once they realize the extent of their inheritance, what with the shipyard and the money as well as this!"

"That is if they're still alive or, in the baby's case, exist at all."

"Too true."

Alex rang the doorbell and presently the door was opened by a formally-dressed butler with grey hair and a very upright manner. After Alex had introduced himself and Katherine, they were ushered into a vast hallway, with a black and white tiled floor and curving staircase up to a galleried landing, back-lit by large windows. The opulent interior spoke of enormous wealth, and large Chinese Ming dynasty pots containing tall ferns, placed either side of the staircase, added to the air of affluence and distinction.

"Please come this way. Madam said you were to have free access to Master Rupert's room," and the butler led them up the plush carpeted stairs, where not so much as a creak disturbed the elegance.

Once they had reached Rupert's room, he spoke again, his manner haughty. "I cannot say that I approve of this. But it is what Madam wishes. Please be very careful."

With that he closed the door and left them alone. Alex and Katherine had to suppress their laughter.

"Poor chap, it must pain him greatly to allow us across the threshold, let alone in here, the inner sanctum of his house," said Alex, looking around the immaculately tidy and clean room with interest.

Katherine agreed. "Strangers invading his territory and coming to pry into his family's private affairs… Still you have to have some sympathy for him."

"Absolutely. So, where shall we begin?"

"Well, I'd like to start with that desk."

"All right and I'll investigate the bookshelf."

"What am I looking for?"

"Anything – letters, notes, documents – anything that will give us a clue as to where Rupert went."

"Surely, he wouldn't have wanted to leave evidence like that behind. If he'd wanted to disappear, then he would have covered his tracks pretty thoroughly," said Katherine, sorting through each compartment in the desk, but finding nothing of relevance. There were old bills, scraps of paper with reminders on them and used, discarded local train tickets. "Some desks have secret compartments, don't they? I wonder if this one does?"

Alex came over to her and they began to pull at the dividers between the compartments but nothing sprang out to reveal a hidden secret. It was very frustrating. Then Katherine tried the drawer underneath the flap. It was locked.

"Of course it had to be!" said Alex.

"Just like all the best mystery novels – you have to have a locked drawer!" remarked Katherine.

"So, where, I wonder, is the key?"

"The key or not the key, that is the question!" said Katherine, intentionally mis-quoting Hamlet.

"Well, I hope we're not going to come across too many slings and arrows of outrageous fortune on this search!" quipped Alex in response.

They both laughed and Alex wanted to take Katherine in his arms and kiss her but, as time was of the essence, they continued with the search.

"There might be something in his coat, you know, where Lady Mathieson found one of Mhairi's letters and the photograph? It might still be in the cloakroom."

"That's a distinct possibility, because it would seem that he left in a hurry. It'll be a bit of a long shot for the coat to still be there after all this time. However, I'll go and investigate and disturb old sour-puss from his afternoon nap." And Alex disappeared out of the room and down the stairs.

Katherine continued to explore the desk. She opened the cupboards underneath the drawer but they revealed nothing of significance. So, she began to look at the crowded book shelves. Rupert had been a prolific reader of both fiction and non-fiction, judging by the variety and scope of the literature before her, but it was among several dog-eared and much read volumes of school-boy adventure stories that she discovered two books about Scotland.

One was a history of the country, which she had come across while at Edinburgh and which laid great emphasis on the rebellions and the clearances. The other was a famous travel book by George Fergus Mayhew, written towards the end of the 19th century, about his journeys in the Outer Islands of Scotland, including Cairnmor.

Katherine couldn't believe it; here was another link to the island. It was a book she knew well for it was on her bookshelf at home. Taking both of them with her, she sat down in the armchair by the window.

The travel book fell open at the chapter on Cairnmor; it had obviously been read many times. It was also annotated with words in the margins: 'Mhairi wants to live here'; 'seems ideal'; 'remote and distant'; 'no one could find us'.

Alex came back upstairs, having had no luck with finding the key; the coat no longer where it had been kept – hardly surprising after so many years, he remarked.

Katherine was so absorbed, that she failed to hear him and jumped at the sound of his voice.

"I'm sorry, darling," he said, "I didn't mean to startle you." He came over to her. "Have you found something?"

"Well, I'm not sure, but yet again, there seems to be some sort of connection with Cairnmor." She showed him the travel book.

Alex was immediately alert. "But no one on the island saw either of them. They didn't go there."

"We can't be certain of that yet," said Katherine. "We keep finding a connection to Cairnmor. Nothing concrete, I agree, but something just the same."

As she spoke, the history book slipped off her lap onto the floor, falling open at the page describing the forced emigration of the Outer Islands population to Nova Scotia. An envelope also fell out and Alex picked it up.

"It's another letter from Mhairi!" he exclaimed. "I recognize the hand-writing."

Carefully, he took the same flimsy paper out of the envelope and together, they read its contents. There was an address this time:

Tumbling Gill Farm,
Grasmere

31ˢᵗ August 1909

Dearest Rupert,
I have to leave Aunt Flora as Ma is ill. I have to go back to Pa's house, even though the baby is due any day now. Aunt Flora says it's a crying shame and that my Pa and brothers can manage perfectly well without me, that it is not fair on me. When were they ever fair? But she is sorry about my Ma. So am I.
I have been very happy here. I wish I could stay.
Please write to me at the house in Govan. I will look out for the post and make sure I get to it before Pa does.
I miss you so. I wish you were here with me. I do not know what I am going to do. I am so afraid they will take our baby away if it is born while I am in Glasgow.
Please help me.
All my love, Mhairi.

"Poor Mhairi," said Katherine, full of sympathy for this girl, separated from her lover and vulnerable to the whims of a demanding father.

"I know," agreed Alex, touching her shoulder. "But just think how exciting this is!" He was unable to contain his enthusiasm. "I can't help feeling this really is something of a breakthrough. We now have another address – Mhairi's Aunt Flora in the Lake District! I'll get Dad to write to her. Hopefully she'll still be there, and he can ask her to tell us everything she can about Mhairi and Rupert and also if Mhairi's family still live at the Govan address… Dad still hasn't had a reply from Jock Hamilton at that address yet. I know it may draw another blank, but…"

Katherine was delighted too, but her delight was mainly focused on Alex, because he was so pleased. However, she was also puzzled. "I'm sure there's a good reason, but why does your father have to write? Why not you?"

"Because Lady Mathieson is Dad's client and so was Sir Charles. As a barrister, I'm not allowed to contact a client directly, be they real or in this case potential, if there is a point of law involved. As their solicitor, Dad can only instruct me on behalf of the client."

"So, the letter to Mhairi's aunt will be a formal request for information because of searching for the legal heirs to the Mathieson estate?"

"That's correct. We'll make a lawyer out of you yet!" added Alex, with a broad grin.

"Thank you, m'lud. But how is it that you can come here and search for information? Or me for that matter?"

"Because Dad has the client's permission for me to carry out that task. He is acting upon the client's instructions."

"What about me?"

"Let's just say that it's pending!"

They continued their search. The bookcase revealed no further clues so, working together now, they turned their attention to the bedside table. Nothing there. A chest of drawers revealed only clothes of varying sizes and the last piece of furniture left to explore was the wardrobe. Inside this, they found ancient (very smelly) rugby boots, an old football (deflated), a pair of rusty ice skates and finally, a large box, with the lid tightly bound by twine.

With great difficulty, Alex undid the string (they didn't like to cut it) and lifted the lid. Inside were childhood toys – a threadbare teddy, a grubby bit of cloth, a couple of toy cars, a clockwork mouse and... a small key. Katherine and Alex looked at each other in triumph.

"It must be!" exclaimed Katherine.

"It has to be!" declared Alex.

Together, they went over to the desk and slid the key into the lock. It fitted perfectly and the draw slid open to reveal five exercise books, similar in design, but in different colours.

"Looks like he kept a few of his old school-books," remarked Alex.

They experienced a momentary sense of anti-climax until Katherine looked inside one of them and exclaimed, "Oh no! It's much, much better than that! These are Rupert's diaries! This one is from when he was very little and this one is from his later childhood. They cover the years 1897 – 1909. Just what we're looking for!"

"Let me see!" Alex was delighted, too. "1909 was the year he disappeared. Let's not read them now, let's take them home with us. It's getting late and if we're on time for dinner, then we can spend the rest of the evening reading them. I've only a little preparation for the trial tomorrow which shouldn't take too long. Does that sound like a good idea?"

Katherine agreed and, having said farewell to Thomas after Alex had shown him the diaries that they wished to take with them, to which the butler reluctantly agreed, they hailed a taxi and drove home.

After they had left, Thomas stood on the top step, a mixture of emotions flowing through him. The grief for Rupert's loss, still potent, he understood; the residual anger against his deceased employer he quickly suppressed; but the tiny beacon of hope and a lifting of his spirits – that was unexpected and unexplained.

Feeling more cheerful than he had for many years, he turned and went inside.

CHAPTER 11

Rupert's Diary

27th August, 1897

My name is Rupert Charles Mathieson. Today is my birthday. I am 7. I had lots of presents but my favourite is the teddy which Mama gave me. I have called him Paul. Miss Cole my governess said I should keep a diary.

16th September

Mama, Papa and I and Miss Cole travelled to Minton House today by train. Minton House is very dark and scary. I like the house in London much better. It has white paint and lots of windows. Glasgow is very noisy and it rains all the time. I like the buildings in London much better.

20th September

Papa took me to the shipyard today. I spent lots of time in his office. He showed me the plans he has drawn for a new ship. I drew pictures of houses on the paper that he gave me. Papa told me I was supposed to draw ships but I like drawing my own made up buildings best.

25th September

Went with Papa to the shipyard again today. He took me down to the place where they make the ships. It was scary and VERY NOISY. I put my hands over my ears. Papa said that one day I would have to run the shipyard. I don't like ships.

After these initial entries, Rupert did not write again in his diary until December of the same year when he was delighted to be back in the Park Lane mansion. Katherine and Alex speculated that perhaps life at Minton House did not capture his imagination; that it was very much a life dictated and dominated by his father's wishes.

23rd December

Hooray! We're back in London. We arrived this afternoon and I ran straight up to my bedroom and bounced on my bed singing I'M HOME I'M HOME so loudly that Thomas the Butler came upstairs and said I had to be quiet. But he was not cross and took me downstairs to the kitchen where cook had baked some cakes and she gave me one straight out of the oven. Yummy!

24th December

Thomas and John our footman have bought a big big tree. It fills the hallway and Thomas and Miss Hansom the housekeeper have been busy decorating it. It has lots of candles on it and sparkly stuff and wooden ornaments. I cannot wait to see it lit up tomorrow.

25th December

Christmas Day! I was allowed to open my presents after lunch. Papa gave me a model ship. I tried my best not to let him see that I did not like it. Mama gave me a castle with soldiers and horses and everything. I did not like the soldiers so I put them in the ship. Thomas gave me a football which I kicked around the drawing room until Papa found out and sent me upstairs to my room.

I had tea in the nursery as Mama and Papa had lots of people coming for dinner. After tea I sat on the stairs and peered through the banisters as the guests arrived. Miss Cole said the ladies were wearing silk dresses. They made a funny sound as they walked. Miss Cole said they rustled. The men all had their tail coats on and white bow ties. Miss Cole said that everyone looked very elegant. The tree looked elegant (I like that word) and the candles sent a glow all the way up the stairs. Miss Cole said I should write a poem about it. Then we played card games and hide and seek. But we had to be quiet so we did not disturb the guests. Here is my poem. Papa said it was not very good but Miss Cole liked it so did Cook and Thomas when I showed it to them. Mama had a headache so she was not able to see it.

Candle, candle burning bright
In the darkness of the night.
Glowing, glowing flickering flame
Electric lights are not the same.

Miss Cole said it sounded a bit like a poem called Tiger Tiger by William Blake.

27th December

Thomas and Miss Hansom took me out to Hyde Park and let me run around to my heart's content. It was cold but I kept warm. Thomas and Miss Hansom keep looking at each other all funny. It was wonderful to be out in the fresh air and free to do what I liked. I felt safe with them watching over me. They gave me bread to feed the ducks.

5th January, 1898

We go back to Glasgow tomorrow. Oh dear. But Miss Cole will be there as always and this time Thomas is coming as the Scotland butler has left. I shall take my diaries with me as I always do, but life in Minton House is so boring I never write anything.

Poor Rupert, thought Katherine. It was not much of a life for an active and intelligent little boy. She said as much to Alex, who totally agreed and said that he would have hated it. There were no more entries until August, when the family arrived back in London.

27th August

I had to say goodbye to Miss Cole today. No one had told me that she was going anywhere until just before she left. Papa has arranged for me to go away to boarding school in Kent. He said I do not need a governess any more. I was very sad and she cried and I cried. Papa told me to be a man and not make a fuss like a baby. I hope she will be all right. She said she would write to me. I overheard Cook say that it was a terrible thing that Miss Cole had to go away on my birthday and that the Master could have at least waited a day or two. She said he was very unfeeling and should have told me when the decision was made and not left it to the last minute.

8th September

My first day at boarding school. I like the building. It's red-brick and quite grand, with a large coat of arms over the doorway. There were lots and lots of other boys all with their trunks and things saying goodbye to their parents. I wanted to cry when I said goodbye to Mama, but I remembered what Papa had said about being a man, so I stopped myself. But it was very hard. I am not a man yet, so I should be allowed to cry. Some of the other boys did.

9th September

My school is called Mersea House School. It's a prep school and you stay here until you are 13. The food is good but not as nice as it is at home. The Masters are very strict and we're not allowed to talk in the dormitories after lights out.

25th October

I had technical drawing today. It is my favourite lesson so far. Mr Newton says I have a real talent for it and an eye for detail. I also had history with Mr Tyler which is another favourite subject. He makes it very interesting and real.

I had a piano lesson today. I quite like my teacher Mr Smith but I have to practise a lot. I'm going to start learning the violin with Mr Frampton next week.

18th December

Home at last! I showed Papa my report. He was not pleased. He said I could have done better. I showed it to Cook and Thomas who said I'd done very well. I was in the top three in the class for all my subjects. Cook said the Master should encourage me and praise me more, that he should be proud of what I had achieved after only one term. Thomas told her to be quiet but I could see he agreed. Cook gave me a slice of cake and said she'd bake me an apple pie for supper. Mama hugged me and said I'd done wonderfully well.

23rd January 1901

Queen Victoria died yesterday. She was very old. Everybody is very sad. Papa and Mama were going back to Minton House today and I was going back to school, but Papa says we must stay for the funeral. Our new King is called King Edward VII. He is Queen Victoria's oldest son. He does look very old in his picture. I saw it in the newspaper.

2nd February

Queen Victoria's funeral was today. Everywhere was decorated in purple and white. I thought that black was the usual colour when someone had died, but Thomas says that Her Majesty didn't like black funerals so she wanted something more cheerful. She is to be buried in Windsor Great Park next to Prince Albert who was her husband. Cook says she'll be happy now as they really loved each other and she missed him very much when he died.

3rd February

Today Mama and Papa have gone up to Minton House. I'm glad I don't have to go. I really don't like that place. Thomas is taking me to school and I'm looking forward to going back and seeing all my friends again. They have all been there since January. Miss Hansom, the Housekeeper, left yesterday and no one will tell me why. I always hoped that she and Thomas would get married one day. Thomas seems very unhappy so I bought him a bar of chocolate with some of my tuck money while we were on the station waiting for the train. He thanked me and said it made him feel much better.

After this entry, the diaries followed a similar pattern for the next few years – holidays at home either in the Park Lane mansion or at Minton House in Govan, and then back to school. Rupert seems to have been happy at Mersea House School and did well with his school work, finishing top of his year.

Before he went to his next school, the family spent the summer in Glasgow. Rupert hated this and couldn't wait for the new term to begin. This was to be Frensham College in Edinburgh, a very prestigious establishment with an excellent academic record.

4th September, 1903

Arrived at Frensham College at 10.00am today. It was good to get away from Glasgow. Edinburgh seems to be a very different kind of place. Apparently, this is one of the best schools in Scotland. Thomas brought me here and as I was very early and the first to arrive, we had our own guided tour which was rather nice. It seems like a good school, though I would have preferred to go to Eton or Harrow with my friends. The buildings are granite and so is most of the city. It looks gloomy on a wet day.

6th September

Settling in well, but there are lots of customs and traditions here to learn. I just want to do my lessons, not mess about with all that stuff. It seems I'm the only boy from England, so for self-preservation, I've set about acquiring a Scottish accent so I fit in better. There's lots of music going on so I shall spend my time in the music department as much as I can and away from the boys who think it's fun to tease and torment me because of my accent. But I'll show them.

10th October

The art department have organized a 'Design a Building' competition. There are all sorts of criteria that this building has to fulfil. I'm going to go in for it. I don't care what the other boys think. I hope I beat them all.

1st November

We got the results today of the design competition and I won!! I earned 50 House Points for Greyfriars House and a special Certificate of Commendation. I've written to Papa and Mama to tell them. I'm so pleased. I love designing buildings. It's fascinating to see them taking shape and being able to control the spaces and structure.

The diary entries between 1903 and 1908 are sporadic and contain the usual schoolboy complaints about food, bullying and playing rugby. Rupert spent a lot of time developing his musical skills, becoming a very proficient pianist and violinist, and also in the art department, where his draughtsmanship earned him further commendations.

22nd April, 1908

Went out sketching in Edinburgh today. Very mild. Just as well as I sat still in one place for ages until I was satisfied with what I had drawn. No matter how many times I've come out into the city over the years, I still find the way that the rock dominates the whole place is very striking. But, as ever, it made me wish for London. It is still my favourite city. Here is nothing compared to the grandeur, variety and historical significance of the buildings back home.

I have decided that I definitely want to be an architect when I leave school. I had a long talk with my Head of House about which university would be the best. Cambridge seems to be the favourite. I would have to take a year out after my final exams in July to study for the Oxbridge entrance exams. You have to know Greek and Latin whatever course of study you choose. My Latin is good enough apparently, but my Greek is fairly rudimentary as we haven't done very much at school, so I'll have to work hard at that next year. I shall have to talk to Papa about this. Something tells me he's not going to like it.

24th May

Arrived home for Whitsun holiday and when I told Papa what I wanted to do, we had the most enormous row, the worst ever. He is adamant that I will be leaving school in July, that I am not going to Cambridge, that I am not going to be an architect but that I am going to work in the shipyard and take over the family firm when he retires and that there was nothing further to say on the subject. I said there was, and slammed out of the house.

I walked for miles, down by Tower Bridge, along the wharves, then back along Victoria Embankment. I am still angry with him. Why does he never listen to what other people want? Why does it always have to be about him? He never thinks of Mama. She has to follow him around between here and Glasgow and I know she gets fed up with the constant travelling and organizing the servants and the packing and unpacking. But she never complains – sometimes I wish that she would. I asked her once why she didn't and she said that she preferred things to be peaceful and that "your Papa can be very difficult sometimes".

10th July

So, this is my last day at Frensham. I feel sad to be saying goodbye to my friends. On the whole I have been happy here. The masters are all delighted with my progress and think that I should get very good exam results. Although I'm pleased and want to do well, whatever marks I get are meaningless. Working at the shipyard makes grades irrelevant, especially as I'm going to be starting at the docks as some kind of labourer.

84

17th July

A welcome end to my first day at the shipyard. I hated almost every moment of it. I was shown around by the manager, Mr Lowrie. He's a gruff sort of man but good at his job. He took me to the offices where the designers work drawing up plans and specifications for the ship's hull. That was quite interesting, but not the same as building design. After this, we went to the marine engineering department where the engines are designed. Next, we went to the loft where full-size patterns of the ship are constructed. That was better because you could see the designs becoming something real.

18th July

My second day. Hated this one too. Went down to the dock itself. I was left with Mr Hamilton, one of the foremen. His particular field is to oversee the welders, but he is very knowledgeable about most of the trades. He's obviously a proud man; proud of his position and of the men who work under him. He showed me the ramps (called the 'ways') where ship's hulls are constructed, then the crane operators and riggers who lift the huge plates and sections into place to form the hull and told me that it was the ship fitter's job to check that each section has been put in its place correctly.

Welding and riveting are important parts of shipbuilding and each man is allocated his specific area. The jobs for each worker are clearly defined and they seem a cheerful lot, on the whole. Seams and joints are made watertight by caulkers. Then there are tool and die makers, patternmakers, coremakers, pipe fitters and boilermakers. The list seems endless. And oh, the constant noise. My ears were ringing after a few hours. I was glad when the day was at an end.

1st August

Spent today learning how to weld plates, having finished my allotted two weeks on riveting yesterday. I'm not very good at this either. Mr Hamilton sent me on several errands to the machine shop and other places where I would be out of harm's way. He said I can try again tomorrow. He says that my heart isn't in it, and that it's dangerous to continue until I've improved. How right he is. One good thing though, his daughter Mhairi brought him his lunch and I sat with them eating mine as well. She's sixteen, very pretty and sweet-natured and I was very sorry when she had to go home.

2nd - 27th August

Have seen Mhairi every day; sometimes with her father, sometimes on her own. Sometimes we've even managed to escape from the confines of the dockyard. She is so special. I think I'm falling in love with her. I'm getting a bit better at welding, but not much.

28th August

We had lunch together on our own today as her father was called away to deal with some problem or other. A photographer was taking pictures of the yard and asked us to pose. He said he'd bring us the photo when he had developed it. Mhairi is very bright and practical and as we were on our own, we talked about our families. It would seem her father is very much like mine and lays down the law in their house. She has three older brothers who all work at the shipyard and her mother is often ill, so Mhairi has to care for the family.

29th August

Mhairi and I managed to go for a walk after lunch. I think Mr Hamilton was relieved not to have to find something for me to do. Father says I have to carry on with welding until I've mastered it. I could be doing this for years. But it does mean I see Mhairi most days, so I'm not complaining. We went to the park and sat on the swings, talking. I think she's wonderful. She has the most incredible blue eyes and curly red-gold hair. I took her back to her house which is one of a row of tenements in Govan near the shipyard.

8th September

Mhairi hasn't been to the shipyard for several days and I've missed her companionship very much. Apparently, her mother is ill and she is nursing her. I can't stop thinking about Mhairi. I just want to be with her all the time. She's the only good thing to come out of this fiasco that is Papa's idea. I feel useless. I'm a failure at everything here and there is nothing that interests me about the job. But as I have no alternative, I'll try to make the best of it.

10th September

I saw my beautiful Mhairi again today. Joy of joys, she has missed me as much as I missed her. We had lunch together and then disappeared out of the shipyard as quickly as we could. Once we were away from everyone, I held her hand and kissed her. She says we will be able to see each other every day now as her mother is better.

26th September

Saturday at last. Mhairi and I are going out on the tram tomorrow into the countryside – if there is any near Glasgow! She says that she knows a lovely

86

little village with a bridge over a burn which flows through a wood. She went there once when she was a little girl with her Aunt Flora. So that is where we're going tomorrow. We've both got to think up some excuse to be out for the whole day, but I'm sure we can manage that. Her mother is well at the moment, her brothers and father out to some meeting, so Mhairi can actually take a day off.

27th September

What a wonderful, wonderful day. I love Mhairi and she loves me. I can't think of anything else except my lovely girl. She is so beautiful, so sweet and clever.

The whole setting was idyllic; the village and the bridge over the stream just as she described it to me yesterday. It will become our special place. We just sat for ages listening to the water as it bubbled and cascaded under the bridge and then we followed the course of the stream through the wood and up, up into the hills, pausing only to regain our breath.

It was warm and sunny and we found a hidden spot where we ate our lunch and afterwards fell asleep, lying close together. We woke up warm and drowsy and it just seemed so natural when we started kissing each other…

We should have stopped there and then, but it was impossible and we couldn't. It wasn't awkward or anything, which it could have been as it was the first time for both of us. She said I was very gentle and it was just the most wonderful, blissful thing either of us have ever known. I love her so much.

Afterwards, I asked her to marry me and she said yes. I'm so happy, I could leap around the room even as I write. But I am worried. What happens if Mhairi has a baby? She says everything will be all right and that I shouldn't worry.

27th October

We've been out together every day for the past month and Jock Hamilton hasn't tried to put a stop to our friendship, which seems very odd. Mhairi and I can't understand it. I think that Jock sees it as a way to keep me away from the docks before I do damage to myself and everyone else around me!

My father has no idea, of course, unless someone from the dockyard has said anything. I don't think they have, otherwise I would have heard about it by now! We go out on the tram to our special place in the hills whenever we can, barely able to wait until we're there, desperate to be close to each other.

The entries between October and December, are full of a young man's ardent passion and romantic longings. The relationship continues to deepen and mature until neither of them feels that they can survive without the other. Rupert expresses his feelings in his poetry, of which he wrote a great deal at this time.

There were two in particular which Katherine loved because they expressed so much within their simplicity:

Music is your soul's essence,
Love is your heart's soul,
And words are your mind's heart.

And the next:

If every second I've spent with you
Were a million years,
I would not grow tired.
If every moment our eyes met
Were a century,
I would not be afraid.
And if every day that I've missed you
Were a second,
It would be an eternity to me.

In other entries, Rupert despairs of the fact that they cannot get married without parental consent as they are too young. Everything looks hopeless anyway as he cannot see his father allowing such a marriage and they are desperate to be together.

Then in the next entry, disaster…

14th February, 1909

The worst day of my life. Mhairi is going to have a baby. Her father has found out and there's been hell to pay. Jock Hamilton came to the house and told my father, who, rather than thank him for his honesty, accused him of deliberately throwing his daughter at me in the hope of making a 'good match'.

Papa wouldn't listen when I told him that Mhairi and I were in love and wanted to get married. He said he wasn't having any son of his throwing away his career (what career I thought?) to marry some upstart young hussy with designs on family money. I told him he was being ridiculous and if he only met her then he would see what a lovely girl she is.

Jock Hamilton said that he had not thrown his daughter at me, but he would be happy to let us marry. At which point, my father sacked him with immediate effect and said he would make damned sure that Jock never worked in any shipyard on the Clyde again.

Oh, what a mess, what a mess.

15th February

I'm to be sent home to London. My father cannot bear to have me near him. He says I'm a disgrace to the family. I called at Mhairi's house today and managed to speak to her for a brief moment. She's in a terrible state. Mrs

88

Hamilton let me inside as the rest of the family were out, but she can do nothing to help us.

I gave Mhairi the Park Lane address and we're going to write to each other. It's all we can do for the moment. I've promised her that I will try and work something out. She's being sent away on her father's orders to her Aunt Flora (her mother's sister) who lives in the Lake District. Mhairi's mother is beside herself with worry.

21st February

Before I left today, I spoke to Papa and begged him to allow Jock Hamilton to have his job back. He said he would consider it. I really do not care if I never see my father again. Mama is coming back to London with me. My father is to employ a 'minder' whose job will be to guard me and stop me from being with Mhairi or having any contact with her.

20th March

A letter from Mhairi! She says that Sir Charles has given her father his old job back but on one condition. He has been ordered to make sure that our baby is given up for adoption immediately after it is born so that there can be no claim financially or morally on the Mathieson family. This is terrible. My father is a heartless bastard.

21st March

I have written back to say that on no condition must she give up the baby. It is our child and no one else should have any say in what happens to it.

22nd April

Mhairi has written to me about the Isle of Cairnmor, and what a wonderful place it would be for us to live and bring up our child. So today, I went to Hatchards and ordered two books – one on the history of Scotland and the other by the author George Fergus Mayhew, all about his travels around Cairnmor and Cairnbeg.

I shall look forward to reading these; it will help me feel closer to my Mhairi. But any hope of us being together anywhere at the moment seems impossible and I am filled with frustration and despair because of it.

The entries between April and August are of similar vein. They correspond regularly and write of their love for each other, which seems to deepen and evolve, despite the increasing time they are apart.

Yet although he pines for Mhairi, he is not idle. Rupert puts his enforced 'captivity' to good use, studying architecture by taking a correspondence course and continuing his violin and piano studies, attending lessons at the Royal College of Music as an external student. He gained a diploma in violin teaching in July and is embarking on a similar one for piano teaching when:

2nd September

I received another letter this morning. Mhairi has been called home to look after her mother, who has been in and out of the Southern General Hospital in Sheldwich for the past month. Jock cannot cope any more, apparently. Mhairi sounds desperate… her time is so near. I must go to her. But how?

4th September

It is all arranged! I am going to go to Mhairi. Maybe if I am there, I can prevent our baby being taken away after it is born. I have written to Mama and explained why I am going.

Thomas got me the train tickets yesterday and has given me money. I said I would pay him back but he said no, he was glad to help, that Sir Charles was being unreasonable and cruel. I have never heard Thomas be so outspoken before.

He and Cook have been true friends to me these past months, especially in making sure that I receive all of Mhairi's letters.

With Thomas's help, I shall make my escape tonight. I have been a virtual prisoner here since February. I cannot stay any longer. I must go to Mhairi. I love her and she needs me…

Here the diaries ended.

CHAPTER 12

London
December, 1936

Almost as soon as they had finished reading the diaries, Alex and Katherine heard Alastair's key in the lock and for the moment, this precluded any discussion. He came in to Alex's sitting room and, after making sure he would not be disturbing them, sat down on the settee, still in his coat and obviously exhausted. Mrs Thringle had gone to bed with a headache, so Katherine offered to prepare him some food.

"Just some sandwiches and a very large cup of tea would be wonderful, thank you." He smiled at her. "You're a kind lady and I'm grateful to you."

"Hard day?" asked Alex.

"You can say that again," replied his father, with feeling.

So Alex did, and had a cushion thrown at him for his trouble. They continued in this vein for several moments and Katherine smiled as she left the room, enjoying the father-son repartee, thinking how fortunate they were to enjoy such a relationship.

While she was in the kitchen, Alastair took off his coat, throwing it over the back of a chair, settled himself comfortably on the settee and began to read the diaries, which Alex had handed to him, glad to escape the pressures of the day.

He was very much absorbed when Katherine returned, having prepared his sandwiches and a pot of tea for all of them.

She and Alex waited patiently for Alastair to finish reading; Alex scanning the evening newspaper he had purchased on his way home and Katherine sitting on the window seat and looking out onto the street below.

Once he had completed the task, having paused only to drink his tea and reach for his sandwiches, Alastair looked up and said, "I'm not surprised that Sir Charles Mathieson wanted to atone for his sins. He treated Rupert appallingly."

"I know. It's hard to believe that anyone could be so callous. During the time he was your client, did you have any idea of the sort of man he really was?" asked Katherine.

"No, he was business-like and forthright and knew exactly what he wanted. But there was never any indication of cruelty or ruthlessness. We never had a personal relationship earlier on, it was always purely professional. When he was in London, he instructed me as to his wishes and I acted upon them. Then, during the time we were drafting the new will towards the end of his life, I became something of a 'father confessor' for him, even though he was considerably older than me. He was genuinely full of remorse for his past actions."

"I would imagine that you hear many life stories," observed Katherine.

Alastair smiled. "Alex and I could write several books with the life histories we have listened to. Not that we ever would, of course. That would be unethical and go against client confidentiality."

"Why did Charles Mathieson need to draft a new will?" she asked.

"Twenty-seven years ago, when his son disappeared, Sir Charles shut Rupert out of his life completely and pretended he no longer existed. He never made any attempt to find him and disinherited him, drawing up that particular will with a firm of Glasgow solicitors. In the last year of his life, when he knew his health was failing, Sir Charles agonized over everything, regretting his past actions where Rupert was concerned and changed his will again. What effect all this must have had on Lady Mathieson over the years, I can't begin to imagine. But at least she had the letter from Rupert the day he left home offering some explanation of why he was going. It was cold comfort but also something to hold onto."

"Do you think she showed Sir Charles her letter?"

"I would like to think that she kept it to herself, perhaps as her means of atonement for not defending her son more vigorously from the cruelty of his father and also to protect Rupert and enable him to live his own life."

"Even at the cost of not seeing her only child again," stated Katherine sadly.

"I'm afraid so."

She was thoughtful for a moment and then said, "It's a pity we can't see that letter."

"I agree. I haven't liked to pursue the matter with Lady Mathieson, as it's obviously still painful for her but I'm hopeful that one day she'll offer to let us see the letter when she feels able to."

"However, in the meantime, I do know what we should do next," said Katherine.

"What's that?" asked Alex.

"I think we ought to go and speak to Thomas the butler. Perhaps he might be able to shed some more light on what Rupert's plan was and what actually happened on the night he ran away to Mhairi. We have the opportunity at last to speak to someone who was actually there! You know, after reading the diaries, Thomas has really gone up in my estimation because of the way he helped Rupert. And we thought him to be such a pompous old man!"

"I think that's a very good idea." Alex turned to his father. "We're due in court at ten-thirty again tomorrow aren't we? It doesn't leave a lot of time beforehand."

"Don't forget we have a meeting with the client at nine o'clock at your Chambers."

"Of course. Would you mind going on your own?" he said to Katherine.

"Obviously I'd rather go with you, but of course I don't mind, if it's possible. Presumably, there's no official, legal reason to stop me doing that?"

Alex smiled. "No," he said. "As long as Thomas is all right about it. Besides which, Lady Mathieson has now written to say that she is 'happy about your involvement', if it helps us to find Rupert! Dad had written asking for her permission."

"I'm pleased about that, because I really want to know what went on!"

"That's my girl!" said Alex. Then to his father he said, "It would be a good idea as well to write to Mhairi's Aunt Flora in the Lake District now that we have her address, even though we don't know her surname."

Alastair laughed. "I can just see the address now – 'Auntie Flora, Tumbling Gill Farm, Grasmere, Lake District!"

92

"She'll think it's from Mhairi if you write that!" Katherine smiled.

"Probably. Anyway, I'll write as soon as I can, possibly tomorrow. Now, I'm absolutely exhausted and need my bed. Goodnight to you both and I'll see you bright and early, Alex. I hope we're finished with this case soon as my other work is piling up; that's why I was so late tonight."

As soon as Alastair had gone out of the room, Alex went over to the settee next to Katherine and she curled up in his arms.

"I'm sorry we haven't been able to spend a great deal of time together," he began apologetically.

"It's fine. I do understand. But you know, I've been thinking that it's quite good actually."

"In what way?"

Katherine perceived a hint of confusion in Alex's voice. "It has nothing to do with your horrible company, Mr Stewart," she said, reassuring him in humorous fashion.

"I'm glad to hear it!"

"You see, I look at it as giving me the opportunity to get used to London on my own terms, to find my way around and really get to know the place for myself. Living here is one of our options and I need to find out whether I could settle permanently in London and make my home here."

"It's very important for you to do that, isn't it?" he observed thoughtfully.

"Very. Besides, I've always loved exploring and discovering new places, even when I was a child, as you know, when I used to wander for miles all over Cairnmor."

"But it's more than that here, isn't it?"

"Yes. It's part of the decision-making process for our future."

"You're not lonely?"

"Yes and no. Yes, because I want to be with you but no, because I've always been quite self-sufficient and happy in my own company."

"Being an only child has its advantages!"

"It does."

Certain that Katherine would come to the conclusion that it was better for them to live in London after they were married, the place where, if he were honest, he thought they should be, Alex kissed her ardently and she responded to him in kind. Eventually they drew apart and he said, somewhat ruefully, "I think we'd better stop there, otherwise our good intentions will be forever lost in a moment of unbridled passion."

"Mm... I might end up pregnant like Mhairi!"

Alex groaned. "Oh, don't!"

"Well, look on the bright side, your father approves of us and I don't have a nasty cruel parent about to banish me into exile!" replied Katherine, smiling and straightening her clothes.

"But that doesn't give us any automatic rights," he replied, serious for a moment.

Although Alex knew he would do his best to uphold their decision, he also had his own reasons for waiting to make love to her. However, he was unwilling to disclose these to Katherine just yet – she needed to get to know the family better first, he thought.

"I know. I was only joking!" she said.

"I'm most relieved to hear you say it."

Laughing together, they went up to their own rooms; Katherine feeling warm and secure in their love for each other and Alex feeling virtuous but very frustrated.

The next morning after Alex and Alastair had left for Chambers, Katherine telephoned Thomas and, feeling very pleased with herself for mastering this unfamiliar piece of technology, she arranged to be at the mansion in Park Lane for ten o'clock.

She was let into the house exactly as the large grandfather clock in the hallway struck the hour, and she could see from his expression that this met with the butler's approval.

Thomas led the way into a very elegant drawing room off to the right of the entrance hall, and indicated for her to sit down on one of the luxurious sofas that, together with the matching armchairs, were carefully arranged throughout the room.

A magnificent grand piano dominated the far corner and Katherine wondered if this was where Rupert used to practice and also, if it was here that he had played football on that Christmas afternoon of so long ago. She could picture him having fun and then being sent upstairs in disgrace – Sir Charles would definitely not have approved.

After observing her briefly, Thomas was the first to speak. "Tea will be brought shortly," he said in his clipped tones. "Now, how can I be of assistance?"

"Well," said Katherine, gathering her thoughts (why hadn't she written down what she wanted to ask?). "Alex and I wondered if you would mind telling me exactly what happened on the night that Rupert left."

"What makes you think that I should be able to do this?" Thomas asked, guardedly.

Katherine drew a deep breath and then said, "In his diaries, Rupert was quite clear that you and he had hatched a cunning plan to evade his 'minder' so that he could go to Mhairi in Scotland. But we don't know exactly what happened after the diary entries stop, and wondered if you could shed any light on what took place. There may be something that will help us in our search," she added persuasively.

Thomas was silent, working through an inner debate; contemplating whether or not to divulge information that he had kept to himself for twenty-seven years.

"It is not an easy thing to speak of events that happened on that day," he said, at length. "It is still painful and distasteful to me even after all this time. I have told no one, not even Madam, though I think she realized that I had some kind of involvement, but chose not to say anything."

He was silent again. Then, abruptly, he got up out of the chair and left the room, returning after a short while carrying the tea tray. "Please follow me," he said, leading the way upstairs to Rupert's room. He placed the tray on a table on the landing while he unlocked the door and then waited for Katherine to enter before shutting it once again.

"We can talk privately here. The staff know that I am the only person allowed in this room, therefore, there is no risk of our conversation being overheard."

"When we came yesterday, I wondered who had been responsible for keeping the room so clean and tidy." Katherine was intrigued. "You must have really cared for Rupert."

Hesitantly, the butler nodded his agreement. "Yes, as though he were my own son. I felt it my responsibility to watch over him and counteract the worst of Sir Charles's behaviour towards him." Thomas poured the tea. "Of course, it had to be done subtly without the Master's knowledge, otherwise I would have lost my position and Rupert would have been without protection."

"Was Sir Charles ever physically violent towards his son?"

"No." Thomas was definite about this. "He just had *his* way of doing things and expected everyone else to comply with *his* wishes. He was a brilliant engineer and designer and had built up Mathieson's to be one of the greatest shipbuilding firms on the Clyde through sheer determination and hard work. He was used to giving orders and expecting those around him to do his bidding. He was my employer and I had served him for a great many years, but he was the most self-centred, dogmatic individual that I have ever encountered. Until the last year of his life that is, when he had something of an Epiphany."

"What happened to prompt this change of heart?"

"In the last year of his life, he began to relinquish his hold on the shipyard. He had worked way beyond normal retirement age and with his physical powers diminishing, he knew the time had come for him to hand over the reins to someone else. With this knowledge came the realization that there was no member of his immediate family to whom he could pass on his life's work. And he realized that there was no one to blame except himself. His actions had caused his only son to leave home permanently and he began to contemplate his life and to see it in a different light. He became aware of past errors, and with this awareness came the burden of guilt for the way he had conducted his relationships with other people."

"And especially for the way he had treated Rupert."

"Exactly."

"So he felt that he had to make up for it in some way by changing his will and hoping that his son was still alive so that he and his offspring would benefit from Sir Charles's fortune."

"Yes. You see, this was the only gift he had left to give and the only way that remained for him to try to make amends." Having thus uncharacteristically unburdened himself, Thomas fell silent once more.

Katherine sipped her tea. Then she said, "So what happened the night Rupert disappeared?"

Thomas cleared his throat. "As you will have gathered from the diaries, Rupert was very unhappy. He was a virtual prisoner in his own home. And I could do nothing to help."

"Other than offering the tacit support you had always done."

Thomas acknowledged Katherine's praise by a gracious inclination of his head. He continued, "Then, one day, he came to me in real distress. It was imperative that he go to Glasgow to be with Mhairi and he came to me for help."

"And you couldn't refuse."

"No, indeed I could not. I went out immediately and bought a train ticket for Glasgow and arranged for him to have sufficient funds for whatever contingency should occur."

"Out of your own pocket?"

"Yes. But the problem remained on how to evade the er..." and here Thomas coughed discreetly before continuing, "... the weasely little rodent that Sir Charles had employed to follow Rupert around. I found it most distasteful to have him in the house at all. He was a horrid little man."

Katherine hid her amusement at this. "So what did you do?"

"I paid a visit to a friend of mine, a chemist, and said that I had difficulty sleeping at night and could he prepare a sleeping draught, a very strong one, for me to take. I have to confess that he did look at me somewhat askance, as it was not a usual request from me, but he prepared some, enough for three nights. 'That will work a treat' he said to me."

"Very clever. So you slipped the 'minder' a sleeping draught?"

"Yes, with a cup of hot milk, which he had every evening without fail. He fell asleep like a baby." Thomas could not help smiling and showing his pride.

"Brilliant!" said Katherine. "I'm very impressed."

"Thank you," said Thomas.

"What happened next?"

"That night, Rupert crept down the stairs, carrying my carpet bag which I had carefully packed with everything he might need – clothes, hair brush, shaving kit, money, tickets, even his birth certificate."

"Surely Rupert wasn't allowed to keep that in his room?"

Thomas cleared his throat. "Um, no, he wasn't. I'm ashamed to say that I liberated it from the Master's bureau."

Very much amused, Katherine could not resist asking, "Presumably this was a locked bureau?"

Thomas looked down at his highly-polished shoes, embarrassed. "I'm afraid so," he said, ruefully.

Katherine laughed, tilting her head back as she did so.

Thomas glanced at her, a momentary frown flitting across his patrician features; his heart beating a little faster.

There was something... he'd experienced a similarly elusive moment before when they had first met... but once again, he was unable to put substance to such a fleeting notion.

However, his thought processes were interrupted when Katherine said, "Well, you did what you had to do! Please go on," she prompted.

Gathering his thoughts once more, Thomas continued the narrative. "So, Rupert went down the stairs, having carefully passed Gerald's somnolent form, which was recumbent in his customary easy chair outside Rupert's room. I am certain that man never slept until that night.

"However, just as he had reached the halfway point in his descent, the Master's dogs came bounding up the stairs barking furiously. The footman had inadvertently and incorrectly allowed them into the main part of the house.

"Naturally, the 'weasel' woke up, despite the sleeping draught, spotted Rupert and came stumbling after him. Fighting off Gerald and trying to avoid the dogs, who were delighted to see him of course, Rupert managed to make a difficult and complicated exit out of the front door. He didn't even stop to collect his coat and disappeared out into the night. Gerald tripped over my foot, which I had judiciously placed at his disposal, as he in turn tried to exit the front door in pursuit. I'm delighted to say he fell flat on his self-satisfied face." Thomas couldn't resist a broad grin at this point, and Katherine smiled too, absorbed by his description.

"There was chaos," he continued. "The dogs were barking and running around everywhere. They were big dogs you understand – golden Labradors, four of them. Gerald was swearing at me, trying to stand up, but the sleeping draught was still very much in his system and he kept falling over as though he was drunk. I'm afraid I offered him no assistance and locked and bolted the front door, thus preventing him from immediately following Rupert.

"Instead, I helped to round up the dogs, treated the footman with kindness, much to his surprise as he had expected a right rollicking, if you'll excuse the expression, Miss Katherine. He had, quite naturally, assumed he would be dismissed for allowing the dogs into the house, or at the very least, severely reprimanded, which if the Master had been at home, would indeed have been the case. However, on this occasion, he went unpunished." Thomas paused for breath, still smiling at the recollection of it. Katherine smiled too, the picture of the events vivid in her mind.

Having been sitting for some time, she got up out of her chair and walked slowly around the room, pausing at the bureau, the bed and the bookcase. Soon, she sat down once again, this time on the window-seat. Thomas observed her discreetly.

Eventually, she asked, "What was Rupert like as a person?"

"He was polite, kind, patient, considerate, and very determined. Very intelligent. He should have been allowed to go to Cambridge. He also had the ability to make the best of a bad situation – goodness knows he needed it! Hated his father and with just cause, especially after he was sent back to London in disgrace."

"How did his mother cope after he left?"

"Lady Mathieson was very distressed at first, but after she had read the letter that I gave her from Rupert, she realized that this was the best thing for her son. He needed to live his own life. She has always held onto the belief that Rupert is still alive and that one day she'll see him again."

"I have one more question. And this is a personal one. Please don't answer if you don't feel able to. Forgive me for asking, but why did Miss Hansom leave?"

Thomas hesitated before replying. "It is all right. I am able to answer you. She left because she was dismissed. We were very much in love you see, and Sir Charles found out about our romance and let her go. I never knew where she went.

I was very upset and angry at the time, of course, but some years later, quite by chance we met each other again in Hyde Park, resumed our friendship and eventually married secretly. The Master's frequent absences made it possible for me to live two lives: one here and the other with Margaret. Unfortunately, she died a few years ago, but we were always grateful to have been given that second chance."

Katherine smiled. "I'm pleased for you. Truly I am."

"Thank you." Thomas hesitated for a moment; watching her, considering. But once again, Katherine spoke, interrupting his thoughts.

"If you wouldn't mind, please may I stay a bit longer and have another look through Rupert's books? There might be something that we overlooked when we were here yesterday."

"Of course. Take all the time you need. I am also anxious that Rupert should be found and like Lady Mathieson, I too have always held onto the belief that he is still alive. Now, if you will forgive me, I have some tasks to which I must attend. Please call for me before you leave." And with that, Thomas was gone.

Katherine went over to the bookshelf. She was curious to have another look at the books lining the shelves. There were the novels of Sir Walter Scott and Charles Dickens, Wilkie Collins and Robert Louis Stevenson; poetry by Keats, Browning, Wordsworth; the complete plays of William Shakespeare; the entire ninth edition of the Encyclopædia Britannica; an atlas of the world and numerous books on the history of art, of architecture and building design. She also discovered a whole set about the history of London, and another on the British Empire. There were also books on motor cars and steam engines, tracing both history and design; the five volumes of Grove's Dictionary of Music and Musicians, a book on orchestration and several biographies of composers. The mix of subjects was truly eclectic and wide-ranging. But anything on ships or shipbuilding was noticeable by its absence; Rupert really did not have any love for this particular subject.

Katherine took down the two books about Scotland that she and Alex had found the previous day before settling herself in the chair by the window and leafing through the pages. She uncovered nothing new with this cursory investigation except to realize that she would need to take them home to Cornwallis Gardens and study them thoroughly in order to decipher Rupert's many annotations.

The Grandfather clock in the hall struck midday and reluctantly she knew that it was time to leave. Taking a final glance round her, Katherine went downstairs in search of Thomas. She found him in the drawing room, looking out of one of the large picture windows with its commanding view of the busy thoroughfare outside across to Hyde Park. He turned and smiled at her; the smile an action that seemed to have been little used for some time, but one that transformed his stern features into friendliness.

Katherine smiled back and said, "I'm so grateful to you. Thank you for taking the time to see me. I realize it can't have been easy."

"It was not as difficult as I had thought it was going to be. And if I can be of further assistance, please don't hesitate to get in touch again."

"Thank you very much." After letting Thomas know she was taking the two books with her, she said, "And if you think of anything, anything at all, please let us know. I've written down Alex's home address and telephone number for you on this…" she handed him a piece of paper, which he accepted with a slight bow of his head, "… where you can contact us."

Then Thomas cleared his throat, and asked. "I'd very much like to know how things turn out…" he left the rest of the sentence unfinished.

Katherine smiled again. "Of course!" she said, reassuring him. "We will let you know." She extended her hand, which Thomas courteously took; the egalitarian gesture surprising him momentarily, but one which he appreciated.

At the front door, Thomas said, "I hope that we may meet again one day."

"I hope so too," replied Katherine, meaning every word. Then she walked out into the street and waited while Thomas hailed a taxi for her.

She turned to him before getting in and said, "Goodbye."

Thomas bid her farewell in turn and, just as he had done the previous day, stood and watched. His thoughts took him down a different avenue this time, but engendered a similar beacon of hope and optimism. He remained where he was until the taxi had rounded the corner out of sight, before going into the house and closing the door reflectively.

CHAPTER 13

London
December, 1936

Katherine paid off the taxi at Trafalgar Square and made her way through the crowds of lunchtime workers and shoppers to Lyons Corner House where she managed to secure a table and have her order taken by a uniformed waitress. While she was waiting for it to arrive, Katherine observed the people streaming out of Charing Cross station, their collective destinations divided between turning right into the Strand, left towards The Mall and straight across into Duncannon Street towards St Martin-in-the-Fields.

She was becoming familiar with the streets and landmarks in the centre of 'Town', as it was colloquially known, and becoming more acclimatized to the bustle and pace of the city. However, could she live here? As yet, she could not answer that very important question but it would seem that ultimately, the decision might well rest with her.

Could she in all honesty expect Alex to give up a highly successful career, which he thrived upon, to live on Cairnmor where intellectually there would be no challenge for him? For all its beauty and sense of freedom and peace, Alex would need more. He didn't have her background and affinity to the island nor the long-standing friendships that she did. Besides which, she had her teaching and the evening classes, both of which she enjoyed and which gave her the mental stimulus she needed. She was also obliged to her friends for their financial kindness to her in paying for her education. She was part of a very close-knit community.

Would this ever be enough for Alex?

Katherine knew that she loved Alex very deeply and that it would be her heart that would make the decision for her. Her need for him; to be with him outweighed any other consideration. But could she make her home here? For the moment, it remained the unanswered question.

The waitress brought her lunch – a vegetable soup and roll; cake and a pot of tea. While she ate, Katherine opened the book on Cairnmor that she had brought with her and began to read the familiar words.

All at once, her island leapt off the page at her, vivid and real. Even though it was Cairnmor from the previous century, it described a way of life that, remarkably, had changed little in the intervening years. The steamer still came once a week, or not, depending on the weather; crofters carried out their tasks in the traditional way; fishermen still plied their trade and the storms still blew with customary force.

It tugged at her heart; calling to her and suddenly, Katherine missed Cairnmor with an intensity that brought tears to her eyes, a tightness in her chest and an overwhelming desire to catch the first train home that she could.

However, with a sigh, knowing this to be an impossibility, she closed the book and paid for her lunch. Reflectively, yet with a lingering sense of loss, she made her way along the Strand towards the Royal Courts of Justice where she was to spend the afternoon at the court case with which Alex and Alastair were involved.

Some twenty minutes later, having more or less recovered her emotional equilibrium during her walk, Katherine arrived at the imposing grey stone edifice built in the Victorian Gothic style, so Alex had informed her, with its many spires, turrets and ornate windows. She wondered whether Rupert had ever visited this building. If so, with his interest in architecture, he could not fail to have been impressed by its dimensions and grandeur. Imagine having this as your place of work? Alex does, thought Katherine with pride.

She entered the building from the Strand, passing under two elaborately carved porches fitted with iron gates and found her way into the Great Hall. Here, she went over to a large glass-fronted cabinet and looked down the list of cases to be heard that day, which Alex had told her was called the 'Daily Cause List'. She knew that his case was being heard in Court Four and saw that the session: 'Before the Honourable Lord Justice Cameron, Stephenson versus Smith', was due to resume in fifteen minutes' time.

Katherine spoke to the man at the desk and gave her name, just as Alex had instructed her to do before he had left for Chambers that morning. The clerk gave her a badge with her name on it and 'Visitor' written underneath in impeccable copper-plate writing. He asked her to wait while he fetched someone to take her to the courtroom.

She pinned the badge to the lapel of her coat and took a few moments to wander round and admire the Hall, which in itself was as splendid and awe-inspiring as the rest of the building had been so far – from the intricate mosaic floor to the coats of arms on the windows and the high vaulted ceiling; from the extensive display of robes to the bust of Queen Victoria and a statue of Lord Russell, whom Katherine discovered from the details written on a plaque beneath the statue, was the first Catholic Judge to be appointed after the Reformation.

She continued her exploration. Facing each other across the hall were two portraits of the judges who settled land disputes after the Great Fire of London in 1666, commonly known as the 'Fire Judges'. It had never occurred to Katherine that there might have been land disputes as a result of the Great Fire. It seemed so obvious now that she was aware of this fact and she wondered how she could have missed that observation during her studies.

Coming back up the Hall, there was a painting depicting the scene as Queen Victoria opened the Law Courts in 1882 and a life-like marble statue of the architect, George E. Street.

At that moment, Katherine's escort arrived and they left the Hall via one of the staircases on the right hand side of the cabinet, going up into the main court corridor. She was shown inside Court Four and took a seat on one of the benches at the back of the book-lined, oak-panelled courtroom directly behind what would be Alex's place. Gradually more people filed in, until all the seats were occupied. It would seem that this case had generated a great deal of interest.

Alex had told her very few details and Katherine had not asked; their recent conversations having revolved mainly around Rupert's diaries and the speculation they had evoked. However, she did know that he was representing the defendant, whom he believed to have right on his side and a very strong case.

First to enter were the clerks and other recording officials. After this, the barristers, their solicitors and their clients, who took their designated places. Alex and Alastair spotted Katherine immediately and her fiancé smiled at her, causing Katherine to blush. His father leaned forwards and said something to Alex and they both grinned at each other and then looked at the papers on their desks with studied concentration.

Lastly, the Judge entered and the Court was invited to stand. Once everyone was seated again, the proceedings resumed. Katherine's heart was beating in anticipation of Alex's contribution but it was the advocate for the prosecution who spoke first. He rose to his feet, lifting a sheet of paper and referring to it. He continued as though there had been no break from the previous session that morning.

"M'lud, it seems to me that my friend has missed the point of these proceedings – I hesitate to use the word trial – as my client is the only son and rightful heir to all the land, property and title of the estate belonging to the deceased. Therefore the case should be simple and clear-cut." He sat down.

Alex stood up. "My Lord, with all respect to my friend, as we heard from the evidence given this morning, it is equally simple and clear-cut in that the deceased chose *not* to leave all his property and estate to his eldest son. This was made with sound and well-considered reasoning and in his view was the only decision that he felt able to make."

Mr Mullion rose to his feet. "I believe there is evidence of coercion on the part of your client to have the will made out in his favour."

Alex's response was immediate. "I can disprove any such allegation, my Lord."

The Judge spoke. "Mr Mullion, if you have evidence of coercion, then the court would be pleased to hear it." There was silence while the prosecution barrister consulted his solicitor.

"We cannot bring the evidence at this time, m'lud."

"Then perhaps you should consider your allegations more carefully in future."

The Judge was stern, and there was a faint ripple of laughter in the courtroom. Mr Mullion looked suitably chastised and remained seated for the moment before turning to consult his solicitor. He stood once again. "We will be able to bring such evidence before the court at a later date, m'lud," and sat down again.

"Not too much later, I hope, Mr Mullion. This Court has other business to attend to," replied the Judge.

There was another ripple of laughter; Lord Cameron seemed to be enjoying himself.

Alex was on his feet quickly. "My Lord, if such evidence exists, then it should have been brought to the court's attention earlier."

The Judge nodded.

"My client has apprised me of this only within the last hour, m'lud," expostulated Mr Mullion.

Lord Cameron remained unmoved and unimpressed. Again, the barrister consulted his solicitor, taking an inordinate amount of time to do so.

102

"Are you ready to move on now, Mr Mullion?" The Judge was beginning to show impatience.

"Yes, m'lud. I turn once again to the question of fraud. My friend's client was for many years in a position of great trust with the deceased. It is our belief that he usurped that position to his own advantage."

Alex said, "This is pure speculation."

"Continue," ordered Lord Cameron.

Mr Mullion cleared his throat. "On twenty-fourth of July last, my client visited his father and came across Mr Smith working at the financial ledgers in his office." He sat down, looking pleased with himself.

Alex was not intimidated and rose to his feet. "If it may please the court, for twenty-five years my client was Sir Joshua Stephenson's Estate Manager and close personal friend. It was part of his job to oversee all aspects concerning the running of the estate, including the finances. It was an essential part of his work to complete the financial ledgers."

Mr Mullion was silent for a moment. "Of course," he acceded. "However, when Mr Smith had left the room, my client studied the books and found a great number of crossings out, numbers changed, columns and rows deleted."

Alex rose to his feet and Mr Mullion was forced to sit down. "My Lord, I have not been given sight of this so-called evidence. I do not believe the court has either."

"You are correct, Mr Stewart," concurred the Judge. "We will recess for fifteen minutes to consider the matter. I would like to see both of you in my Chambers."

The clerk called out, "All rise!" and everyone stood up while the Judge and barristers left the room.

There was a general buzz of conversation. The visitors seated around Katherine were chatting and talking and Mr Mullion's solicitor was in deep discussion with his client, a sallow-complexioned young man in his early twenties, who kept looking around the courtroom, anywhere except at his solicitor.

Even with Katherine's unfamiliarity of the law, it seemed to her that court procedure had not been followed. Mr Mullion was either unfamiliar with it (very unlikely as he was an experienced barrister) or was taking a chance in order to put his case forward, or was just incompetent.

Alastair turned round to her and smiled. She smiled back. Things must be going well from their perspective, she thought.

"I'm going for a quick cup of tea, would you care to join me?" he said.

"Oh, yes, please. Is it allowed?! I mean, can the briefing solicitor be seen with a member of the public present in the courtroom?" she asked.

Alastair chuckled and reassured her. "An essential part of court procedure."

"Especially during a recess when reviving beverages are rapidly sought!"

"Ah, my son has chosen well! A lady after my own heart."

They found the refreshment room and quickly ordered tea. Katherine said, "Tell me about Mr Mullion."

"Our learned friend!"

"Is he as learned as he should be?"

Alastair smiled. "Actually he is, but he's trying to muddy the waters and trap Alex into accepting undeclared evidence; testing his mettle, if you like."

"Can he do that?"

"Lawyers like Mullion will try anything if they think they can get away with it."

"But Alex is too quick for him."

"Yes, especially in pointing out errors in procedure as well as the legal arguments."

"The Judge doesn't seem too impressed with Mr Mullion."

Once again, Alastair smiled. "No, he's not, but he will give Mr Mullion's client a fair hearing, despite the antics of his barrister."

"Which is exactly as it should be." Katherine took a sip of tea before asking, "Alex has said very little to me about this case. I think I need a bit of background so that I can understand what's happening a little better."

"In his will, Sir Joshua Stephenson, a very wealthy landowner, left his entire estate to his Manager and friend, Daniel Smith. Sir Joshua's only son, George, objected to the terms of the will and the whole thing became so contentious, there was no alternative but to bring it to trial."

"But there's no jury? I thought all trials had a jury?"

"In criminal law, yes, but not in civil law. In civil law, the right to a jury is limited to four specific areas: fraud, defamation, malicious prosecution and false imprisonment."

"And am I right in thinking none of those applies in this instance, even though Mr Mullion is trying to imply that there has been fraud?" asked Katherine.

Alastair admired the way she quickly absorbed his explanation and replied, "Yes, you are. This case is essentially concerned with resolving a dispute about the terms of a will."

"Talking of wills, I'm glad Lady Mathieson didn't feel that way!"

"Absolutely, but I think she has been given enough money of her own and is just as anxious for the outcome as we've become! She inherits everything anyway if we can't find Rupert or his heir."

Katherine nodded. "Going back to today," she said, "what I like about the court case is the humour despite the formality and tradition."

"Oh yes, it makes the whole process less stuffy. But I have to say, I always enjoy being in court with Alex. I know I shouldn't say it, as he's my son, but he is a fantastic advocate."

"Well if you can't say it to me, who can you say it to?" said Katherine with pride.

He patted her hand affectionately and they vacated their table, as it was time for them to go back into the courtroom.

The clerks had remained, as had Daniel Smith, in the courtroom. The plaintiff, George Stephenson, and his solicitor had vacated the room and now returned, smelling strongly of cigar smoke.

Alastair retook his place, and was soon joined by Alex in his position at the Bar, along with Mr Mullion.

"All rise," came the instruction from the clerk and everyone stood as Lord Cameron returned to take his seat at the Bench.

Mr Mullion was the first to speak. Nothing further was mentioned about the ledger for the moment. Instead, he began with a different tack. "My client maintains that he has been a devoted son all of his life, taking a great interest in the Estate and the way in which it was run. He feels that he is being deprived of his birthright and has the ability to run the estate in accordance with his father's wishes." Mr Mullion sat down.

"My Lord," said Alex, "it is my painful duty to point out to my friend that on the dates set out before the court, his client was brought home from public houses and other establishments in a severely inebriated state. Also, that his gambling debts – again you have records of these before you, my Lord – are in the region of four thousand pounds, most of which, at this time, have still not been repaid."

An audible murmur went round the courtroom.

Alex continued, after a suitable pause. "The deceased took it upon himself to repay his son's debts, using income from the estate and amending the ledgers in his own hand to cover for his son's indiscretions. I put it to the court that there is no evidence of fraud, merely my client's employer trying to protect his son, even at the risk of endangering the financial stability of his estate. I have proof of the deceased's handwriting, my Lord," which he handed to a clerk who took it up to the Bench. The Judge studied it carefully and Alex sat down.

The visitors seemed shocked by his disclosure and began to talk among themselves. They fell silent as Mr Mullion rose to his feet again, with no choice but to concede defeat on this point of evidence.

"We have nothing further to add at this time, m'lud," and he sat down again. After once more consulting with his solicitor, he rose to his feet and said, "However, the fact still remains that my client is a direct blood relative of the deceased, and therefore by the laws of the land, is entitled to his inheritance. The estate in question has been in the same family for three hundred years, passed down from father to son in an unbroken line."

"May I point out to my friend, that the laws of the land allow any individual who is of sound mind and body to bequeath his property and title to that property to anyone whomsoever he chooses. In this case, the deceased, who was of sound mind and body, chose to bequeath it to Mr Smith and his family, who had proven his loyalty, reliability and devotion over a period of twenty-five years."

"M'lud," began Mr Mullion, adopting an ingratiating manner that made Katherine cringe. "My client lost his mother at a very tender age, and his father, being a much older man, and greatly concerned with the running of his estate, had very little time for him and left him in the care of maidservants and gardeners on the estate."

Alex turned to Alastair and his client and they exchanged a few brief words. He stood up. "My Lord, my client informs me that the deceased was a devoted father, who had not expected to have any children at such an advanced age and therefore this made his only son very special to him. His son was left with servants only when it was unavoidable – and there are witness statements to that effect from the employees concerned – again these are before the court."

When Mr Mullion spoke, it was as if the previous statement had not been made. "May it please the court, my client was sent away to a boarding school he hated and felt he had been forced by his father away from the only home he had ever known. Being sent away from home proved to be a detrimental experience for him and led to a few minor behavioural problems."

"Come now, Mr Mullion," said Lord Cameron. "I am sure that there are several people in this courtroom who have attended boarding school and did not find it a detrimental experience that led to 'minor behavioural problems' as you have so delicately phrased it. I boarded at both a prep school and public school, and to the best of my knowledge never became a juvenile delinquent as a result."

A murmur of laughter went round the court.

"Nonetheless, he was forced to go there."

Mr Mullion had begun to sweat profusely and Alex could see that his opposing counsel had realized he was losing ground.

He took advantage of this with his next words, "My friend is aware that his client was given every opportunity to benefit from an excellent education and that he chose to abuse that privilege. I have placed before the court copies of letters written to the deceased by the Headmaster of this very well-known and well-respected establishment, citing reprimands and punishments given out for…" and Alex consulted the document which his father had just placed into his hand, "… bullying, vandalism and shocking language in front of his teachers." Alex laid the papers on the desk, his lips twitching. "Finally, he was expelled for smoking, gambling and extortion."

Alex paused while a muttering went round the court. "Indeed, it was a constant source of grief to my client's employer that he was not better able to communicate with his son and curb his more, shall we say, wilful impulses. He tried on innumerable occasions to help him overcome his problems, but to no avail." Alex re-took his seat.

Mr Mullion then stated, "We have nothing further to say at this time," and sat down, heavily this time.

Alex knew he had him on the run and his final statement of the day was, "The deceased placed his estate in the hands of my client because he wished to protect and preserve it for future generations. He knew and understood his son well, and felt that he would not be able to cope with the burden of responsibility that running such a large establishment would entail. My client had been successfully running the estate in conjunction with Sir Joshua for a great many years; he understood the intricacies of the process and had proved himself to be completely trustworthy and excellent at his job. Sir Joshua wished to leave his estate in safe hands and in Daniel Smith he found the perfect candidate. I should add that it is my client's intention that the house and grounds should be open to the public during the holiday seasons so that as many people as possible may be able to appreciate its artistic treasures and the beauty of its grounds." Alex sat down, concealing his sense of triumph with difficulty.

"Thank you, Mr Stewart," said Lord Cameron. "Do you have anything further to add, Mr Mullion?"

"Not at this time, m'lud."

"In that case, we shall resume tomorrow morning at ten-thirty a.m. If you wish to submit any further evidence it must be placed before nine a.m., if not, we shall

106

have closing legal arguments from both junior counsel and I shall then give my final judgement on the matter before the court."

"All rise!" called out the clerk and the Judge left the courtroom.

Katherine was present when the session resumed the next day and sat on tenterhooks waiting for the outcome. The prosecution could bring forward no evidence of fraud or coercion and their case collapsed. The legal arguments from Mr Mullion were very weak and Alex was very strong with his.

Lord Cameron stated that having given the matter due and careful consideration, he found in favour of the Defendant, Daniel Smith. The case was summarily dismissed and he left no grounds of appeal for Mr Mullion on behalf of his client. Afterwards, he called Alex to his chambers and privately congratulated him on the thoroughness of his preparation and excellent presentation.

Alastair had difficulty in containing his delight when Alex re-joined his father and Katherine who had waited for him in the courtroom. Alastair put his hand on his son's shoulder and, full of pride and admiration, said, "Well done, my boy!"

"The Stewarts strike again!" exclaimed Alex. Then, acknowledging his father, he added, "But I couldn't have done it without your fantastic preparation."

"We're a good team, you and I!" said Alastair.

As Katherine stood there watching them, Alex grinned at her, coming over to her and hugging her with so much energy that she had to be very quick to stop his barrister's wig from sliding off the back of his head once he had released her.

She shared in his happiness, genuinely delighted for him. But it was in that moment of his pure joy that she knew she would be the one making the sacrifice of not only giving up her career because of her marriage but also leaving behind her beloved Cairnmor. Alex was too good at his job; too fine an advocate to ask him to relinquish all of this for her.

It was Alastair who caught the change in her expression so she concealed it from him quickly, wishing to do nothing to dampen the moment of their celebration.

CHAPTER 14

After Alex had taken off his wig, gown and white neck bands in the robing room and gathered together all his documents and packed them into his briefcase, as well as his court clothes into a small suitcase, he re-joined Katherine and Alastair (who had meanwhile collected his own papers) waiting in the Great Hall. Together they went out of the Royal Courts of Justice into the Strand and walked back to Alex's chambers in Middle Temple Lane.

The Senior Counsel at Royal Court Chambers, whom Alex introduced to Katherine as Sir John Pemberton K.C., was very pleased with the outcome of the case. He congratulated Alex and said he had already had a telephone call from Lord Cameron with regard to his performance. The Judge thought that he was destined for great things.

Pride radiated from Alastair, and Katherine was happy for them both. However, she felt strangely detached, as though she shared their pleasure but was not emotionally involved herself. Perhaps she was tired. It had been a very hectic few days with so many new sights and sounds to absorb.

As Alex was occupied discussing a difficult case with Sir John that involved several members of Royal Court in a complex litigation procedure on behalf of a major client, it was Alastair who spotted Katherine's sudden pallor.

"Are you all right?" he asked, his voice full of concern.

"Yes, I'm fine. Just a little tired."

"It's been a very busy time for you."

"It has. I'd quite like to go home if that's possible, but I don't want to disturb Alex." She could see he was still involved in conversation.

"You don't have to worry. I'll take you home."

"Don't you have work to do?" Katherine was concerned.

"Nothing that won't keep until tomorrow!" he said reassuringly.

Alastair went across to Alex and Sir John Pemberton and interrupted them briefly. The K.C. came over to her and shook Katherine's hand, saying that he hoped they would meet properly at the banquet on Friday.

"I gather that you are coming as Alex's guest?" and after Katherine had replied that she was, he added, "There will be an opportunity for everyone to be sociable during the banquet. That's what these events are all about, young lady."

Although Katherine tried very hard not to, she could not help but notice his patronizing air. However, he did at least have the grace to apologize for keeping Alex away from her at the moment. "He's an invaluable member of my team," he said. "I hope you are agreeable that I keep him away from your company a little longer."

"Of course," she acquiesced graciously, having been given little choice in the matter.

Alex smiled at her in such a way that any concerns she may have been having about their future together temporarily melted away. Alastair, pleased by their response to each other, put his hand under her elbow and gently guided her out of the room.

"Come, my dear, let's get you home," he said.

They walked into the Strand and Alastair hailed a taxi which took them through the busy afternoon streets back to Cornwallis Gardens. During the journey, he observed Katherine discreetly as she looked out of the window before saying, "Are you sure everything is all right?"

When she didn't answer immediately and kept her head turned to avoid him seeing the tears which were in danger of spilling onto her cheeks, he became concerned. Hastily, she wiped the traitorous droplets away, but said nothing.

Once they were home, Alastair suggested that they go out for a walk and some refreshment. Katherine was grateful to him for in her present emotional state, she did not wish to have Mrs Thringle fussing over her, no matter how well-intentioned that might be.

Alastair dumped his briefcase in the hallway; Katherine did the same with her handbag and they set off in the direction of South Kensington Station for a cup of tea in the little café across the road and round the corner from the Underground entrance.

Inside all was quiet and peaceful and Alastair ordered tea and cakes for them both. They sat in silence while Katherine regained her composure and he waited patiently until she felt able to say something.

"I'm a very good listener, if you want to talk," he said after a little while, by way of encouragement.

Katherine smiled ruefully, not sure how to put what she was feeling into words. She said as much to Alastair. "I've been keeping my own counsel..." and they both smiled at the choice of words, "... since my parents died when I was fourteen years old. I'm more used to sorting out other people's... confusion... than my own."

"Everyone needs someone else to talk to at some time."

"It's not Alex; it's not us," she began, struggling to find the right way into what she was feeling. "We love each other and I can't imagine my life without him. But he lives and works here, in London. I live on a beautiful remote island hundreds of miles away in the far west of Scotland."

"And one of you will have to make a very difficult and painful decision in order to be together."

"Yes." Katherine hesitated before continuing. "That much was obvious from the beginning but we've both avoided the issue. Our falling in love happened so fast and as we haven't been able to spend much time together, it seemed more important to enjoy each other's company and really get to know one another before attempting to go down that particular rocky path."

"But something has happened for you to change that, hasn't it?" suggested Alastair gently.

"Yes. Now I see what a brilliant advocate Alex is and how successful he is in his career, I know it is me who has to make the sacrifice." She struggled to control her tears. "And even just the thought of leaving Cairnmor is tearing me apart."

Alastair was silent, considering carefully all that she had said and weighing his words in response. He said eventually, "Have you mentioned any of this to Alex?"

109

"No, he's been so busy with the court case, that I haven't really had the chance. Besides, it was only yesterday that the full force of realization hit me."

"Well, for your own sense of well-being and self-preservation, my advice to you is to say nothing. Keep it to yourself for the time being and let your mind and body get used to the idea slowly and gradually. Be kind to yourself; enjoy every moment that you have with Alex. Be sure that he really is the one, though anyone with half a brain can see that the two of you are made for each other!" he added, making Katherine smile.

"I have no doubts about that," she replied, her face lighting up as she spoke.

"I know, I can see that," he said. He poured them both another cup of tea, hoping that Alex really did recognize that fact. "At the moment, what you have said about the future seems to be the logical and sensible course of action. But life has a way of throwing things up that sends logic out of the window. Hard as it might be, put the dilemma and all thoughts of leaving Cairnmor to the back of your mind for now and enjoy the rest of your time here just being with Alex. Things will work out and remember, I'm always here if you need to talk. You are a very special lady; my son has chosen extremely well." He smiled and Katherine could not help but respond.

"And so have I!" she said. "But in reality, there was no choice for either of us. It's been like some kind of whirlwind. Our feelings progressed incredibly quickly and there was nothing we could do about it." She smiled at him, feeling considerably happier and relieved. "Thank you," she added.

"You're welcome. But now," said Alastair, "you need to go home and rest."

He gave his hand to Katherine as she stood up and vacated her chair. He paid for the tea and they made their way companionably through the rapidly darkening streets back to the welcoming glow of light from the uncurtained windows of 17 Cornwallis Gardens.

The next day was very mild and fine and Alastair left early for his office. He intended clearing his desk before travelling to Oxfordshire by train that afternoon, not returning to London until after the New Year, when his office re-opened. Alex and Katherine were going to join the family on Saturday, travelling down in Alex's car in the afternoon. Friday was the evening of the banquet at Middle Temple Hall and they would be staying in town for that.

Alex had no further court appearances booked until after the first week in January. There was pre-trial work to be done in preparation for that and he had also been given an additional brief to assess and decide whether or not it would be viable to take to court at a later date. He had brought home the necessary books and documents and could work on those after Christmas in Oxfordshire before coming back to London. But until then, he was free and, revelling in this holiday mood, said to Katherine during breakfast, "What would you like to do today? Your wish is my command!"

Katherine raised an eyebrow at him and said, in a very refined English accent, pretending to look down her nose at him, "You mean that you are not required to appear in court today, my learned friend?"

"Nah. I fort I'd take the day orf, miss."

"Is this allowed by your Chambers?"

110

"Yeah, miss. Self-employed ain't I, miss. Please meself, like." And they both laughed.

"You're very good at accents," said Katherine.

"So are you," replied Alex. "But I love the Scottish lilt in your real voice. I find it incredibly attractive." He smiled, took her hand and kissed it and in return, she lifted both their hands to her cheek.

"Just as I love the sound of your voice. It's extraordinary isn't it, that you had to come all the way to Cairnmor for us to find each other?"

"Just as well I did though, ain't it?" said Alex, teasing her and reverting to his Cockney accent. "I dunno what you might 'ave got up to wivout me to annoy you. I certainly don't know what I would 'ave done if I 'adn't met you. Spent me days plying me trade round the Law Courts waiting fer a crumb of justice to be dished out from all them posh lawyers!" he added with mock pathos.

"Oh, be quiet!" said Katherine, laughing so much that she almost knocked the remains of her tea over.

Alex caught it just in time and asked, "So, what are we going to do today, seriously?"

"Well, I'd like to go to the National Gallery this morning, and then come back here for the afternoon," said Katherine.

"Paintings it shall be and we'll find a nice little restaurant for lunch and then come back and relax before you have to endure all the stuffy judges, K.C.s and barristers, and make stilted conversation all evening."

Katherine wasn't sure if Alex was joking. "Surely it's not that bad?"

"No, of course not. On the whole legal people are really nice and the social events are a good opportunity to get together away from the courtroom or the pressure of Chambers and legal issues. But they can be a bit dull sometimes. However, Michael will be there this evening, and he's guaranteed to lift the mood... or wreck it, depending, of course on your point of view!"

Alex and Katherine walked up to Kensington Road and caught the bus to Trafalgar Square where they admired Nelson's column while the famous Admiral, at the very top of his plinth, looked out towards the Thames, as though keeping watch over England and protecting the country from any adversary.

"Now he really was a childhood hero of mine!" said Alex.

"Oh, and mine too. I'd love to have met him. He really was a brave man who led by example. One of the main reasons why the British were so successful at Trafalgar was that he cared about the welfare of his sailors and also trusted the initiative of the captains under him in carrying out his plans."

"Yes – all of that, as well as excellent provisioning, fair discipline and endless battle drill. See, I remembers my history too!"

"Clever boy! What do you want – a gold star?"

"No, I'll settle for a kiss," said Alex, pointing to his cheek and Katherine obliged.

"Did you know," she said, "the British could fire and reload their guns in half the time that the French took?"

Alex nodded. "I did, and Edward says that the innovations Nelson introduced still influence the Navy today."

"Of course!" exclaimed Katherine. "Your brother's a lieutenant in the Royal Navy isn't he? I remember you telling me at the ceilidh. Will he be in Oxfordshire for Christmas or New Year?"

"I'm not sure whether he has leave or not. No doubt my mother will tell us when we go there tomorrow. Anyway, I'm getting cold. Shall we go and inspect these pictures?"

Alex put his arm round Katherine's shoulder and they walked across the Square, past the stalwart but friendly lions and the impressive circular fountains, crossing the road to the National Gallery.

They spent a pleasant couple of hours wandering around the various galleries. They both admired the Flemish and Dutch masters with their vivid, yet sparing use of colour in accurately capturing the people and scenes they were painting. Alex particularly admired the artistry of Vermeer, whom Katherine had not come across before. She was very taken with Constable and Turner and they stood for a long time studying Turner's *Fighting Temeraire*, which had particular relevance to the conversation they had just had outside.

"It says here," said Alex, reading from the guide book, "*that the ship was a celebrated gunship that had fought valiantly at Trafalgar in 1805, only to be broken up thirty-three years later at a Rotherhithe shipyard after being left on the Thames to decay.*"

"It seems very sad doesn't it," remarked Katherine, "that no attempt was made to restore her. I've always thought the past is worth hanging onto, particularly when it's an artefact, something that was actually *there* at the time. We can learn so much from history." She studied the painting, wondering about the old ship being towed to its final destination and the carelessness with which it had been treated. "What else does it say?"

Alex consulted the booklet again. "*Turner's painting pays homage to the gallant Temeraire, while at the same time showing us that it is also the end of an era. Her once proud colours are faded and ghostly behind the vibrant little steamship that takes her on her final journey, while the magnificent sunset is a poignant reminder of the Temeraire's glorious past.*"

"Fitting words," she added, thoughtfully.

They viewed the picture for a while longer, before moving onto another of Turner's paintings, a much earlier one this time, of a boat trying to land at Calais in a very rough sea.

"His style is so different here," observed Katherine, "but the painting reminds me of a stormy night on Cairnmor. This one may have been of Calais, but it's pretty universal. I've witnessed a scene like this several times in real life when a sudden storm has blown up out of nowhere and the fishermen are trying desperately to come into the harbour and safety."

After completing the gallery and eating lunch, they hailed a taxi and returned to Kensington, the driver's route taking them down The Mall and past Buckingham Palace. Katherine was impressed by its stateliness and Alex said, "Queen Victoria was the first monarch to use this as an official Royal Residence and she and Prince Albert had it decorated to suit their style. He was a great collector of works of art and she loved having portraits of the family done."

"I wonder how the new King will fare?" said Katherine. "Of course, Queen Elizabeth is of Scottish descent, being the younger daughter of the Earl of Strathmore," she added, with a smile and no little pride.

"I think they'll make an excellent King and Queen," replied Alex. "I never had a lot of time for the Prince of Wales or Wallis Simpson either; somehow I didn't buy the 'romantic' Prince image that the newsreels and the popular press seemed so keen to project. The Duke of York is a much steadier sort. Honest as they come."

"And with two lovely daughters."

"Yes. But their lives are going to be very different now, aren't they?"

"That is so, my love." *Just like mine*, she thought and seeking comfort, Katherine moved closer to Alex in the back of the taxi.

They spent the afternoon reading; Katherine with her feet up on the settee trying to decipher Rupert's annotations in the two books about Scotland and Alex in the easy chair opposite attempting to read the newspaper. He kept falling asleep and eventually Katherine did the same, unable to keep her eyes open.

Mrs Thringle found them thus when she brought in the afternoon tea, and woke them gently by placing the tea tray on the occasional table in front of the fire, by drawing the curtains and putting on the two table lamps. She put more coal on the fire and went out of the room after making sure they didn't need anything else.

Alex poured the tea while Katherine helped herself to a slice of cake. "I could get used to all this luxury," she said.

He looked at her enquiringly but when she didn't elaborate, said nothing and continued to drink his tea, enjoying just watching her.

She became thoughtful and remarked, "As I'm going to be spending this evening with the 'legal fraternity… '"

"I like that!" chuckled Alex.

Katherine smiled. "I thought you might. Anyway, as I shall be spending this evening in their company, I want to make sure that I understand the background to being a barrister so that I can join in the conversation without looking like an idiot."

"You could never be that," and Alex went down on his knees in front of Katherine, pulled her towards him and kissed her, having first removed her cup from her hand.

After several moments, he sat back in his chair and said, "Right, so what do you want to know?" and was highly amused by her momentary inability to say anything.

She pretended to glower at him and said, "When I have gathered my thoughts…"

"Fire away."

"Qualifications. Now I know you have a Law Degree."

"Yes, the Oxford equivalent is termed 'Jurisprudence'."

"What was the syllabus on the course?"

"Curious young lady aren't you?"

"Yes, I have an insatiable thirst for knowledge."

Alex raised an eyebrow and grinned broadly. Katherine threatened to crumble her cake down his neck if he didn't behave.

"I'm serious. Now, just answer my questions."

"Yes ma'am." Alex pretended to be suitably chastised. "In my first year, I studied criminal law, constitutional law and practised research skills. Then in the second and third years we did land law, contracts law, administrative law, jurisprudence and tort law."

"What's tort law?"

"Civil wrongs as opposed to criminal wrongs. The police can enforce the law by taking the wrongdoers to court – as in a criminal case. A 'tort' is a civil action taken by one citizen against another."

"As in Stephenson versus Smith."

"Exactly."

"What's jurisprudence?"

"Jurisprudence is the theory and philosophy of law, helping to give a greater understanding of the nature of law, legal reasoning, legal systems and institutions." Alex regarded her sternly. "You realize I shall ask you questions on this later…"

"Yes, m'lud," replied Katherine demurely, pulling Alex over to join her on the settee, which he did, willingly.

"So, what happens after graduation?" she asked.

Alex put his arm around her and she tucked her feet up under her and laid her head on his shoulder, both of them enjoying just being close to each other.

"Once a student has graduated, they are then required to join one of the four ancient Inns of Court which have the exclusive right to call students to the Bar. This involves paying a membership fee and attending a required amount of qualifying sessions at their Inn. These can include purely social occasions…"

"Like the one we're going to this evening…"

"Yes, there'll be students present, so you'll feel quite at home as you're a teacher, and also lectures, debates and moots, all of which help students in preparing for advocacy."

"What's a moot?"

"It's a hypothetical case argued by law students as an exercise. Once all these requirements at the Inn are completed, the student is assessed, they take an examination and if they pass, they are then 'called to the Bar'."

"What's the Bar?" asked Katherine, and then added, "I shall have the equivalent of a law degree by the time we've finished this conversation!"

She cuddled up closer to Alex. Thus companionably ensconced he continued, happy to talk about his profession.

"Originally, courtrooms were partitioned off, or enclosed by two bars or rails. One separated the judge's bench from the rest of the room; the other segregated the lawyers engaged in trials from the space allotted to the public and from those appearing before the court."

"Oh, I see. So, what happens after a student has been 'called to the Bar'?"

"They have to secure a pupillage, that is, a period of training at a barrister's Chambers. For the first six months, a student is assigned to a more senior barrister,

114

a 'pupil master'. In Scotland, they're called a 'devil master', and pupillage is called 'devilling'."

"I think I prefer the English terminology," said Katherine. "I wonder why it's called that in Scotland?"

"I've no idea!" replied Alex.

"Och now, Mr Stewart, how could ye possibly not know?! And here was I thinking that ye were the fount of all legal knowledge!"

Alex tickled her and when she was breathless and pleading for mercy, he kissed her. Then they heard the floorboards creak outside the door as Mrs Thringle went about her late afternoon routine and drew apart in case she came in on them unannounced.

"So," he continued, "during the first period of shadowing their senior barrister, the pupil sits in on client conferences and works on papers. Then, in the second six months, you start working on your own, 'getting on your feet' as it's known; starting with case management reviews or bail applications and then doing minor cases, building up advocacy practice. The pupil is still under the direct supervision of the pupil master until finally, when the year is completed, you have to try and 'secure a tenancy' in one of the many chambers following an interview. If successful, you can, at last, start working as an independent barrister, also known as junior counsel." Alex smiled and looking at Katherine asked, "Any more questions?"

"Yes, two more. What's a K.C.?"

"King's Counsel, so called if the monarch is male and Queen's Counsel if female, are barristers appointed to represent the Crown in criminal cases. They must have been qualified and working for at least ten years before being selected as a K.C."

"So, you could never become a K.C.?"

"No, not unless I changed to criminal law, although some K.C.s have been known to work on civil cases. But as a member of the Chancery Division, I could become a judge."

"Would you want to do that?"

"I don't know. Certainly not at the moment. I enjoy what I do too much."

"So, junior counsel, do you think I'm more or less prepared for my trial by social occasion?"

"Honestly, you have nothing to worry about, my love. Just be yourself. View it as a social gathering. I've never worried about what other people might think, nor have I ever gone in for social climbing or overt snobbishness as some people do on these occasions. It's so false and pretentious and I find it irritating. I'm proud to go anywhere with you." And he kissed her very tenderly before saying, "Here endeth the sermon."

"You sermonize very well, dear," Katherine replied, wanting to stay in his arms forever.

At that moment, Mrs Thringle knocked on the door discreetly and came into the sitting room to collect the tea tray. She reminded them that there wasn't too much time before they were due to go out and so very reluctantly, Katherine and Alex disentangled themselves and went upstairs to bathe and change.

Mrs Thringle cleared away the remainder of the tea things and later said to her husband after Katherine and Alex had gone out, "Those two seem to get on like a house on fire. I'm looking forward to the day when they're married. Brings real happiness to the house, she does."

Mr Thringle merely grunted his agreement as his wife settled down in front of their fire and brought out her knitting, her tasks finished for the day, and dreamed of weddings and of children running around the house again.

It had been far too long since that had happened; far too long.

CHAPTER 15

Alex and Katherine alighted from the taxi in the Strand and walked down Middle Temple Lane into Fountain Court where Middle Temple Hall was situated. Many people were arriving at the same time and they found themselves part of a steady stream going up the steps into the attractive building, with its castellated tower and solid oak doors.

The hall porter, James Morris, greeted Alex. "Hello, Mr Stewart. How are you this evening?"

"I'm fine thank you," replied Alex, steering Katherine out of the flow of people and over to the side of the entrance hall where the hall porter was standing. "This is my fiancée, Katherine MacDonald."

"I'm pleased to meet you," said James and they shook hands.

Alex turned to Katherine and said, "There is nothing that this man doesn't know about the history of the building and the people who've lived and worked here over the years. If you have a question, just ask James. He taught me everything I needed to know about Middle Temple when I first came here as a student barrister. I'll embarrass him totally now by saying that he takes the greatest pride in his position here and the place wouldn't be the same without him."

James took Alex's praise in his stride, but was obviously pleased and said to Katherine, "The people who work here are very nice people, very nice." Then, lowering his voice confidentially, he said, "Well, you get the odd few who aren't, but that's the same anywhere, isn't it?" Resuming his usual level of speech, he added, with total sincerity, "But this man here is one of the nicest people that I know. And I know a great many people!"

Katherine smiled. "I may be a little biased, but I do happen to agree with you!"

The lobby was becoming somewhat congested, so it was time for them to move on.

"Enjoy your evening!" said James, as they rejoined the throng of people entering the corridor.

"We shall try!" replied Alex.

Katherine turned and smiled at James, who smiled back and watched them until someone else claimed his attention.

They went downstairs and deposited their coats in the cloakroom, waiting patiently in a queue to claim their tickets. Katherine was very grateful to Mary for providing her with such a wonderful dress that was in no way overshadowed by the elegant attire of those around her.

Alex whispered in her ear, for the second time since leaving home, that she looked beautiful. Feeling confident and relaxed, Katherine put her arm through his and they made their way towards the hall itself.

"I'm taking you here first, rather than to one of the ante-rooms where everyone else is gathering," Alex explained, "because I wanted to show you this before the start of the evening's festivities." He stopped at the top of the stairs and said,

"Now, close your eyes" which Katherine dutifully did and he led her by the hand into the hall, having kissed her first. "Now open them again."

"Oh my goodness!" she exclaimed, looking around her. "This is so beautiful! What an amazing place."

Before her was an oak-panelled room, with long tables laid with pristine white damask tablecloths, silver candlesticks, sparkling crystal glasses, striking red goblets and elegant black place mats with a red and white shield motif emblazoned on them. Each red leather-backed chair had printed on it the emblem of Middle Temple, the Lamb and Flag, in gold leaf and at the head of the hall, behind the enormous top table, were portraits of Queen Elizabeth I, Charles I on horseback and other portraits of Charles II, Queen Anne, James II and William III.

"That's William of Orange, isn't it?" asked Katherine, looking at the portrait on the far right-hand side.

"Yes, the infamous scourge of the Scots!" replied Alex. "It's a good job someone like Mrs Gilgarry isn't here!" he added, recalling his trip round Cairnmor with Donald, the postman.

Katherine laughed. "Yes, the Jacobite rebellion and the punishments meted out by the English to the Clans still run very deep with many Scottish people."

"But not with you."

"No, I prefer to forgive and forget. Besides which, you can't change the past and studying it gives you a healthy objectivity."

Alex pointed to the table positioned underneath the paintings on a slightly raised platform. "This is called the 'Bench Table' – that's where the Master Treasurer, the judges and the senior members of Middle Temple sit. It's twenty-nine feet long, carved from just one tree felled in Windsor Great Park on the orders of Queen Elizabeth I and floated down here on a barge along the River Thames," said Alex.

"It's enormous. I don't think I've ever seen a table as large."

"The table had to be put in place before the Chancellor's window in the alcove on the left there could be glazed and finished and it's never been out of the room since."

They admired the table for a few moments, then looking up, Katherine said, "The ceiling is amazing."

"Isn't it just? It's called a 'double hammer beam roof' and it's incredible to think that this hall, known as the Great Hall, was built during the Middle Ages and has remained virtually unchanged for over four hundred years."

"When I go back to Cairnmor and everyone asks me what I saw in London, I shall say that everywhere I went there were Great Halls – Euston Station, the Royal Courts of Justice and now Middle Temple!"

Alex laughed. "Perhaps you can persuade them to re-name the new hall on the island 'Cairnmor Great Hall'!"

Katherine chuckled. "Now there's a thought!" Her attention was drawn to the oak panelling that lined the room where a coat of arms was fixed to each of the individual panels. "What are these?"

"These are the coats of arms that belong to former 'Readers' at Middle Temple."

"Readers?"

118

"Yes. They organize the moots or debates for the student barristers and give lectures. They also call out the names of the barristers at the graduating ceremony when they're called to the Bar. They really are the most experienced and learned of the members."

"I really love this Hall. It has such an atmosphere of history and learning, and warmth too. You know how some churches have a real sense of spirituality, because people have prayed and worshipped there over the centuries while other buildings, like the Royal Courts of Justice, great solemnity?"

"Yes?"

"Well, this one has heart and there's an almost tangible sense of intelligence here too. Or am I being fanciful?"

"Not at all. It just shows a great sensitivity to your surroundings. It's one that I happen to share..." Alex smiled at her and then thought for a moment. "The composer Edward Elgar always felt there was 'music in the air' in the countryside around his native Malvern and he drew on this as inspiration for his own compositions. He wrote some wonderful music. Unfortunately, he died about two years ago, but Dad and I were lucky enough to go to several concerts of his own works that he conducted, here in London and at the Three Choirs Festival in Worcester Cathedral. An amazing man. It was quite something to see him conduct."

"I'm not familiar with his music, I'm afraid," said Katherine, "being a Scots lass from a remote island, ye ken!" she added lightly.

"Oh, I'm sure you'd like it," replied Alex, not rising to the gentle bait. "I'd love to take you to some concerts at the Queen's Hall when Elgar's music is being performed, if you'd like that?"

"Of course I would!" said Katherine, unable to resist Alex's obvious enthusiasm.

A rising tide of conversation behind them made them aware that everyone else was beginning to flow into the hall. Katherine took a deep breath and Alex took her hand and held her close.

A voice immediately behind them said, "Hello you two!" and Katherine and Alex turned to see Michael coming through the door. They both greeted him warmly, and Katherine found herself pleased to see him again. She liked his easy-going extrovert nature and the obvious regard the two men had for each other.

"Rather splendid all of this isn't it?" said Michael. "In my opinion, it's probably the most spectacular of all the Inns of Court. Apparently, in the Middle Ages, they all vied with each other to see who could produce the most impressive buildings and construct the ultimate status symbol and bring in the richest patrons. This place attracted patronage at the highest levels – Elizabeth I became both a benefactor and a guest. Not bad for a dining hall is it?" said Michael, somewhat irreverently, but still with obvious admiration. "The first performance of Shakespeare's *Twelfth Night* was given here in 1602 and it survived 1666 unscathed."

"No Great Fire in the Great Hall then?" said Alex, and Katherine groaned.

"Only on cold winter nights like this one," retorted Michael.

"I can see it's going to be one of those evenings!" observed Katherine drily.

"Watch out," said Michael *sotto voce* to Katherine, as an under-dressed and heavily made-up, woman approached them. "Behold, the incomparable Lucinda Clifton – beauty and nastiness all wrapped up in one gorgeous body!"

"Ssh, she'll hear you!" said Katherine.

"I really do not care," said Michael, with such feeling that it made Katherine think there must be more to this than just a superficial dislike.

"Hello, *darling,*" she said to Alex in tones of clear-cut glass, kissing him on the lips and totally ignoring both Katherine and Michael. "How simply *wonderful* to see you. I've missed my little *lambikins*. We must get together again, it's ages since we've been out on the town. It's all been so *terribly* dull in my little flat without you to play with."

"Genuine soul, isn't she?" whispered Michael in Katherine's ear to distract her.

She tried valiantly not to giggle, having already cringed at '*my little lambikins*' and suppressed a rising anxiety at the woman's final few words.

Then Lucinda noticed Katherine and Michael. "Oh it's you," she said to Michael, with a barely disguised sneer. She looked Katherine up and down with contempt. "You must be this Scotch woman everyone's been talking about – the one who's taken Alex away from our inner circle," she said, with an unmistakeably malicious tone in her voice.

"Och, aye, ye're reet," said Katherine, summing her up immediately and intentionally adopting a broad Glaswegian accent. "And just to let ye know lassie, I'm a Scot. Scotch is a drink and I dinna tak' even a wee dram, ye ken."

Lucinda, taken aback, said something to Katherine in French, who opened her eyes very wide at this flow of insulting rhetoric. She immediately replied in equally fluent French, finishing off with a final broadside in Gaelic, which caught Lucinda completely unawares.

She spluttered, "I beg your pardon?"

"I was merely answering you in French and Gaelic, my dear," said Katherine, in an impeccable English accent.

Michael meanwhile, had disappeared behind Alex's back and put his fist into his mouth to stop himself from laughing out loud, but the effort made his eyes stream. Alex, who had said not a word or reacted in any way to Lucinda, was also having difficulty keeping a straight face, although if Katherine had looked at him closely, she would have perceived a hint of embarrassment behind the amusement.

Unable to think of anything else to say, Lucinda flounced off with her nose in the air and Michael could at last let go of the laughter that he had done his best to control.

"What did she say to you?" he asked, in between wiping his eyes.

"She said that my dress was disgustingly outmoded, that Alex still belonged to her, and that I was obviously an uneducated bitch!"

"Even for Lucinda, that was quite something!" observed Michael. "What did you say?"

"I told her that my dress was from the 'House of Cairnmor' and was far more fashionable than her ragged apology for a garment, that Alex and I were engaged and she should keep her claws out of him otherwise I'd be out to get her and finally, in Gaelic, I told her to get lost."

120

"Politely?"

"Very impolitely!"

"I must learn Gaelic," said Michael. "It could come in useful. You can swear at people and they'd never know it!"

"Unless you're from Cairnmor or the Highlands," said Alex, laughing almost as much as Michael.

"Oh dear," said Katherine. "I shouldn't have said any of that. It's not like me at all. Not that she would have understood what I said at the end, but even so…"

"Well, she deserved it, silly woman," said Alex, with contempt.

"It took the wind out of her sails though, didn't it?!" remarked Michael. Then he said, in a perfect imitation of Lucinda's English drawl, going down on one knee in front of Alex and clasping his hands together in an attitude of pleading, *"Oh Alex, my little lambikins, please be mine!"* causing three of them to dissolve once more into fits of laughter and Katherine had to exert considerable self-control to recover her breath and her composure.

Alex remarked, "You know, she reminds me of those two awful men we encountered at the hotel in Lochaberdale."

"Yes, when we nearly dropped the tea tray doing imitations of them!"

"You two keep talking about Cairnmor. I think I shall abandon the rat-race and go and live there. And learn Gaelic," added Michael, for good measure.

Katherine and Alex looked at each other. He raised an eyebrow enquiringly at her and she nodded imperceptibly.

"Well, Cinderella," began Alex, "you shall go to the ball."

"What do you mean?" asked Michael.

"How would you like to be my best man when Katherine and I get married next April – *on Cairnmor?*" he emphasized.

"I'd like that very much. Thank you," responded Michael, genuinely delighted and honoured to be asked.

Katherine kissed him on the cheek and said, "I can think of no nicer person to have as best man. And you'll get on famously with my matron of honour."

Michael's face lit up. "Aha! Cairnmor might weave a magical spell on me and it will be my destiny to fall in love with the matron of honour, my island princess!"

"Don't even think about it," said Katherine sternly, wagging her finger at him. "She's married already!"

Michael went into mock agony, placing the back of his hand across his forehead. "Just my luck. Thwarted before I've even met her – the love of my life!" And the three of them laughed again with the warmth of a shared sense of humour and a shared friendship.

There was no further time for conversation, as everyone was invited to take their places. A loud fanfare heralded the arrival of the Master Treasurer, Judges and King's Counsels. They processed into the room and most made their way to the Bench Table or others nearby and sat down in their allotted places. This was the signal for everyone else to do the same and, after a call for silence, formal greetings were expressed and the banquet commenced.

Wives and girlfriends were placed next to their partners. Alex and Michael noted discreetly that Lucinda was seated next to Edwin Mullion, the barrister whom Alex had opposed in court, further down their table.

"What is it with Lucinda and you two? And who is she? She's not a barrister, surely?" whispered Katherine to Alex, having overheard their conversation.

"No she's not!" replied Alex quietly, but emphatically. "I'll tell you when we get home," he added, hoping that the subject wouldn't be raised again and just go away.

Katherine, satisfied with that, did not press the matter further but watched her discreetly at odd intervals and several times caught Lucinda doing the same. She seemed very subdued and this did not go unnoticed by Michael, who winked at Katherine and whispered, "You've really put her nose out of joint!"

The four course dinner was exquisitely prepared and served with care and consideration. The conversation was varied and interesting, though Katherine found it hard work when the wife of another barrister, seated next to her, began to talk about how difficult it was to find a decent nanny and how the shops were no longer stocking her favourite shoes.

Katherine made polite, appropriate answers but did not see any connection with her neighbour as a potential friend. She was far more interested in the discussion that Alex and Michael were having with a colleague and a student seated next to Sir John Pemberton, the head of Royal Court Chambers. Others on the table gradually began to listen and participate as the student, who seemed to feel that he knew everything there was to know, expounded the virtues of law being solely regulation handed down by the state. A few of the barristers seated nearby agreed, but Alex and Michael did not.

Alex said that law should be something that emerges from society as a whole rather than something that is imposed, adding, "The English legal system has developed over a long period of time and law has to be seen as the extension of custom which evolves into law with the passage of time."

The barrister seated opposite, who had previously agreed with the student, observed, "It has always seemed to me a very haphazard way of going about things."

"I disagree," said Alex. "Law at its best should be the redefinition of custom so that it has clarity and can be enforced by legal institutions. We don't have revolution in this country, apart from the time of the Commonwealth which then ran its natural course, enabling the monarchy to be reinstated. We have a way of allowing change to evolve rather than being something that is imposed from the outside."

"But surely it's better to deny the evolutionary link and have the law clearly defined and unequivocal," said the student.

Sir John Pemberton had been listening intently and when he spoke it was not to join in with the debate, which was in danger of becoming quite heated, but to ask Katherine her opinion on the matter.

For a brief moment, her heart beat wildly, as she realized that she was being tested intentionally. She took her time before replying. "Although I'm not a student of law, I do agree with Alex. From the historical perspective, the best changes have emerged over time because they were needed and not imposed by some bureaucrat who wished to alter the law to benefit his particular political party or stratum in society. Change for the sake of it has caused enormous hardship and unfortunate repercussions over the years, especially if that change is ill-conceived and not thought through properly. Good laws should benefit society as a whole and not cause difficulties for the people who are affected by them."

"I'm not referring to change for its own sake, rather that state regulation is better and should replace customary forms of behaviour as a means of making laws," said the student defending himself.

"But surely law has to be the response to developments in the economy, politics and sociological change," replied Katherine, warming to her subject. "Someone in London can create a radical new law and this might adversely affect someone living in, for example, Scotland, whose life bears little resemblance to the politician's experience. Why not allow the law to evolve from custom which in itself has evolved over a long period of time and tends to be more universal?"

Sir John Pemberton nodded and studied Katherine with intelligent interest. Alex, proud of her, joined in again and addressed the student.

"Consider this: in the law lecture delivered by William Blackstone in 1758, he described law as, and I quote: '*This most useful and rational branch of learning*'. It takes great knowledge and wisdom to perceive and define what is needed in evolving new laws and by setting precedents, judges do just that in the courts. They can draw upon past or present judicial experience as analogies to help in making a decision. *Stare decisis* provide certainty and predictability and the '*case of first impression*' provides flexibility. Both make for a stable legal environment."

The student was silent and had sufficient grace to regard Alex with a new respect. "I'll certainly think about all that you've said," he replied.

There the discussion ended and most people returned to conversations with their immediate neighbours.

Sir John Pemberton addressed Katherine. "Alex tells me that you studied history at Edinburgh. I gather you were awarded the equivalent of a First for your efforts."

Katherine blushed and nodded, not quite sure where this conversation was leading. "Yes," she responded simply.

"Alex needs a clever partner. He seems to have found it in you. Where are you from again?"

"Cairnmor – one of the Outer Islands on the west coast of Scotland."

"A long way away," he observed.

Katherine did not reply but merely smiled and let his words linger unresolved in the air. If he noticed this, Sir John did not acknowledge the fact. Instead, he turned his attention to the student and proceeded to engage him in conversation.

Around them, the other guests were beginning to leave their seats and gather in small groups in the Hall, continuing old conversations or beginning new ones. Alex, Katherine and Michael did the same, though presently Michael excused himself when he spotted a colleague with whom he would be working on a land partition case in the New Year and went across the room to talk to him.

Alex and Katherine were left alone together and he took her over to a battered looking rectangular table with legs that seemed to have been added as an afterthought.

"This is the Cupboard," said Alex, with no little amusement, "and it has a very colourful history."

"But it's a table!" declared Katherine sceptically.

"I know," replied Alex, chuckling. "It's actually two separate words: Cup Board. Don't even begin to ask – your guess is as good as mine! Anyway, it was used as a lectern many years ago, but now it's where barristers sign the Roll during the ceremony when they graduate and are 'called to the Utter Bar'. The oak from the table top was given to the Inn by Sir Francis Drake and it began life as a hatch cover on board the *Golden Hind*." Alex lifted up the heavy oak cover protecting the original golden-brown wood underneath.

Katherine ran her hand over the highly polished surface. "London has such a rich tapestry of history. It's my subject and it's wonderful to be so surrounded by it – here in Middle Temple, in the architecture of the buildings in London, in the ceremonies that take place. For me, it's not just words any more that you read in a book or study in a paper; it's tangible, indisputable evidence of the past in a very real present."

"You know," considered Alex, "it's very easy when you live here to take it all for granted and go about your daily business without really thinking about any of that. I've always appreciated the buildings from an aesthetic point of view but since we've read Rupert's diaries, with his love of architecture, and if I add to that all you've just said about the historical perspective, one begins to view things in a wholly different light." Very discreetly, Alex held her close.

Katherine responded to him, equally discreetly and then continued in a similar vein. "I mean, look at that window, all those coats of arms in each of the frames. I'd love to be able to see them properly in daylight. I'd give a guess and say they were Elizabethan?"

"Yes, you're right, most of them are."

"It's funny, but Middle Temple reminds me of being at Edinburgh in many ways."

"Yes, it reminds me of Oxford as well. It has similar architecture, a Great Hall, a chapel, libraries, extensive grounds."

"And a very learned atmosphere," said Michael, coming over to join them, "which some of us would like to exchange for the great outdoors!"

"Are you suggesting that it's time to go?" asked Alex, smiling at his friend.

"Yes, because I've had enough but also because I need fresh air and the open spaces of Shropshire or Cairnmor or anywhere away from stuffy intellectualism."

"Philistine," said Alex.

"Yep, that's me. Call me Phil," he said, extending his hand to Katherine.

"With pleasure, Phil," she said, shaking it vigorously and laughing.

They were unable to go anywhere, because at that moment, Sir John Pemberton came over to them and totally failing to acknowledge Michael in any way, said to Alex that he was impressed by his contribution during the dinner-time debate, also by his recent advocacy work in court and would be considering how best to utilize his talents over the coming months.

"You're destined for great things. A number of people are watching you very closely, Alex." Then he turned to Katherine and said, with deep significance, "Your fiancé is a very talented man. Don't take him away from where his best interests lie."

Katherine thought carefully before replying, trying not to show the sudden surge of irritation she felt at his words. "You may rest assured that I too have his best interests at heart, Sir John." *And I don't need you to point them out to me*, she thought, all the while keeping a neutral expression on her face.

"Thank you, my dear woman," he said, obviously reassured by her words.

Michael, however, had spotted her momentary anger and had every sympathy for her. He smiled at her, trying to lift her mood and while she acknowledged this, she was unable to shake off a lingering resentment.

Alex meanwhile, was engaged in further conversation with Sir John, who had steered him away from Michael and Katherine. When he had said all he wished to say, he bid Alex goodbye and went across to the other side of the room to join his fellow senior colleagues. Katherine could see that Alex too was angry.

"Do you know what he said?" muttered Alex. "He suggested that the best way for me to get ahead now was to mix with the right people, to cultivate the friendship of those who could influence my career path and avoid those whose influence might be detrimental to me. That really riles me, because I'll progress in my job on merit or not at all. He was patronizing to you, Katherine, and very rude in ignoring you, Michael."

"I think he's been a K.C. for so long, he's forgotten all about empathy and consideration," replied Michael, somewhat regretfully. "Not that all K.C.s are like him, I have to say," he added. "But I agree with you totally about getting ahead on one's merit, which is why I have no jealousy of your success, Alex – I mean, I know I'm just hopeless," he added, with customary self-effacing levity.

"No you're not." Alex defended his friend vigorously. "I'd rather work with you than any other barrister I can think of."

"That's nice of you to say, but seriously, this evening has confirmed my opinion that Sir John's a part of what I call the cut-throat brigade; the members who see our job as some sort of competition. Being the cynical chap that I am, I think that if Alex is highly successful, Sir John believes it will reflect well on him as Senior Counsel at Royal Court Chambers."

"It can't be as bad as that," said Katherine. "It's only natural that with someone as talented as Alex, he should want to help further their career. Surely that is part of his role as Head of Chambers?" And then, trying to inject some humour into the discussion, she added, "He's probably afraid that Alex's career will go downhill under my alien influence so he needs to mix with the right sort of people who'll keep him on the straight and narrow!"

Alex, however, would not be drawn. "Michael's right in this particular instance, I'm afraid. Fortunately not everyone in the profession is of the same opinion as Sir John on how to get ahead."

"So, what are we going to do now?" asked Michael, diverting the conversation. "I have no desire to join the gentlemen for brandy, coffee and cigars. I'd really like to go home as I've got an early start in the morning – the land calleth and I'm off to Shropshire. Hurrah! Would you mind if I went?"

"Not at all," said Katherine and kissed him on the cheek, eliciting a swooning response from Michael who said he wouldn't wash his face for a month.

He bid them both a cheery farewell and Alex, having recovered something of his previous good humour, said that as he didn't wish to social climb that evening, he would be quite happy to leave as well.

It had been a long evening and as Katherine wanted to be well rested before they travelled to Oxfordshire the next day, she was more than content to go home. So, they both collected their coats, left the building arm in arm and went out into the Strand to find a taxicab to take them back to Kensington.

CHAPTER 16

Mistley House
December, 1936

Saturday was fine and sunny. In view of the settled weather, Alex thought it would be a good idea to drive down to Oxfordshire in his car, especially as he wished to demonstrate its finer points to Katherine.

"That way," he said, "we can be independent and do a bit of sight-seeing on the journey."

Katherine thought this sounded like an excellent idea and they went into the dining room to eat the large breakfast which Mrs Thringle had insisted on preparing for them before their "long trek."

"It's only forty miles," Alex whispered to Katherine once the housekeeper had left the room after serving them with extra toast and tea.

"Well, if it keeps her happy," replied Katherine, "and she does love looking after the family."

Alex said that she did indeed. "Her life's work!" he added, with knowledge born of many years of experience.

When they had finished, Alex carried both their suitcases down into the hall, and Mrs Thringle brought them a small picnic hamper.

"There's lots of food in there for the journey," she said, "in case you get hungry or suffer any delays."

"Well, if we do, at least we won't starve! Thank you, Mrs Thing, it's very thoughtful of you," said Alex.

"You're welcome, dearie."

"Your Christmas presents are under the tree in Alastair's sitting room, Mrs Thringle," added Katherine. "Don't forget to collect them."

"No, I won't. I'll take them when Bob and I go to our daughter's in Sydenham on Christmas Day. We always have a family day then and on New Year's Day too. My son and his wife and children will be there as well, so what with my daughter's three, it'll be quite a houseful."

Alex went to fetch the car from the garage and Katherine gathered together their presents and put them into a wicker shopping basket, which the housekeeper had supplied, placing this with the hamper and suitcases by the front door. Alex came up the steps, collected all the luggage and they both bid farewell to Mrs Thringle before going down to the car.

When she saw the size of the little sports car, Katherine wondered where everything would fit.

"Don't worry," said Alex, "there's plenty of room!" He proceeded to stow the suitcases in the luggage space behind the seats, and the presents and hamper in the minuscule rear compartment.

The car looked very full but there was still room for them to squeeze into the front seats. After Alex had checked that the retractable hood was secure, they both got in and he started the engine.

"Have a wonderful time," called out Mrs Thringle, standing just inside the front door, waving to them.

"See you after the New Year," replied Alex and with a loud revving of the engine, they set off down the road.

"Do you know," observed Katherine, "this is the first time that I've ever been in a car like this. I've been in taxicabs, trams, buses, trains and Donald's post bus, but I've never been in a sports car before."

"What do you think of it?" asked Alex, who really wanted to know as this was something of a prized possession.

"It's exciting! Everything seems to be going by very fast."

"That's because we're so low down. I can drive more slowly if you like."

"No, no it's fine. I'll soon get used to it. What sort of car is it?" asked Katherine.

"It's an MG TA midget, which replaced the old MG PB, which I had considered buying but wasn't terribly impressed when I went to look at it. I'm told on good authority that the main difference between the two models is that the TA is longer, wider and more comfortable than its predecessor, and has an overhead valve push-rod engine as opposed to an overhead cam engine." Alex looked at Katherine meaningfully, neither of them being any the wiser as to the difference.

"Aye," said Katherine, with an understanding smile. "I presume from the way you looked at me just now that you're not into the mechanical side of things?"

"Not in the least! I leave that to our local garage to sort out, but so far," and Alex touched the wooden trim on the dashboard as a precaution, "the car hasn't caused me any problems!"

"When did you buy it?"

"Last spring when this particular model first came out."

"Was it very expensive?"

"Two hundred and twenty-two pounds exactly," said Alex, with pride. "Apparently, it's very good value for the money."

"I love the colour; it's such a gorgeous shade of blue."

"Yes. That was the thing that drew me to the car in the first place when I saw it sitting on the garage forecourt and then its shape, of course, and I knew I had to investigate further."

"Was it difficult to learn to drive?"

"I'd already driven Dad's Morris at home, but this was very different. Is the seat comfortable?"

"Yes it's fine, thank you."

"Because you can adjust the angle of the back rest if not."

"Any other wonders you care to tell me about?"

"Yes, it has a map reading light for the passenger, hydraulic brakes, a triplex glass front windscreen and removable side screens if you want to drive with the hood down."

"H'm, that garage salesman had better be careful. You'll be taking over his job soon."

"Be quiet or I'll tickle you," replied Alex good-naturedly.

128

"Not while you're driving! Keep your eyes on the road please, Mr Stewart," retorted Katherine with equal good humour.

They smiled briefly at each other and he took her hand for a moment, before traffic conditions meant that he had to change gear.

They travelled on in silence for a while and Katherine watched the changing scenery of London gradually becoming more rural as the A4 main arterial road took them out beyond the suburbs and into the countryside.

"There are so many trees everywhere. I think that's going to be one of the abiding memories I shall take back to Cairnmor with me."

"That and the thousands of Great Halls!"

Katherine laughed. "I know!" Then after a while, she asked, "Alex?"

"Yes?"

"Tell me about Lucinda Clifton. Who is she exactly?"

Alex hesitated before replying. He had hoped that after meeting Lucinda at the Charity dinner, Katherine wouldn't ask about her as he knew it might lead to questions about his previous life-style – something he was beginning to regret, and something he was anxious to avoid revealing.

"She's an ex-girlfriend, I'm ashamed to say. Not one of the things I'm most proud of."

"Why? Did you go out with her for very long?"

"For about six months."

"Was it serious?"

He hesitated again before replying, wondering whether 'serious' was her euphemism for going to bed with someone. Assuming this to be so, he therefore answered evasively, "Fairly, but more on her part than mine. She seemed nice at first, very attractive, but then her true nature gradually emerged and she became very demanding and possessive. Eventually, after giving her many subtle hints that I no longer wished to see her, I was forced to become very blunt and say that I didn't want anything more to do with her."

"What happened?"

"She refused to take no for an answer and things became very difficult. She kept telephoning and writing to me; weeping on the doorstep, that sort of thing. I couldn't get rid of her. Eventually, Michael came up with a plan that he would ask her out, if only to get her off my back."

"Did it work?"

"Yes, it was quite effective and during the few times they went out, he seemed to be able to curb some of her excessive behaviour. Unfortunately, somehow she found out about our plan and for some totally inexplicable reason, laid all the blame at Michael's doorstep and forgave me totally."

"I think she must have some sort of fixation for barristers because she seems to have cornered the attentions of our learned friend Mr Mullion."

"Yes, I noticed that last night as well. Well, they're made for each other. Good luck to them!" Alex chuckled.

"Are there any other ex-girlfriends I should know about?" asked Katherine, not very sure whether or not she really wanted to know. In the back of her mind was the fear that, wonderful as he was, Alex may have had something of a past.

"You're a brave lady!" he remarked, teasing her gently.

"Well, it's better to know now and get it out of the way than dwell on it," she replied, with more robustness than she actually felt.

"That's a very healthy attitude," said Alex, and squeezed her hand.

He thought carefully before replying. Perhaps he would keep certain things to himself as Katherine didn't need to know everything, no matter how brave she was. He was a top-flight barrister but he knew his love life had not been a conspicuous success. He'd had two or three ill-judged affairs with unsuitable women, including Lucinda, while several other attachments had been passing infatuations; short-lived and transient.

No, Katherine didn't need to know about any of those. This was his chance to make a fresh start, to put his chequered past behind him. So he said, without revealing too much, "Yes, I've had a few relationships over the years, it would be a rare man that hadn't at my age, but I'm difficult to please and I never really knew what love was until I met you."

Allowing herself to feel relief, Katherine leant across to Alex and laid her head on his shoulder. "I'm very glad," she said simply.

She didn't wish to probe further. They were engaged and he belonged to her now. Anything that had happened before they met had gone, was over and done with. There was no point in speculating upon it or pursuing it. However, despite her resolve, the confirmation of her suspicions stayed with her and would trouble her from time to time.

Alex rested his head on top of hers, feeling relief after having cleared that particular hurdle. After a while, he asked, "How about you?"

"When I was at Edinburgh, I went out with a boy for about a year. We were just good friends really and had lots of fun. But he wanted the relationship to become serious and even asked me to marry him. Of course, I said 'no' as gently as I could. I was very fond of him, but I didn't want to spend the rest of my life with him. He was very nice about it, but it cost us our friendship, which I was sorry about. Then a few weeks later he began going out with another girl at the University and they got engaged sometime afterwards, so I was pleased for him."

"Anyone else?"

"No, I've lived a very virtuous life. Until I met you, of course!"

"We're still quite virtuous," said Alex.

"Amazingly enough!" replied Katherine, and they both smiled at each other. "But it was the same for me. I didn't fall in love until I met you, and now I can't imagine my life without you."

After she had said this Alex turned the car off the main road, down a very convenient side turning. He switched off the engine and took Katherine into his arms and kissed her. For a few brief wonderful moments, the world outside the car ceased to exist and they lost themselves in a tender, loving embrace.

They had reached the half-way point on their journey and a few miles later, Alex drove a short distance south into Windsor. Enjoying the mild winter sunshine, they ate their picnic lunch in Windsor Great Park, admiring the panoramic view their chosen location afforded them of the Castle.

Once they had finished eating, they followed the Long Walk up to the magnificent building itself, where they found that, unusually, St George's Chapel was open to the public. They decided to take advantage of this and went inside where a guided tour had just begun. They wandered around, enjoying the splendour of the surroundings and listening to the guide as he expounded on the history of the building.

"St George's Chapel is one of the most beautiful examples of late Medieval Perpendicular Gothic architecture in England," he began. "The building was started by Edward IV in 1475 and completed fifty years later during the reign of Henry VIII. It is the Chapel of the Most Noble Order of the Garter, Britain's highest order of chivalry founded by Edward III in 1345. Now, if you'd care to follow me, we shall proceed to the Nave."

"It reminds me in many ways of The Royal Courts of Justice," whispered Katherine.

"Yes, it has a similar style and feel, doesn't it? I wonder if George Street, the Victorian architect who designed the courts, took inspiration from this?" speculated Alex. "He must have been familiar with it."

"Please observe the slender, perpendicular Gothic columns which rise up to the fan-vaulted ceiling overhead," continued the guide, proceeding to give everyone a few moments to appreciate their beauty. "There are seven monarchs buried in the Chapel and here you can see Edward IV's tomb, where he is buried with his Queen, Elizabeth Woodville. Please note how the tomb is protected by these intricate wrought iron gates." Again he paused, making sure that the ironwork was fully appreciated, before resuming. "Now we move on to the Garter Stalls. Most of these were carved between 1475 and 1483. Each stall bears an insignia of a current Knight of the Garter. Brass and copper plates bear the arms of past knights from the 14th century up to the present. When a member of the Order of the Garter dies, then the insignia is returned to the monarch and a new one for the new member put in its place… Let us move on to the West Window." And the group duly followed him.

Alex was ready to make some quip about their guide but when he saw that Katherine was genuinely absorbed in the tour and the history lesson unfolding before them, he had the good grace to refrain from doing so.

"The West Window was completed in 1509 and the stained glass portrays seventy-five members of the Royal family, saints and popes." Again he gave his charges time to view the individual panes of glass. "Now we move onto Edward III's sword. This was his battle sword and it is six feet eight inches long."

"Imagine lifting that, let alone using it in battle!" Katherine said to Alex. "I'd be staggering around all over the place just trying to get it into the right position. The fighting would be over before I'd managed to do that!"

She and Alex giggled at the picture that it conjured up. The guide looked at them sternly, so they immediately suppressed their laughter.

"Now we shall proceed to the East Doors. Please note the beautiful 13th century ironwork frames to the doors. These were built in 1240 and once formed the entry to Henry III's chapel." He paused meaningfully again. Then he said, somewhat abruptly, "This is the end of the formal tour, but everyone is at liberty to study the rest of the building should you wish to do so. Please note that Choral Evensong begins at three o'clock which you are more than welcome to attend. Thank you." The guide then walked off, having discharged his duty, leaving the group to disperse in various directions.

"What do you want to do now?" asked Katherine.

"We must get on the road again as I'd like to be in Maybury before it gets dark," replied Alex.

"It's a pity the rest of the castle isn't open to the public."

"I think some of it is on certain days of the year, but I suppose that as the Royal Family live here for some of that time, they would wish to protect their privacy, which is completely understandable."

"Yes. But can you imagine living here – a thousand year old fortress made into a Royal residence?"

"Not really! But then I'm not Royalty."

"No, just *my* handsome Prince Charming," said Katherine, sweetly provocative.

"Come on then, *my* beautiful Princess," replied Alex wittily, "let's go and find our carriage!"

Hand in hand, they made their way through the narrow streets of Windsor and resumed their journey, arriving at Mistley House just as the light was fading. As they drove up the short gravel driveway, Katherine's first impression of Alex's childhood home was of a well-proportioned, gracious red-brick and flint country house glowing in the last vestiges of a wintry sun.

Alastair had heard them arrive and immediately came to the front door to greet them, a golden retriever exiting at the same time, running up to the car, its tail waving excitedly.

"Sam! Hello, boy! Good dog," said Alex, bending down, stroking the animal's fur and patting him. The dog followed behind him lovingly, having first placed his cold, wet nose politely in Katherine's hand by way of acknowledgement, as Alex lifted their luggage out of the back of the car.

Katherine was pleased to see Alastair, a familiar face in yet another new and unknown setting, and they greeted each other warmly with a hug and a kiss. In the spacious hallway, waiting slightly nervously, her fingers rubbing against each other in small circular movements, was a woman approaching late middle age, impeccably dressed and subtly made up, whom Katherine took to be Alex's mother. The exquisite beauty she must have had in her youth was still apparent in her face, with its perfect bone structure and oval brown eyes framed by long black lashes, but there was something brittle and wary in her expression.

Alex introduced them. "Mother, I'd like you to meet Katherine. Katherine, this is Roberta."

Katherine smiled, hoping to put the older woman at her ease and offered her hand to her future mother-in-law. However, the smile was returned out of courtesy, but without warmth, and her hand shaken limply, without enthusiasm. Katherine swallowed hard and looked at Alastair, who nodded imperceptibly, his lips tightly drawn.

"I'm very pleased to meet you," she began, but her words faltered as Roberta said, slightly imperiously, "Tea is waiting in the drawing room, if you'd all care to come through when you're ready."

Katherine needed to freshen up after their journey and was grateful to Alex when he said, "I want to take these suitcases upstairs first and show Katherine her room. We'll be down directly, Mother. I presume it's the blue guest room?"

"Yes." Abruptly, Roberta turned and went into the drawing room.

Alex and Alastair exchanged a brief glance and, not a little upset by this unexpectedly cool reception from Alex's mother, Katherine followed him up the staircase to her room which faced out over the garden at the rear of the property.

"When it's light, the view from the window is quite delightful, as you'll see in the morning. The garden stretches all the way down to the Thames." Alex looked at Katherine, biting his bottom lip, sensing her discomfort. "This may not be an easy few days, I'm afraid," he began.

"Why didn't you tell me before we arrived?" asked Katherine reasonably.

"Because I wanted to see what sort of reception you might receive; what sort of mood she was in; whether or not she would make the effort. It's not you. It's difficult to explain."

"I bet you never say that last bit to a judge," said Katherine, injecting a little levity into the conversation.

Alex smiled ruefully. "I'd rather stand up in a whole courtroom full of judges than have to deal with my mother when she's in one of her moods."

"What causes them?" asked Katherine, relieved to discover that Roberta's conduct was not an instant personal antipathy towards her.

"It's been like it for as long as I can remember. There doesn't seem to be any rhyme or reason sometimes; just good days and bad days. I had hoped that today would be a good day."

Katherine nodded thoughtfully. "It sounds to me as though I need to allow your mother to get to know me in her own time and in her own way, and try not to take anything personally or worry if it's hard going."

Alex seemed immensely relieved. "I love you," he said.

"I know. I love you too!"

"I know that as well!"

"Well, now that we have all this knowledge, should we not go down to tea before it becomes a dark brown sludge in the bottom of the tea-pot and your mother starts to fret?"

"That sounds like an excellent idea," agreed Alex, smiling at her, his anxieties concerning Katherine's acceptance of his mother's habitual lack of warmth allayed.

CHAPTER 17

It was still dark when Katherine awoke. Unable to return to sleep, she pushed back the covers, found her slippers and padded across the floor to the window, where she drew the curtains. The grey dawn was just beginning to lighten the sky in the east and, not wanting to miss the sunrise, she quickly dressed and crept downstairs to the cloakroom to collect her coat, hat and scarf.

Sam, lying comfortably warm in his basket by the gently glowing cylindrical stove, wagged his tail laconically at her arrival and lifted his head drowsily in greeting. He laid it down again almost immediately onto his blanket; it was as yet too early for his first walk.

A Sunday calm pervaded the house, although Katherine could hear distant sounds of early morning breakfast preparation coming from the kitchen. As she did not wish to speak to anyone, she let herself quietly out of the French doors in the dining room, closing them carefully behind her.

There had been a sharp frost during the night and the white crystals sparkled with reflected moonlight, guiding her way as she walked towards the river across the silvery grass, preferring this route to the stone path which was slippery despite her trusty walking shoes.

As she approached the river bank, she could hear the water lapping around the supporting struts of a wooden pontoon which ran the whole width of the garden.

There was now sufficient light to distinguish the characteristics of the river bank – an upturned clinker-built boat on the pontoon; a wooden boathouse to the left with a large motor-boat inside, half-concealed under its winter covers. Bare-branched trees lined both river banks – graceful willows dipping yellow-red tendrils into the water; proud elms, ash and chestnut; sturdy oaks, the convoluted shapes of their branches forming patterns only visible in winter or early spring. A gentle mist hung over the calm water and then, unexpectedly, dappled sunlight emerged through the trees, lighting the house behind her with pale wintry light.

Katherine stood still for some time, absorbing this idyllic English country scene, so different from all that she had been used to on Cairnmor, with its dramatic mountain scenery, the wide open spaces of the machair and the Atlantic Ocean which pounded the white-gold sand beyond the dunes with frequent regularity.

And yet, she felt an affinity with this gentle scene before her; a familiarity that seemed to come from somewhere deep inside her which she could not explain. She had always loved trees and this place had them in abundance, but it was more than that; more than the sum total of the scenery around her.

Suddenly, Katherine shivered in the cold air. Reluctantly, she turned away from the river and back towards the house. Smoke was rising from the double chimney and the household was stirring. She wondered what the day would bring and whether there would be a repeat of the stilted conversation at both tea and supper the previous day.

Alex and Alastair had kept the conversation going as much as they could, but Katherine had found herself unable to join in with her characteristic ease and sociability; her words seemed to freeze on her lips in the frigid atmosphere that Roberta created around her. Despite her resolution not to be affected by the older woman's manner, Katherine had found it disconcerting to think that she had not made any headway at all. Roberta seemed to have closed her mind and it appeared that there was nothing she could do to change that.

Alastair had excused himself early and gone upstairs to his room more dejected than she had ever seen him. When she and Alex said goodnight, he seemed as much at a loss how to deal with his mother as Katherine, and they too went to their bedrooms feeling somewhat depressed.

However, today was Christmas Eve and she hoped that this would help to lighten the atmosphere. Alex's sister Lily had been staying at a friend's house for a few days and was coming home sometime that morning. Katherine wondered who she took after – Alastair or Roberta?

Katherine deposited her outdoor garments back into the cloakroom. Sam's basket was empty and he was nowhere to be seen when she went into the main part of the house. Taking a deep breath, she opened the door to the dining room and there, seated at the table, munching her way through a large cooked breakfast while reading a book was a very pretty girl of about fourteen years of age. She looked up and smiled as Katherine came into the room, and Katherine sensed that with Lily at least, everything was going to be all right. She smiled back.

"Hello. You must be Katherine," said Lily, without preamble. "I'm Alex's sister, the second apple of my father's eye – Alex is the oldest apple – and the bane of my mother's life! Has she been giving you a hard time?"

Katherine laughed and said, "Well…"

"I thought as much. Something's gnawing at her, so Alex and Daddy had better watch out – they're the ones that get it in the neck when she's like this! I just go and hide in the kitchen with Cook or in my bedroom and stay out of the way until she's calmed down. I'm probably one of the few people in my class who actually likes going away to boarding school!"

Katherine wasn't quite sure how to respond to this uninhibited flow of words, so she said, diplomatically: "Surely it's not that bad?"

"Well," said Lily, meaningfully, "let's put it this way. She's my mother. I love her, I think, but things are a lot calmer out in the real world. It's a shame because she's so beautiful and can be lovely and charming when she wants to be. Especially when Edward's home. Now he really *is* the apple of her eye and seems to be the only one in the family who can cheer her up or deflect her moods!" she added, without a trace of jealousy towards her eldest brother. "Can I see your ring?" Katherine extended her left hand and Lily took it and examined the sapphire and diamonds closely.

"Ooh, it's gorgeous! I'd like a ring just like that when I get engaged." She paused, collecting herself. "Sorry, I'm forgetting my manners. Breakfast is on the sideboard – there are various things under the lids. Do help yourself and then please tell me everything – how you met, how Alex proposed! Was it very romantic?"

Katherine did as she was directed, coming back to the table with her breakfast and proceeded to tell Lily enough details to satisfy the younger girl's curiosity, while retaining her own and Alex's privacy.

"You're very lucky, you know. Alex is a real catch. Any school friends I've dared to bring home have all ended up wildly in love with him, just like all his real girlfriends. And he's had *lots* of those. But most of them haven't lasted very long because he's *so* wrapped up in his work that I'd begun to think he'd wind up a stuffy old bachelor doing boring court cases for the rest of his life. Which would have been a shame, because he's far too attractive to just do that. When and where are you getting married?" she asked, changing the direction of the conversation almost in mid-flow.

"At Easter on Cairnmor, the Scottish island I've just told you about," replied Katherine, this time taken aback by Lily's remarks about Alex's love life. Just how many girls *had* he been out with?

"Oh how wonderful! Definitely appeals to my romantic nature! Have you chosen your bridesmaids yet?"

"Well sort of. My best friend Mary is going to be my matron of honour."

"That's all?! Oh. Would you think me very rude if I asked you if I could be a bridesmaid – I mean, you *must* have another one…" she asked beseechingly.

"I recognize that wheedling tone!" said Alex, looking at Lily through narrowed eyes as he came into the room. Lily leapt up from the table with a broad smile on her face and greeted her brother with a huge hug. "Careful," he said. "You're getting too tall to do that now. You'll knock me over!"

"No I won't! I remember when I used to run and hug you when you came home during the holidays and you used swing me round and then throw me on the settee. You did it so skilfully that I always felt safe and it was such fun!" She paused for a moment, and looked at him with her head on one side. "I like Katherine. I think we're going to be friends and I'd like to be a bridesmaid at your wedding, *please*!"

"Minx," said Alex. "It's up to Katherine, though. The bride always gets to choose the bridesmaids." Then turning to her he said, "Don't be pressurized or cajoled. She's probably the only person in the world who really could charm the hind leg off a donkey!"

Katherine laughed, putting her insecurities aside; once again feeling reassured by Alex's warmth and humour. "I'd be delighted, honestly. I'm sure that Mary won't mind making you a dress too when I tell her you're going to be a bridesmaid."

Lily hugged her in a rush of gratitude. "Thank you," she said. "Is Mary making your dress?"

"Yes, and hers. She's a wonderful dressmaker."

"I can vouch for that. She made a gorgeous evening gown for Katherine. When you want to hide from Mother, take Katherine upstairs and get her to show it to you. Talking of Mother, where is she?" asked Alex.

"Gone to early morning service at church. She was just going out as I was coming in. She didn't even bother to ask why I'd come back from my friend's house so early. Just insisted that I accompanied her but I didn't want to go as

136

we're going to Midnight Communion tonight and Christmas morning service tomorrow. That's enough church to last me for a year. We nearly had a row about it. She's in such a bad mood today." Lily sighed.

"Where's Dad?"

"Had his breakfast with Mother and then took Sam for a walk. He didn't seem very happy."

"He's not, I'm afraid."

"What shall we three do this morning?" asked Lily, changing the subject and watching Alex as he helped himself to breakfast. "Daddy and I decorated the tree the day before yesterday. Mother wouldn't let us do it today as it's Sunday, though I don't see what difference that makes, it's still Christmas Eve and we always do it on Christmas Eve. I've wrapped all my presents. So I've got nothing else to do."

Alex raised an eyebrow at Katherine, who nodded her agreement.

"Right then, squirt. Any suggestions?" he said.

"How about a game of 'Knowledge Matters', you know the one that Granddad Stewart gave us last year? Mother hates it and I never get to play . Have you ever played it?"

"No, I haven't," said Katherine. "I've not come across it before."

"It came out a couple of years ago," said Alex. "It's a good one to keep for a rainy day – ideal for Cairnmor during a storm. Just like the storms, it can go on for ever!"

"Ooh, are there really big storms on Cairnmor? How exciting. I like storms!"

"Strange child!"

"So shall we?" begged Lily.

"What, go to Cairnmor now?" teased Alex.

"No, stupid! Play 'Knowledge Matters'?"

"If you insist. You must go and find it though."

"All right then. Wear my little legs out first."

"Yes, us oldies just want to sit around and rest our ancient limbs."

"I hate big brothers!" said Lily, with a smile as she went out of the room.

"I'm not too keen on annoying little sisters!"

"Beast!"

When Lily was safely out of earshot, Katherine said, "I like her very much."

"Yes, she's not bad for a sister!" replied Alex, with genuine affection.

"Which school does she go to?"

"Benbridge House in Kent – rather exclusive, but very friendly and academically top-notch which is good for Lily as she's very bright."

"Does she have any idea what she wants to do when she leaves school?"

"She's desperate to be an actress and I can quite see why, as she has the sort of personality that lights up a room when she walks in and a real stage presence when she acts."

"I would imagine your mother isn't too keen on that," observed Katherine drily.

"That's an understatement!" said Alex, with feeling.

They both finished their breakfast and cleared the table, placing everything on the sideboard ready for the maid to come and remove it, which she did almost immediately.

Lily returned, bearing the game. They set out the board with forfeit and advantage cards, subject and question cards, distributed the tokens and uncovered the dice and a shaker.

"The game is basically word play on 'matters', quite clever really. Having knowledge matters when you play this game in order to progress, but it also has to do with things about that knowledge which you need to be able to use."

And very clearly, Alex proceeded to explain how the game worked, the three of them becoming so absorbed that they failed to hear Roberta return from church. They only stopped playing when the maid came in to lay the table for Sunday lunch.

"I won, I won!" said Lily, triumphantly when they had added up the totals against any forfeits remaining in their hands.

"Luck, I think," said Alex.

"No, it was skill, skill!"

"You'll have a job getting out of the door if you're not careful."

"You're just jealous because you lost!"

"That's a really good game," said Katherine, as they packed everything away in the box. "I'll see if I can buy it when we go back to London. It's perfect for whiling away time during a prolonged storm! It will make a change from cards."

"Do you play cards?" asked Lily, ever curious.

"Yes"

"Which ones?"

"Goodness. Er… whist, rummy, canasta, bridge, sevens. Probably some more as well."

"Mother plays bridge – she belongs to a club and they have tournaments and things. Really tedious, old fogey stuff."

"I'll remember the 'old fogey' bit when I tell Mary how to make your dress," said Katherine.

"Oh goodness, I'm sorry, I didn't mean…"

"It's all right, I was only teasing!" and Katherine reached out to Lily and they took each other's hands briefly. At that moment Roberta walked in and immediately walked out again, without saying a word.

"For goodness' sake…!" muttered Alex, annoyed.

He could say no more as Alastair came in with Roberta in tow, and shortly afterwards, Sunday lunch was served by the maid. The meal took place in strained silence and Katherine could sense Alex's patience dissipating rapidly. She excused herself after dessert, much to Alex's consternation, and went upstairs, followed shortly by Lily who ran to catch up with her.

"Can I come and see your dress now?" she asked, as anxious to be out of the room as Katherine was.

"That sounds like a very good idea."

And the two of them disappeared into the blue guest room. Alastair left the dining room soon afterwards and went into his study with Sam who came up the hallway wagging his tail, pleased to be with his master.

Alex and Roberta went into the sitting room and waited for coffee to be brought. He eyed his mother speculatively. She appeared to be completely oblivious to the impatience in his manner and Alex knew that he had stayed silent long enough.

After a while, Katherine and Lily could hear the sound of raised voices and they crept out of Katherine's room to see what was going on. They found Alastair seated about half way down the stairs, facing the door of the sitting room which was slightly ajar, listening to the argument in full flight. Katherine and Lily joined him.

"Shouldn't we stop them?" asked Katherine, her voice full of consternation.

"No," said Alastair. "Not at the moment. It's best to let them argue it out, otherwise it could simmer for days."

"Do they often row?"

"It's been known."

"I hate rows," observed Katherine.

"So do I. Unfortunately, my wife seems to thrive on them."

"Ssh," said Lily. "I want to listen."

Her father threw her a reproving glance.

"Well, you are!" she said, and of course, there was no disputing the logic and indefensibility of that statement.

"I am monitoring," said Alastair, with an air of finality.

"But you come from such different backgrounds," said Roberta peevishly.

"Actually, we don't. Katherine went to boarding school and then Edinburgh University, so our backgrounds couldn't be more similar and the educational experiences that shaped us are exactly the same."

"I'm not talking about education. I'm talking about breeding and wealth."

"Those things don't matter to me one jot but someone's character, their intelligence and their abilities do. You can be such a snob at times, Mother."

"But she comes from a poor rural background, just like Grandfather Stewart," persisted Roberta. "Your life in London is sophisticated, what can she know of society?"

"My life is work, work and more work, Mother. I don't socialize except with my friends and when it's absolutely necessary at Royal Court or Middle Temple." That wasn't strictly true but as Alex was building a case to defend himself, he was not about to reveal this fact to his mother. "I don't know what you imagine I do in London."

"She'll hold you back in your career, you mark my words," said Roberta, trying to find anything that she could to express her objections to Katherine.

"How on earth did you work that one out?"

"Because she hasn't had the advantages you've had and she'll make you live on that island of hers – Cranmore, is it?"

"Cairnmor," said Alex, finding it increasingly difficult to contain his temper.

"Well, whatever it is. And then you'll leave behind everything you've worked for, throwing it all away. I'd set my heart on your becoming a judge one day."

"Your wish not mine, Mother. And where we choose to live is our business, not yours; what career path I follow is my business. It is my life and not for you to dictate how I live it."

"You're my son, of course it's my business! But I don't know why I bother. You have too much of Grandfather Stewart in you. No ambition. He would have been happy just to be a simple shepherd if your Grandmother hadn't taken him in hand."

"That's not how Dad recounts it. And he should know – he was there. Granddad became a farm manager on his own merit and through his own hard work with the support of a loving wife. And very successful he was at it too. He and Grandma were very happy and gave Dad every opportunity that they could afford. And now that Granddad's retired, it's given him the chance to pursue his painting and writing. Not bad for a man of limited education."

"Yes, your father is very generous towards them financially," responded Roberta, choosing to ignore Alex's observation of Grandfather Stewart's abilities.

"He also looks after you very well too, Mother. Your father gave you and Dad this house as a wedding gift, but Dad pays for its upkeep and the life you lead here."

There was no denying this, so Roberta tried a different tack. "Then tell me, why do you want to marry her?"

"She's intelligent and understanding and I know she'll make me the ideal wife. Besides which, I love her," he added for good measure.

"You could easily give her up. *I* gave everything up to marry your father."

"You and Dad had to get married because you were pregnant with Edward! You've drummed that into all of us enough times over the years. Fortunately, he wanted to marry you, but for the sake of argument, if it was anyone giving anything up, it was Dad not you," said Alex emphatically, striding round the room, trying to control his anger once again.

It was then, in the heat of the argument, that Roberta let slip the bombshell; a secret kept and buried for twenty-eight years: "I loved Edward's father more than anyone or anything, certainly more than Alastair." The words escaped before Roberta could prevent them.

Alex stopped dead in his tracks. "Say that again," he said slowly and deliberately.

"You heard me." Roberta was defensive now and frightened, immediately regretting her hasty words. Alex was stunned into silence.

Out in the hallway, Alastair went very pale. Lily sat on the stairs with her mouth open and Katherine knew that the argument about her own suitability as a wife for Alex had come to an end. However, with the disclosure that had just been made there would be more disagreements to follow, of that she was certain.

She looked at Alastair. "Did you know?" she asked softly.

He nodded, very close to tears.

"Then what you did was very noble and kind." Katherine went to sit beside him and tucked her arm through his, offering comfort and consolation.

He took her hand in his and held onto it. "I loved her very much," he said quietly, by way of explanation.

Katherine nodded, full of empathy for Alastair, a lovely, kind and patient man; full of sympathy for the family where change and disruption were now inevitable. "But she's not made your life easy, has she?"

He shook his head, regretfully.

Katherine moved aside to let Alastair take Lily into his arms in order to comfort his daughter, who was crying silently, the tears pouring down her cheeks.

"You are *my* real father, aren't you?" she asked, knowing the answer, but still needing the reassurance of being told.

Alastair's manner was expansive in his support. "Of course I am, my little one. And, so that you can be sure, Alex is *my* son, too."

"Is that why you've always been closest to us and Mother to Edward?"

"Yes, my child, it probably is."

Katherine sighed. "Perhaps you need to go in there now," she suggested gently. "Alex will need your reassurance too and you will both need to support each other. He will want to know why and how. I'll stay with Lily. We also have some talking to do, I think."

As Alastair got up to go, Lily took hold of his hand and said, "You will tell me the story of how it all came about too, won't you?"

"Of course I will," he said. Then to Katherine, with grateful affection in his eyes, he mouthed the words, "Thank you."

She smiled a half smile in return and nodded her head in acceptance.

Taking a deep breath, he opened the door and entered the sitting room where Alex immediately went over to Alastair and embraced him and his father knew that here, at least, all would be well.

CHAPTER 18

After Alastair had gone into the sitting room and closed the door behind him, Katherine suggested to Lily that they go for a walk and, well wrapped up against the December chill, they first made their way towards the pontoon at the bottom of the garden where Katherine had begun her day.

"I see you have a motor-boat," she said, indicating the boat-house.

"Yes. That belongs to Daddy. He's had this one about a year. He owned another one before, which we all really liked but last summer the engine kept going wrong, so he sold that and he bought this one instead. She was brand new and he called her *Spirit of Adventure*. We had a proper launching as well. It wasn't down a ramp or anything, but just here by the pontoon after she was delivered. Daddy let me break a bottle of champagne over the bows just like they do for all the big ships and we had a bit of a party."

"Has your Dad always liked boating?"

"Yes, he has. I suppose it's just as well really, with the Thames at the bottom of the garden."

Katherine smiled. "It would seem to be appropriate!"

"For the last ten years, Daddy has always taken us on the boat for holidays in the summer. We've been to all sorts of places – Essex, Suffolk, along the South Coast."

"Do you sleep on board when you're on holiday?"

"Yes, but we also stay in hotels or bed and breakfasts. Much more civilized."

"But not as much fun!"

"Why, would you like to stay all the time on a boat?" asked Lily.

"If it was one like this, of course I would! Apart from going ashore for the occasional bath. How long is it?"

"Thirty-eight foot, six inches."

"Does the whole family spend the summer on the boat?"

"No. Since Edward got his commission which was years and years ago, he hasn't been with us and Mother won't go near it. She always goes to stay with her twin brother in Berkshire when we're away. He inherited the family estate and is *very* rich."

Curious, Katherine asked, "Do you have much contact with your uncle?"

"Not really. I don't know him that well. He's never taken much interest in us as a family, only in Mother. He and his wife and son train racehorses and they're totally involved in that. Mother loves horses, as she was brought up with them, so she's in her element when she goes there. I don't like them, personally, and it's yet another area where I've been a disappointment to her. She tried to teach me to ride when I was little but I was useless at it, so she gave up in the end."

Katherine, sensing a downward turn in Lily's mood and looking towards the boat house again, said, "I like that little dinghy. It's a very pretty design."

"Yes. Before I was born, Daddy taught the boys how to sail in it. When he thought they were competent, he let them take it out on their own. They never went too far, just up and down between the two locks. It's only a few miles, but it's where Edward discovered his love of being on the water. Goodness! Edward! Do you think he knows?"

"Only if your mother has told him. If not, he has a tremendous shock to come."

"What's going to happen, do you think?" asked Lily, suddenly becoming very young and vulnerable.

"I honestly don't know. I would imagine that there will be some sort of family discussion – it could be going on right now. We'll find out when we get home. Anyway, shall we go on?" and for the moment, Katherine steered the conversation again away from the subject.

Lily led the way through a wooden gate set into the fence on the left-hand side of the garden, which brought them out onto the tow-path beside the Thames. She seemed preoccupied and Katherine allowed her to gather her thoughts.

After a while, Lily said, "Daddy has always been just the same towards Edward as he has been with us but there was never the same affinity between them as there is with Alex and me; especially Alex. They are *really* close." Again, there was not a trace of jealousy in Lily's manner and Katherine admired her, both for her maturity and her generous nature.

"I know and it's wonderful to see. But your Dad really loves you too."

"Yes, I know he does. He's very protective of me and always takes my side if Mother is having a bad day."

"There's a big age gap, isn't there, between you and Alex?"

"Yes. I'm the afterthought and Mother never tires of telling me so!"

"How old is Edward?"

"Twenty-eight. He's done very well in the Navy. We don't see him very much now. Mother travels to Portsmouth or Dartmouth or Plymouth or Chatham or wherever his ship has docked to see him." She paused reflectively and then said, "I wonder who his father is?"

"Yes, I've been wondering that."

"I never imagined anything like this happening to us. It happens in books but they're just fiction, the product of someone's imagination. But not to us, not in real life, which seems so ordered. Difficult sometimes, yes, but there's a regular pattern to it that you accept as the norm." And Lily fell silent.

"Things do happen in families. You remember I told you the reason why Alex came to Cairnmor?"

"Yes, he was helping Daddy out by searching for the heirs to the will of one of Daddy's clients, Sir Charles Mathieson?"

"That's right. Well, we didn't find any trace of them on the island, or any clues. But, after I came down to stay in London, we were given permission by his widow to go to Sir Charles Mathieson's home in Park Lane..."

"Park Lane?" interrupted Lily, her eyes opening wide.

"Yes."

"Was it *very* grand?"

"*Very*! Anyway, Alex and I searched through his son's room, which had been left exactly as it was when Rupert disappeared..."

"Rupert is the heir, yes?"

"Yes, and we found some diaries that Rupert had written, hidden in a locked drawer."

"How exciting!"

"We thought so. Now, if you want some family drama and the things you think only happen in fiction, then you should read these! It's a very real and human story and if you're not drawn into it, you're not the girl I think you are!"

"*Can* I read them? They're not for lawyer's eyes only?"

"No, I'm sure it will be just fine!"

"I like the way you say that," said Lily.

"What?"

"'Just fine'!" They both laughed and linking arms, continued on their way until they reached Maybury Lock with the old Mill and the Mill House next to it, both falling into a state of disrepair.

"Someone needs to buy both of those and restore them before they fall down. They've been lying derelict for several years now," observed Lily sadly. "When I was little, I used to come here with Alex and we imagined that the Mill belonged to us. We pretended to grind the flour and bake the bread, and that people came from miles around to buy it from us because our bread tasted so wonderful. And we lived with our families in the Mill House next door. Such are the fantasies of childhood!" And Lily sighed.

"Poor old thing!" said Katherine, teasing her gently. "Anyway, it's beginning to get dark, so I think we ought to go back home very soon."

"To face the music, but not to dance."

"I beg your pardon?"

"Fred Astaire and Ginger Rogers in the film *Follow the Fleet* – you know, the song written by Irving Berlin? It's from their latest film." Lily seemed most anxious that Katherine should understand.

"Ah, of course," said Katherine, none the wiser and hoping she had been vague enough for Lily not to have noticed. She knew of Irving Berlin and had music by him at home, but who were the other two? She would obviously have to do some research. Perhaps Mary would know; she seemed to be more in touch with films and film stars than Katherine. She obviously had some serious catching-up to do.

They walked in silence for a few moments before Lily said, "I'm really glad you're marrying Alex. You're kind and sensible and he needs someone like you, especially after some of the other…" and she stopped, glancing quickly at Katherine to make sure she hadn't realized what she was about to say. When Katherine didn't react, Lily continued, reassured that was so. "I feel as though we're friends already… even though you have no idea who Fred Astaire and Ginger Rogers are!" she added, with her tongue very firmly in her cheek, ducking out of the way protectively in case she received a physical rather than a verbal retort.

"You don't miss a trick, do you?!" said Katherine, not succumbing to the temptation and trying to ignore the implication of the words *some of the other…* "And I thought I'd hidden it very well! Astute young lady! Though I do have to say in my defence that there is no electricity and consequently there are no

144

cinemas on Cairnmor, and I haven't been to the cinema on the mainland since I left teacher training college in Glasgow five years ago."

"Well, I'll let you off then. But how do you manage without electricity? It must be terribly primitive."

"Aye, that it is. We primitives have to make the most of what little we have and put up with the terrrible, terrrible conditions!" replied Katherine in a very pronounced Scottish accent.

"Now you're making fun of me," said Lily, pretending to pout.

"No, just teasing you very gently. If you dish it out, you must expect a little in return."

Lily laughed and Katherine knew that her companion's spirits had been lifted for the moment for which she was glad as it was time to go home

When they arrived back at the house, all was quiet inside. There was no one in any of the downstairs rooms, though they could hear the low murmur of voices from Alastair's study. Of Roberta, there was no sign and they assumed she must be in her bedroom.

Lily declared that she was hungry so, after divesting themselves of their outer garments, they went to the kitchen in search of food. With mutterings of displeasure at being disturbed, Cook prepared them a pot of tea, some sandwiches and cake, which they took up to Lily's bedroom. Katherine went to hers and collected Rupert's diaries and her book and, after putting more coal on the fire, they settled themselves companionably to read and eat their tea.

Katherine explained some more about the background to the diaries and how she used to walk past the Head Office of Mathieson's Shipyard every day when she was at college in Glasgow.

"So it really is real then?" asked Lily, before turning the first page.

"Oh yes, very real."

It took a couple of hours for Lily to read the diaries and when she had finished, she was silent for a long time, just staring into the glowing embers of the fire.

Katherine observed her covertly, looking up occasionally from her book and waiting for Lily to begin the conversation.

"Rupert really loved Mhairi, didn't he?"

"Yes."

"It must be wonderful to know a love like that."

Katherine smiled, partly to herself because of Alex and partly at Lily's remark. "It's called true love."

"Imagine giving it all up – all his wealth and status just to be with her. What a sacrifice!"

"All the wealth and status in the world is hollow and empty without someone to love and be loved in return."

"Would you?"

"Would I what?"

"Give up everything for Alex?" asked Lily, with the directness of youth.

"If I had to; though it wouldn't be money, because I have very little. It would be a different kind of wealth that I would be sacrificing."

"What do you mean?"

Katherine was thoughtful, trying to find the right way to phrase what she meant. "The richness of my life on Cairnmor – the beauty of the island, my friends, my work, being part of a very close community. All the things that money can't buy."

"Alex would give everything up to be with you as well."

"Really? Are you sure?" Katherine was surprised because even though Michael had intimated as much the first time she had met him, Alex had never given her any indication of this. "How do you know?"

"Because he said so to Mother during a row they had when he came back from Scotland. She was livid. I suppose she's been brooding about it ever since and that's why she's been so awful to you since you arrived."

"It would explain a lot."

"You and Alex are really in love, aren't you?" It was almost a statement rather than a question.

"Yes, I think we are," replied Katherine carefully, trying to understate the depth of her feelings but her smile betrayed her joy and Lily was not slow to discern this.

"I hope I meet someone and fall in love with them the way you and Alex love each other; the way that Rupert and Mhairi did; the way that Daddy loves Mother." After saying that Lily fell silent then she said, with a sudden flash of insight way beyond her years, "But I don't think that Mother has ever really loved Daddy."

"I think you've just hit the nail on the head. It would go a long way to explain her bitterness, her resentments, but it's not everything. I think there's something more."

"If you're right, then I wonder what it could be?"

"Mmm, at the moment I have no idea," and with that, the conversation came to a natural conclusion.

After Katherine had gathered together the tea things and placed them back onto the tray, she suggested to Lily that as it was getting rather late, it might be a good idea for her to go to bed as none of them knew what the next day might bring.

"Will you stay with me for a while?" asked Lily.

"Of course."

She moved her chair next to the bed and sat reading in the gentle glow of the table lamp until Lily had fallen asleep. Katherine shut the door quietly behind her and crept downstairs, leaving the tray in the deserted kitchen. Then she went back up the stairs to her room, undressed and climbed into bed. But she was too restless to stay there and putting on her warm, thick dressing gown, she went over to the window where she drew back the curtains to reveal the full moon shining directly through the glass, illuminating the room with its pale, ghostly light. There had been another frost and the garden shone silver once again in the moonlight, just as it had early that morning before the sun rose.

Then Katherine heard a faint knock and turned to see Alex in the doorway, an expression of uncertainty and hesitancy in his eyes. She smiled, beckoning for him to come into the room which he did, closing the door behind him.

Immediately, he came over to her and held her in his arms. His need for comfort and consolation was very obvious but they remained sensible and after a while, Katherine suggested that they should get into bed as it was very cold,

146

despite the fire. However, she instructed him that he should lie under the eiderdown but on top of the blankets.

"Why, are you afraid that I might ravish you?!" teased Alex.

"No, but I might ravish you!" she replied smartly.

"Promises, promises!" and they both laughed and held each other close. "Goodness, it feels good to laugh after this evening," he said.

"Has it been difficult?"

"Very."

"What happened after Alastair went into the sitting room?"

"Not good. Mother started hurling recriminations at him. Why, I don't know. The poor man has done nothing wrong and acted very honourably in standing by her all those years ago. He deserves a medal for that and for all he's put up with over the years." Alex was visibly shaken and took a moment before continuing. "If Dad had got her pregnant, sorry to be so crude…"

"No, it's fine. I'm an island lass, remember? My sensibilities are very robust!"

Alex kissed her lightly on the forehead and said, "Anyway, if it was his responsibility, which is what we had always assumed, then she might have grounds for her resentment. But as it is, I really don't understand."

"I think there's something more," suggested Katherine gently.

"I'm inclined to agree with you," replied Alex. "Though at this stage, I have no idea what." Then he paused before saying. "One of the several reasons why I think we should wait until we're married before we make love is that I don't want either of us to have any grounds for resentment; to feel that we were trapped into marriage by you becoming pregnant, were that to happen. Of course, it's also your reputation that I'm thinking of, that goes without saying…" he added hastily as an afterthought.

Alex knew he had been lucky so far and had managed to avoid getting any girl into 'trouble', although he recalled having a worryingly close shave on one particular occasion. However, he also had the idealized perception that his future wife should remain a virgin until they were married.

"Thank you, but it works in both our favours, because I would prefer to conceive after we're married, rather than run the risk beforehand." She took his hand in hers and kissed it. "But there is one distinct difference," she continued. "You and I both love each other and want to be married, whereas, I think that, unfortunately, Roberta does not love your father."

Sadly, Alex acknowledged that Katherine was correct.

Curious to know more, she asked, "What happened next?"

"In the end, Dad couldn't cope with it any more and left the room, disappearing into his study. I followed him shortly afterwards leaving my mother to her own devices, not particularly caring what she did or how she felt, I'm ashamed to say."

"That's understandable in the circumstances."

"Dad and I talked for a very long time and he told me what transpired."

"Go on," said Katherine encouragingly.

"Mother's family is very rich."

"So Lily tells me."

"And she was quite a society belle, beautiful and much sought after, especially at seventeen when they first met. Dad was eighteen and in his first year at Cambridge University studying law. A friend of his knew my mother's family and was invited down to the country estate in Berkshire for the weekend. He brought my father with him as his guest.

"Dad fell in love with Mother at first sight, absolutely head-over-heels stuff. He was totally smitten but Mother only had eyes for a certain Edward Fothergill, the errant middle son from the neighbouring estate who had a real reputation as a ladies' man, to put it mildly."

Alex was glad the room was in darkness, so that Katherine would be spared his own embarrassment as he spoke those particular words.

"Anyway, Dad became a frequent house guest at these weekend social gatherings and he and Mother became something of a couple. He spent every moment with her that he could spare from his studies.

"However, unknown to everyone, Mother and Edward Fothergill were having a secret liaison and when she became pregnant, Edward dropped her like the proverbial hot-cake as he had no intention of marrying her. He disappeared abroad and her father stepped in and offered Dad a considerable sum of money to marry his daughter and save the family's reputation. Dad refused the money point-blank and said that he was very happy to marry Roberta, but only if she would have him. Left without a choice, she accepted and, much against his parent's wishes – who had been very proud of the fact that their son had earned a place at Cambridge and who gave their consent only reluctantly – a month later they were married. My father did accept this house as a wedding gift from his new father-in-law.

"In order to support my mother and the child for whom he had become responsible, he left university at the end of the academic year and joined a solicitor's firm in London, accepting the sponsorship of Roberta's father. I was born the following year, much to my father's joy. He continued to study, earning his degree by correspondence course and later becoming an articled clerk.

"After serving with great distinction as an officer in the Royal Naval Volunteer Reserve during the Great War, he eventually became a partner in a solicitor's firm in London. I think Dad always hoped that one day, my mother would come to love him but that obviously never happened."

"Poor Alastair. I do feel for him. He made so many sacrifices for her."

"He did."

"How is he now?"

"Asleep, just. What about Lily?"

"The same."

"I'm so grateful to you for being with her."

"We went for a walk and talked a great deal and then I told her all about Rupert and Mhairi and gave her the diaries to read."

"A very good distraction."

"Yes, among other things." Katherine sighed, too tired to go into detail. That would have to wait for another time. But she did say, "What happens now?"

"I don't know."

"There would seem to be no easy resolution."

"No, it is something of an impasse."

"Well, we can only wait and see what the morning brings. Christmas morning."

"Some Christmas!" said Alex, with considerable irony.

"Aye, it will certainly be different." Feeling her eyes closing with tiredness, Katherine said: "I'm nearly falling asleep…"

"So I'd better go, though I don't want to…"

"I know. Goodnight, my love."

"Goodnight, dear Katherine."

And very quietly, Alex crept back to his own room, which seemed very cold and lonely, doubly so as the fire had nearly gone out.

Having re-kindled it, he got into bed and eventually fell into an uneasy slumber.

CHAPTER 19

The next morning Alex, Katherine and Lily went to Christmas morning service at the local parish church but Roberta reluctantly stayed behind with Alastair, who with gentle insistence suggested that they needed to talk things over and try to repair some of the damage caused by the previous day's emotional upheaval.

It would have been magical for the rest of the family as they walked along the frost-covered pavements, with the bare-branched trees and crisp grass sparkling in the sunlight and passers-by wishing everyone a 'Happy Christmas', had not each of them been preoccupied with the trauma of the previous day. They were hardly aware of the pealing church bells – sending out their evocative greeting, calling the faithful to worship – as they entered the lovely old parish church through the West door.

The Christmas morning service of Nine Lessons and Carols in Maybury was traditionally an ecumenical one, and as it was not a Communion service, anyone was welcome, regardless of denomination. Katherine had never been to a Church of England service before and although she knew that one of this nature was very rare, she appreciated the egalitarian way of thinking very much.

While at university, she had explored different churches in Scotland and experienced various types of liturgy, much to the consternation of the local priests. But she was curious and wanted to learn about other ways of worship.

Ultimately, she had come to the conclusion that she preferred the services on Cairnmor, finding them much freer and less constricting than those elsewhere. There seemed to be a good balance between traditional modes of worship and the expression of the islanders' independence in their way of doing things. Father McPhee understood this very well and had had some battles of his own with the Bishop on the mainland, who questioned this deviation from strict adherence to rules that should be followed without hesitation. A few of the hierarchy even considered him a heretic, which of course he was not. In the end, they opted to leave him to his own devices and ceased interfering, just maintaining the occasional foray onto Cairnmor to keep a weather eye on one of their more 'problematic flocks and difficult priests'.

At the end of the service, Alex showed Katherine round the church.

"The Lady Chapel is the original part of the building and is over eight hundred years old. The glass in the east and south-east windows is medieval and French in origin, having come from a ruined abbey in St Omer. But it's this I want you to see." And he took her to a part of the building which obviously dated from a later time. "The church underwent restoration in the Victorian era – and look who the architect was who was responsible for the designs…" With boyish pleasure, he showed her a plaque on the wall by the chantry steps.

Katherine read the name aloud. "George E. Street." His name seemed familiar and she had to think before she realized why. "Oh, he was the architect who designed the Royal Courts of Justice! What a coincidence!"

"I know. If I were given to fanciful thoughts, I could say it was some kind of portent but as I'm not, it's just a very neat connection."

Various people came up to Alex and he introduced Katherine. They expressed regret that Roberta had not come to the service that morning and enquired after her health, as they thought she had looked very pale at Midnight Communion. Alex replied diplomatically that a very bad headache had kept her at home.

"If only they knew!" he whispered to Katherine, who nodded, also widening her eyes in acknowledgement. "I wondered where she had gone last night. I'd forgotten about Midnight Service," continued Alex. "As she wasn't around when I left Dad, I went to bed."

When they arrived back at Mistley House, everything was very quiet and delicious smells of Christmas dinner emanated from the kitchen.

Nonetheless, Alex felt uneasy and knocked on the door of Alastair's study. No reply.

Lily ran up to Roberta's room. No reply.

Tentatively, they opened the door of the sitting room. Alastair and Roberta were sitting in different chairs, facing away from each other in an atmosphere of icy silence. Alastair was pale and drawn and Roberta's mouth was set in a thin determined line, her expression hard.

She was the first to speak. "Please come in and sit down. We have been waiting for you."

The three of them did as she requested, cautiously and guardedly.

"We have an announcement to make."

Alex saw his father wince.

"I have decided that I am going to leave," continued Roberta, her voice matter of fact. "It is better for all concerned."

To his father, Alex said, "Is this what you want?"

"Of course not," replied Alastair, shaking his head despairingly.

"I am going to do what I want, for once," said Roberta, totally disregarding Alastair's reaction to Alex's query.

"So what's new?" interjected Lily sullenly, her voice low.

"Don't be impertinent, young lady," said her mother imperiously. "From now on, I am not going to pander to everyone else's needs. I am going to please myself entirely."

Alex threw her a resentful look and said, in an ominously quiet voice, "I see. We were under the impression that you had always done exactly as you wished."

"Well, you were wrong."

"I think not."

Katherine put her arm around Lily, who had sunk back into the settee, hiding her face in her hands. Katherine looked up at Alex and saw the controlled anger in his eyes. When he continued, his voice was steady, betraying nothing of what he was really feeling.

"Where will you go?"

"I have telephoned my brother in Berkshire. I am going back to live in my family home. Harold says I can stay there as long as I wish and that I can set up a separate domestic establishment within the main house. It is quite big enough."

"A risky strategy, Mother."

"Perhaps. But at least I shall be free to live my own life as I wish. I feel an enormous sense of relief at having made this decision at last."

"What about money?" This was from Alastair.

"My brother has agreed to give me an allowance; a very generous one, I might add. He can easily afford it."

"And your brother's money is better than Dad's has been for all of your married life?"

Roberta was momentarily thrown off-balance by Alex's searching question. "Well, no, not exactly, but Harold's generosity does mean that I shall be able to live in the manner to which I was accustomed when I was young and not in the way I've been living since marrying your father."

It took all Katherine's self-control not to say anything, so angry was she, so furious at Roberta for her utter self-centeredness and self-absorption, for her total lack of appreciation of the care and consideration that her husband and her children had obviously shown her over the years.

Alastair observed Katherine's contained fury and shook his head imperceptibly, gently warning her not to say what she was thinking. She sent him what she hoped was a look of sympathy and support and remained silent. He understood.

Alex, who had been standing by the fireplace, facing away from the family, trying to exercise his own self-control by adopting the emotional detachment of his profession, then asked,

"What about all the organizations you belong to here in Maybury?"

"I am tired of them," replied Roberta. "They have become too tedious for words. There is too much effort involved; too much pretence for their petty enthusiasms. I shall resign from them all." She addressed Alastair. "You can write the letters."

For the first time during the discussion, he looked directly at her and said calmly, but very firmly, "I will not."

"Very well, they can just get used to my unexplained absence."

Alex, beginning to think of legal issues, did not take her to task on her obvious discourtesy and asked instead, "What about the house?"

"Your father can have it. I don't want it. The deeds are in his name anyway."

"The deeds are in your name, Roberta," said Alastair. "If you recall, I insisted that it was so when we were married."

"Well, instruct your partners to change them. I want nothing. I am going to make a completely new life for myself. I don't want to be held back by any vestiges of my former existence."

"And Lily?" asked Alex, very concerned now for the welfare of his family's youngest member. "She can hardly be described as a 'vestige'."

"I have said nothing to you, Alastair, about this yet but I suppose it's best if Lily comes to live with me in Berkshire during the school holidays." Her tone was resigned; disinterested.

Alastair looked horror-struck and it was this statement that finally roused Lily from her passivity. She leapt up from the settee and turned passionately on her mother.

"I will not. I absolutely refuse to go and live anywhere with you. *This* is my home; *this* is where I belong, with Daddy and Alex and now Katherine. They are *my* family."

Roberta seemed puzzled. "But so am I."

"Really? I'd never have guessed. You've always treated me as though I was some kind of nuisance, an afterthought that ruined your ordered existence. We've always made light of it and treated it like some kind of joke as though you didn't really mean it. But it isn't a joke, is it, Mother? You were serious and that hurts; it's always hurt." Lily paused, making her point. Then she added, with a perfect balance between condescension and firmness, "I *may* come and visit you sometimes but it will be when *I* choose. My home life outside of school will be here or in London with Daddy. Not with you." And she ran into Alastair's arms, who held her close and whispered, "My darling girl."

With hardly a flicker, Roberta said, "You are far too young to make such a decision."

Katherine could stay silent no longer and when she spoke it was with such quiet conviction that Roberta was silenced temporarily.

"Forgive me, but she is not. My parents died when I was fourteen, the same age that Lily is now. I made the decision that when I came home from school for the holidays, I wanted to stay in the cottage where I had lived all my life. It was my home, my security. I had lost my parents but I was determined to remain in an environment that was familiar and safe. I was very fortunate that I had good friends and neighbours who made that possible for me and generously looked after my home when I was at boarding school, and looked after me when I came back to Cairnmor."

Roberta looked at Katherine with contempt and was uncompromising in her reply. "Lily is not an orphan."

"No, but she is an intelligent, loving girl who should be allowed to make her own decisions." Katherine was resolute and single-minded in her support of Lily, leaving behind any attempt to tread carefully with her future mother-in-law.

"This is none of your business."

"Actually, Mother, it is," said Alex assertively, joining in the fray once more. "Whether you like it or not, Katherine is part of the family now and anything she has to say is valid and appropriate. If you are determined to go ahead with this plan of yours, then Lily should be allowed to make her own decision as to where she lives.

"It is *your* choice to leave, Mother, not *ours* that you should go. You must therefore allow all of us to deal with the ramifications of your actions and overcome them in our own way. Lily is not a pawn to be moved from pillar to post on someone's whim. She is a human being who is capable of deciding things for herself, with our love and support. If you try to challenge this legally, I shall oppose you in every court in the land if necessary."

Roberta was visibly shaken by this glimpse of Alex's formidable courtroom manner. Alastair, of course, knew it well, and could not help smiling to himself at the effect it was having on his wife. It sustained him and carried him over the nadir of his life, the moment he knew that he was going to lose forever the only woman he had ever loved.

But Alex had not finished. He added, "I hope for your sake that your brother and his family really mean what they say in offering you a permanent home with them. If not, then you could find yourself in a very difficult position in a few years' time."

"He will stand by me."

"Then if you are going, it is better that you are ready to leave sooner rather than later."

"I have packed the immediate things I wish to take. The rest can be collected later. My brother should be here within the hour." Then, without a further word or glance, Roberta left the room.

A stunned silence followed. Alastair slumped back into the sofa; Lily remaining upright and unmoving next to him. Katherine, sitting on the other settee and Alex, still standing by the fireplace, looked at each other in disbelief.

Lily was the first to break the silence. "Some Christmas Day this has turned out to be!"

"Impeccable timing, as ever," responded Alex, his voice tinged with bitterness. Then to Katherine he said, "I'm so sorry."

"So am I," she replied, with real concern in her voice. "But not for me, for all of you. To say that it's a terrible thing to have happened doesn't even begin to come close." Then, trying not to appear as though she was taking over, but wanting to help, she said, "But I think it's important that we should eat something now, even if we don't feel like it or can't manage very much. A walk would be good too – Sam would like that. Let the rest of the day take its course, then tomorrow we can begin to be practical."

The last to go out of the room, as they stood in the doorway, Alastair laid his hand on Katherine's shoulder, silently thanking her for her gentle pragmatism and support. She put her hand over his and smiled at him.

Reluctantly, they all went into the dining room for a very desultory Christmas dinner, which had been laid out on the table in readiness.

That afternoon, they walked for miles over the bleak and wintry Chiltern Hills; not talking much, each of them dealing with their individual pain and attempting to adjust to their changed circumstances.

Alex – trying to stem the rising tide of animosity and anger he felt towards his mother; Lily – coping with the sense of rejection that she had always felt, but never acknowledged, and which now had become overpowering and inescapable; and Alastair – numbed and bereft, defeated and saddened that he was unable to provide the woman he loved with all she had needed, either emotionally or practically. He had tried so hard, tried his very best, sacrificed so much, but it had not been enough, had never been enough and he felt himself to be a failure.

Alex and Lily had gone on ahead looking for Sam, who had disappeared. As if sensing his thoughts were at their lowest ebb, Katherine fell into step beside Alastair and put her hand through his arm.

"All this isn't your fault, you know," she said gently and simply.

"Oh, but it is," replied Alastair despairingly.

154

"No, it's not. It's just the way it is. But it's a terribly hard thing to accept."

"Yes. But there must have been something more I could have done."

"I don't think so. No one could have done more than you. I think Roberta is a fool not to have seen the wonderfully kind and considerate man that she was married to."

And Katherine held him and supported him as he finally gave way to the grief he had been so careful to conceal from everyone.

"I'm sorry," he said apologetically and with a tinge of embarrassment as they let go of each other.

"Don't be," replied Katherine. "It's necessary for your own emotional well-being and a natural part of the grieving process. I know that only too well."

"Yes."

By the time the others came back to join them – Sam had been busy digging up a rabbit burrow – he had recovered his composure but the release of emotion enabled him to carry on. It also deepened the developing bond between Alastair and Katherine.

They all made their way home through the late afternoon chill to find the house in darkness, silent and apparently deserted. There was no sign of Roberta.

Katherine and Lily went upstairs to her room and were met with the detritus of hasty and haphazard packing – drawers left open; half-filled trunks and suitcases; the bed strewn with clothes. Alex went in search of the maid and cook, hoping for some tea, but found the kitchen deserted.

Alastair went into the sitting room and found a note from Roberta on the mantelpiece. It stated baldly that the maid and cook had gone with her to be part of her new household and that she wished for the rest of her things to be packed and sent on.

When they joined him in the sitting room, Alastair showed the others the contents of the note, before tearing it up and throwing it into the fire, where it quickly turned to ash in the smouldering embers.

Katherine prepared tea for the four of them and later that evening, went upstairs with Lily and stayed with her until eventually she fell asleep. Alex kept Alastair company in his study, where they talked late into the night. When Katherine managed to go to her room, she found Alex, fully clothed, fast asleep on her bed. Carefully, she took off his slippers and covered him with a couple of spare blankets which she found in her wardrobe.

After banking up the fire, she drew the curtains back and sat by the window, framed in moonlight. There was no choice now. She was part of this family. Not through some marital 'joining' but really part of it, emotionally and with a profound sense of commitment.

Taking a deep breath, knowing what it would cost her to leave Cairnmor, she resolved to speak to Alex as soon as she could. There was no reason for any further delay in talking to him about her decision. This was where she now belonged and the place where she was needed the most.

Having made that decision, she tried not to dwell upon it further and without getting undressed, lay down under the covers with Alex beside her. They both slept until the morning light drifted in through the uncurtained window.

CHAPTER 20

After breakfast the following morning, they sat around the table in the dining room and had a family conference, beginning to plan the shape and tenor of their lives without Roberta and temporarily, the maid and cook. Katherine offered to write down the things to be done and who was to do them.

"This isn't the first time I've wished I could do short-hand," she observed, with paper, pen and ink at the ready. "Perhaps I'll have time to teach myself one day. Now, where to start? What about household things?"

"Couldn't Mr and Mrs Thringle come down from London, like they used to when I was little and we came here for the weekends?" suggested Lily.

"That would be really nice but they have their own plans and at this short notice, it would be very unfair on both of them," said Alastair.

"But it's certainly something to bear in mind for the future," observed Alex, smiling at her, giving due regard to Lily's idea.

"In that case," said Katherine, "it's going to be up to us, as I would imagine it will be difficult to find hired help during the festive season. I presume we're not going to go back to London still until after the New Year?"

"No, if that's all right with everyone. I'd rather stay here as we'd planned, despite everything," responded Alastair. "There's a lot to be done and I'm not sure I can face thinking about work just yet, which I will inevitably do if we go back to Town."

"So, we need to decide who does what," said Katherine affably, but still sounding like the schoolteacher that she was. "Lily and I can do the cooking."

"But I can't cook!" protested the younger girl.

"Then I shall teach you."

"It's just as well I'm not marrying a flighty social butterfly who can't lift a fork without some servant to do it for them!" observed Alex, with a flash of his habitual humour.

"You wouldn't be the person you could be if that were the case," responded Alastair drily, raising an eyebrow at his son.

Alex understood the inference and smiled slightly ruefully. Katherine, busy with her writing, failed to notice this exchange and continued, "And you two gentlemen won't be allowed to get away with being idle, because if we're doing the cooking, you are both doing the washing-up!"

"Bossy isn't she?" Alex said to his father, grinning at Katherine.

"I like her just the way she is." Alastair took Katherine's hand and kissed it in a courteous gesture of appreciation. She smiled at him in acknowledgement of this and then, business-like, said, "What about cleaning?"

"Mrs Towers comes in twice a week from Maybury," replied Lily. "She's quite nice – moans a bit about Sam's hairs on the carpet in the hall and Daddy's study, but she's very efficient."

The four of them looked at Sam, lying comfortably on the dining room floor, who immediately sat up and began to wag his tail on hearing his name and in recognition of their attention.

"Well, she'll have cope with other rooms having dog hairs on the carpet now!" observed Alex stroking Sam's head. With Roberta gone, the golden retriever had been given the run of the house, to which he was cautiously becoming accustomed, having hitherto been restricted to the cloakroom, hall and study.

"It's not the only thing Mrs Towers is going to have to adjust to," said Katherine, with a certain irony.

"That's an understatement," replied Alex.

"What about the garden?"

"I do some of it myself when I'm down from London," said Alastair. "And Tom comes in once a week from spring until late autumn to mow the lawn or do the weeding if I haven't been able to get back at the weekend. As it's the middle of winter, we don't really have to worry about the garden until March."

"Who's Tom?" asked Katherine.

"Mrs Towers's husband," said Lily.

"Right. What about Sam?"

"He'll have to come and live with Dad and me in London. In that case, I suppose Mrs Towers will only need to come in once a week with someone only being here at weekends. I don't expect she'll be too pleased about that," said Alex.

"No, she'll lose income and as she's been with us a long time, I wouldn't want her to go elsewhere. We'll have to think about that one," observed Alastair.

"I'll speak to her," said Alex, as Katherine wrote that down. "I hope you're keeping up with all of this," he added, teasing her and once again using repartee as a means of maintaining a semblance of normality in a potentially upsetting situation.

Perceiving this, Katherine pretended to be important and replied, "How dare you doubt my note-taking abilities and my efficiency, impudent person! I'll have you know, I was secretary on the new hall committee."

"You mean they trusted you even though you can't do shorthand?"

"Huh!" Katherine glowered at him, then said genuinely: "Actually, Mary and I shared that task as it was a very complicated and time-consuming one. And, what's more, neither of us can do shorthand!"

"I can't begin to tell you how much I appreciate all this," said Alastair. "You are all so wonderful..." and for a moment, he was unable to say any more. Lily went round the table from her seat and, standing behind him, put her arms round her father and laid her cheek against his, comforting him.

After a moment or two, Alex brought them back on task. "We'll deal with all the legal stuff like the deeds of the house when we get back to London. If Mother keeps her word, then it should be quite straightforward. But if Uncle Harold persuades her to follow a different path, then it could become difficult."

"Yes, I've been thinking about that too. But let's cross that particular bridge when the time comes, if it does," replied Alastair.

Neither of them voiced the fear they both held that at some stage, Roberta might demand that Alastair divorce her. Legal separation, though not very pleasant, was relatively uncomplicated but divorce raised all kinds of potentially nasty issues that neither man wanted to think about at that moment with the shock of Roberta's departure so recent and the wound still raw.

They sat in silence for a few minutes and then Katherine said, "As we can be fairly confident that Roberta won't contact the organizations that she belongs to, I think we shall have to do it. It's not very fair on the people in them if she just disappears, and it will raise more difficulties than it is worth if they start asking questions."

"We could say that she's gone to stay with her brother in the country, which is true, but say that it's for health reasons and that she'll be gone some time," said Lily, pleased with herself for thinking up this very simple but effective line of reasoning.

"I bet you come up with all sorts of excuses for not doing your homework when you're at school – you seem rather good at them," teased Alex.

Lily immediately defended herself. "I always do my homework, you horrible beast. I bet I get better marks than you did at school!"

"You two are about even, if I remember correctly about Alex's marks, though it's a long time ago," said Alastair placidly, kissing his daughter on the cheek, having successfully deflected Lily from starting an argument. "And I'm very proud of both of you; you've always worked very hard."

"Thank you, Daddy," said Lily. But she couldn't resist grinning at Alex, who smiled back at her.

"I hate to interrupt this mutual admiration society," said Katherine good-naturedly, "but which organizations does Roberta belong to?"

Lily thought about this. "The bowls club, the bridge club, the W.I. – she's just coming to the end of her stint as chairwoman of that – and she does flower arranging at the church."

"I'll write to them," replied Alex. "And I'll use your excuse, horrid little sister."

"Thank you, and not so much of the 'little' if you please."

"Yes, ma'am," said her brother contritely.

"Who were her friends here in Maybury?" asked Katherine.

"She didn't have any *particular* friends. She wasn't someone who enjoyed a good gossip, nor did she have any one person that she confided in, except for Uncle Harold of course, but he's family. But she did socialize with the people associated with the organizations she belonged to. Her soirées were held for them and she often had W.I. committee meetings in the house. But that was all." Lily couldn't think of anyone else, and neither could Alastair.

With this, the family discussion reached a natural conclusion having covered just about everything they could think of, so Alex and Alastair took Sam out for his morning walk while Katherine and Lily went to investigate the kitchen, to see what food had been left and if there was anything they could prepare for lunch and supper. They found potatoes, carrots and cabbage in the larder and the remains of the cold turkey in the refrigerator.

"I still think this is a brilliant invention," said Katherine, opening the door and feeling the icy blast of air that emanated from inside. "I'd never seen one before I came to London."

"How do you manage to keep your food cold on Cairnmor without electricity?"

"The walls of the cottages where we live are made from thick stone which keeps the inside very cool during the summer. I have a larder which is very cold inside and a marble slab on which I store things like cheese or puddings which need to be kept cold. Meat and fish are smoked or salted and eggs collected every day from the hens, along with milk from the cows. Fish and lobsters can also be eaten fresh from the daily catch and there are crabs that live on or near the sea-shore. I also put things in a sturdy container with a lid in the stream that runs through my croft. The water is very cold and that works very well summer or winter. Some people use the fresh-water lochs which are very deep and chilly and there are a great number of lochs on Cairnmor."

"Don't you buy any food from the shops?"

"No, for two reasons. Firstly, because there are no food shops on the island and secondly, because every crofter tries to be self-sufficient. We grow our own vegetables and store them ready for the winter in the outhouses. During the summer we cut peat for fuel from the peat-bog, storing it beside the cottage under the eaves after it has been turned and dried. We have to be completely self-reliant because sometimes, the winter storms are so bad that the steamer may not be able to reach us for a couple of months at a time."

"What about bread?"

"We bake our own from wheat, barley or oats grown on the machair."

"What's the machair?"

"A flat expanse of fertile soil where every crofter has a large strip that is his to cultivate."

"Do you do all of that – cultivate the wheat and milk the cows, as well as teach?"

"No, it would be physically impossible. I do some during the school holidays, but I have an arrangement with my neighbours that they do all the farming of my land, I pay them for what I need, and they keep the rest for themselves. It works very well and enables me to do my job."

Lily was fascinated by this glimpse of island life, and being fourteen, was curious about other things like baths, to which Katherine replied, "I have a tin bath which I use, heating up the water on the stove and bathing in front of the fire."

"Don't you have taps?"

"No, I have a pump which my Dad designed to bring water from the stream directly into the kitchen. Some people still go and collect water from their nearest loch each day. However, at the hotel in Lochaberdale there are real baths like you have here and hot running water. It's the only place on the island that has hot running water."

"Don't you find it a pain to have to heat the water up every time you want a bath?"

"Not really because it's what I've always been used to. And what you don't have, you don't miss!"

"Will you miss that now you've experienced it here and in London?" asked Lily astutely.

"Probably. It will certainly seem very strange to go back to having to fill a tin bath. I have to confess, I'm enjoying the conveniences of modern living, particularly just being able to put on a light at the flick of a switch and, until today that is, having all my meals prepared for me. Talking of which, we'd better get on."

"But thank you for telling me all that. I'm really looking forward to seeing Cairnmor."

"I hope you'll like it, it's a very special place."

And with that, the two of them proceeded to peel potatoes and carrots and prepare the cabbage, thus establishing a pattern that was to continue for the rest of the week. They talked about all kinds of subjects while preparing the breakfasts, dinners and teas, and Katherine was gratified to see her future sister-in-law become calmer and much more thoughtful as time progressed. Lily also discovered a talent for inventing puddings. There were a few disasters along the way, but the successful ones were delicious and much appreciated.

The four of them took it in turns to do the shopping. Alex and Alastair proved to be very efficient at washing up, but drew the line when Lily tried to make Alex wear an apron, spraying her with soap bubbles as she attempted to tie one round his waist.

At other times, they played cards or board games and when the weather was fine, they went for long invigorating walks, always taking Sam with them, exploring the Thames Path and the Chilterns, or driving in Alastair's Morris Oxford over to the Cotswold hills, passing through picturesque villages with thatched honey-coloured stone cottages.

They kept themselves busy and occupied, trying to be positive and not dwelling on Roberta's departure too much. However, it was inevitable that the pain of circumstance pervaded their innermost thoughts and feelings. It took time for the shock to lessen but even longer for the heartache to heal. Their strategy afforded them some protection, but the road of change and acceptance was long and hard and for Alastair in particular, was to prove a very difficult journey.

On their last evening before returning to London, they gathered round the piano in the sitting room – a beautiful walnut Steinway grand, just over five foot in length, which Katherine had admired greatly and had been playing from time to time throughout the holiday whenever she had had the opportunity in between all their other tasks and activities. This was usually when Alex was working on the brief for his court case, the latter being due almost as soon as they returned to London, and when Lily was occupied with her studies in preparation for her new term at school. Alastair was very complimentary about Katherine's playing the first time he heard her, and from then on, whenever she started to practice, he would come into the room and sit reading the newspaper or a book or, more usually, just stare out of the French doors to the garden beyond, losing himself in the Chopin Nocturnes and Rachmaninov Preludes that she played.

He found solace in the music: a consolation and escape from the conflicting emotions and sadness that he could not dispel and which had made him quiet and withdrawn since Roberta's departure. Katherine sensed this and any shyness she initially felt at having him in the room while she played, quickly disappeared to the extent that on the rare occasions when he was unable to come and listen, she missed the company of his unobtrusive presence.

160

As they gathered round the piano that last evening, Katherine commented on the vast quantity of music that she had discovered in the spacious cabinet close to the piano.

"Many years' accumulation," observed Alex. "A lot of this belongs to Mother, doesn't it, Dad?"

"Yes, she brought it with her when we were first married," replied Alastair. "I wonder if she'll want it back? I bought the Steinway for her the year Lily was born. It replaced the elderly upright we had had until then and was intended as a gift to celebrate our good fortune in having a daughter, as well as our fifteenth wedding anniversary. I hoped it would encourage her to take up the piano again. But it was to no avail," he added sadly.

"Did she play well?" asked Katherine.

"Exceedingly well. She wanted to be a concert pianist but her father was against it. He thought that *'music for young ladies should remain an accomplishment and not a career; particularly young ladies of good breeding.'*" Alastair's mild impersonation of his late father-in-law made everyone smile, even if, as in Katherine and Lily's case, they had never met him.

Privately, Katherine thought she could see where Roberta must have acquired her supercilious attitudes but she also had sympathy for the thwarted aspirations of the talented young woman. Aloud she said, "Would she have made a concert pianist, do you think?"

"Without a doubt. In fact, just before she knew she was expecting Edward, she was secretly making enquiries about studying at the Royal Academy of Music. She had managed to make an appointment with the Vice-Principal and persuaded me to come along as support, not that I needed much persuading to go anywhere with her in those days," added Alastair morosely, taking a deep breath. "He heard her play and offered her a place there and then, so impressed was he with her abilities."

"But falling pregnant with Edward put a stop to all of that," said Alex.

"That's right." Alastair didn't offer anything further on the subject and it was not pursued.

Katherine began to understand her absent future mother-in-law a little better – the loss of her career, frustrated before it had even begun, and losing the man whom she had loved. Surely Roberta should have resented the child or the lover who had absconded, rather than Alastair; after all, it was the fact of her being pregnant that had forestalled her ambitions. Perhaps her love of Edward's father really did outweigh all other considerations and she saw the baby as the one remaining tangible link with him.

Again, as with the reasons for Roberta's departure from the family home, Katherine felt there was another piece to this puzzle; some facet that was missing. However, for the present, it had to remain a mystery. Just like Rupert and Mhairi, she thought.

"So, what shall we do first?" asked Lily.

"How about some madrigals?" suggested Alex. "Dad here has a very good voice."

But Alastair declined, saying he wasn't really in the mood for singing and would prefer just to listen to everyone else. So Lily got out her flute and, accompanied by Alex, gave them an impromptu concert.

Katherine was very impressed by her musicality as well as her technical skill and said as much. Alastair too observed that he hadn't heard her play as well as that for a very long time.

Lily was thoughtful for a while and then said, "I know I shouldn't say this but I've felt so much freer since Mother left. I can be myself and therefore, I can express what I feel without fear of criticism or being put down, whatever I'm doing – whether it's music or just general conversation."

"My poor darling, has it really been that bad?" said Alastair.

"Sometimes," replied Lily honestly. "But then, it's not been that easy for you either."

"No," admitted Alastair.

And, lifting the mood once more, they finished the evening with songs from Alex and Katherine, accompanied by Lily, this time on the piano.

That evening after supper, they packed and checked that everything had been done in the house that was needed to leave it safe and secure. Roberta's belongings had been despatched earlier in the week, with Katherine and Alex sharing this difficult task. They went through the whole house but found very few personal effects anywhere except in her bedroom. Once all her belongings had been removed, very little of her personality remained. In her bureau, there were no letters or diaries, no indication of what she thought or felt, only folders containing minutes of committee meetings and a few photographs of the children when they were young. There was nothing in the attic either: no personal mementoes, no baby clothes or toys.

It seemed to Katherine that Roberta had invested no emotional attachment in her home; nothing that would bind her to it. It was as if she had wanted to be prepared and ready to leave at a moment's notice. She did not say any of this to either Alex or Alastair, but it made her feel very sad that Roberta had been so cold and distant towards her family, when they were so warm and loving and could have given her so much had she chosen to accept it and open up to them.

Katherine took the opportunity to talk to Alex about her decision to leave Cairnmor and live with him in London after they were married. He was secretly relieved, knowing that it really was the only possible course of action. He was very well aware that crofting would not suit him, nor the restrictions of island life. And as for the weather… its unpredictability would be just too much to bear if he had to contend with it all the time. In any case, it would be his responsibility to provide for her once they were married, and as a barrister, he could do that extremely well. He could not have done so on Cairnmor.

Katherine was very upset after she had told him: not because she would find being with him difficult, but because of the enormity of what she would be relinquishing. He understood this and held her for a long time while she recovered her equilibrium, kissing her and wiping away her tears, more convinced than ever that she was the right person to be his wife.

162

The next morning they departed for London – Alastair and Lily with Sam in the Morris, and Katherine and Alex in the MG. Every available space in the Morris was taken up with luggage, school clothes and equipment, for Lily was returning to school the day after Katherine's departure for Cairnmor. None of them was looking forward to her return to Scotland, and Katherine for her part dreaded leaving them. They had all become very close.

There was little time to spend together in London before she was due to go back and, inevitably, that day arrived all too soon. On the platform at Euston station, they said tearful farewells amid prolonged hugs and promises of letters to be written.

As the *Princess Elizabeth* drew away from the platform at ten o'clock precisely, in keeping with the long-standing timetable of the Glasgow-bound express, the picture that Katherine took with her on her long journey was of Alastair with his arm around Lily, both of them waving, and of Alex, her Alex, standing alone on the platform, blowing her a kiss.

CHAPTER 21

Letters
January-February, 1937

Katherine to Alex

My darling,
I arrived home safely after a <u>very</u> long journey. The train journey was good from a travelling point of view but terribly lonely from my personal perspective. It was awful to leave you standing there on the platform at Euston and Alastair and Lily too. I just wanted to leap off the train and come back to you all but of course that was impossible. I miss you all so much.

Just before we arrived in Glasgow, the guard informed us that we had covered the four hundred miles in seven and three-quarter hours and the engine had touched eighty miles an hour in places. Someone in our compartment (obviously a train buff) asked what the average speed had been and the guard replied about fifty-two miles per hour. After the guard had gone, this man regaled us with other engine 'facts' – apparently the Princess Royal Class, the engines that haul the 'Royal Scot' expresses out of Euston, are one hundred and fifty tons in weight; the tender holds four thousand gallons of water and a scoop underneath picks up water from specially constructed troughs every forty miles. This can be done at sixty to seventy miles per hour and enables the train to run non-stop for the whole journey (apart from a brief stop at Carlisle to change crew). The engines are designed by Sir William Stanier and train journeys are (and I quote our itinerant expert) 'one of the great sensations of life'.

Fortunately, we arrived at Glasgow Central before any of us non train buffs could nod off. (But I hope you're impressed with my remembering all this information... !)

It was raining in Glasgow; a typically miserable damp drizzle that made everywhere look grey and depressing. It matched my mood absolutely. I caught the train to Oban, to find it was very wet there too. My room at the hotel was serviceable, but no more. However, I slept well, I was so tired, but next morning I awoke to find that the wind had got up during the night and was now blowing with considerable force.

There was some debate as to whether the steamer should sail, but the Captain, a doughty, dour, grizzled old man of the sea, whom I'd not encountered before (apparently Captain MacTavish is ill) dismissed the Harbour Master's reservations and off we went.

It was a dreadful journey – one of the worst that I can ever recall. Lochfoyle was tossed about by the mountainous seas as though she were a toy. Up, up, up, we went until it seemed we could go no further and then we would come straight down, hitting the trough of the wave with a tremendous crash which sent a fearsome shudder throughout the boat. Then it was up again to the top and down again to the bottom for nearly the whole journey. Even I found it frightening and I'm well used to the vagaries of the voyage from the mainland to Cairnmor.

All we passengers could do was find something to hold onto tightly and stay there. I wedged myself on the floor between the wall of my cabin and the bunk bed and held onto one of the posts. It was impossible for any food to be served (no one felt like eating anything anyway) and we endured this torment for fourteen hours.

Throughout it all, our intrepid Captain, to his credit, kept the ship under control, bringing the valiant little steamer safely into Lochaberdale. When we disembarked, he said cheerily, "There, that wasn't too bad was it?!" If everyone hadn't been so shell-shocked from the journey, he might have received something a little ruder than the quickly mumbled, "Thank you", before we all scuttled down the gangplank as quickly as our very wobbly legs could take us, onto the safety of terra firma.

I had quite a reception committee to welcome me home. It was wonderful to see everyone again – they kept saying that my accent and way of speaking had changed, that I sounded very English. Do I? I haven't noticed. I suppose for people like you and I who are good at accents and receptive to syntax, then some influence is probably inevitable. However, a few days of speaking Gaelic again will soon sort that out from their perspective!

Everyone seemed pleased with their presents and Fiona and Gordon had brought Misty and Breeze along too. Breeze has grown so much but is still very close to her mother.

I'm very worried about Mary, though. She seemed very pale and quiet when she met me at the quayside and not her usual self at all; there was none of her normal gaiety and spontaneous chatter. Adam is away at the moment apparently but where, she wouldn't say. Something is definitely wrong. I hope that she will feel able to talk to me, but I shan't pressure her to do so; I'll wait for her to do it in her own time. I'll take her off for a walk on the next fine day we have and see if that yields any results.

It's very quiet here. The cats are asleep next to the range in their basket and I'm sitting at the kitchen table looking out over the bay. School starts tomorrow, but everything seems very strange and it's going to take me a while to readjust.

I shall write to the Highlands and Islands Education Authority tomorrow, sending in my resignation. I still can't believe I'm about to do that but it is the correct decision, my darling, indeed it is the only decision.

Thank you for all your love and support when I told you that day. I needed it very much. It isn't easy, and I'm not going to pretend otherwise, but it is right and will work out for the best, I'm sure. I'll take it one step at a time, and be kind to myself, just as Alastair advised. I'll be very happy living at Cornwallis Gardens and at Maybury – both places are large enough for us to have our own privacy and independence as well as having company when we need it.

You know how fond I am of Alastair and Lily, and how I am content for us all to live in the same house, just as we did at Christmas and New Year. The four of us get on so well and I'm very thankful for that.

But I miss you more than I can say. It feels as though no sooner are we together than we have to part and I don't know how much longer I can do that. I comfort myself with the thought that we'll be married in a couple of months (I can't quite believe it and have to keep telling myself that it's not a dream!) and it really isn't that long. But I so want to be with you and to feel your arms around me and just to be able to talk to you without having to wait a week when the mail-boat comes to read your reply! I love you beyond anything I could have imagined and I want to be with you all the time and for us to make our own life together.

The clock has just chimed eleven and reminded me that I must stop now as I have to do some preparation for school tomorrow, though I would much rather carry on with this letter to you.

All my love and hugs and kisses,
from your own Katherine.

Alex to Katherine

Dearest Katherine,

Thank you so much for your letter. I'm sorry you had such a rough crossing, it sounds horrendous. I would have been beside myself with worry if I had known you were travelling in conditions like that. I'm glad you arrived safely without any mishap. Oh, and yes, I am <u>very</u> impressed with your locomotive knowledge!

I've been thinking about you so much and missing you dreadfully. I know exactly what you mean about meeting and parting. It is incredibly difficult, and to console myself, I have to picture you and imagine holding you in my arms too. I wonder if it would work if I sent that picture to you via the telepathic network (if such a thing exists!)? There... can you feel my arms around you and my hand stroking your gorgeous hair and my kissing you... and you kissing me back and us... ? (I'd better stop there otherwise we'll both be in trouble... When we're married we won't have to stop and I can't imagine anything more wonderful than that, my darling.)

I'm so glad you feel you could be happy for us to live in London and at Maybury sharing both houses with Dad, and Lily during the holidays, but living our independent lives. As you say, the four of us do get on so well, and if the circumstances had been different, Christmas would have been a joyous time. They are both very fond of you as well, and send their love.

I drove Lily back to school the next day after you'd gone (it seemed an age!) and spoke briefly to her Head of House about the events of Christmas. She was very understanding and sympathetic and said she would keep a gentle eye on Lily and let me know if she felt that Lily was upset in any way or if her work was being affected. I was grateful for this, as you never can be sure how people will react to a situation like ours – I've no doubt that there are those who will be very disapproving and judgemental.

My court case is going well and I think I'm going to win, which is always gratifying. I have another two lined up at R.C.J. after this one – the Head Clerk seems to be giving me all the advocacy work! I'm not complaining at all as it is this aspect of being a barrister that I most enjoy.

Generally however, things are not very happy in our Chambers at the moment. Sir John (Pemberton – do you remember meeting him at Royal Court Chambers and at Middle Temple?) seems to be putting pressure on all and sundry, interfering with nearly everyone's cases, rather than trusting his lawyers and allowing us just to get on with the job.

With me, he's trying his level best once again to persuade me to further my career by attending social functions and mixing with the 'right people'. How I dislike that phrase and the sentiment behind it! I'll attend the usual events at Middle Temple but I really do draw the line at weekend house parties designed for that purpose. I've always been happy to stay at country houses for purely social gatherings but not for that. So I'm doing my best to deflect him tactfully from arranging this type of thing.

Surely my record as a barrister should speak for itself if I am to move forward in my career?

Michael on the other hand is really unhappy, as he seems to be getting all the minor Briefs. While these are important to the people who need the help, it's good to have a mixture of subject matter to deal with. Michael is convinced that Sir John has something against him for some unknown reason and has instructed the Head Clerk to give him all the tat. I told him he was being slightly paranoid but there may be an element of truth in what he says. I'm not sure what's going on here.

Sir John has been head of Royal Court Chambers for a year now. In that time, the atmosphere has changed considerably since the K.C. whom he replaced retired. He was a very kind and considerate man, who had the most balanced perspective of anyone I've ever known and for whom the welfare of his staff was paramount.

Sir John has a very different personality and seems to be most concerned with enhancing the reputation of his Chambers. It's very worrying, and if he continues along these lines, there is the danger he will start to alienate those around him, who may decide to take their skills and expertise elsewhere. We shall see.

I'm worried about Dad too, as he seems very tired and dispirited. I'm not sure how he's managing at the office. I think I may have a discreet word with one of the partners and just check that he's all right. He may not have said anything to anyone, but they would have to be very unobservant not to see the change in him.

Poor man, he feels as though he's tried so hard over the years to keep the family together and now it's all falling apart. I've told him that it's not his fault and pointed out to him that Lily and I have no intention of going anywhere, that we want to be with him and that you can't be much closer than the four of us were at Christmas this year. That seemed to console him, but I know Mother's departure has robbed him of his self-esteem, which is understandable, given the circumstances. It will take some time for that to come back.

Well, it's getting late and I must do some more work on my case notes for court tomorrow – we both seem to be doing preparation work of some kind or other, don't we?!

Goodnight, my love, sleep well. May your dreams be sweet and your mind content with the knowledge that we'll be together soon and that I love you.

Your very own,
Alex

Mary to Lily

Dear Lily,
I hope you won't take offence if I write and ask you to provide me with some measurements for your bridesmaid's dress. Katherine told me that you would not mind and gave me your address but I wished to make sure. I have written a list of requirements on a separate piece of paper. Please could you fill in the blank spaces and return the paper to me? I have also enclosed a sketch of my design for the dress and a small sample of the material. I hope that you will like it.

Yours sincerely,
Mary Wallace

Lily to Mary

Dear Mary,
Thank you so much for sending me the sketch of my dress, it looks wonderful! Katherine said you were very clever, and I agree. I can't wait to wear it. I love the colour too. I've filled in the blank spaces as you requested and I enclose the piece of paper with this letter. I couldn't do the measurements by myself, so I asked Matron to help me, which she did. Fortunately, there was no one in sick bay at the time. Though, the next day, two girls at my school went down with what has been diagnosed as influenza and are now keeping Matron busy. She's hoping there won't be an epidemic and is keeping them isolated. Sick bay smells even more of carbolic soap than it did before! I shall keep well clear of anyone with the slightest sniffle, I think. Anyway, do let me know if you need anything else. I'm really excited about the wedding!

Yours sincerely, Lily

Messrs Haynes, Poulton-Smith and Sansom, Solicitors, to Mrs Roberta Stewart

Dear Mrs Stewart,

We have been instructed by our client, Mr Alastair Stewart, regarding the transfer of the deeds into his sole name of the property known as Mistley House in Maybury, South Oxfordshire.

We enclose a copy of the request and wait to hear from your solicitor regarding this matter, so that it can proceed expeditiously.

Yours sincerely,

R.R. Haynes

Messrs Tamer and Stubbs, Solicitors, to Messrs Haynes, Poulton and Hansom, Solicitors

Dear Mr Haynes,

We are in receipt of your client's request for the transfer of deeds to the property known as Mistley House in Maybury, South Oxfordshire into his sole name. However, our client, Mrs Roberta Stewart, is not yet ready to progress with this matter and has given us instruction to instigate additional proceedings.

We shall contact you in due course regarding these.

Yours sincerely,

N. Tamer

Katherine to Alastair

Dear Alastair,

How are you? Keeping well, I hope. We have a nasty influenza bug here on the island at the moment. Several of the children have been absent from school and although I try to avoid close contact with the remainder in situations like this, it is almost impossible when the children bring their work to my desk for me to mark, and breathe all over me, or when the little ones need hugs!

It doesn't seem to be the sort of germ that spreads quickly but rather takes its time, and when it eventually strikes, it can be severe. We're all blaming the postman, Donald MacCreggan, and his wife Annie. They went to visit their son and his family, who live on the mainland, and brought the 'flu back with them. Donald was ill first of all and then Annie succumbed a week or so later. They have both recovered now but passed it on to a couple of the children's parents who came into the post office, and it is now 'going the rounds' as we say.

My friend Mary and Lily have been in contact regarding the bridesmaid's dress, and Lily said that the 'flu is at Benbridge House too. It seems to be pretty widespread across the country, so stay clear of clients that come and see you with coughs and sneezes!

I thought you might like to hear a little about life on Cairnmor and about some of the people you will meet when Alex and I get married at Easter.

In Lochaberdale, the main settlement on Cairnmor, the hotel is being redecorated. Apparently the owner of our island (he owns several of the smaller outlying islands, including Cairnbeg, as well), who is very elderly now, is, according to John Fraser the manager of the hotel, inviting some important guests whom he wishes to impress with the accommodation his island can provide.

Fishing, if you like that sort of thing, is excellent here, with both fresh and sea water lochs giving a variety of breeds to catch. Apparently, he wants the accommodation to match this (the excellence, I mean, not increase the variety of available breeds in the hotel – sorry, couldn't resist that!).

A couple of days ago, several of us were gathered in the hotel lounge for the evening and spent a pleasant time speculating as to who these dignitaries might be. Father McPhee (our priest) and Robbie MacKenzie (well-respected fisherman, philosopher and weather expert) both think that he's having delusions of grandeur in his old age and anticipating the new King and Queen. Gordon MacKinnon (Mary's father) suggested it might be the Prime Minister, Stanley Baldwin and his adviser, Thomas Jones. His wife, Fiona, told them not to be daft and said it's probably just for the proprietor's usual cronies who come every year. Jimmy Gillies (odd-job man and game-keeper) said he hoped it was the King and Queen, as her father was Scottish and he'd make sure the boiler was working properly so they'd have plenty of hot water. Everyone laughed at that (not unkindly) and then Jimmy said he'd catch the best trout he could and ask John's wife (Marion) to cook a rare supper for them.

We all agreed (solemnly) that we'd have to invite Robert and Andrew MacClennan (excellent musicians who live in the northern part of Cairnmor) to bring their bagpipes and accordion, to compose and play a special royal reel to accompany Jimmy's specially prepared trout dinner. Jimmy said he'd look forward to that and immediately disappeared to check the boiler and his fishing tackle! Poor man, he wasn't the brightest when he was at school, apparently, but his heart's in the right place and there isn't anything that he wouldn't do to help someone if they needed something mending or moving!

The speculation became more extreme after that, as you can imagine, when everyone tried to out-do the previous person, with the suggestions becoming more fantastic and implausible by the minute. It was one of those occasions when you had to be there to appreciate the humour and wit fully, but I hope I've given you something of its flavour and an indication of the verbal silliness we occasionally get up to here!

How is your work at the moment? I expect there has been quite a lot to do after the Christmas and New Year break. It must seem difficult sometimes to focus, but work can be a great escape. I know that only too well. Please let me know how things are. I can only begin to guess what you must be going through. I'm only at the end of a pen if you want to write.

Love from Katherine xx

Alastair to Katherine

My dear Katherine,
Thank you so much for your cheerful letter. I enjoyed reading your account of the conversation you had with your friends, and it has enabled me to know

something of the people on Cairnmor. I shall look forward to meeting them at Easter.

Work in the office has been mainly catching up with the accumulated backlog that inevitably follows the Festive Season and I'm plodding my way through my part of it. You are quite correct – it isn't easy to keep focused and I have to try very hard not to dwell on things too much. I hope I'm succeeding, but I have my doubts sometimes. I appreciated your last paragraph a great deal and I thank you for that.

However, I do have one piece of very good news. I've received a reply from Mhairi's Aunt Flora in the Lake District – you recall I wrote to her asking for any information she could give me about Mhairi and the time she spent there.

I enclose a copy of the letter (Alex has read it, of course) as I think you will enjoy the story it tells, and it may help us further along the path of solving this particular mystery. Please do let me know what you think after reading it – you are as involved in this quest as we are and I value your opinion on this, or indeed, any, subject.

Warmest regards, Alastair

Mrs Flora Finlay to Mr Alastair Stewart of Messrs. Stewart, Patterson and Faraday, Solicitors

Dear Mr Stewart,

Thank you for your letter regarding my niece Mhairi. I am afraid that I cannot give you any help as regards her current whereabouts. The only contact I had was some months after she returned to Glasgow to care for her mother. She wrote to thank me for the time she had spent on our farm and said that she would like to have stayed. She also said that she and Rupert were together and very happy. She made no mention of the baby. She said that her mother (my sister) was very poorly. The letter was postmarked Cathcart, a district of Glasgow, but she gave no address.

I travelled to see my sister in hospital and was with her when she passed away. But I didn't see Mhairi and no one knew of her whereabouts. She apparently disappeared the day she came back from Grasmere after taking her mother to hospital, and has not been in contact with her family since. But she must have been aware of her mother's precarious state of health when she wrote to me.

You also asked if I could tell you about Mhairi's time on the farm with us. That I can do, although it is a long time ago now. When she first came to us, she was very pale and undernourished. My first task was to make sure she had lots of good food, so that the baby would grow healthily and Mhairi remain well enough to nurture the infant. She was young and strong, despite her skinniness, and she soon put on weight and began to have a healthy glow about her.

I have always felt that books and learning are very important. I saw to it with my own children and my second task was to encourage Mhairi to follow suit. This she did, taking to it like a duck to water and making rapid progress.

Her schooling had been very limited as she was frequently absent to nurse her mother who was frail and often ill. Mhairi then had to look after her father and brothers too, doing all the cooking, cleaning, washing and shopping. She last attended school when she was eleven years old. But she continued with her reading, spending time in the local public library whenever she could. She was not able to take books home because her father thought that books and learning were not for girls and women. So it was a delight to see her hunger for studying when she was with us.

I gave Mhairi writing tasks and arithmetic as well as books to read and she helped the younger children with their schoolwork. She showed herself to be a natural teacher. Like the rest of the family, she had a ticket for the public library in Kendal and we went there once a fortnight in the pony and trap to buy supplies and change our library books. Mhairi was always very quick to learn and very intelligent. My sister had been like that and as a family, we had all been encouraged to try hard at our studies by our parents.

Mhairi stayed with us for most of her pregnancy and kept up a regular correspondence with Rupert, which I supported. They were obviously very much in love. Mhairi was very upset that she had to leave. It made me very angry to think that her father put his own welfare before that of his daughter, insisting that she come home to look after him and her brothers. And I was angrier still that he and Rupert's father were adamant that the baby was to be taken away as soon as it was born. It was inhuman and unfeeling, even if Rupert's father was a Baronet. As I said to you before, she did not mention the baby in her letter to me.

You asked me about Cairnmor, as this featured in the letters you found from Mhairi to Rupert. My parents, Iain MacNeil and Catriona Ferguson, were from Cairnmor and my brother Fergus and I were born on the island. When I was eight years old, my father found a good job on the mainland in Glasgow, so we left Cairnmor and made our home in the city. Mhairi's mother, Anna, was born there. When she was little, she caught scarlet fever and was very ill for a long time. This left her prone to bouts of ill health for the rest of her life, although she managed to have four strong sons and a lovely daughter.

I told Mhairi many stories about my life on Cairnmor. I have very good memories of my early childhood there and wished to share them with her. Mhairi was so taken with my description of Cairnmor that she wanted to make her home there with Rupert after the baby was born. I have no idea if she got her wish.

I am not sure if this is helpful, but Jock Hamilton, Mhairi's father, is still alive and is a resident in the Glasgow Royal Mental Asylum. He had always been partial to the drink and this became so bad after Mhairi disappeared and Anna passed away, that he frequently drank himself into a comatose state and eventually had to be admitted to the asylum. I gather that he has moments of lucid thought before slipping back into a dream world.

I am now seventy-five years old. Jock must be about eighty, if not more, and has been living in the Asylum for fifteen years. Mhairi's brothers are called Angus, Donald, Fraser and Hamish but they no longer work at Mathieson's

Ship Building and Engineering Company. It was Hamish who wrote to tell me about his father. However, I have not heard from him in a long time.

I hope that you will find this helpful.

Yours faithfully, Flora Finlay (Mrs)

Katherine to Alex

My darling,

In the light of Flora's letter, I think we should go to Glasgow and visit Jock Hamilton, even though he's in the Asylum, don't you? I have a <u>very</u> strong feeling that it would be the right thing to do. The school here is closed for a week at the end of February, so I'm a free agent for that time. It's being re-decorated inside. It was fine as it was but the owner seems intent on sprucing up the public buildings in Lochaberdale, including the hotel – I wonder why? We're becoming suspicious now. Especially as he could have waited just a few weeks for the Easter holidays when the children were officially not at school.

Could you manage to get the time off at the end of February? We could spend the week together and try to make some headway on this case? We could also go through plans for the wedding. What a wonderful excuse for us to meet! I hope it's possible…

Your Katherine xxxxx

Alex to Katherine

Dearest Katherine,

Michael is going to take on my case load from the week before so that if any court cases should run over, as they often do, I'm covered. He's delighted to do it, but the Head Clerk's face was a picture of disapproval. My name will probably be mud now and it will be both Michael and I being given all the dross after this!

However, I shall risk it all just to be with you. I'll catch the 10.00 a.m. train from Euston on that Monday and be in Glasgow Central at 5.45. I've booked us into the Central Hotel. We'll have until the following Friday when you have to begin your journey back to Cairnmor.

I can't wait to see you, my love.

Alex xxxx

P.S. I wonder if I'll encounter your train buff?!

CHAPTER 22

Glasgow
February, 1937

The early evening express drew into the station with a hiss of steam. Grease on the rails caused the engine wheels to slip erratically for a brief moment, creating an explosion of exhaust from the chimney.

Waiting behind the arched 'Royal Scot' ticket barrier before platforms one and two, Katherine watched the steam and smoke rise up to the glass and metal roof overhead, and as the passengers left the carriages, she anxiously searched the crowd for Alex.

She couldn't see him at first, then suddenly, there he was – a very familiar figure striding towards her, suitcase in hand. She could hardly contain her delight, and when at last he came through the barrier and reached her, he put down his case and they threw their arms around each other, holding each other as though they would never let go again.

It was several moments before either of them spoke and then Alex said, "It's so good to hold you, to see you!"

"Are you really here?!" said Katherine, looking up at him, her eyes full of emotion and relief.

"Oh, yes, I really am here, my love," replied Alex, taking her face in his hands, looking deeply into her eyes and then kissing her on the lips. If passers-by disapproved, they neither noticed nor cared; being together was all that mattered.

"Our lives seem to be a series of meetings and partings at railway stations, don't they?" he murmured, breathing in the scent of her hair.

"And harbours," she replied. "Don't forget the first time we met!"

"How could I possibly do that?" said Alex, smiling and gathering her into his arms again. "I can see it as clearly and vividly as though it was yesterday. And even if we never find Rupert and Mhairi or their elusive offspring, I shall always be grateful to them, because it was through the search for them that I came to Cairnmor originally!"

"And your Dad, because he asked you to come in his place."

"Yes."

They had at last drawn apart. Alex picked up his suitcase, and with his arm around Katherine's shoulders, they walked away from the ticket barrier onto the circulating area of the station with its brimful newspaper, magazine and confectionery stands, advertising bill-boards and posters, and two very large clocks – one suspended from the rafters and the other on top of the largest oval-shaped stand.

Crowds of people were hurrying to catch their trains home in the latter part of the evening rush hour, and Katherine and Alex had to manoeuvre their way past the destination board, where travellers stood and stared at the train times clearly delineated under the semi-circular platform numbers before heading off in the direction of their advertised platform.

174

The station itself was very distinctive with deep mahogany-coloured wood on all the interior buildings and walls, contrasting with the metal and glass beamed roof above.

In the middle of the concourse they passed a howitzer shell.

"Oh!" exclaimed Alex. "I didn't notice that when I came here last time."

They went over to examine it more closely.

"It's known as 'The Shell,'" said Katherine. "And it really is one – or at least it was," she added mischievously.

"Unlike the Cup Board at Middle Temple," observed Alex, reading her thoughts.

"Exactly." And they smiled at each other. "It was converted into a Charity Collection Box after the First World War and it's become a favourite meeting place for courting couples."

"Well, we'd better take advantage of that, hadn't we?" said Alex, and kissed her again. After a few blissful moments, they resumed their way towards the hemi-spherical entrance of the Central Hotel, the warm reddish stone façade of which was clearly visible rising up behind the entrance, the latter part of the hotel contained within the structure of the station roof.

The interior was a haven of calm after the bustle of the station and once Alex had signed the register and collected his key, they took the lift up to their adjoining double rooms situated on the fourth floor.

"What time did you get here?" he asked.

"Just before lunch. I had a meal downstairs in the restaurant and then slept for a couple of hours this afternoon. I was really tired after all the travelling."

She watched him while he unpacked and when he had finished, he kissed her again. Arms round each other, they stood looking out of the window at the night-time view of the city; the darkness alleviated by pools of light from the street lamps and the cars which moved below them. It had started to rain but they felt warm in each other's company.

Presently, they went downstairs for dinner, finding the restaurant well lit and fairly full. They chose a table in the corner away from the other diners and ordered their meal. Alex took Katherine's hand in his and kissed each of her fingers in turn and smiled at her, his eyes bright with desire.

"There's a lot to catch up on," he said prosaically without any urgency of intention in the tone of his voice.

"Yes," said Katherine dreamily, not taking her eyes off him, wanting to hold him close.

"It's very tempting, isn't it?" he said, echoing her thoughts.

"Incredibly tempting," she replied.

"Our resolve does seem to be weakening." This was a hopeful statement, rather than a regretful one. Despite his good intentions, he knew how much he wanted her.

Katherine regarded him thoughtfully. "Well, after this week, just think, the next time we are together will be for the wedding and when we're married, the waiting will be over."

"Yes," he replied dutifully, his hope fading.

Their soup arrived. It was adequate in quality but not as good as that which was served at the Lochaberdale Hotel.

"How are things on the island?" asked Alex.

"Fine, except the 'flu epidemic is really taking hold now. Lots of people have got it, or are recovering from it. It's probably a blessing in disguise that the school has been closed for this week. It may help to stop the spread of germs, and also there probably wouldn't have been that many children at school. Touch wood, I seem to have avoided it so far."

"Lots of girls have been sent home at Lily's school, and if any more contract it, they're considering closing the school."

"I'm not surprised. It's very nasty for about five days but after that, everyone seems to recover quite quickly, apart from feeling very tired for about a week. I had something similar when I was at Edinburgh, so perhaps I have some immunity to this version."

The waiter came to collect their plates, and they began the main course.

"How's Alastair?" asked Katherine.

"Coping."

"Have you heard anything further from Roberta's solicitors?"

"Not as yet. They seem to be taking their time."

"I wonder what the additional proceedings could be? Surely it can't be a divorce?"

"Dad and I worried about that for a while."

Then suddenly, Alex seemed reluctant to talk further; it was as though she had reached a barrier. Katherine knew that he was concealing something and that whatever it was, he found it deeply upsetting.

She looked at him, her expression one of concern and empathy, and Alex took her left hand and held it, turning round her engagement ring between his finger and thumb. She could see he was trying to find the right words to use and also, as they were in a public place, although secluded from the other diners, to control his emotional response to whatever it was he was about to say.

"You remember that we both thought there was something more to Mother's leaving than the reasons she gave?"

"Yes."

"Well, we were right. Unknown to Dad, I hired a private detective to follow her and to try and find out what was going on."

"You must have found that a very difficult thing to do."

"I did. It went against every instinct that I possess. I felt sullied and humiliated after I had set it in motion, as it was my own mother whom I'd asked to be investigated."

"My poor love. But you had to know."

Alex looked at her, relief showing in his eyes for her understanding; for not judging him; for not thinking less of him and finally, for being able to tell someone at last. "Yes."

Katherine then said gently, "What did he find out?"

"The obvious. That Mother's erstwhile lover from her youth, Edward Fothergill, had returned from abroad, was newly divorced and had made contact

176

with her some months previously, after which it would seem they renewed their affair almost immediately. Behind Dad's back. While she was still living at Maybury," he added bitterly.

Despite herself, Katherine was shocked and scandalized. Alex saw this in her face and muttered, "You probably won't want anything to do with me or my family now."

She looked at him aghast and said, "Why on earth should I think that? How could you possibly believe such a thing of me? You know I'm not prejudiced in that way and I'm certainly not concerned with what bigoted idiots might think of your family circumstances. People have affairs. She's not the first married woman in the world to be in love with someone else and then pursue her feelings. I don't condone it; I don't agree with it, but it happens."

"I can never see that happening to us. We love each other far too much." Alex was passionate in his assertion, all too aware of the superficial nature of his previous relationships, and needing to reassure himself as much as Katherine.

"Yes, my love. We are indeed fortunate," she responded, taking his hand in hers, hoping that nothing would ever diminish their mutual trust and fidelity to each other.

The waiter, who had been hovering discreetly, waiting for an opportunity to collect their empty plates, came over to their table a few moments later and completed his task.

They both declined dessert, not feeling that they could eat anything further, and made their way up to Alex's room, both still distressed at his revelation.

"Have you told Alastair yet?" asked Katherine, as they sat on Alex's bed with their backs resting against the headboard and their feet up on the counterpane.

"No, I've kept it to myself for the past couple of weeks. I've told no one except you. I don't know what to do. In the law of the land, Dad has grounds for a divorce but he's reluctant to drag her name through the courts." Alex struggled to control his emotions. "I've dealt with many divorce cases, but it's a very different feeling when it involves your own parents. It's a horrible mess."

"Dear kind Alastair, he doesn't deserve any of this. You have to tell him, my love, before he finds out through another source," said Katherine gently.

"I know. But I'm so afraid it will break his spirit."

They talked long into the night until eventually Alex slept. After getting off the bed, Katherine covered him with spare blankets which she found after searching through the wardrobe, just as she had done at Christmas when Alex had come to her at Mistley House. Then she went into her room and, tired out, she too fell fast asleep.

She was awoken early the next morning by a discreet knock on her door. On answering, she found Alex there, pale but recovered, dressed and shaved.

"How did you sleep?" he asked, following her back into the room and admiring her body beneath her figure-hugging silk dressing-gown and night-dress, his heart beating wildly.

"I was out like a light and slept the whole night."

"So did I, amazingly enough."

Then, catching her by surprise, he pulled her into his arms and there was no more conversation for a long time.

It was Katherine who resisted him finally and said firmly but gently, "It's only a month to go before our wedding and we've managed so well. If we succumb now at the final hurdle, it would negate all that effort."

Reluctantly, Alex had to agree. "I know," he said, resigning himself to another period of celibacy. He was beginning to regret suggesting that they wait, despite the risks.

"Now," said Katherine briskly, hiding her own frustration, "I must get bathed and dressed if we are to stand any chance of going anywhere today. Besides which, I'm really hungry."

"Breakfast sounds good to me," he replied with more enthusiasm than he felt.

Alex amused himself while he waited for her by reading the newspaper she had brought with her on her own journey to Glasgow the day before, and when she was ready, they went down to breakfast, choosing the same table that they had occupied the previous evening.

"How's Mary?" asked Alex, still trying to overcome his frustrated desire from earlier that morning. "Did you manage to find out why she didn't seem to be herself?"

Katherine hesitated before answering. This was not going to be easy. "It's not very good, I'm afraid. You remember I told you that Adam has a drink problem? Well, Mary confided in me eventually, saying that it has been getting much, much worse in recent months. He's drinking nearly all the time now and he and his friends, who together own the fishing boat, have been going on two or three day binges, ordering alcohol from the mainland and carousing all over Cairnmor. In the past few weeks, he's become violent too, which scares her. When he's like that, she walks out on him and comes to stay with me, which is sensible. Then she goes home and tidies up the mess he's left while he sleeps it off. But it's no way to live."

"No, it isn't. Alcohol is a terrible thing and very destructive when the addiction takes hold. I've seen too many court cases resulting from its misuse and the heartache that brings. It's one of the reasons I'm teetotal."

"And I don't drink because I don't like it. I don't see the point of it."

"Mary can't carry on like this."

"No. I persuaded her to go to Father McPhee, which she did. He has told Gordon and Fiona, and Adam's parents, and they all had a crisis meeting. As a result of this, Adam and his friends have promised to stop drinking. They have little choice now that they are under pressure to do so from the community. But how long this latest resolution will last, I don't know. There have been so many of them in the past."

Thinking of the main subject matter of their conversations since his arrival in Glasgow and the terrible events in the Spanish civil war that he had just been reading about in Katherine's newspaper, Alex said sombrely, "The world seems to be beset by problems at the moment and going slowly insane."

"Isn't it just? And to add to it, today we're going to visit an ex-alcoholic in a lunatic asylum!" she exclaimed.

178

They were both unable to resist laughing at this, even though they felt slightly guilty for doing so, but it did serve to lift their spirits again. They collected their coats and went out onto the station, finding a taxi to take them to the Royal Mental Asylum situated on Western Road.

"If it hadn't been raining, I would have suggested that we take the tram, which I've always enjoyed. But it would be miserable on a day like today and we would have got very grubby. When it rains here, all the soot from the chimneys and other industrial waste seems to attach itself to the water droplets. Everywhere and everyone tends to get filthy." Then she added, "Did you know, the name Glasgow is derived from the Gaelic word meaning 'dear green place'."

Alex chuckled and said, "If they came back today, whoever named it that would be horrified to see the difference in how it must have been then and what it's like now."

"Can you imagine it?! Though I must admit, I'd always quite fancied travelling in H.G. Wells's time machine – wouldn't that be a fantastic way to study history and really see for yourself what life must have been like in days gone by?"

"Yes, complete with plagues and wars and deprivation!"

"That's right, depress us both further! No, I'd like to think that you'd be immune to all that – no one would know you were there and you would have no effect on historical events. You'd just be able to observe and learn and *feel* what it was like. We could even go back to 1909 and try to find Rupert and Mhairi and see what happened to them!"

"Talking of which, Dad wrote to the principal psychiatrist at the Hospital, paving the way for our appointment to visit Jock Hamilton today. He had a really helpful reply from a Dr Cameron, who said that he would be glad to meet us and show us round. He was rather intrigued by what we are trying to do, as he feels it would help Jock greatly to know that we are searching for his daughter."

The taxi soon reached their destination and dropped them off at the roadway below the Royal Mental Hospital, which loomed above them like some medieval castle emerging through the rain and the misty gloom, with its tall chimneys and castellated walls.

They walked up a narrow, winding, tree-lined road, which led them to the ornate gates of the entrance. Soon, they came to an imposing front door where Alex pulled the bell cord and the door was opened by a nurse dressed in a stiffly starched apron and cap over a dark blue uniform. She greeted them with a friendly smile and introduced herself.

"Hello, you must be Mr Stewart and Miss MacDonald. I'm Sister Waverley, the Matron. Welcome to our hospital. If you'd like to take a seat by the desk, I'll tell Dr Cameron that you've arrived."

She disappeared away from them along the corridor, with its highly polished floor and cream and white paint. Neither Alex nor Katherine had quite known what to expect but what impressed them was the quiet air of efficiency that pervaded this part of the building at least.

A receptionist sat behind the large horseshoe desk which was situated opposite the front door, typing briskly, pausing every so often to consult the notes in front of her, and to her left sat a nurse, writing in a large ledger. Portraits of eminent doctors lined the walls on either side of the corridor and pot-plants on stands completed the agreeable first impression.

They did not have long to wait, as Dr Cameron, a man of medium height with a shock of white hair, startling blue eyes and a commanding presence came down the corridor and shook hands with them.

"Ah, yes, Miss MacDonald and Mr Stewart. I'm Dr Cameron, and you're both welcome, indeed. I had a very clear letter from your father, Mr Stewart, explaining the circumstances of your desire to visit here, and I think it may be a good thing, a very good thing indeed."

He led them through a door to the left of the main entrance and up some stairs.

"I thought I'd begin by taking you on a wee tour of our facilities. I've been here for five years now and in that time have implemented many changes. We have a policy of care for our residents that aims to promote maximum independence for those that are able to cope, while at the same time acting as advocates – and I'm sure that as an English barrister yourself, Mr Stewart, you'll appreciate my deliberate use of that terminology – for our most vulnerable patients. We also try to provide practical help and emotional support for relatives. We offer secure accommodation for those who may be a danger to themselves and others, but we try to maintain an ordered and calm atmosphere at all times so that the patients will have consistency in what for them is very often an erratic inner existence."

"Very impressive," remarked Alex. "It seems very forward-thinking, even revolutionary."

"Aye, I've had my battles with the hospital board. But they can see that my methods are working and we have a good success rate in returning a number of residents to their families. We offer occupational therapy in the form of arts and crafts and basket-weaving, and we've also found that music has a great healing and calming effect on even our most, shall we say, difficult inmates. People with mental illness are human beings and should be treated as such, not shut away like outcasts to society, which is how it often was in the old days. We understand much more about treatment these days and here we try to use that knowledge to benefit the individuals in our care." He stopped talking suddenly and said to Katherine apologetically, "I'm afraid I'm pontificating."

"Please don't apologise. I really admire your vision and philosophy. In the work that you do, passion and commitment are so essential and no one should ever be afraid of showing that," replied Katherine. "I am a teacher, so psychology interests me, and as a barrister, Alex will be employing his skills in that area too. But obviously, an institution such as this will take psychology into a different realm." And Katherine stopped, afraid she had said too much.

But Dr Cameron's reply showed his immediate measure of her intellect. "Indeed, here we deal with anxiety, moving through neurosis all the way to psychosis. The problems in the mind caused by excessive consumption of alcohol is another specialist area of responsibility for us, as well as treating and containing the most violent members of society in a secure unit. And this is where we are now."

180

He stopped outside a solid-looking door which he unlocked with a large bunch of keys attached to a key ring that he was holding. Inside was a small entrance hall with two male orderlies seated at a desk. On the wall was a large bell with the word 'Panic' written above it in capital letters.

"For emergencies only," said Dr Cameron. "It safeguards our staff and the inmates too should there be a problem. Someone can be here in a matter of seconds in the event of an emergency. I'm afraid I'm not able to let you in through that door, but beyond it there is a long corridor with rooms made up of padded walls and floors. We have the facility to use straitjackets should that become necessary in extreme circumstances. There are two orderlies the other side of the door outside the rooms."

Katherine and Alex peered through the wire mesh strengthened glass panel set in the door, seeing two burly men walking up and down checking each room and they could hear muffled thumps and shouts from the other side.

Dr Cameron continued, "Most of the men here today will be able to return to their ward when they have calmed down."

They left the secure unit and continued their tour, walking along several corridors, each containing rooms that resembled sitting rooms as well as wards which were high-ceilinged and well ventilated. There was a good ratio of staff to patients and both Katherine and Alex appreciated the care that was being shown and the help given to those who needed it.

"We also have an infirmary and a laundry unit, which in itself is a major undertaking, as you can well appreciate. This is one of four dining rooms. We have found it best to have compatible residents eating together. It saves a lot of fuss and bother!"

He took them to a further sitting room, which again was well lit, even on a dank dismal day such as this one, and which was laid out with a variety of easy and dining room chairs. Two of the residents were playing cards at a table, and by the window, staring vacantly out at the garden, was a white-haired old man in a wheelchair.

Katherine's heart beat faster; she knew they were about to meet Jock Hamilton, Mhairi's father.

"Is that Jock?" she asked.

"Indeed it is. Before we go and meet him, I should first explain that he has days when his thoughts are clear and logical, and others when his mind wanders and he enters a dream-like state. Either mind-set can last for a couple of hours or a couple of days. His drinking has caused irreversible damage to his brain but he has responded particularly well to the therapies we have been administering during my time here and his lucid times have increased in number. However, he is eighty-two now and old age is beginning to play its part in diminishing his mental faculties."

"Would he ever be able to leave here?" asked Katherine.

"I'm afraid not, for two reasons. Firstly, he's lived here for fifteen years now and has become institutionalized in that time – an inevitable consequence of long-term stay, I'm afraid. And secondly, because he still needs our care. He felt the demise of his wife and the disappearance of his daughter Mhairi very acutely and this, together with a burden of guilt for his part in all of that, caused him to drink heavily until he was unable to contain his addiction and everything spiralled out of control. For his own safety, he was committed here and has remained in our care ever since."

They walked over to the other side of the room where Jock was seated. Just as Dr Cameron was about to introduce them, Jock Hamilton turned his head, looked piercingly at Katherine and exclaimed, "Och, my Mhairi, my Mhairi. Ye've come back, ye've come back to me at last!"

CHAPTER 23

Later, when Jock had let go of Katherine's hand, when she and Alex were sitting in Dr Cameron's office and when Katherine had recovered from the shock of being mistaken for Mhairi – and, moreover, being unable to deny or clarify it while they were still with Jock because she was afraid that it would cause him distress – Dr Cameron looked enquiringly at her and said, "Is there any remote possibility that you could be related in some way to Mhairi or to Jock's family?"

"None whatsoever," replied Katherine unequivocally. "My parents never spoke of any relative on the mainland. Both my mother and father were born on Cairnmor and always lived on the island. All the time I was growing up, I never knew them to travel anywhere except Cairnbeg for a wedding, which I also attended. No, I'm sure they would have told me if I'd had any relatives elsewhere."

"Are they still alive?"

"No, they both died in a diphtheria outbreak on the island when I was fourteen."

Dr Cameron was thoughtful for a few moments. And then he shrugged his shoulders. "Well, it would seem that Jock is mistaken and under an illusion. However, it has made him very happy and he looks calmer and more relaxed than I have ever seen him. I would like to thank you for that and also for not immediately denying that you are not his daughter – that would have upset him greatly."

"You are welcome."

"Now, I have a favour to ask you both. Please don't feel obliged in any way, but is it possible that you could pay him another visit? It did him a great deal of good today, and I would like to see if we can continue with that frame of mind tomorrow."

Katherine looked at Alex, who nodded his agreement. "Then we shall be glad to do that," she said, "though I hope he doesn't ask me too many questions about 'my childhood'! I have very scant knowledge of that!"

Dr Cameron smiled. "I think you'll be quite safe in that respect," he replied.

He walked with Alex and Katherine to the door and before they parted, he said, apologetically, "I'm afraid that I won't be here tomorrow as I have to attend a conference in Edinburgh. However, Sister Waverley will be able to assist you. If you can come about nine o'clock that would be ideal, as Jock tends to be at his best first thing in the morning."

They shook hands and bid each other goodbye. After the door had closed, Katherine turned to Alex and said, "That was unexpected."

"Absolutely," he replied.

They walked down the lane, back to the Great Western Road. The rain was falling heavily now but they were very fortunate, as in the distance, they saw the welcome sight of the gold, green and cream livery of a Glasgow tram travelling towards them in the direction of the city centre.

There was a tram stop a few yards away so they ran to that, splashing through the puddles and laughing at their bedraggled appearance as the rain soaked them further.

"Well, at least we can get changed back at the hotel," said Katherine, as they stood in the tram, dripping water all over the floor of the middle aisle, unable to sit down as all the seats were taken.

The tram stopped in Argyle Street under the glass-walled railway bridge that carried the platforms of Central Station above the road. As they alighted from the tram, grateful to be still in the dry, Katherine explained to Alex that this was known by the local nickname of Heilanman's Umbrella.

"It's a very famous landmark because after the second phase of the clearances in the nineteenth century, tens of thousands of Highlanders who could only speak Gaelic came here looking for work. They were spread out all over the city and used to keep in touch by meeting here at the station, mainly at weekends. 'Heilanman' is a corruption of 'Highland man' and 'umbrella' originated because as it rains so frequently in Glasgow, this area offered a large sheltered meeting place! But over time, the Highlanders became integrated into Glasgow culture and the tradition ceased."

They went into the hotel, and after they had changed and had lunch, they sat in Alex's room drinking coffee and discussing what to do.

"I had hoped to show you around the city this afternoon," said Katherine, "but I think perhaps that isn't such a good idea as it's still raining very heavily outside."

"No, I'd rather be warm and dry in here," replied Alex, secretly glad they were not going out.

However, first things first. They needed to discuss the business in hand. So, being strong-minded for the moment, he said, "I do think that we ought to review what we know so far about Rupert and Mhairi and see if we can come up with any ideas as to what we should do next. I don't think that Jock is going to be a lot of help; his mind is not sufficiently reliable to give us anything concrete." Alex sighed. "It seems that any discoveries we do make always create more questions than they answer. It's incredibly frustrating."

"I agree," said Katherine. "So let's start at the beginning. Sir Charles Mathieson, shipping magnate, dies, leaving his entire estate – personal fortune, mansion in Park Lane, Minton House in Govan, Mathieson's Shipbuilding and Engineering firm on the Clyde – to his only son Rupert and his heirs."

"After first ensuring that his widow is well provided for financially," added Alex.

"Many years prior to this, as a young man, Rupert was sent by his father to Mathieson's to learn the trade of shipbuilding with a view to him taking it over from Sir Charles on his retirement. However, Rupert falls in love with Mhairi Hamilton, whose father, Jock, was a foreman at Mathieson's and whom we have just met and will see again tomorrow."

"Mhairi becomes pregnant, but the two lovers are not allowed to get married. Mhairi is sent to the Lake District to stay with her mother's sister Flora. Rupert is sent back to London."

"Her own mother, Anna, who has always been frail, falls ill and Mhairi is called back to Glasgow to look after her. She then disappears."

"After receiving a letter from Mhairi in distress, Rupert runs away from London, where he has been kept a virtual prisoner, in order to be with her."

184

"They obviously meet up because in her letter to Flora, Mhairi says that she and Rupert are together and very happy."

"And there the trail ends," concluded Alex.

"There are two other things to bear in mind," added Katherine. "You remember when you came to Cairnmor, and we were asking everyone whether they knew of any strangers who had come to the island with a baby about twenty-seven years ago? And that Robbie became quite grumpy when we asked him? He knows something, I'm sure, but won't reveal what it is. I've quizzed him a few times since then, but he closes up like a clam each time and becomes taciturn. I tried again just before I came over here, to no avail. So for the moment, he's no help."

"No, but I do agree with you that he knows something."

"Also, there seems to be no mention of the baby. Did it survive? Was it given away for adoption as Jock had been asked to do by Sir Charles?"

"That's something we need to find out." Alex picked up his briefcase and extracted a folder which he opened and said rather formally, "Next we need to look at the documentary evidence."

Katherine smiled and resisted the temptation to say that he was beginning to sound as though he was in court.

If Alex noticed her amusement, he didn't remark upon it but merely listed the contents of the folder. "We have the will, Rupert's diaries, Flora's letter to my Dad, the two letters from Mhairi to Rupert."

"Also Rupert's two books about Cairnmor and Scottish history with his annotations," added Katherine. "I still haven't been able to decipher all of them yet and those that I have done offer no further clues as they are just comments on various geographical or historical items in the books."

"And then we have the photograph of Mhairi and Rupert." Alex picked this out and studied it for a few moments. "You do look a bit like her, you know," he said, holding up the photograph and comparing it to Katherine.

"Don't be daft," she said, coming over to where he was sitting. "Firstly, you can't tell anything from that picture. If I had a photograph of my parents, which unfortunately I don't, then I expect you'd see a real resemblance, not just this purely speculative one," she concluded, slightly irritated by the mention of any resemblance to Mhairi.

"Well, in one of Mhairi's letters to Rupert she did say she wanted to call the baby 'Anna' if it was a girl, and your middle name is 'Anna'..." he said, teasing her, having sensed her annoyance.

"Mean person. Well, if we're going down that road, *your* middle name is Michael, but that doesn't mean that your friend Michael is your long lost twin brother. I am *not* Rupert and Mhairi's daughter, so there's an end to it!" and she threw a pillow at him.

"All right, I surrender. I accept defeat! Aagh!" as she threw another pillow, which landed squarely on his head.

"Right, that does it!" and he chased Katherine round the room, caught her and picked her up into his arms, and threw her down on the bed and began to tickle her.

"Enough, enough!" she exclaimed, giggling and gasping for air.

Alex, being very kind, ceased immediately and managed to resist the temptation to take off all her clothes and make love to her. He really did want to wait for this woman but it was taking all his resolve to do so, perhaps more resolve than he possessed.

"Be good though, wouldn't it?" said Katherine.

"What would?" he said distractedly, still wondering whether or not to give in to his desire.

"If I were the elusive baby."

"Why?"

"Just think of all that lovely inheritance money... ! I'd be rich! Ha-ha!" she said, rubbing her hands together, pretending to be gleeful and avaricious.

"I have enough to look after you very comfortably," said Alex, feigning indignation. "We wouldn't need anything else."

"I know. I'm only after you for your money. It's the only reason I'm marrying you, didn't I tell you that? I mean, I didn't fall in love with you *before* I knew how much you earned..." Katherine smiled at him, fluttering her eyelashes, sweetly provocative.

"Huh." Then he was serious. "That is, if I've got any work when I go back."

"What do you mean?"

"Before I left Chambers on Thursday, Sir John invited me to spend the weekend just gone at some Lord or other's country estate, returning to London on Monday morning as there's some important function or other that he thinks would be good for my career."

"He's beginning to sound like a record where the needle's got stuck!"

Alex chuckled. "Anyway, he was not best pleased when I said I was coming to see you in Glasgow and would be away for the whole week. When I informed him that Michael was handling my court case, I thought he was going to have apoplexy."

"Ah!"

"Quite. I expect I shall find I'm *persona non grata* when I get back on Friday."

"Surely he wouldn't do that? It would be incredibly short-sighted of him. No chambers can afford to alienate and lose any one of their top barristers."

"Who knows what goes on in that man's mind? I certainly don't, neither does Michael."

"Perhaps we should send him a referral to Dr Cameron at the Mental Hospital!"

"Good idea!" Pulling her towards him, he kissed her again, saying, "Goodness, I'm hungry!"

"Why don't we ring for tea?" suggested Katherine, intentionally obtuse. "And then we can carry on considering what we do next. We have rather distracted ourselves," she said, smoothing out her rumpled clothes and putting her hair back in place.

Alex grinned at her. "We have."

They placed their order and very soon, their tea arrived, served with cakes. While they consumed this repast, they looked at the documents.

Katherine's attention was drawn to the phrase in Flora's letter saying that Mhairi's letter to her had had a Cathcart postmark. When she pointed this out to Alex, he was immediately alert.

"Where is Cathcart?"

"It's south of the River Clyde. It's a mainly residential area, with a mix of tenements, terraces and villas. On the whole, it's quite a wealthy district, as the Cathcart and District Railway brought a lot of prosperity to the area when it first opened."

"Is it very large?"

"Quite large. It extends from Mount Florida and King's Park in the north-east to Muirend and Newlands in the south-west. It used to be part of Govan, but was incorporated into the City of Glasgow about twenty-five years ago."

"Why do you think it might be significant?"

"I was wondering if perhaps they made their home there."

"That's certainly possible. Although Mhairi could have deliberately posted the letter away from where she and Rupert were really living."

"That's a thought. But somehow I don't think so. Don't ask me why though. Do you think they got married?"

"I'd like to think that they did. How well do you know the area?" asked Alex.

"Quite well. I know Govan very well because I did my main teaching practice there, but a friend of mine on the same course lived in Cathcart. I used to stay with her at her parent's house at weekends sometimes, so she showed me quite a lot of the area."

"Are you still in touch with her?"

"No, unfortunately. The family moved away to Aberdeen and we lost contact."

"I think we should go to Cathcart tomorrow after we've visited Jock Hamilton again. It's a long shot, but we might turn something up."

"When people get married, they have to sign a marriage register, don't they?" asked Katherine.

"Yes."

"Where are those registers kept?"

"Usually at parish churches. I presume it's the same in Scotland," said Alex.

"There's a public library in Cathcart, attached to the Couper Institute in Clarkston Road. They might be able to help us."

"Then that, my love, is what we shall do! We have a generic letter from my Dad which gives an 'official' communication that we can show to anyone we need to and which adds authenticity to our search. He also wrote to Mathieson's asking if we could look round the shipyard. He made it open-ended so as not to tie us down to a particular day or time. They replied that they were quite happy for us to go there at any time. I'd quite like to see the shipyard, having read so much about it."

"So would I. Your Dad's very efficient isn't he?" said Katherine.

"Very."

"And don't forget, Flora thought that one of Mhairi's brothers might still work at Mathieson's."

"Of course. He may be able to tell us something."

The next day was fine and sunny and Glasgow took on a somewhat more pleasant mantle. They took the tram this time to the Royal Mental Hospital and were met by Sister Waverley, who showed them the way to the lounge where Jock Hamilton was seated by the window again.

"This is his customary place," she explained.

"How is he today?" asked Katherine.

"In his own world, I'm afraid. We had hoped that yesterday might have wrought some kind of change that lasted a little longer than usual, but that hasn't proved to be the case. Anyway, see what happens. You're very kind to do this," she added.

"It's very strange having to be someone else, but if it helps him, then I'm quite willing to do that."

"Thank you. I'll take you over to him."

They crossed the room towards him, but there was no spontaneous recognition, no acknowledgement of their presence. He sat there, perfectly content, muttering to himself, saying the same words over and over again.

Sister Waverley was about to apologize for bringing them here under false pretences, but Alex, politely, shook his head and indicated for her not to say anything.

He was listening intently to Jock's words and as he became accustomed to the syntax, he found he could distinguish what the old man was saying. Katherine stood very still so that she too could try to understand what Jock was muttering; both of them listening closely in order to interpret words which superficially appeared to be nonsense.

"Over the sea, over the sea, my Mhairi went over the sea. Over the sea, far, far away. Gone away over the sea. Too late, too late. Her poor old Pa was too late." He repeated this again and again, sometimes with the sentences in a different order, but always including the words 'over the sea' and 'too late'. Eventually, he grew tired, and sat there silently, vacant and staring, withdrawn into his own dream world once again.

Alex and Katherine looked at each other, wondering what it could all mean. They felt enormous sympathy for this broken man, who was still grieving for his long lost daughter; they were all too aware that even his diminished mental capacity appeared to offer no defence against the pain he still suffered.

Jock's withdrawal from his surroundings on that day was absolute and there was nothing further they could do to help him as there was no recognition, no connection. Thoughtfully, Katherine asked for a piece of paper and a pencil, which Sister Waverley immediately produced from her apron pocket, and wrote down the exact words that Jock had spoken before they could be forgotten or lost in translation. This might help them later on in trying to decipher their meaning, if there was one.

She felt very strongly that there would be and if there was, she knew instinctively that this could prove to be an important breakthrough.

Sister Waverley expressed her regret that their visit had proved to be not as they had anticipated. But Alex and Katherine were far more concerned about Jock's well-being than their own situation.

188

"I can see that he's in excellent hands," said Alex, "and we both really admire the work you're all doing here."

"Thank you. I shall pass your kind words onto Dr Cameron. He'll be delighted to hear it."

They bid farewell to Sister Waverley and made their way down to the tram stop, catching a tram back to the city centre before continuing south to their next destination – Couper's Institute and Public Library in Cathcart.

CHAPTER 24

Katherine and Alex arrived at the Library just before half past ten and were relieved to find that it was open. The building was constructed from blonde sandstone that complimented the reddish variety characteristically used in so many Glasgow tenement blocks and other buildings. However, like the majority of places in Glasgow, even out here in the suburbs, it was ingrained with the soot of hundreds of coal fires. Fortunately, Cathcart was far enough away to escape the worst of the industrial pollution which additionally affected much of the city.

The Institute itself had an air of elegance, with a first floor Venetian window, stone bracketed balcony and a bell tower with a spire. It had been built in 1887, with the library and hall being added in 1923.

The library was situated on the right of the Institute and Katherine and Alex ascended the stairs into the building. They were met with the hushed atmosphere that all libraries manifest and approached the librarian, seated at the central desk. She looked up from her task of sorting returned books, and listened attentively while Katherine explained what they were looking for.

"Yes, it is the Parish Churches you'll be needing. They hold records for births, marriages, deaths and baptisms. It will depend on which religion you are after as to which church you go to. I can give you a list if that would be helpful."

She wrote down a list of churches, road names and their denominations on a piece of paper. "The nearest ones to here are Cathcart Old in Carmunnock Road, and Cathcart South, which is just next door. I think they both keep records, actually, even though the church next door isn't the parish church. Those two are Church of Scotland. St Gabriel's is just round the corner in Merrylee Road, that's Roman Catholic, and the others are some distance away, but I've listed them all here. In the library, we also hold trade directories, which can be quite useful in certain circumstances."

"Thank you very much – this is so helpful," said Katherine, with genuine gratitude.

"We have guide books and tram timetables for sale as well if you need them."

"We may well come back for one of those a little later on."

"We are open until four o'clock today." And with the briefest of smiles, she returned to her work.

Alex and Katherine decided that they would begin in the obvious place with Cathcart South Church situated beside the Institute. The door creaked as they opened it but as the church was deserted, they decided to continue into Merrylee Road and St Gabriel's.

"I hope we have more luck here," observed Alex.

The church was constructed of grey stone and flanked by several coniferous trees, lending evergreen colour to the surroundings throughout the year. The lawns were well-manicured and the gardens neat and tidy, even in late February, with stone paths giving access to all points of the building.

They went up the stairs, through glass-panelled oak doors and into the interior calm, where a mixed scent of candles, bees-wax polish and incense pervaded the atmosphere. The priest had just finished hearing confession, and as his parishioner went on her way, he came over to where Katherine and Alex were standing and greeted them.

"Hello! I'm Father O'Donnell. I've not seen ye here before, I think."

They concurred, and this time it was Alex who explained why they had come and showed the priest Alastair's 'generic' letter.

"Ah, yes. We do keep all the records here. If you'd care to come with me, I'll show you."

He led them across the nave into a side room, which was obviously the vestry judging from the book and paper strewn table and the wardrobes bulging with white surpluses.

From a floor-to-ceiling cupboard on the far side of the room he extracted four large volumes, which he placed on the table, after first clearing a space by consigning the papers to the chair. Katherine thought that his gardener could give him a few lessons in tidiness and then immediately chastised herself for being uncharitable towards this genial, helpful man.

"From about 1909 onwards ye say?" He paused, and opened the first book, after checking the dates on the spine. "There ye are. Ye do the looking. I left my glasses at home this morning, so it's no good me doing anything – waste everybody's time it would," he added good-humouredly. Alex obliged, sitting at the table, and turning the pages slowly, checked each entry very carefully.

"Where are ye from?" asked Father O'Donnell, conversationally.

"Alex is from London and I'm from Cairnmor," replied Katherine.

"Cairnmor!" exclaimed the priest. "Well I'm blessed. Is that old renegade Aidan McPhee still there?"

Katherine laughed at this description. She must remember to tell him when she got home. "He is indeed."

"Och, we were at theological college together. He was always a bit of a rebel even then, never afraid to take on the hierarchy. We meet up from time to time at various symposiums up in the city or in Edinburgh and he always causes a stir, gives the powers that be a run for their money."

"I think the hierarchy have decided to let him alone now – they know they get short shrift every time they come to the island and try to change the way he does things. Father McPhee suits us very well though, we couldn't hope for a better priest."

"Well I'm of the opinion that's all that matters." Then he addressed Alex, "Have ye found anything?"

"No, nothing in 1909. Is this 1910?"

"Yes, it is – do help yeself. There's one or two things I must see to before I go home this morning and write my sermon for Sunday. I always write it on a Wednesday, otherwise I just keep putting it off. Give me a shout if ye need anything," and he disappeared out of the vestry door and back into the main part of the church.

Katherine went over to Alex and sat down beside him after first carefully lifting the pile of papers onto the floor beside her.

They pored over the books together: 1910, 1911, 1912… January, February – then, "Look, look!" exclaimed Katherine. "Here it is, here it is! A record of their marriage!" she said, unable to contain her excitement.

"At last, a real, tangible breakthrough!" responded Alex, equally delighted.

"They did get married – I'm so pleased! And look, this priest was certainly one for detail, because he seems to have written everything down. What a find!" Katherine got out her note-book and began to copy, reading aloud as she did so:

"16th February, 1912 at 2.00pm by Special Licence in St Gabriel's Roman Catholic Church, Merrylee Road, in the District of Cathcart. Rupert Charles Mathieson, Bachelor, of 43A Clarkstone Road, Cathcart – that's just where we've come from!" exclaimed Katherine. "Age 22, profession: Music Teacher – oh, that's a surprise! – and Mhairi Anna Hamilton, Spinster, of 43A Clarkstone Road, Age 21, Shop Assistant, in the presence of witnesses Elsie Anderson and Albert Anderson." Katherine hugged Alex. "So, they were living here in Cathcart, and at the same address, and it's not too far from the library! How amazing is that!"

The priest must have heard their exclamations, as he came back into the vestry. "Have ye found what ye're looking for, then?" he asked.

"Definitely," replied Alex. "It's just what we've been looking for. It says here that the witnesses were Elsie and Albert Anderson. Do you know them?"

"I did. When I came here about fifteen years ago, they were running the bakery in Clarkston Road…"

"Number forty-three?"

"I think it is; yes, it must be. Why?"

"Because the couple we're looking for were living at number forty-three at the time of their marriage." Katherine smiled up at Father O'Donnell, who smiled back, sharing in their pleasure of discovery.

"What happened to Elsie and Albert?" asked Alex. "Are they still there?"

"No, they retired a few years back and went to live with their daughter in Edinburgh. I don't have a forwarding address, unfortunately," and the priest scratched his chin, as though this might help him find the address out of thin air, or come up with some other suggestion.

"What happened to the bakery?"

"Och, it's still there, and still called 'Anderson's Bakery', but it now offers lunchtime rolls and soup as well as selling bread. Ye'd be as well to go there if ye want some lunch; they do very good soup. Ye might pick up some more information," he added, giving a knowing wink to Katherine and Alex. "Many people who go there have been around the area a great number of years; it's become quite a meeting place. Now, is there anything else I can be doing for ye?"

"Well," said Katherine, "could we look at the Baptism records as well?"

"For the same years?"

Katherine nodded. "If it's not too much trouble, that is."

"Och, it's no trouble at all!"

The priest collected up the books that they had finished with and replaced them carefully in the cupboard before selecting three tomes equally as cumbersome as the previous volumes had been. These he placed on the table in front of Katherine

192

and Alex. Yet despite searching through every one of them, they could find nothing; no record at all of Mhairi and Rupert's offspring.

They didn't talk about this, wanting to wait until they were alone, but they thanked Father O'Donnell for his time and his help.

"Och, don't mention it. I'm only too pleased that ye found what ye were looking for. Now, mind ye give that old rebel Aidan McPhee on Cairnmor my very best wishes when ye next see him."

Katherine promised that she would, and she and Alex waved goodbye to the priest as he stood on the church steps watching them turn once more towards Clarkstone Street.

They decided to go back to the library to look at the trade directories before going on to the baker's shop for their lunch.

"This is just so exciting," said Katherine.

"It's certainly fortunate that you knew about this library, and then finding out that this was the very part of Cathcart where Rupert and Mhairi lived and were married... It's almost too good to be true! I can't quite believe it."

"I think it's fate, or whatever you care to call it. I think we're meant to find them."

"Well, there's still a lot of research to do yet, we still don't know where they are."

"Wouldn't it be wonderful if they were still around in this part of Cathcart?"

"I think Father O'Donnell would have said if they had been."

"Pessimist! But wasn't he helpful? I wonder what Father McPhee will say about him?"

"Probably call him an old reactionary!" and stifling their laughter, they entered Couper's Institute Library once more.

They asked for the trade directories for 1909–1912 as their starting point and searched carefully through all the entries, but there was no mention of Rupert anywhere in 1909. They turned to 1910, and Alex found a violin teacher named Robert Murchieson, advertising '*reasonable rates*; *will travel*'.

"Looks like Rupert had competition," said Alex, speaking *sotto voce* and sounding disappointed.

But Katherine wasn't put off so easily. "There must be a contact address." But the page was torn, and they were unable to make out the wording.

So, they turned to 1911. The same teacher was there again, this time with a much fuller advertisement: 'Robert Murchieson, Teaching Diploma from the Royal College of Music, London. Fully Qualified Teacher of Violin, Piano and Music Theory. Lessons given in All Standards. Reasonable Rates. Willing to travel. Also available for Music Recitals at Weddings and Birthday Parties etc.'.

"And the address?" asked Katherine, a rising note of excitement creeping into her whispered question.

Alex chuckled. "I suspect our minds may be working along similar lines."

"They often do," replied Katherine, "especially now," she added and promptly blushed.

Alex quickly looked round to check that no one was watching and then kissed her lightly on the lips.

"Come on, tell me. It's 43A Clarkstone Road isn't it?!"

"It is indeed!"

"Ha!"

Her exclamation reverberated around the library, disturbing the studied calm. Some unseen person said, "Ssh" and Katherine and Alex suppressed their laughter.

Alex whispered, "He wouldn't have used his real name because that would have been too obvious and might have led to them being discovered."

"Exactly. And Robert Murchieson and Rupert Mathieson have enough similarity to give Rupert an alias that he could feel comfortable with…"

"And the names are just different enough to be an effective disguise," finished Alex.

They turned to 1912, which contained the same advertisement. They asked for 1913 and 1914 but were disappointed to find that 'Robert Murchieson' was not in either of them.

"What's happened to him, I wonder?" said Katherine, her mood of elation dissipating rapidly.

"Any number of things, I suppose. They could have moved to another area of Glasgow or somewhere else in Scotland…"

"It's too early for him to have been caught up in the Great War. Oh dear, the possibilities are endless…" She sighed. "I hope we haven't come up against another dead end."

"So do I. It's so tantalizing. But now I think it's time for lunch – soup and rolls at number forty-three sound very appealing!"

They returned the directories to the librarian and purchased a *Seeing Glasgow by Tram and Bus, 1937* guide book, which brought back memories for Katherine, as she still had her *Where to Go by Tram and Bus* guide book from 1932, which had cost her all of tuppence and had served her well during her Diploma year. They thanked the librarian and set off on the next part of their search, wondering what this might bring forth.

The café was quite small, with only five tables and a long counter across the width of the wall at the back. There was a hinged section in the counter allowing movement into the main part of the café to and from the kitchen. All available seats were taken, and a few people had propped themselves up against the counter.

A lively buzz of conversation ensued, and Alex had to speak loudly to make himself heard above the level of voices surrounding them. Father O'Donnell had been correct; it was quite a meeting place, with any number of subjects being vigorously discussed at the same time.

"We're very full at the moment, but if ye don't mind standing up, ye're welcome to soup and rolls," said the proprietor in response to Alex's enquiry. "It's vegetable broth today." He called out to the back: "Soup and rolls for two," then turned back to Katherine and Alex. "Would ye like anything to go with it – cup of tea? Cake?"

"Both would be fine, thank you," replied Alex.

They had already aroused considerable interest when they walked into the café, and now, Alex's well-spoken English accent caused the conversation gradually to cease, starting at the counter where he could be heard and gradually filtering its

194

way towards the tables positioned near the doorway, until everyone had stopped talking.

Alex and Katherine found themselves the object of close scrutiny and exchanged the briefest of raised eyebrows with each other, as the situation now demanded that they offer some sort of explanation for their presence They had to decide who was going to speak first – both were used to public speaking – but would Katherine's Scottish accent yield a more favourable response in this environment?

Deciding that perhaps it would be better for her to lead the way, she discreetly pointed to herself, and Alex nodded his agreement.

Clearing her throat, nervous despite her classroom experience, she said, "We're looking for two people who used to live here over twenty years ago – they were called Rupert and Mhairi Mathieson?" When these names drew no response, only blank stares, she added, "Someone here may have known one of them as Robert Murchieson – a violin and piano teacher?" Again, silence. Katherine and Alex stood there with bated breath, not quite knowing what to do next.

Then someone spoke – an elderly lady in the corner of the room. "Now what would ye be wantin' to find them for exactly?"

Alex took up the thread of the conversation. "Er… Robert… has come into an inheritance and we're trying to trace him and his wife in order to tell them of this. They er… lost contact with their families all that time ago. His father died about six months ago and… Robert… is his legal heir."

"Is it a big inheritance, then?" asked a man propped up by the counter.

"A fair amount," said Alex.

"And who might ye be?"

"My name is Alexander Stewart, and this is my fiancée Katherine MacDonald. I come from London, where I'm a barrister"

"An advocate, ye mean?"

"Yes, that's right and Katherine comes from Cairnmor, where's she's a teacher."

"What's you're connection to all this?"

"My father's a solicitor and… Robert's… father was one of his clients. I'm acting on my father's behalf."

"Do ye have proof?"

Suspicious lot, thought Alex. "I do. My father has written this letter to explain why we're doing this." He handed the letter to the man, who glanced at it briefly.

"It says here though that ye be lookin' for Rupert and Mhairi Mathieson."

"That's correct," replied Alex. "We understand that Rupert used a different name professionally so that his real identity could be… protected."

"I suppose that's wise if ye're the son of *Sir Charles Mathieson* owner of *Mathieson's Shipyard* and wanted to remain anonymous," declared the man, reading on and emphasizing the important words, having taken on the role of spokesperson for the gathered customers. There was a gasp from one or two quarters.

"We have a photograph of the two of them, if you'd like to see it," said Katherine, and Alex handed it round.

A few people nodded to each other. "Aye it's them all right."

195

"Oh, you knew them!" exclaimed Katherine, with relief. "Please tell us about them. It's become sort of personal to Alex and me now, and we'd really like to know what they were like and what happened to them. We so want to find them, and not just because of the inheritance."

"Och, there can be no harm in helping, can there?" suggested the old lady. "Who would have thought that our Robert and his lovely wife Moira were related to the owner of Mathieson's? Robert taught my son the piano and a very fine teacher he was too. He taught many youngsters round and about and earned a nice living from it, I imagine. A good reputation round here is worth its weight in gold and word of mouth is the best kind of advertisement."

"He was good on the violin, too," joined in another woman seated at the side of the room. "Played for our wedding he did. His wife made the food. A rare cook she was too. Worked here in the shop with old Mr and Mrs Anderson. Very kind the baker and his wife were to Robert and Moira; they looked after them well."

Someone else took up the story, a woman in a headscarf. "Aye that's reet. Moira had been ill and had just come out of hospital when they first arrived. Elsie and Albert took them in and wouldn't take rent until Robert had got his teaching all set up and Moira was on her feet again and could earn her keep."

"Did you know why she'd been ill?" asked Katherine, thinking it might have something to do with the baby.

"Och no. It was not our business to pry, but her choice if she'd wanted to tell us, but she didn't, so we never knew. We were curious, mind you."

Katherine asked one of the two important questions to which they needed an answer, "Did they ever have any children?"

"No, no. There were no bairns. We always thought it a great shame as Moira was lovely with the wee ones."

And Alex asked the other, "What happened to them?"

"Och, they emigrated to Canada!"

Katherine and Alex looked at each other open mouthed, both of them recalling in an instant Jock's words, "*... over the sea, over the sea, my Mhairi went over the sea...*" They knew then that he had spoken the truth; that it wasn't the incoherent rambling of a senile old man, but the very real pain of loss.

The woman wearing the headscarf continued, "Aye, that's what they'd wanted from the start and they saved up all their money for the fare. We missed them very much when they left. A lovely young couple. They were here for about three years, I think."

"Do you know whereabouts in Canada they went to? I'm sorry to ask so many questions," said Alex apologetically, "but it is very important."

"No, I'm afraid not. I don't think they said. It was just Canada. They wanted to make a new life for themselves – and who could blame them?"

Katherine and Alex thanked the people who had spoken, and for the moment, when no one could tell them anything further about Robert and Moira, they both ate their soup before it was completely cold.

Soon, people came up to them and asked them questions about Mathieson's Shipyard and said how they would never have guessed that there was any connection with their Robert. Robert and Moira were well-liked but were very

196

private people they explained, and were very protective of their personal lives. However, they had been very close to Elsie and Albert, that much was certain, who unfortunately, had both passed away now.

The café closed at two o'clock, and reluctantly, the discussion came to a close. The people of Cathcart, though initially reticent, ultimately had provided Katherine and Alex with information that took them on yet another stage in their journey of discovery.

They bid farewell to their lunchtime friends with gratitude and took the train from Cathcart Station back to Glasgow Central. Once at the hotel, they sat in the lounge drinking tea and eating cakes and discussing what their next steps would be given all they had learned that day. They had discovered much but Canada was a huge area in which to search.

Once again, trying to find Rupert and Mhairi had become the proverbial looking for a needle in a haystack, although they knew two things for certain. Tomorrow, they would visit Mathieson's and then somehow, try to ascertain Rupert and Mhairi's exact destination in Canada.

That night, Katherine sat up in bed studying Rupert's books on Scotland, looking at them afresh in light of their recent discovery; hoping they might reveal some clue as to the couple's whereabouts. In the early hours of the morning, she found just what she had been looking for – annotations that finally made sense.

Satisfied with what she had discovered, but unable to tell Alex until the morning, Katherine turned out the light.

CHAPTER 25

The main office of Mathieson's Shipyard was of an ordinary redbrick construction, but with attention to the kind of detail, such as turreted pillars and arched windows, that rendered it distinctive.

Katherine and Alex entered through large wrought-iron gates that led into a very small courtyard and then went into the building itself through a glass-panelled door, straight into the administrative offices.

A receptionist took their names, after hearing Alex's explanation, and telephoned through to the manager's office. Presently, a good-looking man in his early forties and with a pleasant, open manner came through the door of the room behind and introduced himself.

"Hello! I'm the deputy works manager, Laurence Hart. The manager is away on sick leave at the moment, and won't be back at work for some months, I'm afraid. So I'm running the place for the time being." He indicated with his hand the room he had just vacated and said, "Please do come into the office. I've read the letter your father wrote explaining the circumstances of your proposed visit – in fact it was me who answered it – and I'm very glad that you were able to come here."

Katherine and Alex did as they were asked and followed him into a large room containing a mahogany desk and enormous book shelves, some neatly lined with folders and ledgers, and others with text books which seemed to cover all aspects of ships, ship-building and engineering.

On the floor were piles of paper, which gave the initial impression of chaos, but took on a different aspect when Laurence Hart explained that in the manager's absence, he was sorting through documents and papers and books that had accumulated over the years and were in desperate need of filing, amending or discarding.

But it was the painting on the wall behind the desk that dominated the office – an imposing portrait of a grey-haired man, whose powerful personality seemed to leap from the frame and fill the room. His countenance was stern and his jaw set in a determined line, and yet there was humour and intelligence in the blue eyes that seemed to reach out to Katherine as she studied the face before her. Despite all that she knew about him, she could not help taking to him and found it fascinating to see what he actually looked like.

"Is that Sir Charles Mathieson?" she asked.

"It is indeed. A remarkable likeness, apparently. I've only been here six months, so I never met him personally, though I'd like to have done. He was both respected and feared, even hated by some people. But no one could doubt his engineering prowess, nor his eye for detail in his ship designs. He was a brilliant businessman as well as a remarkable engineer and draughtsman. Did you know that he built up this company from virtually nothing? He's something of a hero of mine, actually."

And, slightly shamefacedly, Laurence Hart stopped, afraid that perhaps he had said too much in front of two people he had only just met.

Alex, who had been studying the portrait while the manager was speaking, now turned his gaze to Katherine and smiled at her thoughtfully as she made her reply.

"That's really good to know because we have only come across the more negative side of his character through reading his son's diaries," she said, wishing to reassure this very human man.

"Are you any nearer to finding Rupert Mathieson?" enquired Laurence.

"We discovered yesterday that he and his wife emigrated to Canada," replied Alex. "That is something, but it throws up more problems than it solves. Canada is an enormous place, and they could have travelled anywhere. But Katherine has an idea, which may or may not be helpful."

Katherine threw him a slightly quizzical look. She had felt her idea to be very plausible and slightly resented the implication that it might not be as good a suggestion as she believed it to be. However, ignoring this, she said, "Rupert had two books on Scotland – one a travel guide to Cairnmor, and the other a history of the country. He made annotations in both of them, most of which I've been able to decipher, some I haven't. Until last night, that is. The page most heavily written on in the Cairnmor book is about Colonel Rowan Clancy and how he forced hundreds of islanders to go to Canada. The other is in the history of Scotland, describing the Highland clearances. But the place that both pages have in common is Nova Scotia and the annotations are to do with travel, passports, possible routes and how Mhairi would be happiest, if she were in a new place, to be surrounded by her own people. All the notes are hastily scribbled, but there nonetheless."

Katherine's idea was treated with enthusiasm by Laurence, who replied without hesitation, "That is perfectly possible. Ships still left Glasgow taking emigrants to Canada, the United States and Australia at the beginning of this century. Let me see, if I remember correctly, the Anchor Line went to New York and Boston, Donaldson's sailed to South America and I think it was the Allan Line that went to Canada. Of course, all the companies went to other places as well, but those were their main destinations. The Allan Line's Head Office is in Bothwell Street, I think. It would definitely be worth your while paying them a visit. With any luck, they may have passenger lists and copies of ships' manifests from way back."

He seemed slightly hesitant, then said: "I'd very much like to come with you if I may."

"Of course," said Alex, liking this man's immediacy of response and willingness to help. "But we wouldn't want to take you away from your work."

"I can justify it totally – at Mathieson's, we need to know as much as your father does where Rupert is now. This is a public limited company; we have shareholders and we are without a chairman, which is not a good place to be. Even in his last year, Sir Charles Mathieson kept the shipyard under close scrutiny and the orders placed while he was alive are still being built. In fact, we have eight ships under construction at the moment. Mathieson's reputation will carry it through for a long time, but any firm needs stability and someone at the helm."

Alex regarded this likeable man astutely and asked, "What about you?"

Laurence's response was immediate. "Me? Oh, I'd love the chance to run it – it's an amazing place to work and I find every aspect of the industry totally absorbing. My father used to bring me down to the Clyde when I was little to see the ships being built and I've always wanted to be a part of it. It's noisy, dirty and dangerous but I love it!" He stopped talking again, but Alex had one more question for him.

"What about the legal side of things?"

"We have a small team of solicitors, whom we employ 'in house' and known advocates we can call on should any dispute arise. This is a huge firm, with over five thousand employees, so we need clear representation. In fact, we're trying to stop a hostile take-over bid at the moment from Dunbar-Moncrieff."

"Will you be successful?"

"I hope so. Our cash-flow situation is excellent, so we should be able to fight them off. So, what would you like to do now? I can show you round the shipyard, or we could go to the Allan Line offices first."

"Shall we look round the shipyard as we're here?" said Alex, and Katherine agreed.

"In which case, I'll ask my secretary to telephone the shipping office, find out if they can help us, and if so, book us an appointment. Please excuse me for a moment." He went out of the room, returning a few minutes later, a smile lighting up his face. "Good news! They do have passenger lists at the office and I've booked an appointment for us this afternoon at two-thirty. So, I shall now take you on a guided tour here and then we'll have lunch in the canteen."

They left the office and proceeded up the stairs to the drawing offices, and thence out of the administrative block to see the engine, joiners', sheet metal and mechanics' shops; the brass foundry, stock yard, power house and then on to the ship berths and fitting-out basin.

All through the tour, Laurence spoke to the men at work, asking questions and being asked questions himself, which he was able to answer immediately. He was very knowledgeable, spoke with authority and seemed very well respected by the men working in all the departments that they visited. He may have been there only a short time, but he knew the firm inside out and Alex guessed that for the moment, Mathieson's was in a safe and capable pair of hands.

Laurence guided them expertly throughout the tour, giving clear explanations at every opportunity, and Katherine and Alex ended the morning with a real understanding of how a shipyard functioned.

However, the physical aspects of the industry were overwhelming. They felt dwarfed by the sheer height of the ships under construction; by the enormity of the wooden scaffolding and towering cranes; they were stunned by the deafening cacophony of sound produced by the riveting, and the crackling and sparking of the welding. They admired the skill and focus of the men who carried out this work, marvelling at their faultless teamwork and appreciative of their sense of humour, which was legendary, according to Laurence.

"The Clyde is one of the most important ship-building areas in the world," he added, as they came to the end of their tour, walking in the shadowy area between the buildings and the ships. "And Mathieson's is regarded as being one of the greatest," he concluded, with obvious professional pride.

As they re-emerged into the sunlight, he said, "Now, let's go and see about lunch."

He led the way once again, taking them back through the stock yard to a building set some way back from the others, from which emanated delicious smells of food.

"This was built around 1920, when one of the union representatives went to Sir Charles and requested that all the workers had a subsidized lunch as part of their working day, and an hour off to eat it. He was very reluctant at first, as you can imagine, but relented and this was the result. As with everything he did, once he had made up his mind, he was determined that it should be the very best. I always eat here; the food is second to none."

Laurence was not wrong, and having consumed a satisfying meal, they left Mathieson's and travelled back towards the city centre, crossing the Clyde, and onwards to the West End.

Bothwell Street was lined with tall, elegant three-storey sandstone buildings. Just beyond the junction of Boswell and Wellington Street was Allan House, its name carved into patterned stonework above the door. Inside, there was a purposeful atmosphere, with customers who wished to travel booking their passage abroad.

A clerk led the three of them into a room in the depths of the building, which contained filing cabinets that extended almost to the ceiling. He opened a large drawer in one of these, and produced several volumes of documents which he laid out before them. These covered the years 1910 to 1914 and were clearly marked with the Allan Line flag – a distinctive red, white and black funnel design emblazoned with the company crest. The documents contained passenger lists, ships' manifests and general information for the passengers on a voyage, as well as instructions and duties for the crew.

With a sense of great anticipation, they each began their individual search – passenger lists for the S.S. *Pretorian...* the ship's manifest... the S.S. *Virginian...* the ship's manifest and passenger lists... names of hundreds of people starting a new life in Canada and the United States... destinations to Quebec, Montreal, New York... 1910... 1911... 1912... the S.S *Scotian* – Katherine did a double take – Glasgow... Liverpool... *Halifax...* Boston. Her eye travelled back to Halifax.

"Where's Halifax?"

"Nova Scotia, I think," replied Laurence.

With renewed intent, Katherine immediately began to scan the manifest:

Passengers: 1348 + 28 children + 4 infants
Saloon – 0   2nd Cabin – 339   Steerage – 1041
1. Captain: Gavin Hamilton, Commander
2. Chief Officer: Robert Kinloch
3. Purser: Ivie Alexander
4. Surgeon: Dr Carruthers

5. Chief Engineer: John T. Cummings
6. Chief Steward: William Campbell
7. Matron: Mrs Morrison
8. Stewardess: Mrs Ferguson
Port of Embarkation:
Glasgow   Mar 30 1912
Liverpool   Mar 31 1912

then further down the page:

Arrived at... Halifax... April 8th 1912

After this were the details of the cabin inspections for Second Cabin and Steerage, both of which were given a clean bill of health. Everyone arrived safe and well, and no one was hospitalized. There were no deaths, births or marriages.

Katherine moved onto the passenger lists. She discovered that the most expensive way to travel was Saloon Class, followed by Second Cabin and then Steerage.

In which were Rupert and Mhairi most likely to travel? Steerage? Second Cabin? They had had to save hard for their fare, so she presumed that they might have travelled in steerage. But having scanned over a thousand names (not in alphabetical order), she had no joy.

Beginning to feel dispirited, she turned to the Second Cabin list. Once again, they were in no particular order. Her eyes travelled quickly down the list of names, selecting all those beginning with 'M': McKenzie, MacCleod, Murray, Muir, Morgan, Munroe... Katherine developed a crick in her neck; she stretched her back and moved her head from side to side. And then her eye fell on the name *Mathieson... Mr Rupert Mathieson, Room 17 and Mrs Rupert Mathieson, Room 17.*

"I've found them!" she exclaimed.

Alex and Laurence immediately came over to her.

"They're here! 30th March, 1912 to Halifax, *Nova Scotia*! You see, I was right!" She couldn't resist a dig at Alex for his less than enthusiastic reception to her prediction.

"I never doubted you in the slightest," he said, grinning at her.

"Huh!" said Katherine.

Laurence was highly amused by this and turned to look at the list. "That must be them." He scanned the next document. "Look, this appears to be a personal history questionnaire of all the passengers on the ship. There's pages and pages of it! But it does seem to be in alphabetical order."

"Thank goodness for that!" exclaimed Katherine.

They found Rupert and Mhairi easily this time and the three of them examined the list together.

Name: Mr Rupert Mathieson. Age: 22 years. Sex: Male. Occupation: Violin and Piano Teacher. Religion: Roman Catholic. Family: Mr and Mrs Albert

Anderson (and the address). Intentions: to begin a new life in Canada; to continue with music teaching and to train as an architect.

Name: Mrs Rupert Mathieson (Mhairi). Age: 21 years. Sex: Female. Occupation: Cook. Religion: Roman Catholic. Family: Mr and Mrs Albert Anderson. Intentions: to begin a new life in Canada and to work as a cook.

"So they gave Elsie and Albert's name as their family," mused Alex.

"Who are they?" asked Laurence.

"They were the two people who looked after Mhairi and Rupert when they first arrived in Cathcart. They were witnesses at their wedding," answered Katherine. "But it's interesting that Rupert still wanted to be an architect. I wonder if he ever realized his dream?"

"Well, it will make Dad's task easier when he starts writing his letters to Halifax to try and locate them, whatever Rupert's occupation was," said Alex.

"But there's one thing we haven't looked at," said Katherine. "All the passengers with children have them documented on the passenger list. There's no mention of Rupert and Mhairi's child, who I suppose would have been about three years old by then."

"They had a child?" asked Laurence, now hooked on this search.

"Well, this is something we're not too sure about," she replied. "Mhairi was pregnant when she and Rupert disappeared. Sir Charles Mathieson was insistent that the baby should be adopted immediately after it was born and Mhairi's father was instructed to carry out the dreadful deed. We presume it was to escape this fate for their baby that they decided to run away. But we can't find any record of the child. The people we spoke to in Cathcart yesterday who knew them said they didn't have a baby. So that leaves two possibilities – either the baby was adopted, or died when it was very young. We have no way of knowing now, unless we manage to locate the two of them. Either way, it would have been awful for them."

Laurence was sympathetic. As a father himself with a growing family, he could well understand Rupert and Mhairi's plight. He couldn't wait to go home that evening and tell his wife all about his day. Thinking of that, he said, "Look, it's getting late. The office here will close soon." He hesitated again. "Would you like to have supper with my wife and me this evening? I'm sure she won't mind."

Katherine and Alex looked at each other. It was their last evening together before they had to return to their respective homes. But they sensed a developing friendship between the three of them and neither Katherine nor Alex wished to seem churlish and refuse.

Laurence picked up on their hesitation and said that he hoped he hadn't appeared presumptuous. Alex reassured him and, after raising an eyebrow enquiringly at Katherine who nodded in reply, thanked him and said they would be glad to accept his invitation.

So it was arranged. Katherine copied down all the necessary information and they left Allan House with a shared sense of achievement, but also the knowledge that there was still an enormous amount of ground to cover. Alex hoped that it could be done by judicious correspondence which would yield the results that they hoped for.

Laurence arranged to collect them that evening at seven and returned to Mathieson's to finish his working day. Katherine and Alex walked the short distance back to the hotel, from where their host collected them promptly at the appointed time and drove them to his home – a fine, unpretentious detached villa in Riverside Road in Newlands, not too far from Merrylee Road where Katherine and Alex had been the previous day.

His wife Dorothy, very welcoming and hospitable, was some years younger than her husband and the same age as Katherine. They had two small children of three and five years, with another baby on the way.

Alex and Laurence were immediately deep in conversation, disappearing into the latter's study, and Dorothy introduced Katherine to her children. They were very polite and well-behaved and Katherine commented on this.

"Well, you should see them sometimes," she said, looking at the youngest meaningfully, who promptly plugged his thumb into his mouth and demanded to be lifted up. Dorothy did this expertly and safely, balancing the little boy on her hip. Thomas laid his head on his mother's shoulder, tired and a little shy, and observed Katherine intently through his long eyelashes.

His older sister Daisy, who was a confident young lady, said to Katherine, "He's tired. Mummy took us to the park today and we ran around for the whole afternoon. It didn't rain at all."

"Well that's good," replied Katherine. "It rains a lot in Glasgow, doesn't it?"

"Yes. How do you know that?"

"Well, I lived here for about a year."

"Oh."

"Come on, Daisy," said Dorothy. "It's time for bed."

"Can Miss MacDonald read me a story?" Daisy asked her mother.

"Do you mind?"

Katherine smiled. "Not at all."

"This is definitely going to be our last!" Dorothy said to Katherine, patting her stomach, as they took the two children upstairs. "We always wanted three, and that's going to be quite enough. But I wouldn't have it any other way. Do you want a family?"

"Of course," replied Katherine. "But we haven't specified a number, they're just vaguely 'children' at the moment."

"When are you getting married?"

"At the beginning of April."

"Not too long to wait then?"

"No. But we don't manage to see a great deal of each other as I live on Cairnmor and Alex lives in London."

"Where will you live after you're married?"

"We plan to live in London, although I'm hopeful that we'll visit the island as often as Alex's work allows us to." She smiled encouragingly at the children. "Now about this story…" and while Dorothy pottered round the bedroom tidying up the children's things, Katherine read Beatrix Potter's *Tale of Samuel Whiskers* to her captive audience, who when the tale was finished, snuggled down under their blankets and went to sleep.

It proved to be a very enjoyable evening, with plenty to talk about. Laurence and Dorothy had met because her father, a fellow engineer in the same firm as Laurence, had invited the younger man back to his house for supper – in order to meet his daughter. The plan worked. They fell in love and, after a lengthy courtship, during which time, Laurence saved all the money he could, they were married. Once he had secured the job at Mathieson's, they were able to move out to Newlands, an area they had always liked and regarded as an ideal place in which to live. They were genuinely interested by Katherine and Alex's story, but especially that of Rupert and Mhairi.

Time passed swiftly and eventually Alex and Katherine had to say farewell to Dorothy. Laurence drove them back to their hotel.

"Thank you so much for a wonderful evening," said Katherine, as they bid goodbye to their host.

"I hope it won't be too long before we meet again," he replied.

They promised to stay in contact. Alex said that Laurence would hear from his father very shortly, and that they would keep him up to date with any developments concerning Rupert and Mhairi.

The next morning, Katherine took Alex to the Argyle Street Arcade, where he found himself surrounded by glittering jewellery shops.

"I thought…" began Katherine.

"Yes…" said Alex cautiously.

"… that we could buy our wedding rings here."

"Oh you did, did you?" he said, putting his arms on her shoulders, looking deep into her eyes, teasing her a little. "Trying to make sure of me, huh?!"

"Yes."

He smiled and kissed her. "I'm not going anywhere, my darling. You and I are together now," he said, in all seriousness. "We shall be married, I promise you that absolutely."

"I know." She smiled at him, her niggling doubts about the strength of his commitment reassured by his words. "You see it's *the* place in Glasgow to come to buy jewellery and I thought…"

"Yes…?"

"… I thought it would be a good idea to do that before we go home, because the next time we see each other will be just a week before the wedding…"

"And there won't be the time…"

"… or the opportunity," finished Katherine. "It's a good place to come. Look, it's even got a hammer beam roof…" (they both looked up at the glass ceiling above their heads to the ornate roof trusses) "… and I thought you'd feel at home, even though it is just a single one and not a double hammer beam like Middle Temple…"

Alex threw his head back and laughed. He led her into the nearest shop, where they found exactly what they were looking for.

Later, after they had said a very reluctant farewell, Katherine sat on the train to Oban with her ring case open in her lap admiring her shining gold band.

Suddenly, the wedding was no longer just a dream on the distant horizon, but had become a reality. The joy of this outweighed her sadness at having to face yet another separation from the man she loved with all her heart.

Unbeknown to her, Alex was doing the same with his ring, as the 'Royal Scot' express carried him rapidly back to England. The next time he made this journey, it would be to bring Katherine home as his wife and this knowledge was to sustain him through the month he had to endure before they could be in each other's arms again.

CHAPTER 26

Cairnmor
April, 1937

The day dawned quietly, just like any other day, but Katherine was already awake, alert and excited. She lay in bed with her hands behind her head, contemplating the ceiling and the grey, early light reflected onto it through the uncurtained windows.

Today was the beginning of the rest of her life. Alex would be arriving on the steamer later that afternoon, and in exactly a week's time, the waiting would be over for both of them and they would be married, finally together. The time since they had last seen each other had gone quickly; the week in Glasgow, a distant dream.

Katherine reached into the drawer of her bedside table and pulled out the ring case containing her wedding ring. She had gained much comfort from this sparkling gold band during the past month and also, as always, from Alex's letters which were full of affection and the absorbing minutiae of his life.

She took a deep satisfying breath. At last she could relax, knowing that this had been their last separation; the last time that their emotions would be battered by the constant meeting and parting. She longed for Alex, she ached for him and today, he would be here.

She put the ring away and got out of bed, too restless to linger. The sky outside had not changed from uniform grey, but even this slight concern about the weather could not undermine her happiness and sense of anticipation.

Katherine dressed quickly and replenished the fires with peat, firstly in the sitting room, where an empty tea chest stood in the corner, waiting to be filled with her books.

She had listened and adhered to Alastair's sound advice, given before Christmas while she was in London, and had not rushed into packing up her belongings. She had been kind to herself, still unable to bear the pain of leaving her beloved Cairnmor. To be surrounded daily by the evidence of her departure would have been too much; there would be time to complete that task later. After she was married. Meanwhile, there were enough changes with which to contend.

The first change concerned the cottage which had always been her home. In accordance with Scots Law, the tenancy of the croft would become Alex's on their marriage, but he had said that it would always be hers to do with as she wished and she was grateful to him for his consideration.

The second change affected her career. The round table by the door was now devoid of the children's exercise books waiting to be marked, and a small involuntary sigh escaped from Katherine's lips.

Her resignation had been accepted, with regret but with understanding, by the Director of the Education Board, who had been instrumental in appointing her to the post on the island originally. Her replacement, a young man of great promise, would be starting after the Easter break. She had not yet met him, but she wished him well.

It had been very hard to let go of her school and although she would still see the children when she came to visit Cairnmor, she would no longer be a part of their lives in the same way and have the joy and privilege of watching them grow up, knowing that she had had some influence in drawing out their latent talents and abilities. Nor would she be an integral part of her friends' lives, no matter how often she returned to the island.

Her close friendship with Mary would always remain, of that she was certain, but there were many other people whom she would miss seeing every day; friends with whom she habitually exchanged pleasantries and shared the small details that made living in a close community so special.

Resolutely, Katherine took a deep breath, not allowing herself to dwell too much on these things. After putting peat onto the fire in the kitchen range, she ate her breakfast and decided to go out for a walk.

Yesterday had been very mild and sunny but, in typical island fashion, today was a complete contrast: cold with a rising wind, so she needed both her coat and shawl. It was quite possible that *Lochfoyle,* with Alex, Alastair, Lily and Michael on board, would have an unpleasant crossing.

Her early morning optimism was gradually replaced with mild anxiety, which, later that afternoon when she went down to Lochaberdale and the steamer did not arrive at its appointed time, developed into real concern. Four o'clock passed, then five, then six…

At first, Katherine and Mary sat together on the harbour wall, watching the white-flecked sea outside the harbour, engaging in gentle conversation. Around them was the usual bustle of activity that preceded the arrival of the steamer every Saturday. But gradually even this ceased as, leaving crates, boxes and more general luggage stacked on the quayside, people began to disperse; homewards, if they lived nearby, or up to the Lochaberdale Hotel which afforded a good vantage point, enabling them to see *Lochfoyle* as it approached the sheltered haven of Loch Aberdale.

John and Marion were kept busy serving tea and cakes to those who requested them, and soon Katherine and Mary joined their fellow villagers, chilled by the wind and unwilling to remain by the quayside any longer. They found a quiet corner of the dining room by a large picture window, looking out onto a dreary landscape, where rain had begun to fall from the leaden skies. The hills surrounding the bay had disappeared into a fine grey mist and Katherine was sorry that Alastair's, Lily's and Michael's first impression of Cairnmor would not be a more auspicious one. She said as much to Mary, who agreed.

"Aye, it's a shame all right," she replied, stirring her tea, which John had just brought in for them, and selecting one of the cakes. "Adam's going to go out with his fishing boat again tonight. The three of them seem to go out in all weathers. He won't listen to anything I say."

"Has he kept his promise and is not drinking?" asked Katherine.

Mary was hesitant. "He was, ever since I spoke to Father McPhee. At least I think so," she added, uncertainty colouring her voice. "Sometimes, though, just recently, he's come home from his fishing trips with his breath smelling of the alcohol, though he thinks he's hiding it from me by sucking peppermints. There doesn't seem to be a lot of fish being landed either."

"Oh Mary. You can't let him get back into all that. Have you said anything to Fiona and Gordon?"

"Not yet. They'd have a fit. Dad would thump him one, for sure."

"Not that I condone violence in any shape or form, but it might do some good if that errant husband of yours had some sense knocked into him. Monitor it, Mary, please don't let it go on for any length of time again."

"I promise," replied her friend, tears welling up in her eyes, her bottom lip trembling.

Katherine looked at Mary's face, pale and drawn with the strain and constant anxiety; dark smudges under her eyes from lack of sleep. There seemed to be no easy solution to this problem and she felt helpless, especially as she would soon be going away and unable to protect and support her friend.

The grandfather clock in the hall struck seven and then, emerging through the rain-soaked gloom, *Lochfoyle* drew near, steaming its way gently into the harbour. There was a flurry of activity, as everyone vacated their seats and made their way down to the quayside to greet the arrival of the steamer.

Katherine's heart was thumping and her breath seemed to catch in her chest. Mary squeezed her hand and they smiled at each other, Katherine barely able to conceal her excitement.

It was several minutes before the lines of the ship were secure and the gangplank lowered for the passengers to disembark, but then Katherine spotted Alex immediately, and suddenly they were in each other's arms, holding each other tightly, the waiting finally over.

Alastair and Michael followed close behind, with Alastair greeting Katherine warmly with a wonderful hug, saying how glad he was to see her again. Michael kissed her on the cheek and Katherine said she wouldn't wash it off for at least a week. He placed his hand against his heart and said he was overwhelmed by her grace and beauty, and offered her his undying devotion. Alex pretended to be jealous and, folding his arms and putting his nose in the air, went into a theatrical sulk before grinning broadly at Katherine and Michael and relaxing his stance.

The friendship between them all, forged so many months previously, was once again there, intact and immediate, and they all delighted in it.

Mary had been watching this miniature pantomime in amazement and laughed in a way she had not done for many months. Accordingly, when Michael was introduced to her, he saw a very pretty woman with real liveliness in her expression. He was instantly smitten.

He was very quick to hide it, though unfortunately, not quick enough before Alex spotted it. So Michael play-acted and kissed Mary's hand in a flamboyant but gentlemanly fashion, saying that he was delighted to meet her, adding solemnly, without any recourse to flirtation, that he hoped he would be able to live up to the expectations of the matron of honour in his duties as best man.

Mary blushed, and withdrew her hand gently so as not to cause offence, for she was not in the least upset by Michael's actions. On the contrary, she found his personality a relief and a balm after the trauma of the past few months.

Both of them remained very quiet for several moments, each covertly observing the other. Mary's throat had inexplicably gone very dry and her hand was tingling where Michael had held it. For his part, he was shocked by his own reaction to her, but acknowledged Alex's subtle expression of warning.

However, there was one person who had not appeared, and whose absence had not been explained amid the greetings.

"Where's Lily?" exclaimed Katherine, anxious as to why Alex's younger sister had not arrived.

"She's succumbed to the 'flu, I'm afraid," replied Alastair. "She's so upset at not being able to be here."

"Devastated is the word," added Alex. "But she's been very poorly for the last couple of weeks. Her school was finally closed two weeks before the end of term and all the girls sent home. Lily thought she was one of the few who'd managed to escape it, but a couple of days after she arrived back in Kensington, she developed a terrific sore throat and the next day, a very high temperature, becoming quite ill. Dad stayed home from work to look after her because he was so worried about her. She's well on the way to recovery now, but she's certainly not fit enough to travel. She insisted that Dad came, however, and that she was going to be all right. Mrs Thing has taken charge…"

"Which Lily will hate," interjected Alastair regretfully, suddenly looking very tired.

Alex agreed. "Poor girl. But she sends her love and says she'll see you in a few weeks."

The rain was fast becoming a heavy downpour and the wind increasing in intensity, making standing outside very unpleasant. So, before they became any wetter than they were already, they made their way up to Lochaberdale Hotel; all, that is, except Mary, who apologized and said she had to go home and prepare tea for Adam.

Katherine watched her disconsolate figure as she turned and walked away from them towards the main street. She was not alone in her observation, however, as Michael followed Mary's movements as long as it remained possible to do so without arousing attention.

They arrived at the hotel soaking wet and cold, to be welcomed by John, who showed them to their rooms immediately. The three men enjoyed the luxury of hot baths (the hotel possessed five bathrooms) and a change of clothes in warm, fire-lit accommodation.

Katherine, meanwhile, had been given a room, also warm, where she too could change – having brought extra clothes with her, an expert in the vagaries of island weather conditions. She declined a bath, saying it wasn't essential for her as she had not just spent twelve hours on a boat. Her refusal was much to the relief of John, who was worried about his boiler with so many guests needing baths at the same time; Alex, Alastair and Michael were not the only visitors who had come to stay at the hotel.

Their sodden garments were whisked away by Marion to be washed and dried, including Katherine's, who said that it really wasn't necessary.

"Och, it's fine," said Marion, kindly efficient. "Can't have your clothes growing mildew now, can we?"

There was no arguing with that, so Katherine, who was changed and ready first, waited in the dining room for the others to appear.

This being their first night all together on Cairnmor, they had naturally arranged to eat their evening meal together and soon, the four of them had gathered at their table and were being served by John, somewhat later than planned, but all safe nonetheless.

Since their arrival, the wind and rain had continued to increase in strength and were now lashing against the windows of the dining room, shaking them with an almost primeval fury.

"I'm glad we didn't have to travel in this," remarked Michael, looking askance at the conditions outside.

"How was the trip?" asked Katherine.

"Terrible, terrible," replied Michael, with characteristic humour. "We were tossed about like matchsticks on the water. And Captain MacTavish fed us salted meat and dry biscuits. Such deprivation, such hardships we endured. We were lashed to the mast and assaulted by the wind and the waves." Then, having caused much laughter (and incipient indigestion), he said more normally, "It was all right, actually. A bit choppy; well quite rough really. I have to be honest and say that sailing is not my favourite mode of travel. I'm more of a solid-wheeled wagon man myself," he added, unable to resist one last bit of humour.

"Luddite," said Alex, good-naturedly.

"I thank 'ee for that, sir," said Michael, tugging at an imaginary forelock. "I promise I'll 'ave me looms mechanized by sun-down. No more opposition to progress. No, sir, not from me, guv, sir. Not no more."

"I really shall have indigestion soon," said Alastair, laughing as much as the others.

"Sorry," said Michael, chuckling.

"Please don't apologize. I'm enjoying it."

The banter continued in a similar vein for several more moments and then, when the laughter had subsided, Alastair turned to Katherine and said, "Thank you very much for supplying me with the address of Mrs Gilgarry's relative in Nova Scotia. It's proven to be a most fortunate connection."

"Why, have you found Rupert and Mhairi?!" exclaimed Katherine, barely able to contain her excitement.

"Not exactly, not yet, but I'm optimistic that we're very close to doing so," replied Alastair calmly. "You see, Mrs Gilgarry's great-nephew had music lessons with Rupert, who apparently has a position of some responsibility in the musical life of Halifax. We're now waiting for this nephew to find and send us contact details for him. I haven't disclosed why we're looking for Rupert, of course, I merely said that we were looking for him in a professional capacity, which should be sufficient. It's going to call for a great deal of tact and diplomacy for the news to be broken to Rupert and Mhairi in the right way and for legal reasons, I have to be the one to do it."

"I made that clear to Mrs Gilgarry too when I asked for her nephew's address. Bless her she understood perfectly. And she appreciated your letter of thanks too, Alastair. I translated it and when I was done, she said that young people nowadays have few manners and it was a pleasant change to find someone that did." Katherine smiled at her future father-in-law.

"I like the young people bit…" chuckled Alastair.

"I thought you might… So they're still there, in Halifax," murmured Katherine, almost to herself, and then to the others she said, with her usual energy, "But this is wonderful news; it almost seems too good to be true. I can't believe we're so close!"

"Who is Mrs Gilgarry?" asked Michael.

"When I came to Cairnmor in October," replied Alex, "Donald the postman took me on his rounds one day to see if we could find anyone who might have come across Rupert and Mhairi, Dad's missing heir. Well, we visited a feisty little old lady called Mrs Gilgarry who gave us quite a vitriolic history lesson on the clearances on Cairnmor and how everyone was forcibly shipped off to Canada, including most of her immediate family to Nova Scotia. So Katherine, with yet another of her bright ideas…" Alex paused to smile lovingly at his bride to be.

"Go on, get on with the story. Let's have less of this lovey-dovey stuff," said Michael good-naturedly.

"As I was saying before your untimely interruption…" said Alex, narrowing his eyes at him, "Katherine thought that although it might be a long shot, it was worth asking Mrs Gilgarry if any of her family over there had come across Rupert or Mhairi in their professional capacity."

"And you struck gold?" said Michael.

"We did indeed," replied Alastair. "The Immigration Office has also been very helpful and replied to my letter almost immediately to let me know that they were looking into the matter for me and 'were hopeful of a propitious outcome'. I haven't heard back from them since but it's only been a month since Katherine and Alex discovered Rupert and Mhairi's whereabouts, so I feel we've made very good progress in a very short space of time, given the inevitable time delay in trying to communicate across the Atlantic Ocean."

Once they had finished their meal, they left the dining room and stood in the lobby for a while discussing what they wanted to do, as it was nearly midnight. Katherine spoke to John about keeping her room, as she didn't fancy the idea of a long walk back to her croft in the appalling conditions outside.

"Och, of course ye can. I wouldn't have let ye go out there in any case. Keep the room for as long as ye need it," said the ever hospitable manager, who often accommodated stranded islanders during inclement weather. True, they couldn't always pay in cash, but afterwards the hotel was never short of smoked ham, eggs, milk or butter.

Alex eyed Katherine speculatively, but she shook her head imperceptibly. He understood. He could wait a week.

Alastair was just about to say that he thought he would go on up to bed, as he had a headache and was very tired – he failed to mention the prickly feeling at the back of his throat, hoping this was just the after effects of a very strenuous day – when suddenly the door of the hotel burst open.

The sound of the storm reached them in all its attendant fury and out of this maelstrom came Mary, bleeding profusely from cuts on her forehead and cheek, drenched to the skin, and shaking uncontrollably.

She managed to gasp, "He's gone, he's gone! The stupid man has gone out in his boat. I tried to stop him but I couldn't! Please can someone help me…" before passing out.

Michael was by her side instantly and caught her in his arms.

CHAPTER 27

Michael carried Mary to the sofa in the hotel lobby and laid her gently onto its leather surface, taking out a clean handkerchief from his pocket to try and staunch the flow of blood that obscured most of her face.

Alex rushed to secure the door against the wind and rain, while John went to collect Marion, who came into the lobby almost immediately, armed with blankets, towels, clean cloths and a bowl of water.

Dressed in a Macintosh and sou'wester, John went to fetch the doctor and then see if anything could be done to stop that imbecile Adam. However, by the sound of things, it was already too late. 'Imbecile' was not the only thing that John called Adam as he went out into the tempestuous night, but he had the good grace to keep it to himself.

By the time the doctor reached the hotel, Marion and Michael had managed to stem the worst of the bleeding, and he had carried Mary up to Katherine's room, where they laid her on the bed wrapped in yet more dry blankets. By banking up the fire and changing her covers frequently, they made her warm and dry very quickly.

Katherine, Alex and Alastair could only help by fetching clean water and bringing up peat from the basement.

During this time, Mary regained consciousness very briefly, opened her eyes and looked at Michael before slipping back into her insensible state, holding onto his hand as though she would never let it go. Indeed, nothing would have induced him to allow her to do so, even if she probably did have no idea of what she was doing.

When he arrived, Dr Armstrong took one look at Mary, saw that she needed stitches in both cuts, and diagnosed severe concussion and shock. He carried out his task expertly and efficiently, sterilizing the needle before threading it with silk and joining the two halves of each wound together. He remarked that it was just as well that she was still unconscious.

"She may have a small scar on her cheek, as that is the larger cut of the two, and there will be bruising as well. How did this happen?"

"We don't know yet," replied Marion, "but it has something to do with Adam who seemed intent on taking his boat out to sea."

The doctor shook his head. "He's a stupid, stupid man. Did his friends go with him?"

"We don't know that either. John was going to find out."

Dr Armstrong closed his bag. "Mary needs to rest quietly for a day or two. I presume she's all right to stay here?"

Marion nodded.

"Good. Then I'll come and see her again in the morning. When she comes round, she might well be sick, so be prepared for that. She's nice and warm, but if you can change her clothes, then I would do so and get her properly into bed. Thank you," he added, giving a brief smile to Marion, Katherine and Michael, who had remained in the room with Mary. "I'll show myself out. Goodnight to you all." With that he left the room, went downstairs, put on his waterproof clothing and battled his way back to his house through the driving wind and horizontal rain.

"Now, young man," said Marion to Michael. "We have to get this poor lass undressed, so I think that for the moment yere job is done. But I thank ye for all yere help and I'll let ye know when ye can come up again and see her."

There was a natural acceptance on her part that Michael should want to be with Mary, but because she was busy, Marion didn't analyse why that should be so, nor indeed, why she should feel it at all. It was only much later, as she eventually crept into bed beside her sleeping husband just as dawn was beginning to lighten the sky, that she thought about it. As far as she was aware, Michael and Mary had only just met and it took her by surprise that his presence with her in the room had seemed so very *right*.

The storm continued unabated for nearly the whole of Sunday. Even the safe haven of Lochaberdale was not immune to the effects of what came to be described as 'the worst storm in living memory'.

Spumes of white-flecked water battered the harbour wall, and gusts of wind sheared off the tops of the waves, sending drenching spray over the line of shuttered cottages that huddled beyond the quayside. Within the harbour itself, churning waves were sent into confusion by the elements, and fishing boats on their moorings were thrown haphazardly in all directions, in danger of collision.

Lochfoyle remained at the pier, unable to leave on her return journey, tugging at her restraining ropes, buffeted by the wind and waves. Further along the shore, huge breakers engulfed the rocks, sending white foam rivulets running down the rock face as the water retreated, only for them to be swamped again with the next sea-surge.

Gulls sat hunched and still on the grassy bank above the rocks, the wind ruffling their feathers, unwilling to move. Those that tried gave up, unable to fly anywhere except backwards in the teeth of the gale. Orange-legged oyster catchers took to foraging on the grass, rather than the sea-shore; always busy, always moving.

Skywards, the storm clouds remained black and menacing and the atmosphere oppressive. No one could go anywhere. No rescue attempt – because that is what it had inevitably become by now – could be launched until the storm had run its course.

At the present time, there was nothing anyone could do other than sit and wait.

Mary regained consciousness at about breakfast time. Katherine was with her, having relieved Marion in the early hours. She went over to her friend's bedside immediately. Mary wasn't sick, but her mouth was dry and she was in desperate need of a drink of water. She put her hand up to her cheek, which felt stiff and sore, and winced with the pain. One eye was virtually closed and her face bruised and swollen. Her head ached and her shoulder felt as though it were on fire.

"Hello," said Katherine softly.

"Hello," said Mary, her voice cracking. She tried to moisten her lips, but her tongue was too dry.

Katherine helped her to sit up and drink some water from the cup on the bedside table. Mary could manage only a few sips and she lay down again, falling instantly asleep once more.

She had woken up properly by the time the doctor came at about eleven o'clock. He examined her thoroughly and asked her a few questions. He informed Marion that she had severe bruising to her right shoulder, as well as the obvious wounds on her face and concussion, and reinforced the need for bed rest.

When he had gone on his way, Katherine and Marion took her up some soup, but Mary refused to eat until she knew whether Adam had come home.

"I'm afraid he hasn't yet," said Katherine, as gently as she could. "But as soon as the storm dies down, the search and rescue parties will go out."

"It's my fault, all my fault," she muttered, tears streaming down her face.

"How can that be so?" soothed Marion, stroking her hair and not saying that she thought Adam one of the biggest fools ever to walk the earth. "I'm sure ye did everything ye could to stop him."

"Oh, I tried so hard, so hard, but it wasn't enough," she sobbed, her voice full of anguish and defeat.

She drank a little of her soup, with help from Katherine, and when Marion had taken the bowl downstairs, Mary felt strong enough to be able to recount to her friend all that had taken place.

After she had left Alex and Katherine at the harbour, she had arrived back at the croft to find Adam was not there. He eventually returned much later that evening to collect his gear, or so he said. He had obviously been out drinking with his mates; he could hardly stand upright and his breath stank of alcohol. By the door, she found at least half a dozen bottles of spirits in a bag.

Mary picked these up and began to empty them down the sink in the kitchen while he was gathering his things together in the bedroom. When Adam came back into the kitchen and saw what she was doing, he was furious. He tried to yank the bottle out of her hand and a bitter struggle ensued which he won, not just by virtue of his superior strength, but because he shoved her violently against the wall. That was where her shoulder had been hurt. He then became abusive, shouting at her and threatening to beat her up if she ever did anything like that again. As he couldn't drink at home, he said, he was going to go out in *his* boat where a man could do exactly as he wished without his wife nagging away at him all the time.

Mary remonstrated with him, begging him not to go, saying he was too drunk to know what he was doing, even saying he could drink at home. But Adam brushed her aside, weaving his way down the path towards the jetty where his boat was tied up and his friends were waiting.

Mary followed him, out into the wind and pouring rain, and begged him again to stay with her and not to be so stupid as to take the boat out in weather like this. He almost listened to her this time, but both his friends egged him on, saying that he was a spineless coward (or words to that effect – Mary preferred not to repeat exactly what they said) to be told what to do by a woman.

216

Sensing a chink in his resolve, despite the goading of his cronies, she placed herself between her husband and the boat to try and prevent him physically from going. But he pushed her aside with such ferocity that it sent her reeling onto the ground, where she hit her head hard on the rocky shoreline and blacked out for several moments.

During that time, the three men managed to launch the boat, with great difficulty in the face of the ever increasing gale, leaving Mary sobbing on her knees on the beach. It was when she could do no more, that, with great difficulty, she made her way to the hotel where she knew she would find help from her friends.

After she had finished speaking, Mary lay back exhausted onto her pillow, tears streaming down her face. Eventually, comforted by Katherine, she was overcome with exhaustion and slept once again.

Shocked by what she had just heard and checking that Mary was all right to be left for a moment or two, she went downstairs to find Alex and Alastair sitting with John and Marion in the lounge. Michael joined them almost immediately and Katherine briefly recounted the tale that Mary had just told her.

Wordlessly, Michael left the room and went upstairs, sitting by Mary's bedside for hours while she slept, watching over her. Eventually, Marion gently persuaded him that perhaps it was time that he went downstairs and that she would stay with Mary for a while and make sure she was all right.

That afternoon was one of the unhappiest that Katherine could remember. She was in tears by the time she had ended Mary's story, hardly able to believe that all this could have taken place, yet knowing it to be true.

Alex consoled her as best he could and both he and Alastair looked at each other, deeply troubled by what they had just heard, well aware that Mary had grounds to prosecute should she so wish; that is, if Adam and his cronies managed to survive.

By late afternoon, the wind began to lessen and the rain to ease, heralding the end of the storm. In somewhat calmer conditions, John walked up to Fiona and Gordon's croft to tell them what had happened to their daughter. They arrived in Lochaberdale early in the evening upset and angry, and as Mary was awake, went upstairs to see her.

By eight o'clock the storm had dissipated completely, though there remained a heavy swell out at sea.

A meeting was convened in the village hall, to which all able-bodied men came, including Alex and Alastair, to work out a strategy for the rescue attempt which would begin at first light. The men were divided into teams, with at least two people to each boat, and search areas were designated, taking into account tides, wind direction and the make and size of each boat involved in the search.

Alex and Alastair were impressed. This was an experienced group of people who were used to working together and who knew exactly what they were doing. They felt privileged to have been invited to be a part of it, once, that is, it was discovered that both of them had sailing experience and that Alastair was a member of the Royal Naval Volunteer Reserve.

Alastair chose to ignore his headache, sore throat, aching legs and developing cough. He was needed here and besides, it was something of an adventure as well; albeit one with a serious purpose.

Alex was assigned to Gordon, whom he had met when he first came to Cairnmor in October, and the two men greeted each other as old friends. Alastair was with Robbie, whom he was interested to meet, knowing that Alex had told him that he reckoned Robbie had some secret that he was withholding, which might have a bearing on the search for Rupert and Mhairi.

A sea voyage was often a good time to exchange confidences, thought Alastair, and perhaps this would prove to be one such opportunity. However, he knew that it might have to wait, given the seriousness of the undertaking upon which they were about to embark.

They left just before first light: an armada of boats of varying lengths and design, pushing off with the ebb tide, with sails hoisted and oars positioned, and engines started for the few who possessed them.

Katherine and the other women were there, standing on the quayside in time-honoured fashion to see their menfolk away. Some would return that evening while others, like Robbie and Alastair, would be away for longer, searching the myriad uninhabited islands that surrounded Cairnmor or travelling further afield out into the Atlantic.

Robbie's boat was a twenty-eight foot transom-sterned Clyde smack with a bowsprit. They towed a small rowing boat, necessary for landing on small islands where the water was too shallow to take the smack close into shore.

The first port of call for Robbie was to be Cairnbeg, as their brief was to explore the area to the south, criss-crossing the channels, searching the outer archipelagos and landing wherever it was deemed necessary in order to eliminate from the search any land mass that remained uninhabited.

A fairly stiff breeze was blowing and they made good progress out of the harbour, having wind and tide with them. But once they had cleared the headland and turned towards Cairnbeg, they were almost head to wind and their pace slowed for a short while until Robbie had adjusted the sails and they began to tack.

Alastair was grateful for the warm clothes that Robbie had lent him, and glad of the oilskins to protect him from the spray thrown up by the boat as they ploughed their way through the sea. If he had felt better, he would have been enjoying himself. As it was, he tried to put his state of health out of his mind and concentrate on keeping a constant lookout for any sign of the fishing boat and its occupants. Despite himself, he gave a cough, deep and chesty which Robbie could not help but notice.

"That's a nasty cough ye have," he remarked, looking sideways at Alastair.

"I'll be fine," he replied. "Nothing that a good dose of fresh air won't sort out." Alastair sounded more convincing than he felt.

"Aye, there is that. Last month I had this 'flu that's been goin' the rounds. Had a cough just like that." Then he looked up at the sails. "Can ye take the helm for a while? I've got one or two things to sort up for'ard."

Alastair took the tiller, wondering if Robbie, canny sea-dog, was testing him. He took his time, adjusting to the feel of the wind in the sails and the way this

218

unfamiliar boat handled, as well as keeping a steady course. He must have passed muster, because Robbie came back to the cockpit seemingly very relaxed, sat on the transom, and lit his pipe, leaving Alastair at the tiller.

"How was it ye learned to sail?" Robbie asked presently, trimming the canvas every so often and suggesting minor course adjustments.

"My father kept a ketch on the River Orwell in Suffolk where we lived. He taught me to sail when I was a boy. He had learned from his father on Skye, where he was born. My father also had a friend who raced East Coast smacks on the River Blackwater in Essex and we often went there as crew, though this is the first time I've actually been at the helm of a smack. This boat is very similar to the ones I knew as a child."

"Aye, it's a practical design and she handles well."

Alastair succumbed to a coughing fit, for which he apologized. It passed quickly but his chest was painful afterwards.

Presently, Robbie asked, "How did your father come to be in Suffolk if he was born on Skye?"

"He was a shepherd like his father and grandfather before him but when life became difficult on the island, his parents encouraged him to leave in order to find a better way of life. So, at the age of eighteen, he left his home on Skye, travelling through Scotland and on into England, finding employment as and when he needed it. He worked his way down through the industrial north of the country before journeying along the south coast and up the east coast doing a variety of jobs along the way. He worked as a labourer, a dairy herdsman, a pig farmer, a blacksmith, a shepherd and then, after several years' travelling, he found a job on a farm near Pin Mill where he met my mother. And that, as they say, was that. She was the farmer's daughter and eventually, after they married, my father took over as farm manager."

"Did ye not want to become a farmer?"

"No. I always had my head buried in a book," chuckled Alastair. "I was fortunate in that my parents recognized that my abilities were going to take me in a different direction from theirs, and they made sure I had a good education. I became very interested in the law and eventually became a solicitor."

Robbie was quiet, taking all this in and thinking about Alastair's story. They had been sailing for about four hours and Cairnbeg was growing ever closer. Robbie brought down the sails, slipped the anchor and they transferred to the rowing boat to go ashore.

The good people of the little island were dismayed by their tale, but there had been no sighting of the fishing boat so Alastair and Robbie returned to the smack and resumed their journey, still without success.

The weather remained fair. At dusk the wind dropped and they landed on a small uninhabited island, rich in wild life, with a colony of seals lolling lazily on the beach in the last warming rays of the evening sun while oystercatchers and dunlin fed busily along the water's edge.

Previously, while they had still been on board and at anchor, Robbie had cast his line over the side and caught their supper, which they now ate on their island by a camp fire, with home-made wholemeal bread and a large slab of Robbie's fruit cake.

Terns and gannets wheeled overhead, incessantly raucous as they competed for the best nesting spaces on the rocky cliff face further along the shore. The clamour persisted until late and Alastair found it difficult to sleep. Also, he felt cold and shivery and could not get comfortable, even though Robbie had supplied him with plenty of blankets and they were warm by the fire, and sheltered in the lee of protruding rocks.

He must have drifted off to sleep eventually, because he was awoken by Robbie gently shaking his shoulder and the smell of bacon and eggs frying in a pan. The sun was just visible over the horizon and with great effort, Alastair roused himself. He felt embarrassed that he could only manage to eat a tiny proportion of the delicious breakfast that Robbie had prepared, but his companion told him not to worry. He could see Alastair was not well, although he kept the observation to himself. They washed up and broke camp, returning to the smack and their quest.

The sailing was exhilarating for all of that second day and the visibility excellent, but Alastair was feeling steadily worse and it took all his concentration to focus on keeping a lookout. They sailed for several miles out into the Atlantic to the last island in their brief, and having completed their search area to no avail, it was time to return home.

They spent their final night on board the fishing smack, Alastair's cough keeping both of them awake. He was most apologetic the following morning, but Robbie was more concerned for his companion's health than anything else.

It wasn't the first night he'd had without sleep, he said, with a twinkle in his eye, nor would it be the last. But he knew they needed to get home as quickly as they could, as there was a front approaching and he could see cumulonimbus building on the near horizon. Robbie was anxious to reach landfall before the worst of the weather caught up with them.

At first they made good progress but the downpour reached them about three hours away from Cairnmor, the rain heavy and penetrating, giving both of them a thorough soaking despite the protection of oilskins and sou'westers.

The wind, gusty and unpredictable in the squall, made sailing difficult and their progress erratic. Robbie was forced to reduce sail, taking in a reef, thus lessening the amount of canvas exposed to the wind. This slowed them down still further and it was not until early evening, two hours later than expected, that they reached the southernmost tip of Cairnmor.

Here, Robbie took the decision to anchor in a small sheltered cove, transfer to the rowing boat and land, making for Katherine's croft, which even if she was not at home, would be somewhere to get Alastair warm and dry. It would take another four hours to sail back round the headland into Lochaberdale with the present conditions, and that would not do.

Katherine was at home, seated in the kitchen with Alex and Gordon, the three of them engaged in deep conversation. They looked up immediately as the kitchen door opened and Robbie came in supporting Alastair, both of them dripping wet.

Carefully he set him down on the settee by the fire and said in Gaelic, for his English failed him after the exertion of helping Alastair up the hill. *"He's not well, he has the 'flu I think. We need to get these wet things off him as quickly as possible and someone needs to go for the doctor."*

Gordon was out of the door almost before Robbie had finished speaking, grabbing his oilskins and sou'wester and walking down the hill yet again to Lochaberdale. His animals would have to wait; young Iain would have to manage on his own. It would be an hour and a half before the doctor would be able to reach the croft and Gordon quickened his pace as the poor man had looked very ill, very ill indeed.

He was not wrong. Alex was shocked by Alastair's appearance and he and Robbie helped his father into the bed in Katherine's spare bedroom, after first helping him to undress and ensuring he was dry.

Meanwhile, she went next door to Gordon and Fiona's cottage and found some pyjamas the right size, telling Iain what had happened. Alastair put these on, all the time worrying that he was being a nuisance. His forehead was burning and he was shivering uncontrollably. There was a gurgling sound in his chest every time he coughed and Alex was beside himself with anxiety.

Katherine suggested that Robbie take off his wet things before he too caught a chill. He obediently complied once she had discreetly removed herself from the room, having first given him blankets with which to cover himself.

She took a bowl of cold water and some cloths into Alex, instructing him to place these on Alastair's forehead as they needed to reduce his temperature as quickly as possible. She also gave him water for Alastair to drink, as he would need plenty of fluids.

Katherine returned to the kitchen where she placed Robbie's sodden clothing on a wooden clothes-horse, standing it in front of the range, before stoking up the fire. Finally, she made a hot drink for all of them. There was nothing else they could do now except wait for the doctor.

It was only much later, after Robbie had walked home having ensured that both his boats were secure, and Dr Armstrong had been, that Katherine realized that because of her concern for Alastair, she had forgotten to tell Robbie that Alex and Gordon had found one of the missing fishermen tenaciously clinging onto life after three days on an uninhabited island out to the north-west of Cairnmor, with the upturned fishing boat floating nearby.

CHAPTER 28

Dr Armstrong diagnosed bronchopneumonia, a dangerous complication arising from the influenza which, on further questioning his patient, he discovered Alastair had been ignoring. His temperature was worryingly high and both his lungs were congested.

The doctor had specific instructions for Alex and Katherine. "Keep him warm but not too hot, and sponge his body down with *warm* water, as he mustn't be chilled any further. The evaporation of the water will help to reduce the fever. But continue with the cool cloths on his forehead, as this is soothing and will help his headache. Keep the window open to allow the air to circulate, but avoid exposing him to any draughts." To Alastair he said, "I'll come and see you again tomorrow." And his patient nodded weakly, unable to reply as a paroxysm of coughing rendered him speechless.

After placing a sympathetic hand on his arm, the doctor went out of the room into the kitchen, asking Katherine and Alex to follow him.

Dr Armstrong hesitated before saying, "There isn't an awful lot I can do, I'm afraid. Pneumonia is a tricky one. I have to be honest and tell you, Mr Stewart, that your father is very, very ill. On the mainland, he would have been hospitalized." He put a reassuring hand on Alex's shoulder, seeing his expression of acute alarm. "It will be his physical strength and ability to fight off the illness that will bring about his recovery. But your father appears to have a good constitution, his heart is not affected and I've absolutely no doubt that he'll receive the very best care."

"Thank you, doctor," said Alex, acknowledging the doctor's assessment.

"There is a new drug called penicillin which is good for treating bacterial infections," continued Dr Armstrong, "although I'm not sure that's what he has, given the pathology of his pneumonia. Unfortunately, it's not yet available for general use, and we'd probably be the last to receive it up here in our remote corner of Scotland even if it were," he added, somewhat despondently.

Just as he was going out of the door, he turned to Katherine and said, "Mrs Gilgarry would probably be the best person to turn to. I would pay her a visit if I were you, but sooner rather than later."

"You took the thought right out of my head," replied Katherine, with a tight smile of anxiety. "It's too late to go there tonight, as the path will be dark and treacherous, especially after all this rain, but I'll go first thing in the morning. Could you speak to Donald for me and ask if he will give me a lift in his post bus as far as the track to Mrs Gilgarry's croft? Tell him I'll walk down to Lochaberdale at first light and meet him at the post office."

"I'll be glad to. And try not to worry, just keep Mr Stewart as comfortable as possible and work hard to get that fever down."

With that, the doctor went out of the door and back into his pony and trap. It had been an eventful couple of days and it was not over yet. He gave a chirrup of encouragement to his horse, who trotted along the stony path with a sure foot and practised eye, taking his master back down into the village to continue the sombre task of consoling two bereaved families. It was from this endeavour, working alongside Father McPhee, that he had been summoned by Gordon to tend to Alastair.

Dr Armstrong sighed. It was an unpleasant business; very unpleasant indeed, and one which could have been avoided altogether. Two strong young men lost forever and all because they were unable to keep off the drink. Such a waste, such an unnecessary waste. A salutary lesson if ever there was one. He hoped the survivor would take heed.

Katherine and Alex took it in turns to keep a vigil by Alastair's bedside, cooling his burning forehead and sponging him down. His cough was becoming worse and occasionally, he would have difficulty in breathing, his intake of air hoarse and painful. Then he would cough up phlegm and for a short while that made things a little easier, though it was very painful for him to do so.

Neither Katherine nor Alex could sleep, even when it was their individual turn to rest, so they sat together with Alastair and supported him, ministering to his needs to the best of their combined abilities.

Just before dawn, Katherine prepared breakfast for herself and Alex and, after making sure that he and Alastair had everything they needed, she set off down the hill to Lochaberdale in the cold light of early morning, light-headed through lack of sleep and only dimly aware of the sunrise, which usually she would stop and admire.

She called first at the hotel and spoke to Marion enquiring after Mary. She sent her love, saying that she would visit her later, knowing that Mary's mother Fiona was by her side and looking after her. She then spoke briefly to John, hatching a little surprise for Mrs Gilgarry should she so desire.

Leaving the hotel, Katherine walked along the harbour road to the post office, where Donald was ready and waiting. An atmosphere of sadness hung over the village; there were few smiles abroad that morning and the early greetings took on a sombre tone. It was a community in mourning and the tragedy of the previous few days sat heavily upon everyone.

The post bus took the route that Donald had followed when Alex had been with him six months previously, stopping a couple of miles away from Mrs Gilgarry's croft as the track was unsuitable and the vehicle could travel no further. Together, Katherine and the postman walked across the stony and difficult terrain to their destination.

The old lady listened carefully to Katherine's description of Alastair's illness; the drowning of the two young men and the story of the lone survivor. Mrs Gilgarry then agreed to come and treat Alastair, even though she was getting on in years, she said, and deserved her peace and quiet. "But," she added, "because his son rescued one of the fishermen and is going to be your husband, and because Mr Stewart wrote me a very kind letter of thanks, and because he is a special man who is loved, I will do this thing. I shall help him recover, you may be sure of that."

Katherine gave the old lady a hug, partly in gratitude for her perspicacity, and partly because Katherine herself, being very near to tears, felt an overwhelming sense of relief at the old lady's confidence in her own ability to help Alastair.

However, Mrs Gilgarry brushed the gesture aside, saying, "Now, now, there's no time for that," even though she was secretly pleased at this show of gratitude. "Now then, Katie, I need you to do certain things for me. I shall stay overnight to make sure that the poor man is on the mend, so I need a nightdress and dressing gown and one change of clothes. That will be quite sufficient. You will find everything in that chest of drawers and there is a carpet bag behind that curtain."

Having completed this request, Katherine then followed the old lady out into her garden. It was large and rectangular, sheltered by a high wall on the side of the prevailing wind, but open on another to allow maximum sunlight, as well as incorporating an area always in shadow.

In this cleverly designed enclosure there grew a profusion of herbs – elderflower, lungwort, plantain, horsetail, thyme, peppermint, horseradish and many, many others. But it was these seven herbs that Mrs Gilgarry instructed Katherine to pick, along with garlic and linden, guiding her to the best specimens. She filled an enormous wicker basket brimful with them, her nostrils suffused with their aromatic scent and her fingers fragrant with their perfume.

Then, the redoubtable octogenarian left a note for her son informing him of her whereabouts, added to the basket three jars of honey and a small earthenware pot with a lid, and led the way out of the croft, using her stick to help her navigate the uneven ground once they had reached the narrow path. Donald came next, carrying her carpet bag, ever watchful in case the old lady stumbled, and Katherine followed at the rear, with the basket of precious herbs, loosely wrapped in a dampened muslin cloth to keep them fresh on the journey.

Mrs Gilgarry was as sure footed as either of her two younger companions and was very impressed by the post bus, this being the first time she had seen it. People usually travelled to see her for cures to their ailments these days; it was now very rare that she went to them, and she had not been away from her croft or the immediate vicinity for many years. She took a lively interest in the journey and noted several changes in Lochaberdale since her last visit.

They stopped briefly outside the hotel, because this was Mrs Gilgarry's favourite place in the village and she wanted to see it, even from a distance. Donald and Katherine exchanged a quick smile, knowing that something special was being planned for the old lady after she had completed her task.

Mrs Gilgarry set to work immediately she arrived in Katherine's cottage, even while Donald remained. She said, "*Halò*," to Alex and he enquired after her health, saying, "*Ciamar a tha sibh?*" in Gaelic, having been primed with a few words by Katherine before she had left that morning.

Their guest was very appreciative of this courtesy and responded by saying she was well with, "*Tha gu math, tapadh leibh.*" She then went into Alastair's room, introducing herself, feeling his forehead, and taking his pulse. She listened while he coughed, didn't seem at all concerned that she might catch his illness, and spoke several words, none of which Alastair could understand. Katherine interpreted, saying that, "She is pleased to meet you and she is sorry that you are ill. But she will help you to get better."

He nodded and tried to smile his thanks.

Then Mrs Gilgarry went back into the kitchen and conversed with Katherine for a while. "He's very poorly indeed, Katie, and you will have to nurse him very carefully. I can treat him and help him. He will be all right, I think, but he's not out of danger yet."

Having observed his tired and haggard look, she spoke to Alex next, with Katherine interpreting, "I suggest that you go back down to the hotel with Donald in his post bus, and get some sleep yourself before you too become unwell. We can manage here for now. Come back when you are rested."

Alex was about to protest but Katherine silently warned him not to say anything.

Obediently, he complied, thanking Mrs Gilgarry for her help by saying, "*Tapadh leibh,*" to which the old lady smiled and replied, "*'s ur beatha*" ("You're welcome").

Katherine went outside with Alex and said goodbye, adding, "Can you bring clean pyjamas for your dad, as many as he has brought with him as well as his shaving things and anything else you think he might need?"

Alex said he would and climbed into the post bus beside Donald. After waving them farewell and thanking the postman for all that he had done, Katherine went back inside to the kitchen where Mrs Gilgarry asked her to put a kettle of water on the range and take out the herbs from the cloth, each variety having been kept separate with twine.

"First we must make an infusion of elderflower and linden," said Mrs Gilgarry. "This will make Mr Stewart perspire and help reduce his fever. He must drink a cup of this tea three times a day." She showed the herbs to Katherine, "This is elderflower and this is linden."

Katherine knew that the only way she was going to remember the appearance of all the herbs was to make labels for them, which she did, writing in Gaelic so Mrs Gilgarry could check that she had done each one correctly.

Once the kettle had boiled, they made the tea and Katherine helped Alastair to take as many sips as he could manage before he lay back on his pillows again. She returned to the kitchen.

"I shall stay here tonight but after that you will have to manage. Therefore, I need to teach you what each herb is for. The horseradish will help fight off the infection. Make a syrup, like so," and Mrs Gilgarry demonstrated. "And then add a teaspoon of honey for every half cup of horseradish juice. The medicinal power of any herbal preparation is made stronger when honey is used in the mixture."

Katherine wrote down the instructions for the various concoctions, striving for complete accuracy, well understanding their importance.

Soon it was time to give Alastair the horseradish syrup, and she had to wake him to do so. He was sweating profusely, the herb tea having worked almost immediately, and Katherine wiped his face and upper body with a clean dry cloth. He took the syrup easily and went back to sleep virtually straightaway.

Mrs Gilgarry had her next set of instructions ready for Katherine. "If you mix chamomile and peppermint, this makes a very good steam which can be inhaled. It is a very good way of soothing and healing the lungs. For this you will need ten drops per bowl of steaming water. However, we shall do that a little later as Mr Stewart needs to rest completely after the preparations he has already had."

Katherine learned how horsetail was excellent for restoring and strengthening the lungs and helping the body to repair damaged tissue; she learned about the best way of making nourishing soups and broths and how important it was to incorporate garlic in the recipes as this helped to fight infection and restore normal body temperature.

"Take plenty yourself," suggested Mrs Gilgarry. "Make sure you keep well. Mr Stewart is going to need you over the next few weeks. I always have masses of garlic – enough to frighten a whole coven of witches!" and she chuckled to herself, making Katherine smile.

The next preparation they made was of lungwort, plantain and marshmallow, as Alastair needed to have this three times a day during the "acute phase," said Mrs Gilgarry.

By the time they had finished, Katherine was very glad she had made detailed notes of all that Mrs Gilgarry had imparted. There was so much to remember. She had learned of infusions and syrups, of the best combinations of herbs and their healing properties, when they should be administered, and how long to leave between each dose. Her mind was reeling and she suddenly felt the room swim.

She must have gone very pale, as the old lady gave her some peppermint tea to drink and made her go and lie down. Katherine's guest sat with Alastair, seeing to his needs, giving him her remedies and supporting him through the pain that racked his chest every time he coughed.

She gave him an infusion of plantain and thyme to help ease his symptoms, and fetching her earthenware pot, spread onto his chest a thick pungent-smelling yellow ointment which seemed to send a deep heat right into his lungs. As he lay back, she sang soft, soothing Gaelic songs which he found comforting, and it was to this sound that he fell into a deep healing sleep.

Mrs Gilgarry took out her knitting and sat in the easy chair, which Katherine had brought in for her, with her feet up on a footstool, knowing they had done everything they could for the time being.

She contemplated her patient. He must have been under considerable strain over a long period of time for the malady to affect him so badly. The wise old lady was very aware of the power of the mind in leaving the body vulnerable to illness and also its importance in the healing process. This man would need much positive encouragement in that direction.

By early evening, Alex too had rested and shaved and felt considerably restored, especially after a hot bath. He was worried about his father still, but felt instinctively that he was in very capable hands. Dr Armstrong had come to the hotel to see Mary, and on his way out, he talked to Alex to find out how his father was. When he discovered that Mrs Gilgarry had arrived, he said that there would be no need for him to go up to Katherine's croft as Alastair would be well tended to and there was nothing he could add to the elderly lady's remedies.

After the doctor had left the hotel, Alex went upstairs to see Mary, as he had not spoken to her since the awful events of the previous couple of days. She had been unavailable when he had returned to the hotel that morning.

When he entered the room, she was sitting on the window-seat looking out onto the bay, her face full of grief and pain, a sodden handkerchief screwed up in her hand.

For Mary was a widow after only five months of marriage. The sole survivor of the tragedy was not Adam, but one of his friends. She was angry, grieving, wanting to lash out at the remaining idiot who had led her man astray and who had somehow managed to survive when Adam had not. Her world had been crumbling during her marriage, she knew that, indeed she had always known that, but now it had fallen apart completely and whatever his faults had been, the man whom she had loved was gone.

After greeting Fiona, Mary's mother, who had not left her daughter's side since arriving at the hotel, Alex went over to Mary and sat down next to her, taking both her hands in his and saying how sorry he was. She accepted his sympathy and thanked him for it and then enquired after Alastair.

"Not too good, but Mrs Gilgarry is there with him at the moment."

"Then he will be fine," replied Mary, reassuring this kind man whom her best friend was very lucky to find. "What's going to happen about the wedding?" she asked.

"I haven't thought about it. At all," replied Alex, shocked that it had completely slipped his mind. He wondered if it was the same for Katherine. "With everything that's been going on..."

"That's very understandable," said Fiona gently.

Apart from saying goodbye, they didn't converse further as Alex felt he needed to get back to Katherine's cottage. On his way downstairs, he met Marion and asked if she had seen Michael, as he was not in his room and nowhere to be found.

"Och, he went out first thing. He's been tending the animals at Mary's croft these past couple of days. He doesn't want her to know though; not yet at least. He said he'd walk up to South Lochaberdale tomorrow and see all of ye. He wanted to talk to ye." She hesitated before adding, "He'd be a... He's a... very considerate man."

It was not what she wanted to say at all but at the last moment her courage failed her.

How could she put into words that Michael would make an ideal husband for Mary when Mary had only been a widow for two days? How could she say that they would be good for each other? It was not seemly or proper for her think it, let alone say it, but nonetheless, Marion knew it to be absolutely true.

"Thank you, Marion," said Alex knowing exactly why his friend wanted to see him.

He gathered together the things he needed to take and began the long walk up to South Lochaberdale. A car and a decent road would be useful, he thought.

Alastair, meanwhile, was sweating so much that he needed yet another change of pyjamas. So Katherine went next door once again and Iain supplied her with another pair.

Mrs Gilgarry helped Alastair to put on the dry clothes, sensing a slight awkwardness on his part as she did so, and reassuring him by saying, with a broad smile, "Don't fret. I'm an old woman and take no notice of men's bodies. We were born naked and that's the way God made us. We should never be afraid or ashamed of our nakedness, whatever the scriptures say."

And Katherine, blushing, was obliged to interpret this at Mrs Gilgarry's behest, much to her embarrassment. Alastair, poorly as he was, tried to laugh but ended up with another coughing fit. However, it was enough for the old lady to see that he had a healthy sense of humour.

That night, after Alex had returned from Lochaberdale, he and Katherine took it in turns to look after Alastair, but Mrs Gilgarry remained in the easy chair, watching over her patient, getting up only to give him the potions that she asked Katherine to concoct for him throughout the long hours of vigil.

That night, his life hung in the balance, his breathing laboured and noisy and his coughing protracted and debilitating.

But just before sunrise, they saw a change. His breaths seemed to come more easily and he seemed to be sleeping more peacefully. Mrs Gilgarry felt his forehead. It was much cooler: the fever had broken.

Katherine and Alex clung to each other with relief, which the old lady was delighted to see. She was even more pleased with her reward – a kiss on one of her remarkably smooth cheeks from Alex.

"*Tapadh leibh,*" he said.

"*'s ur beatha,*" she replied.

Just before three o'clock that afternoon, there was a knock at the kitchen door. When Katherine answered it, John was standing outside with his pony and trap, smiling broadly. Mrs Gilgarry, seated at the table and drinking a cup of tea, said, "Now what is going on here?"

"Your chariot awaits you, Madame!" he said, indicating the vehicle with a flourish of his hand.

Katherine laughed. "It's a thank you from me for coming all the way over here to look after Alastair. I've arranged that you should spend the night in the Lochaberdale Hotel. If you would like that, of course. If not, then John will take you directly home in the pony and trap."

Mrs Gilgarry sat there with her mouth open. She was overcome and said as much. There couldn't be a better treat for her and she accepted the offer gladly. "What luxury!" she said.

Before she left, she gave some pertinent advice to Katherine. "He will take many weeks to recover and should stay in bed until the worst is over. His fever will return, but it will be much less. When it has gone completely, then he can get up for a little while each day until he gets his strength back, when he can stay up for longer. Lots of fresh air, lass, lots of fresh air and nourishing broths," said Mrs Gilgarry, as she bid farewell to Katherine and Alex, who helped her into her seat.

They both waved to the venerable lady until she had disappeared from sight.

"That was a lovely thing to do," said Alex, who had not been party to the setting up of this treat.

"I thought of it when I was walking down the hill to collect Mrs Gilgarry. The hotel is her favourite building of all time, apart from her home. She would never stay there of her own volition, so it will be something a bit special for her."

Alex took her in his arms and kissed her. "You are the special one," he said, holding her. Then he added, "This hasn't turned out to be quite the week we planned, has it?"

"No," said Katherine. "We need to talk, I think."

They checked on Alastair, who was still fast asleep, and went back into the kitchen and sat down next to each other, with yet another cup of tea.

"Our wedding…" began Katherine.

"Yes, our wedding…" said Alex gently.

"We're going to have to postpone it, aren't we?"

"It looks like it."

"It wouldn't be right for it to go ahead."

"No."

"We'd always associate it with what's happened and there's no mood for celebration anywhere at the moment. It wouldn't be the same if Alastair couldn't be there, not to mention Mary."

"And Lily."

"Yes."

"Shall I speak to Father McPhee?" asked Alex, thinking practically, as Katherine was needed here to look after Alastair. She would become the main carer now.

"Yes please. When shall we set the new date for?"

"It depends when I can get away. The beginning of June is most likely. I have a lot of work lined up before then…"

"When we should have been together in London…"

"Yes."

"So, let's aim for June then, shall we?"

"Yes." Alex kissed her tenderly. "We'll get there."

"I know." Then she added, "When do you have to go back?"

"Saturday week."

"At least we'll have until then to be together."

"Yes, my love."

The day before he left, Alex took the time to walk along the beach and speak to Robbie, knowing that he would find the fisherman sitting by his hut tending to his nets. There was a question he wanted to ask and he felt that Robbie could no longer deny him an answer.

He was correct in this assumption and the old man took him into his confidence, transferring the burden of responsibility for the secret he had kept for so many years onto Alex, who, when they had concluded their conversation, went away from Robbie, smiling to himself, walking contentedly along the beautiful white-gold sands of Cairnmor.

CHAPTER 29

April – June, 1937

When Alex and Michael departed on *Lochfoyle*, there were many people at the quayside to bid them farewell. Along with Gordon, Alex had become something of a celebrity for being the man who had discovered and rescued the fisherman from his lonely island.

The story of how the fishing boat had been overturned by a tremendous wave, how the young man had managed to swim to the rocky shore, and how he had survived for three days on bird's eggs and crabs, had reached most of the island. If he, his friend and Adam hadn't been such idiots beforehand as to cause the tragedy then he, Fergus John, would have become something of a hero. As it was, there was sympathy and rejoicing for his parents, but censure for the man himself until he had mended his ways.

So, the good folk of Lochaberdale turned out to see Alex and Michael away, back to the mainland. It had not gone unnoticed either that Michael had been looking after Mary's animals on her croft since the loss of her husband. She had been staying with her parents once she had recovered enough to leave the hotel, so they looked upon it as an act of real kindness. They were also impressed that a stranger from London was able to do this thing; it needed skill and knowledge and this man obviously had both.

Katherine was indeed fortunate to have found such a man as Alex, and for him to have such a friend as Michael.

The steamer left on schedule and there was yet another painful parting for Katherine and Alex. No matter how many times they had done this, they could never become used to the way it affected them. But Alex knew that following his conversation with Robbie, he had an important task to complete and he went away from Lochaberdale with a different feeling and a sense of purpose.

He had said nothing of what Robbie had told him to Katherine or Alastair; there would be plenty of time for that if things worked out the way he hoped. So for the moment, he kept Robbie's shared confidence to himself and bid farewell to his love, with the promise of the wedding to come sustaining them both. This time, nothing could possibly stand in their way, or so they hoped...

After *Lochfoyle* had departed, Katherine did not linger by the quayside, and she and Mary walked back up to South Lochaberdale together. Mary's outer wounds had begun to heal – much bruising remained on her face and the cuts were still very much in evidence, even after the stitches had been removed – but the injury to her inner self would take a great deal longer.

She had become very quiet and withdrawn since Adam had gone and spent much of her time going for long solitary walks, which was most unlike her usual busy, cheerful self. It was inevitable that there would be a change in her. Her parents and Katherine knew that she needed time and space to come to terms with the loss for herself, as well as times when she would need comfort. Mary spent a great deal of time in Katherine's cottage, helping her with household tasks while

Katherine looked after Alastair. Mary even made him a pair of pyjamas, for which he was most grateful.

After his fever had finally left him, Alastair made slow but steady progress. He slept a great deal at first but, as time went on, he gradually stayed awake for longer periods. His cough continued to trouble him but this began to ease as the weeks progressed. All his belongings had been brought up from the hotel and Katherine's spare room became his for the duration of his convalescence.

Kind people from Lochaberdale came most days with little gifts for him; from cakes and scones to soups and sweets – all given for the "father of the man who found that imbecile Fergus John, and who caught his illness after helping with the search, and whose own father was a shepherd from Skye."

Small groups of children, standing shyly at his bedroom door, came with posies made from the wild flowers that had begun to grow on the machair: buttercups, marsh marigolds, dandelions, primroses, wild pansies and daisies, all clutched in their little hands. Katherine and Alastair were touched by their kindness and generosity and it helped in no small measure to aid his recovery.

While he was still very weak, Katherine continued to perform the intimate duties of a nurse towards her patient, tending to his well-being and comfort without embarrassment, caring for the needs of this brave and special man. The bond between them, forged initially in London and Maybury, deepened further during this time, developing into a close and lasting companionship that was to extend beyond the bounds of his convalescence.

Until Alastair was strong enough to read for himself, Katherine would spend time in the afternoon or evening reading aloud to him from one of her many books, or just sitting in the easy chair, which had remained in his bedroom, with her mending or sewing, keeping him company. Alastair grew to treasure these times as he drifted in and out of sleep, comforted by the sound of her voice or her presence. Knowing that he loved music, Katherine played the piano for him, leaving the doors open to both the sitting room and his bedroom so he could hear, recalling the time at Maybury when she had done so before.

Talking about the house in Oxfordshire brought back other memories for him, painful ones, but Alastair resolutely pushed those aside. They had no place here, and because he did not allow them to intrude, their importance began to recede and their adverse effect on his spirits to diminish.

Then one day, he felt well enough to come into the kitchen and sit at the table for the first time. It was only for a few minutes but it heralded the start of his real recovery as his strength returned. Eventually, he was able to get dressed and stay up for the morning or the afternoon.

People came to visit him then, staying for just a short time at first, but extending their stay as his health improved – Mary's parents Gordon and Fiona, Donald the postman and his wife Annie, and John and Marion from the hotel.

Sometimes there was quite a crowd and Katherine was looked after as well, as they insisted she "put her feet up" while they made the tea or did the washing up. The doctor looked in from time to time and examined Alastair, saying that he was making rapid progress under Katherine's ministrations and Mrs Gilgarry's potions. And Robbie was a frequent visitor.

The two men had established quite a friendship since their escapade together and Katherine was pleased for them, quietly enjoying their conversations while she sat near the range with her book open but unread, listening to them expound on philosophy or whatever subjects took their fancy.

Alastair was happy to let other people do most of the talking at first but as his strength increased he felt able to join in with the discussions, exchanging the occasional raised eyebrow or expression of amusement with Katherine when someone said something outlandish that made them all laugh.

The visitors never outstayed their welcome. They were considerate of his needs and never objected if he excused himself and retired to his room to rest. For his part, Alastair never minded that the conversation continued without him; indeed he quite liked that, and fell asleep to the gentle murmur of talking from these good people who were rapidly becoming his friends.

On the occasional warm sunny day, he would sit outside enjoying the fresh air and delighting in the stunning view across the bay, well wrapped up at Katherine's insistence as she was afraid he would become chilled; yet surreptitiously removing the blanket when she had gone indoors.

Good-humouredly, she would tell him off when she came back outside some minutes later, but he was unrepentant, saying that he was fine and knew how to look after himself.

"Don't you be difficult with me," she said, gently admonishing him. "I seem to remember a man who ignored the fact that he had the 'flu and gave himself the pneumonia instead."

"You've got me there. All right, I give in. I'll wear the blanket as you are *so* insistent!"

"Thank you, patient."

"You're welcome, nurse. Now how about that tea?"

"I don't know," she retorted, "there's no peace at all round here! Up and down, up and down I am, on my feet all day…" and Katherine, pretending to be grumpy, began to walk into the cottage.

Alastair caught her hand as she went by and held onto it. He said, deeply serious, "I can't ever thank you enough for all of this…"

Katherine put her other hand over his and replied earnestly, "Don't even try. Please. I'm just so glad that you're getting better." And before either of them became too emotional, she went inside and made the tea.

After Alex had heard from Katherine that his father was getting stronger, he began sending him documents to work on. Before he had left Cairnmor, he and Alastair had agreed that Alex would take over the correspondence involved in the search for Mhairi and Rupert, with Alastair ostensibly in charge but in fact leaving his son to make the contacts and proceed as he saw fit in Alastair's name. Consequently, Alex sent copies of all the documents to his father, who signed them and made annotations and suggestions as to how to proceed, instructing Alex to act on his behalf.

The rest of Alastair's work was taken over by one of his partners and he remained on indefinite sick leave, trying not to fret as to the way his clients were being handled. The work ethic was very strong in him and unwell as he still was,

Alastair found it hard to relinquish the strict habit of a lifetime. However, as the weeks went by and he began to feel better, he found that he could relax, and eventually it became quite easy to let go.

The irresistible magic of Cairnmor had seeped into his soul and he knew that he could quite easily make his home on the island. He said as much to Katherine one day while they were out for a gentle stroll along the sands in the warm, late May sunshine.

"Yes, it's a wonderful place to be, apart from the storms and the wind and the rain! But even that pales into insignificance beside its beauty and character, and the wonderful sense of community," she replied.

Sadness tinged her voice and Alastair's thoughts turned to their conversation soon after her arrival in London: how upset she had been at the mere contemplation of leaving here after her marriage. How well he understood that now; how well he appreciated her reluctance to leave and relinquish all of these things.

"You were quite right, you know," she continued, as though echoing his thoughts.

"About what?"

"About being kind to myself in leaving here; letting myself down gently. As you can see in the cottage, I've taken you completely at your word. I have done no packing at all! I keep putting it off, and yet it is the right decision to live in London after Alex and I are married."

Alastair was silent, thinking of the right way to phrase what he wanted to say. Having found it he said, "It's almost as though by not packing, you can cope with the moving because it doesn't make it seem permanent."

Once again, Katherine had cause to be grateful to Alastair for his insight. "Yes, that's it exactly."

They strolled slowly along the beach, resting every so often to ensure that he didn't overdo it. It was their furthest distance to date and Alastair managed to walk as far as Robbie's hut. The fisherman was there whittling a piece of wood and greeted them both with a cheery wave.

"And how are ye today?" Robbie asked Alastair.

"Doing quite well. But I think this is as far as I can go. May we join you?"

"Of course."

However, Katherine wanted to continue further and left the two men together. Alastair watched her as she made her way along the beach, an expression of tenderness in his eyes, and something else that he wasn't even aware of.

"Aye, she's a bonny lass, all right," said Robbie following his glance and seeing his expression.

Alastair smiled. "That she is."

"The bond between you is very deep…"

"Yes it is. Very." Then Alastair paused, concerned by what Robbie might be meaning. "What are you implying exactly?"

"Nothing. Absolutely nothing," said Robbie quickly and firmly, intending to leave no doubt that that was exactly what he meant. He did not wish there to be any misunderstanding between them. "Nothing at all other than it's natural ye should become close as she's been nursing ye back to health."

"For which I shall always be profoundly grateful."

"Aye."

"My son is a lucky man."

"That he is, that he is." And companionably the two of them continued with gentle conversation until Katherine returned. She and Alastair then bid farewell to Robbie and returned home.

But something of the conversation stayed with Alastair, and that evening he said to Katherine that maybe it was time he went back to the hotel, as he had imposed upon her hospitality long enough.

Katherine was horrified by the suggestion, called him an ungrateful wretch and said she would not even begin to entertain the idea, it was so ridiculous. Alastair, much relieved, laughed and said that he would stay as he dare not risk such wrath again.

"I should think so, too," she said, laughing as well. "Whatever brought that on?" she asked, puzzled.

"Oh, nothing. Just something that Robbie almost sort of intimated, that's all."

"I hope you told him to get lost."

"Not exactly, but he backtracked."

"I should hope so. I think he was testing you, knowing Robbie."

Alastair chuckled. "Well, I must have passed, because he was very affable for the rest of our conversation."

"Which he wouldn't have been if you hadn't, whatever the level of your friendship."

"He's very protective of you."

"Yes. He's sort of watched over me all my life. He made a considerable financial contribution to my education when I went away to the mainland, but especially so whilst I was at University. He felt he had a vested interest, I think, as he had taught me how to read and write in English before I started school."

"He taught you to read and write English?" asked Alastair, surprised.

"Yes. When I was little, we only spoke Gaelic at home and I grew up with Gaelic as my first language. My mother spoke some English but couldn't read or write it very well. My father only spoke Gaelic and couldn't read or write at all. At school all the lessons were conducted in English, a leftover from the dreaded retribution for the Jacobite rebellion. Island children had a reputation for being unintelligent as they all came to school with Gaelic as their mother tongue and suddenly found that they were having to do all their school work and tests in what was to them a foreign language."

"That's very unfair."

"Yes. Only the brightest managed to cope, or those who had parents who knew English. Mine didn't, so Robbie took it upon himself to make sure I had a head start on the other children before I went to school. Once the war started and he went away, he used write to me and continued to help me with my English as I always wrote back."

"And look where you are now," said Alastair.

234

"Yes, in the kitchen doing the washing-up!"

"Seriously though, he must be very proud of you."

Katherine blushed. "Yes, I think he is. Along with Gordon and Fiona and John and Marion, he came to my graduation ceremony at Edinburgh, bought himself a new suit for the occasion and was very honoured to act in *loco parentis* for the whole day."

"I can imagine." Then Alastair said, "Coming from Skye, my father was a Gaelic speaker but for some obscure reason, he refused to utter a word of it after he married my mother and settled in England. It was as though he had renounced his past completely. Is it a difficult language to learn?"

"Quite difficult. Strangely enough, having learnt to read and write in English, it wasn't until I was about eight years old that I decided I ought to be able to read and write Gaelic as well, especially as I spent so much time speaking the language. The spelling seems impossible at first as it doesn't appear to match the pronunciation, which can be a bit of a problem, but once you get used to that it's all right."

"I'd be quite interested to learn, I think, as it might help me understand something of what people are saying. Though most of the time, those who can, speak in English if I'm around, which is nice of them. And it's also a link to my father's heritage."

"I can teach you if you like."

"Thank you. I was hoping that you'd offer!"

The weather continued fine and Alastair and Katherine spent much time out in the fresh air, even managing to walk as far as Lochaberdale, although John offered to bring them home in his trap when he saw how tired Alastair was, and Marion insisted that they ate supper before going home. He read a great deal, dealt with his correspondence, made good progress with Gaelic and, something he had always wanted to do, began to learn the piano as well under Katherine's tutelage.

Every week he ordered newspapers from the mainland, and it was on yet another sunny day during the second week of June, when Alastair was reading the last of his out-of-date newspapers, sitting at the kitchen table with the back door open, his sleeves rolled up, feeling relaxed and well, that two strangers appeared in the doorway. They were smartly dressed (though the word 'sharp' leapt into Alastair's mind) and asked to speak to Miss Katherine MacDonald.

Alastair felt the hairs on the back of his neck rise; something that always happened to him when he was dealing with people he didn't trust. Cautiously, acquiring a Scottish accent, he replied, "Och, she's not here at the moment. But she'll be back directly."

The strangers stared at him. "We'll wait," one of them said.

And they did, seating themselves on the wooden settee, without waiting for an invitation to do so. This discourtesy did not go unnoticed by Alastair and he wondered what they were after. It was only a few moments later that Katherine returned from visiting Mary, surprised to see two strangers sitting in her kitchen.

As she came in the door, Alastair, who while he was waiting for her, had been thinking about how he could put her on her guard, said in Gaelic, not knowing whether it was grammatically correct or even whether he was using the correct words in the context said, "*cha'n'eil uile dithis,*" (not trust two persons).

Katherine's lips twitched at his inaccuracies but she understood his meaning and was immediately on her guard. "*Tapadh leibh,*" she replied.

"Are you Miss Katherine MacDonald?" demanded the shorter of the two men.

"I am. And who might you be?"

The taller man gave her his card, which she glanced at before passing it to Alastair, who read it with some dismay. He knew of these people: a London-based law firm with few scruples. They had been referred to the Law Society on at least one occasion that he knew of. His reaction was not lost on Katherine but went unnoticed by the two men.

The spokesperson for the pair continued, after consulting his clipboard. "Do you have the tenancy of this property?"

"I do."

"May we see the agreement, please," he said officiously.

Katherine looked at Alastair, who nodded imperceptibly. She went to the bureau in the sitting room, returning shortly and giving the document to the man, who immediately passed it over to his companion, who read it closely.

"Would you consider relinquishing your tenancy at any time in the future?"

"I would not."

"And if someone were to make it financially worth your while?"

"I still would not."

The man was silent, pulling down the corners of his mouth. "I see. This is not good at all for you, Miss MacDonald, not good at all."

Alastair was now very concerned; this was sailing very near to the wind. He remained silent for the moment, waiting to see what the man said next. He did not have to wait long.

"I am here to inform you, Miss MacDonald, that the island of Cairnmor and all its associated lands and properties have been sold to my client, Sir Roger Caitiff, who is of course, a well-known industrialist and millionaire. I am also here to inform you that there are going to be many changes taking place, for everyone including you, once we have completed our survey of the island and its inhabitants and advised Sir Roger of our findings."

"And what might those changes be?" said Alastair, losing his Scottish accent.

The man was taken aback by this sudden reversal and said, blustering, "I'm afraid I am not at liberty to reveal that at present."

"Why not?" responded Alastair pointedly.

"Because I am acting under the instructions of the new owner and he does not wish those to be made public at this time."

"What is he afraid of?"

"Er... n-nothing," stammered the man.

"Then why is he hiding his intentions?" Alastair was unrelenting.

"I am not at liberty to reveal my client's intentions at this time."

"I see. Has there been any formal notification of the sale of Cairnmor to the people who live here?"

"No. It was carried out as a private sale."

"The appropriate notification should still have been given whatever the method of sale. It is a legal requirement. Until this information has been made public, no survey of any property or sight of tenancy agreements should have been made."

"Not under Scottish law."

"Is your client a Scot?"

"No, he's English."

"And you are conversant with Scots law?"

The man hesitated. "Not exactly."

"Then please do not quote Scots law at me."

"Who are you?"

"My name is Alastair Stewart, of Stewart, Patterson and Faraday, Solicitors – you may have heard of us – and Miss MacDonald is my client. I suggest that before you return with any further veiled threats or attempted bribery, you make sure that you and your client act in accordance with the law, English or Scots. Now, good day, gentlemen. And please return the tenancy agreement before you leave."

After they had departed in some disarray, Katherine looked at an exhausted Alastair and said, with open admiration, "I can see why you and Alex make such a formidable team. All I can say is that I'm very glad that you're on my side!"

And over a cup of tea they discussed the matter at some length. During the next few days it transpired that the two men had been on the island for a few weeks and had imposed themselves upon a great number of crofters, spreading alarm with their attempts at coercion, especially among those inhabitants who could not speak English. To make matters worse, some of them had had their tenancy agreement document taken away by the men at the end of their visit, leaving them without proof of their right to live on their crofts.

After hearing this, Alastair paid the two men a visit at the hotel and demanded that they return the documents. This they did, not having any legal right to retain them and, with Katherine acting as interpreter and scribe, Alastair spent several days documenting the conduct of the two men and taking sworn statements, so that the islanders had legal evidence which could be produced in the future should the need arise.

However, at the end of that week, the two men left Cairnmor, not having troubled the residents any further because of Alastair's swift intervention. Their imminent departure was noted with satisfaction by both Katherine and Alastair as they waited with Mary on the quayside in great anticipation for the steamer that Saturday, exactly a week before Katherine's wedding.

Alastair was looking forward to seeing Alex and Lily again, especially now that he was almost well. He had missed them both.

And as for Mary? Mary had heard of the kindness of Michael, Alex's friend; had returned to her croft after his departure to find it well cared for and the animals well-tended; and had remembered their previous meeting, and his charm and good manners. She could not help her heart that now beat so quickly at the thought of seeing this man again, of meeting him properly. But she was anxious. What would she say? She wanted to get to know him very much and hoped that he would want to do the same with her.

And what of Katherine? Katherine couldn't wait. The wedding was going to happen this time; there would be no more disasters, no more delays, no more separation from the man she loved. It was going to be the perfect occasion of which she had always dreamed, of that she had no doubt.

Lochfoyle took an age to dock. It was a lifetime before the steamer was made secure. The gangplank was lowered and Lily and Michael walked down together. But there was no sign of Alex.

He had not come.

CHAPTER 30

"But I don't understand," said Katherine. "Why hasn't he come? Where is he?" She was angry, hurt, dismayed that Alex had not arrived. All her fears and doubts about him suddenly re-surfaced. How could he do this?

"He had important business to attend to…" said Michael, somewhat apologetically.

"Important business?! What important business? Surely nothing is as important as our wedding? We've already postponed it once, endured endless separations, storms, searches for missing people. Surely he can put his work or whatever it is aside for once and put us first."

Sensing her mounting anxiety, Alastair suggested that they move away from the quayside, to a place where they could talk properly. He had to admit that he too was very concerned; his son had better have a very good reason for this. It was most unfair on Katherine.

"It's all right," said Lily, when they had moved away from the harbour and were standing on the path leading up to the hotel. "Don't worry; it is something really important, apparently, though Michael won't tell me what it is, the beast. He says even he doesn't know, though I don't believe him." She glowered at her travelling companion. "Alex gave Michael some letters…"

"Yes. There's one for you, Alastair, and one for you, Katherine. They both contain the same information and an explanation of why he isn't here…"

"Though yours won't be a love letter, I'll bet!" interrupted Lily, addressing her father and displaying her usual frankness. Mary couldn't help laughing at this and even Katherine managed to raise a smile.

"There are also some documents for you to sign, Alastair, and Alex said that those need to go back with the steamer today," continued Michael.

"I'll make sure that's done," said the ever efficient solicitor.

Katherine tucked her letter into the pocket of her dress, deciding that she would read it later. Alex was not here and there was nothing she could do about that, so she decided there was no point in pursuing the matter or fretting about it. Feeling subdued, they all made their way up to the hotel, where Michael and Lily were shown to their rooms.

Alastair had moved back into the hotel, having brought his things earlier that day, in order to be with Lily during her first visit to Cairnmor. She was beside herself with excitement.

"I'm *so* pleased to be here," she said eagerly to him as he sat in the easy chair in her room, while she unpacked. "I have to confess that I was glad when the wedding was postponed. It was selfish of me, I know, but I was so upset when I thought I would be missing it. But I was very sorry for Alex and Katherine, and for you. You really are better now, aren't you?" she said, an expression of genuine concern on her face.

"Yes, really better," replied Alastair reassuringly. "But I still get very tired."

"Poor Daddy, I expect you do. Thank you for all your letters. I was so worried about you, but I'm glad that Katherine has looked after you so well."

"She's been wonderful."

It was a simple statement and yet it contained such a wealth of gratitude and feeling that Alastair knew he would never be able to put into words. He remained thoughtful before saying, "I enjoyed reading your letters too. You have a gift for writing, you know. You make everything seem so vivid and funny; oh, so funny!"

Lily laughed. "There were lots of things to describe." Then she brought the subject back to the present. "Alex was very kind to arrange the wedding during my half-term but the extra week I've had to take means that I've got to do my end of year exams on my own when I go back. Therefore, I've got to revise while I'm here, worst luck. But I think I'm pretty much up to speed with most subjects, so it shouldn't be too odious a task." And Lily chattered on happily, while her father listened, pleased to be with his daughter again.

Michael was first downstairs and found Mary on her own, Katherine having disappeared to speak to John and tell him that Alex would not be coming that week. Michael and Mary had not spoken since his arrival, but had merely exchanged shy smiles as they walked up the path to the hotel.

Now, Michael swallowed hard, thinking about what to say. His feelings for her had not diminished. He had dreamed of meeting her again, pictured it in his mind. But now that it was actually here… His mouth was dry, he couldn't swallow, no words would come out. All he was able to do was look at her as she stood by the window, framed in the sunlight.

"How are you?" he managed to say at last.

"Much better, thank you."

"I'm glad."

"Thank you for looking after my croft."

"You're welcome." Then he said, "How are the animals?" After he had uttered the words, Michael wanted to curl up in embarrassment. Of all the stupid, inane things to ask… *how are the animals?* He couldn't believe he had just said that.

But Mary merely smiled and told him exactly how they were, as though it was the most natural thing in the world: how the hens had escaped one day and had to be rounded up from the beach, how the pony's cough was now better and the cow had been giving extra milk ever since Michael had looked after her, and how Mary was so grateful to him for all that he had done.

So deeply were they involved in their conversation that when Marion came into the room with the tray of tea things, her presence went unnoticed. She smiled to herself as she went out again without disturbing them. Yes, everything was definitely right with the world.

It was not until much later, after she had left the hotel following the evening meal and walked home up the hill in the extended summer daylight, that Katherine had the opportunity to read her letter from Alex.

She lit the Tilley lamp and sat at the kitchen table with the door open, allowing the mild late evening breeze to flow over her as she gazed across the sweeping view of the bay. The cottage seemed empty without Alastair. He had been living with her for three months and she missed him. She wondered if he had read his letter yet.

Katherine opened the envelope. Inside were two others; one written on in Alex's familiar, comforting hand and the other addressed to her in an unfamiliar script – or was it? Surely she had seen it before, but where?

On the outside of Alex's letter, were instructions asking her to *'Read this one first. A. xx'* Which she did. And she was stunned by what she read.

My darling,

Please forgive me for not being there with you. Believe me when I say that only something of the utmost importance would keep me from you at this time – what should be our special time, when we should be together, sharing the joy of anticipation in our wedding to come.

You see, my love, I have found Rupert and Mhairi. Yes, they are real and do exist! Isn't it wonderful? I have been in very close contact with them, on a personal as well as a professional level. I can't begin to tell you how exciting it was, after all our months of searching, to receive their first letter, acknowledging mine and its contents. They are the reason that I'm not with you today, my darling, because they are coming over here, over to England, but their boat doesn't dock in Southampton until Monday. I felt it was vital that I meet with them.

What you are going to read next will change your life forever, totally and irrevocably. I've agonized over the best way to tell you these things; whether to leave it as a complete surprise until I see you or to tell you everything in a letter. After much heart searching, I have decided to write it down for you. Then you will be able to adjust and get used to the idea before our wedding, as I shall arrive on the day itself and it would not be right to leave it until then.

Turn to Dad if you need to talk to anyone. He will know everything, as I've told him in his letter, but I've asked him not to reveal the contents until you are willing for them to become public knowledge. You will understand once you have read my words.

This is the hard bit; how do I tell you? There is no easy way. If we were together, I would take you for a walk along the beautiful sands near your croft, put my arms around you, bury my face into your gorgeous hair, look deep into your eyes and tell you that even though your world is about to be turned upside down, you are, and will always be, the same person I have come to love; that you are uniquely yourself and nothing can ever change that or the way I feel about you. Then I would tell you very gently what it is you have to know.

You see, my love, Mhairi and Rupert are your mother and father. The kind people who raised you were not your real parents but brought you up as their own child. You are the baby Rupert and Mhairi had all those years ago and gave up because circumstances meant they couldn't look after you. You are the 'elusive baby' we struggled to find, but of whom there seemed to be no trace. It was you. You were there. All the time. But of course, we didn't know it then.

I will leave you to read the other letter that I have enclosed and then you will understand. It is to you from Mhairi. She asked me to read it first before sending it so that I would know and understand everything and be able to share it with you fully. It is quite a journey.

Remember, I love <u>you</u> and always will.
Your own, Alex xxxx

Katherine sat there, shocked. She read Alex's words again. She didn't know what to do. She couldn't bring herself to read Mhairi's letter. Not yet. The hurt was too great; the feeling of betrayal on so many different levels too much to cope with, too much to be able to take in any more details, or the reasons *why*. It was too soon.

Her whole world had indeed been turned upside down, just as Alex had predicted. Her whole notion of who she was, the whole security of her past life had been wiped out with that short, bald statement, *'Rupert and Mhairi are your mother and father'*.

She needed someone to talk to, someone who would understand this momentous change in her life. Alex's letter was incredibly sensitive and kind. He had known how it would affect her; he understood how she would feel after reading his letter. And she loved him for his insight, his perspicacity. But he was not here, *now*, at this moment when she needed him the most. *'Turn to Dad if you need to talk to anyone,'* he had written. But how could she? It was nearly midnight. Alastair would be asleep.

That notwithstanding, she knew she had to go to him and began the long walk down to Lochaberdale, taking Alex's letter and the other envelope with her. But there, in the distance, in the diffuse light of a northern summer night, she saw the dear, familiar figure of Alastair walking up the hill towards her. She started to run and when she had reached his outstretched arms, she wept tears of confusion and bitterness.

Alastair held her close for a long time, stroking her hair, offering silent consolation. Once her grief had begun to subside, he put his arm round her shoulders and led her the few hundred yards back to her cottage, where he sat her down on the wooden settee and made them both a cup of tea.

"I'm sorry," she said.

Alastair shook his head. "Don't be."

"I needed you."

"I know. That's why I came."

She smiled a very watery smile up at him and gently, he smiled back. The kettle boiled, its whistle intrusive. Alastair made the tea, poured it out and then came to sit down beside her.

How could he best comfort her? What could he say that would give her world back the solid base she had always known, the very roots of her identity? But there was nothing that could ever do that. Only time would lessen the shock of such a momentous discovery as this. He understood that only too well.

Katherine laid her head against his shoulder, and he put his arm round her and began to speak.

"When Roberta left, my whole life changed, just as yours has now. My responses to the world around became different. I wasn't the same person any more. I felt I had lost my identity, my *raison d'être,* if you like. We hadn't been close for a long time; indeed, looking back, I'm not certain that we were ever

242

close, but there was a security, a familiarity about our marriage that gave me the basis from which to go out in the world to do my job, to go about my business, to live my life. She wasn't always very loving towards me, but I loved her and tried to make her happy. After she left, as you know, my world fell apart. But, with your support, I have now put it back together again, just as you will yours. You are loved by so many people..."

Katherine looked up at him, very still, listening to his words, her cheeks wet with silent tears. For the moment, Alastair struggled to continue, his own emotions threatening to spill over.

"You are loved by so many people, for yourself, for who you are, for who you have become. You've lived independently for so many years now, you are very much your own person. That is your identity, your security. Hold onto these things for they are very important. From what we know of them, Rupert and Mhairi, as your biological parents, have given you many gifts – your intelligence, your musicality. Who knows what else you might find when you read Mhairi's letter?" He regarded her with compassion, with empathy. "Do you feel strong enough to do that now?" he asked gently.

"Yes, I think so. But will you read it with me?"

"If you would like me to."

"Yes."

"Then I will."

And, with trembling fingers, Katherine opened the second envelope.

Dear Katherine,
This is not an easy letter to write. We do not know one another, but Rupert and I hope that soon we will...

How strange it was, thought Katherine, recalling the hours and days that she and Alex had spent searching for these two people. How well she had thought she knew them; how little she had in reality...

... be able to meet and change that. It will be harder for you, because you will only just have discovered that Rupert and I are your parents, whereas we have always known and thought of you as our child.

Then why didn't you make contact with me? There was plenty of opportunity; twenty-seven years in fact, thought Katherine, bitterly.

I understand from your fiancé Alex that you have been instrumental in the search for Rupert and me. I am so glad to know that. It makes some things easier to say.
I gather also that you have received a letter from Aunt Flora and that you know many details of our lives up to the time I left the Lake District. Therefore, I shall take up our story from there.

And both Katherine and Alastair were drawn once more into Mhairi and Rupert's world, a world that Katherine and Alex had been fascinated by, an adventure in which Alastair had become involved way beyond his initial professional capacity.

Despite her emotional state of mind and the tears that kept welling up and spilling over onto the page as she read, intellectually, Katherine could not help being curious as to what had happened and, yes, even experiencing an evanescent pleasure in at last knowing the rest of the story.

It was also quite something, when she thought about it, that it was actually Mhairi who was writing these words to her, Katherine. Rupert and Mhairi had seemed so vivid and yet sometimes, it had also felt as though they had been mere characters in a book. But they were now real; very much so. She read on…

After leaving the Lake District, I had a very difficult journey back to Glasgow. My time was very near and I left Aunt Flora against the express wishes of the doctor, whom she had called to try and persuade me to stay. But my mother needed me. When she was ill, Pa was unable to cope and I always had to look after her.

When I arrived home, I found my mother to be very poorly indeed and she needed to go to hospital immediately. I went with her to the Southern General Hospital, which was in Shieldhall and not too far from where we lived in Govan. It had become like a second home for Ma and the staff had got to know me very well. Pa had been called from Mathieson's and arrived very quickly. He was glad to see me, but I was very angry with him.

Then I began to get bad pains in my stomach and realized I was going into labour. I kept it to myself – I couldn't have my baby in this hospital as Pa would know where I was and would arrange for the child to be taken away. So I decided I would run away. I had no notion of where I would go, or where I would find shelter. I just knew I had to get away. And then, miracle of miracles, as I came out of the main entrance, my beloved Rupert appeared – no coat or hat – just a carpet bag and his violin case. I couldn't believe it. We got on the first tram that came along, changing three times to cover our trail just in case we were being followed. You must remember we were very young and the power of our parents over our lives was very great.

By the time we reached a place called Mount Florida, the contractions were coming very close together and I could travel no further. We got off the tram and walked as far as I could manage. In desperation, Rupert knocked on the door of the nearest house and a very kind lady called Rose and her sister, who was staying with her, seeing my predicament – I was clinging onto the railings in agony – immediately let us inside and you were born in her front room.

It was a long and difficult birth, you were round the wrong way and it needed a lot of skill on the part of this lady and her sister to deliver you. The sister's name was Grace MacDonald – the lady you knew as your mother. Rupert and I called you Anna Katherine.

Grace had come to Glasgow to be with her sister Rose who had just had her fifth child. She was needed before the birth as Rose had been ordered to take bed rest until her baby was born and Grace came to look after the family. Rose's husband was away in the Merchant Navy. Grace had been staying there for three months when we arrived. Her home, of course, was Cairnmor. Despite my agony, this fact was not lost on me and I took it to be a good sign.

I was bleeding very heavily, and there was nothing Rose and Grace could do to stop it. They called their doctor who immediately arranged for me to be taken to the Victoria Infirmary which was very close by. I was so weak after the birth and losing so much blood that I was ill for several weeks. Rose fed the baby – fed you – for me and Rupert stayed with you in their small cramped house. We were so grateful to them.

Searching for work, Rupert answered an advertisement in the newspaper for a violin teacher. He used a false name, Robert Murchison, as a precaution, and soon picked up a few pupils. We were soon able to pay for our keep with Rose and her sister.

Rupert went to the Southern General several times, always careful that he was not seen, but there was no change in my mother's condition. Then one day, not long after I had left hospital, there was a knock at the door. Grace answered and was confronted by an unknown man demanding to know my whereabouts as he had a court order to take my baby away for adoption.

Unknowingly, despite his precautions, Rupert had been followed back to Mount Florida by this man. We had taken Rose and Grace into our confidence, so she was very unhelpful to the stranger and was not intimidated, even though he waved an official-looking document in her face and threatened her with the police if she failed to hand over the baby.

When he was refused entry, the man forced his way into the house. Rupert and I escaped out of the back door, leaving you with Rose, who quickly began to feed you to hide your true identity. The man searched the house with great difficulty, with the babies and children getting in the way, but of course found nothing. Rupert and I ran as fast as we could. I had still not recovered fully.

We stayed away for hours, sitting in the park for the whole night, not a pleasant experience, and going back to the house in Mount Florida before first light. This was no way to live our lives. We would have to go far away. But we had no money and nowhere to live, as we knew we could not stay with Rose and Grace any more. There was no sign of the man when we got back, and that day we had a long talk with Rose and Grace.

Rose then got in touch with their other sister Elsie who, together with her husband Albert, owned a bakery shop in Cathcart. It wasn't very far away, but it was far enough. They had a spare room above the shop where we could stay, and when I was better, Elsie said I could help out in the shop.

But little Anna, would she be safe? What would happen if the detective found us again? We were young and very scared that you might be taken away without our knowledge. Grace offered to look after you, to take you home with her to Cairnmor where you would be safe. Then, when we were able to, we could come and collect you. We knew you would be well cared for, because she had been wonderful with you when I was so poorly and couldn't look after you properly. And we would also know exactly where you were. And I had always *dreamed that one day my baby would grow up on Cairnmor. It was almost as though it was meant to be and seemed an ideal solution. It was heart-breaking to say goodbye to you, but I knew that you would be safe.*

The man came to their house on many other occasions, but eventually stopped. He never found you or us and we were not troubled after that.

Elsie and Albert were lovely people and treated us as their own. Rupert and I had been incredibly lucky. He built up a very good teaching practice, travelling all over Cathcart using the district railway, and gained a very good reputation. He turned out to be a very fine music teacher, a career which he had not anticipated!

Once we had come of age, we were married. I paid for our keep by working in Elsie and Albert's shop and we saved all of Rupert's earnings, apart from what we needed for day to day living. We were intent on starting a new life in Canada where we knew you would be completely safe.

After three years, we had saved enough money. I travelled to Cairnmor to collect you. Rupert stayed in Glasgow as there was only just enough money for one of us to make that journey. I had written many times to Grace, but received no reply. After I arrived, I found out where you lived and, well hidden, I watched you playing outside your cottage, so happy and contented with Grace and her husband. I didn't have the heart to upset your settled life on Cairnmor. It was an incredibly difficult decision; a heart-breaking decision, as Rupert and I had spent the last three years working towards this moment.

Was it the right decision? I still don't know. Only you will be able to tell me that. But all I could think about was not disrupting your life, taking you away from everything you had ever known, to live with two strangers. Because that is exactly what we had become – you would have had no idea who I was. It was something we had not thought of when we originally came up with the plan of your coming to the island. At that time, I had to think about what was best for you, to keep you safe.

Agonized and upset, waiting for the time when the steamer left on its return journey, I walked along the beach and came across a fisherman tending his nets by an old wooden hut. I had to talk to someone and I poured out Rupert's and my story to him, and then made him promise that he would never tell a living soul. I am told he kept his promise, but has also done far more than that. He has watched over you and made sure that you had everything you needed. It was indeed a lucky day when I spoke to him.

So, I caught the steamer back to Oban that same day and travelled on to Glasgow. Rupert understood my reasoning, but like me, was very upset. Some weeks later, we set off for Nova Scotia.

We have made a good life out here. The cultural life is vibrant and varied. Rupert is Director of the Music Academy in Halifax, as well as conducting the Philharmonic Society Orchestra and the Halifax String Orchestra, which he founded. He never became an architect, as music took over his life and he has made a very good living from it. Rupert is also a successful composer and says that the structure and appearance of the music on the page is very important to him and satisfies that side of his creativity.

246

I am involved with running the Academy on the administrative side and sing in the local choral society. Much to our regret, we have never had any more children. The difficulties that I had after you were born meant that I was unable to.

So that is our story. There is more to tell, but Rupert has just looked at the clock and said that I must stop as he needs to post the letter (he is sitting here by my side while I have been writing).

For us to have found you is a miracle; for you, your fiancé and future father-in-law to have found us is a miracle. I hope that soon we will be able to see each other, and that we can at least become friends.

We send our love to you.

Rupert and Mhairi.

CHAPTER 31

When they had finished reading, both Alastair and Katherine were silent: no words were needed, and there would be time for talking later. Alastair lifted his arm from around her shoulders as it was beginning to feel cramped but Katherine remained close to him, leaning against him, not wanting to move, finding comfort in his presence.

Eventually, she said, "I'm glad you're here."

"So am I," he replied.

"Would you like to stay?"

"Yes please." For a few brief moments, Alastair held her to him, before kissing her forehead and gently releasing her. He smiled at her as he stood up and said, "Goodnight, Katherine."

"Goodnight, Alastair." She sensed that he knew of her gratitude; she did not need to speak the words.

Emotionally drained, Katherine fell asleep immediately but next door, in the spare room, Alastair stayed awake, thinking of Katherine, his son's future wife, before he too eventually drifted off to sleep.

During that week, Katherine walked for miles, sometimes with Alastair and Lily, sometimes with Mary, but more often than not on her own, preferring her own company and the healing power of silent thought and contemplation. Cairnmor had always been her solace, a place of peace and solitude, and it did not fail her now. Gradually she came to terms with her altered heritage, accepting her life as it was now, and as it had been.

She ceased to feel angry with Mhairi and Rupert for 'abandoning' her, reasoning – especially after talking to Robbie of Mhairi's terrible dilemma and abject misery in her realization that to take her child away would cause unnecessary cruelty to both little Anna and Grace – that it was her *love* for Katherine that had guided her.

She worked her way through her resentment that Robbie had known all along and had not told her, even after her adoptive parents had died. But ultimately, she was glad for his sake, so that he could meet Mhairi, as he inevitably would, with a clear conscience and the knowledge that he had kept his word. To someone like Robbie, that was very important. In any case, he had not known where Mhairi was to be found, so to tell Katherine would have proved pointless.

She began to analyse and acknowledge the intellectual void that had always existed between herself and the people she had known as her parents; a void that had always mystified her. Now she was able to understand why.

Katherine looked back on her life as a whole, tracing its journey. She had grown up in a loving and caring household, and had been granted great opportunity to develop her own resources, both physically, by being allowed to roam the island unhindered when she was very young, and also mentally, through learning to manage without her parents.

She had become close to an incredible community of people who had supported her, taking responsibility for her well-being and financial needs. And she came to realize that she did not wish her life to have been any different. It was indeed as Alex had written – nothing had changed, she was still the same person, with the same past; but simultaneously, everything had changed and her world would never be the same again.

That was as far as she could go for the moment. The rest would reveal and resolve itself with time. She began to feel the first stirrings of curiosity to meet Rupert and Mhairi in their new guise as her parents rather than the two people whom she and Alex had spent so many days, weeks, and months searching for; indeed, they were the very reason that she and Alex had met. There was an intriguing connection here, eddies and currents of life bringing them together with an inevitability that was almost tangible.

Towards the end of the week, Katherine emerged from her self-imposed isolation and went to find Mary. Together, they sought out Lily at the hotel and had great fun trying on their dresses. Lily said that Katherine was going to look beautiful and the three of them admired themselves in the mirror in Lily's bedroom, pretending to put up their hair and walk down an imaginary aisle.

After they had changed back into their everyday clothes, they met with Father McPhee at the church, along with Michael, as best man, and Gordon, who was to give Katherine away, and he went through the ceremony with them; at least as best they could without the groom.

Lily suggested that Alastair pretend to be Alex, but he declined politely, saying, however, that he would stay and watch. Michael, therefore, fulfilled both roles and had them all, but especially Mary and Father McPhee, in fits of laughter with his antics and repartee, so that by the time they had finished, none of them was any the wiser as to what they should do when.

Alastair observed, from his position on the front bench, that whenever Michael was supposed to be the groom, a role which produced rare moments of sensibleness, he always moved back slightly to hold Mary's hand. This did not go unnoticed by Father McPhee either, and the two men exchanged an understanding smile. Her father Gordon, however, seemed oblivious; intentionally or otherwise, neither man could be sure.

Their next task was in the new village hall or Great Hall, as it had been re-christened by John from the hotel after Katherine's return from London, when she recounted to her friends the story of all the Great Halls she had visited.

Fiona, Marion and Annie, Donald's wife from the post office, joined the gathering. Together they swept and dusted the main hall where the reception was to be held, followed by the ceilidh later in the evening. Into this larger hall they moved the benches and tables from the ante-room, laying them with cutlery, plates, napkins and glasses, which Alastair polished with great care.

As with all weddings on Cairnmor, everyone was contributing to the repast and all who brought food came to the reception; no one was turned away. The same applied to the ceilidh. Robert Campbell was to bring his pipes, his brother Andrew his accordion, and the MacClennan brothers their fiddles. A sense of high expectation and anticipation settled over Lochaberdale.

After supper, the working party all gathered in the hotel lounge: a group of friends sharing an evening together. It turned into one of those occasions that

Katherine had described to Alastair in a letter several months previously, with wit and laughter, serious conversation and games.

On this occasion, they played charades, dividing into teams, with Katherine, Alastair, Lily, Michael and Mary being on the winning side, narrowly defeating Gordon, Fiona, John, Marion and Annie. Father McPhee kept the score, devised the words and sentences, and made sure there was no cheating. If Alex had been there, thought Katherine, it would have been a perfect evening.

And so, her wedding day dawned. She was ready, her suitcase packed for her honeymoon and taken down to the hotel the previous day. She still had no idea where she and Alex would be going: Mary, Fiona and Marion had masterminded whatever it was as a surprise and refused to tell her. Lily had become involved as well, but, with her eyes dancing and sparkling with fun, she merely said that Katherine and Alex would *love* it, and she had kept silent about the details, much to her credit.

Katherine lingered over her breakfast, the kitchen door open, looking out over the view she loved, grief catching in her chest and tears filling her eyes, knowing this would be for the last time in this way, and that her married life would take her far away. She sat very still, treasuring the moment when suddenly, in the far, far distance, from her vantage point way above Loch Aberdale, she saw the tiny plume of smoke from *Lochfoyle*.

Excitement replaced sadness; reflection became anticipation. Trying not to hurry, for there was plenty of time, she washed up her dishes and put them away. Closing the door to her cottage, she paused, touching it gently, reverently, saying 'thank you'.

Yes, she would come back, yes, she would stay here again, it would always belong to her, always be her home, but her past life would be gone and a new future awaited her – a future that she had anticipated and one which she had not, that which was unknown and unexpected.

Slowly, Katherine walked down the hill to her new life, and once the steamer had docked, straight into Alex's waiting arms. They held each other for a long, long time. She was almost in tears with joy and relief that he had actually come, that he was *here*, and that there would be no more waiting, no more agony of separation.

And then, lifting her head and opening her eyes, looking over Alex's shoulder, she saw them, standing uncertainly on the quayside... older than in the photograph, but still unmistakable, watching her, sharing the first glimpse of their daughter for twenty-seven years: Rupert and Mhairi.

Katherine put her hand to her mouth in an effort to control her emotions, but failed miserably and smiling through her tears, she went over to them. They stood together in silent contemplation for what seemed an eternity, but was in reality only a matter of seconds; none of them knowing quite what to do or say; the three of them overwhelmed.

It was Rupert who spoke first.

"So," he said, with a mock-serious expression, "as it was your wedding we thought we might as well come and see you." Suddenly his face was wreathed in smiles while Mhairi looked on horrified, knowing his impish sense of humour only too well and wondering what he was going to say next, especially at this most delicate of times.

"Nice of you to think about me," said Katherine, responding in kind. "I suppose you'll want to give me away." She creased up her face with agony at the unintentional double meaning contained in her words – words which could so easily be misconstrued. She took Mhairi's hands, reassuring her, and the older woman held onto them tightly. "I'm so sorry, I didn't mean..." she said.

"I know," said her mother.

"Yes, I'll certainly walk down the aisle with you," said Rupert, taking their hands in his, showing that he too understood what she had meant.

"You'll have to fight a duel with Gordon first," added Katherine, taking a chance that they shared the same sense of humour, testing, probing.

"That's all right, I brought my violin, I can use the bow. I presume you have arrows on the island?"

"Yes, you can buy them at the post office."

And suddenly, the three of them were laughing, crying and hugging each other all at the same time, and soon, everyone was there, waiting to be introduced: Alastair, Lily, Michael, Mary, Gordon and Fiona.

To Gordon, Rupert said, "I gather we have to debate who'll perform fatherly duties at the wedding."

"Och, it's fine," said Gordon, "I think ye have prior claim! I'll talk ye through the ceremony if ye like."

"Thank you," said Rupert graciously.

At the hotel, John and Marion were delighted to welcome them and very soon, it was all round Lochaberdale that the son of Sir Charles Mathieson, the man who now owned *the* most famous shipbuilding firm on the Clyde, was here on the island, and that he'd come to his daughter's wedding. And moreover, that said daughter was their own Katherine.

If Katherine had been party to these conversations and gossip, she would have been jolted into awareness by what they were saying. Because in all of her reflections during the past week, not once had she thought about the fact that her father was an exceedingly wealthy man.

Events moved swiftly after this. There was not much time before the wedding. Katherine, Mary and Lily disappeared into Lily's room and dressed in their finery. As soon as Mhairi was ready, she joined them, proud that her daughter was so lovely; so thankful to be here.

They all told her that she looked lovely as well, and Lily said that the resemblance between them was striking. Katherine and Mhairi stood together looking in the mirror, and saw that this was indeed the case, though Katherine was taller than her mother by an inch or so.

While Mhairi was helping Mary to adjust her hat, Lily said to Katherine, very quietly, "I really like your mother, she's sweet and kind. I wish mine was like that."

Mhairi overheard and immediately resolved to get to know this pretty girl whose mother had walked out on her.

Alex had been very open about his family and he, Mhairi and Rupert had come to know each other well during the past week. They approved of their future son-in-law very much indeed, and wished him and Katherine great happiness in their life together.

Mhairi and Rupert had decided that they would call her Katherine, her middle name; the name by which she had become known, her identity. She was still their daughter. They had the birth certificate to prove it.

In accordance with Cairnmor tradition, both bride and groom walked to the church with their respective families; the groom preceding the bride. Alex, Alastair and Michael had already gone, and would have arrived there by now, so Katherine, Mary, Mhairi and Rupert, and, of course, Lily, as the other bridesmaid, made their way up the hill from the hotel to the white-washed stone building that had seen the celebration of so many island weddings.

The church was full to capacity: people were standing at the back and down the sides, lining the path outside and waiting for their first glimpse of the bride. They were rewarded for their patience, admiring her dress, saying how beautiful she looked.

Katherine could only smile at them, overwhelmed that so many people had come to the church on this her wedding day. Father McPhee greeted them at the door, and escorted Mhairi down the aisle, so that she would not have to walk alone.

Mary adjusted Katherine's veil and dress, arranging the train so that it fanned out on the floor, the white satin shimmering against the grey flag-stones. The signal was given and the music began – played by a professional string quartet hired from Glasgow by John and Marion (after consultation with Alex).

To the ethereal, uplifting sound of Elgar's *Chanson de Matin*, Katherine walked down the aisle on the right arm of her proud father Rupert, whose eyes kept filling up with tears, as did those of his daughter – it being a very emotional journey for both of them.

There waiting at the altar, his eyes alight with love and desire, was the wonderful man who was to be her husband. Rupert gave her hand to Alex and then stepped back to the pew-like bench, where he took his place next to Mhairi, who smiled up at him and squeezed his hand. Mary came forward and took Katherine's bouquet of roses, and she and Lily stood behind the bride and groom.

Alex, handsome and smart in a morning suit, whispered in her ear that she looked beautiful, and held her hand tightly, as nervous as she was emotional. As the ceremony progressed, they relaxed and began to savour every moment: Father McPhee friendly and warm in his presentation, the wedding service itself rich in tradition and liturgy.

In his introduction, the priest welcomed everyone by saying, "Marriage is a sacred opportunity for the couple to join with family and friends in witnessing their vows and dedicating their marriage to God."

Then followed the chosen readings, hymns and the psalm, after which Father McPhee gave his address to the bride, groom and congregation. He promised not to go on for too long, saying that as he was delivering his talk in both Gaelic and English, that alone would be sufficient reason to keep it short. It also gave him a good excuse to say everything twice, which he was more than happy to do, as those who knew him well would be only too glad to testify.

This observation was greeted with general amusement and he proceeded to elaborate on the marriage theme and give pertinent advice to the bride and groom, a homily filled with humour and grace.

Then came the Rite of Marriage itself, and Katherine and Alex expressed their mutual consent to the marriage, making their vows of fidelity and love before the whole congregation. Michael avoided the temptation to pretend he had mislaid the rings, much to Alex's relief, and gave them simply and carefully to Father McPhee, who blessed them.

They were very special moments when Alex and Katherine placed the rings on each other's fingers: shared intimate moments full of sensitivity and tenderness, moments that held all the depth of commitment and longing that had preceded this day.

Father McPhee gave the Nuptial Blessing and invited Katherine and Alex to seal their union with a kiss, which they did much to the delight of the whole congregation.

The wedding party moved across to a table at the side of the church to complete the civil declaration and sign the register while the string quartet, together with Lily playing her flute, performed a selection of music of a suitably romantic character. Lily began the proceedings, with a brilliant solo demonstration of her musical flair.

Rupert took an immediate professional interest in Lily's talent, recognizing her potential. He resolved to talk to her about her playing after the wedding. He was so taken with her abilities that Mhairi had to bring him back gently to the task in hand as together with Alastair, they signed the register as witnesses.

At the completion of the formalities, they resumed their original places and with great pleasure, Father McPhee introduced Alex and Katherine to everyone as husband and wife, kissing the bride on her cheek and shaking hands with the groom, much to the amusement of the watching congregation. With this touch of informality, the final hymn was sung with great spirit and the service ended with the Blessing and Dismissal.

Alex and Katherine walked down the aisle, happy and smiling, together at last, followed by Mary and Lily, both families, and then the rest of the congregation. They emerged into bright sunlight, to be greeted with a shower of rice confetti and cheering.

Alex had arranged for a photographer to come from Glasgow and they stood patiently while several photographs were taken, first with the church and then the view across the bay as the backdrop – Alex and Katherine alone; then with Michael, Mary and Lily; Rupert, Mhairi and Alastair; close friends; and finally, as many people as could be fitted into the frame.

But it was not over yet. From behind the church, the sound of pipes could be heard and there was Robert Campbell, resplendent in full Highland regalia, to lead the way for the wedding party, in time-honoured tradition, on their journey to the Great Hall, where a transformation had taken place.

Marion and Annie, along with several of the villagers, had laid out the food which everyone had been bringing since first thing that morning, and had decorated the rooms with wild flowers from the machair. It looked beautiful and the hall was completely filled by the guests and friends. So many people came that an impromptu picnic took place outside on the sea-shore adjoining the road, and the islanders had been so kind and generous, that there was even enough food for refreshments at the ceilidh that evening.

After the speeches had been made and the bride and bridesmaids toasted, with Michael delivering what was generally agreed to be the funniest wedding speech ever heard on the island, Rupert's the most moving and Alex's the most eloquent – all three evoking tears of laughter and joy in turn – there was time after the meal for people to wander outside in the fresh air.

Katherine and Alex took advantage of this, needing a moment to themselves amid the celebrations and many conversations. But it was not to be, for as soon as they left the hall, Father McPhee wanted to introduce Alex to the Factor of Cairnmor, Ross Muir, and the three men became involved in conversation.

Katherine excused herself, and as she continued on her way silently mouthed, "Don't be long" to Alex, who nodded his head in acquiescence.

She had removed her veil earlier before leaving the hall, and thus unencumbered, walked along the sea-shore where she encountered Alastair, seated on a rock, looking out across the bay, lost in thought.

"Penny for them," she said, sitting down carefully beside him, mindful of not snagging her dress.

Surprised, Alastair turned towards her and smiled. "Oh, too many to count," he responded enigmatically. "You look so beautiful," he said, before he could stop himself.

"Thank you," she replied simply, accepting his compliment graciously. "You look quite smart yourself."

"Only quite? Huh!" and they both chuckled. Then he asked, "How are you doing, with Rupert and Mhairi, I mean?"

"They're really nice people."

"I know they are. I would have been very surprised if they weren't!"

"Doesn't always work out that way."

"No, it doesn't." Alastair sighed.

Katherine second-guessed his thoughts. "Do you wish that Roberta was here?"

"No, but I do wish that she had been more courteous and less cold in her wedding invitation refusal."

"It would have been nice. Alex said he was so angry that he tore it up."

"I can't say I blame him." Alastair paused, before turning to Katherine and said, with some slight trepidation as to her reaction, "I suppose you ought to call me 'Dad' now…"

Katherine put her hands up in the air in pretend abject horror. "No, save me… help… too many parents! Argh!"

Alastair threw back his head and laughed. "I like that," he said.

"But I'm afraid I can't call you 'Dad'," she said in all seriousness, hoping he wouldn't be offended.

"Why not?"

"You are and always will be Alastair to me. You are my friend and we have our own very special relationship that goes beyond that of father and daughter-in-law," she replied, her eyes warm with affection.

"Yes, we do indeed," he replied quietly, much relieved. He put his arm round her shoulders and kissed her on her forehead.

"Though I am very proud to have you as a father-in-law," she added, with suitable decorum.

"Just as I am to have you as a daughter-in-law," he responded, equally circumspect.

They smiled at each other and she laid her head against his.

"Now, now, what's all this?!" said Alex good-humouredly, walking along the beach to where Katherine and Alastair were seated.

Katherine reached out and touched his cheek as he knelt down on the sand. He took her hand and kissed the palm.

"We were talking about your mother."

"Oh, don't. You'll wreck a perfectly lovely day," he replied, though he knew that nothing could spoil or diminish his enjoyment. "She's been very quiet, hasn't she? We haven't heard any more from her solicitors in ages."

"Long may it stay that way!" said Alastair, with deep feeling. "I think I'll just stay here and escape forever," he added, looking wistfully across the bay.

Even though he had been so ill, he couldn't recall feeling as happy and contented as he had been in the past few months. It would be incredibly difficult for him to leave.

"This place gets to you doesn't it?" said Alex, brushing some sand off his trousers. "Every time I come here, it becomes just that bit harder to go away again. Not that you have anything to do with that, my darling," and he kissed her hand again.

"Huh," was Katherine's humorous response. Then she continued seriously, and without any hint of admonition, "Perhaps now you can understand my reluctance to leave. If you're finding it hard, imagine what I must be feeling."

"We'll come back as often as we can," said Alex, his eyes full of promise.

"Yes please," and Katherine tenderly stroked his hair.

Alastair looked on discreetly, smiling to himself, delighted to see the caring in their relationship, glad to be so close to both of them.

Then he said, catching sight of people beginning to move back into the Hall, "I'm sorry to bring to an end our small sojourn, but I think it's probably time for us to go back. But in case I don't get the chance to say this later," and Alastair paused, trying to find the right words, "I think you make a wonderful couple and I wish you both all the happiness in the world."

Alex hugged his father in gratitude, as did Katherine, laying her head on his shoulder, moved by the words of this man who was so loved by both of them.

Alex and Alastair both stood up, brushing the sand from their grey pinstripe trousers, and helped Katherine carefully to her feet.

Then, with her arms linked in one each of theirs, happy in their kinship and rapport, the three of them returned to the Hall, to discover that all was nearly ready for the ceilidh and the evening's celebrations and festivities.

After it was all over, when the musicians had played the dancers outside during the last dance of the evening, Katherine and Alex went back to the hotel to change and collect their luggage ready for their honeymoon. They still had no idea where they were going, having been told mysteriously, and pointedly, not to be long.

Obeying instructions, they returned to the harbour as soon as they could, where the final surprise of the day awaited them. They were invited to step aboard Robbie's fishing smack, complete with pennants festooned on the stays, fluttering in the gentle breeze.

They bid farewell to their family and friends, stowed their luggage, and then Robbie hoisted sail, the boat gently moving away from the quayside and out into the Loch. They waved until they could wave no more, until the gathered crowd were mere specks in the distance. Only then did Robbie tell them where they were heading.

"There's an uninhabited island about an hour's sailing away – ye know the one, Katie."

"You mean Eilean nan Caorach?"

"Aye, that's the one. They've done up the old cottage for ye both and ye've got enough provisions for a month, even though ye've only got a week. There'll be plenty to eat even if the weather turns, though it seems settled fair for the time being. I'll come and collect ye both next Saturday. Ye'll not be disturbed, I reckon," he added, chuckling to himself.

This was more than they could have hoped for. After all the delays and the separations, it was a dream come true.

Alex took Katherine into his arms and contentedly, they leaned back and let Robbie take them across the calm, late-evening sea to their very own desert island.

CHAPTER 32

They stood on the beach and waved farewell to Robbie as he raised the sails and set off on his return journey. When he was far enough away, Alex pulled Katherine towards him and kissed her possessively. There would be no more disappointment, no more frustration, no more waiting. She belonged to him now.

Without saying a word, he swept her up into his arms and carried her over the threshold of their little cottage, taking her straight through to the tiny bedroom where he laid her on the bed, kissing and caressing her with such passion and practised ease that she could not help but respond to his embrace as he made love to her for the first time.

Afterwards, Katherine looked at her husband, quietly asleep beside her. She wondered how often he had done this before and the thought troubled her slightly.

However, just as she had done so many times before, she put this aside. His previous relationships were not relevant any more. They were married; he was her husband. As his wife, her body belonged to him but at the same time, she liked to think that he belonged to her in exactly the same way. Katherine also knew that despite her relative inexperience, she wanted more from him. Gently, she woke him up and he responded eagerly to her touch, but this time showing greater sensitivity and more consideration to her needs.

And so, they embarked on their first week as a married couple. For Alex, every hour stretched out before him like some glorious treat where there were no barriers or restrictions, only unmitigated freedom. For Katherine it was a journey of discovery that she could enjoy with a clear conscience; their union sanctified by marriage.

On warm, still days and nights on the beautiful golden-white sands, they made love under a radiant sky; on cooler days, in front of the glowing peat fire, revelling in its warmth and cosiness.

It was an idyllic time, the happiest they would ever spend together.

Katherine was more deeply in love than ever with this man who was now her husband, and wondered what their future life together might hold.

On the Monday morning following the wedding, Donald and Annie were sorting through the large hessian bags of post that had arrived on the steamer at the weekend. There were two envelopes for Ross Muir, the Factor of Cairnmor – an honest, decent man, who had always represented the islanders' interests with great fairness to their former proprietor.

The previous owner had been a kindly man, who had allowed his tenants and employees free rein, trusting them to carry out their crofting obligations and pay their rent on time. This they did, but he was always generous in extenuating circumstances, allowing Ross to guide him. He visited the island once a year, stayed for a month or two and always went away satisfied with the state of his 'kingdom' as he called it. He knew his tenants, and they knew him. This new owner had not evoked the same confidence as yet.

Donald stopped off first at Ross's cottage, said hello to the Factor's wife, patted the dog, teased the children, delivered the letters and went cheerfully on his way, bidding the Factor a "Good day to ye" as he walked down the path.

Ross sat down at his desk and opened the smaller of the two envelopes. His wife, Eve, brought him a cup of tea, as she always did after the post had arrived, and saw his face white with shock. Silently, he handed her the letter. He had been given six weeks' notice; his services were *'no longer required.'*

She stared at him, open mouthed. "Why, for goodness' sake?"

He shrugged his shoulders. "Who knows?"

"You've done nothing wrong."

"I know."

He opened the second letter. This made him leap up from his chair in anger, knocking over his cup and spilling the tea all over the desk. It dripped down the side onto the floor and hastily, he mopped it up with his handkerchief while his wife went to fetch a cloth from the kitchen. Together they rescued the sodden papers and spread them round the room to dry. He showed her the second letter.

"But surely they can't do that?!" she exclaimed, shocked and angry. "You have to do something," she said. "They may have given you the sack – goodness knows how we're going to manage – but this, this is awful! And to expect you to deliver the bad news as well... it's totally... immoral."

"These people have no scruples, obviously. They have their agenda and they're going to push it through regardless of how it affects the lives of everyone else."

"Are you going to speak to John?"

"Yes. Straightaway."

John was equally dumbfounded. Together, they pored over the document. It was in this position that Alastair found them as he came down the stairs on his way out for a walk. They called him over. He was equally appalled by what he read:

We, the undersigned, hereby inform you that the Island of Cairnmor will undergo substantial alteration and changes. It is our wish to transform our land into a place fit for the tourist trade and associated industries. There is a need to diversify and expand if we are to make the land pay its way. In the first instance, we propose the following:

1. *To build a Championship golf course and other amenities on the land known as the 'machair'.*
2. *To build a new hotel in South Lochaberdale and construct an access road. The existing hotel is to be demolished and the site used as a car park.*
3. *Access roads across the island are to be constructed for use by motor vehicles.*
4. *The harbour is to be extended to enclose the entire northern shore of Lochaberdale.*
5. *Deer and additional sheep are to be introduced on the hillsides.*

258

6.   *Fishing and shooting rights granted only to those persons approved by the Laird.*
7.   *Peat bogs to be drained and the land turned into moorland suitable for grouse shooting.*
8.   *An application seeking approval for the above changes has been made.*
9.   *Tenants affected by these changes will be given notice in writing of the termination of their tenancy agreements.*
10. *New Tenancy Agreements or Transfers of Title will only be drawn up with the express consent of the Laird.*

"We have to fight this" said Alastair, without any hesitation. "I hope to heavens they've left us sufficient time legally to be able to do so." He turned to Ross. "How much do you know about Scots Land Law?"

"Enough to know that in order to make the changes they're proposing, they have to apply to the Land Court because they are altering the status of the land. It's called 'resumption' of crofting land. What the objection process is, I'm not sure. No one here has ever had to make a legal objection: any disputes or grievances have always been dealt with amicably and resolved here on the island. So we've never had to make any official enquiries. I wish I'd kept more up to date with the legal process. I suppose I thought I'd cross that bridge when I came to it." Ross shook his head regretfully.

"Don't worry about that for now. It's to your credit that you've never had to resort to the legal system," said Alastair reassuringly. "But we have to pay the Land Court a visit, that's for sure. Where is it?"

"In Edinburgh."

"Then that's where we go next Saturday when the steamer comes. This is one of those occasions when I wish we could just get on a train!" Then he added, "We need to get Michael in on this. One of his specialisms is land usage; there may be some useful parallels in English law which can help us here. Then we must put our heads together and come up with a suitable plan of action." Which they did, and quickly too.

The notice from the new owner went up in the post office. Marion and Mary laboriously set out to type out at least a hundred copies on the typewriter at the hotel, using up the entire island stock of carbon paper in the process. When Mhairi volunteered to help them, impressing all and sundry with her typing speed, the task was soon completed, especially when she revealed a working knowledge of Gaelic.

Donald distributed the leaflets in the post bus, taking with him Alastair or Michael, with Mary acting as interpreter, or Ross, who spoke Gaelic, or all three of them, to explain what was happening and ask the island folk to sign a petition objecting to the proposed changes, and finally, to tell the residents there was to be a meeting the following Friday evening in the Great Hall at six o'clock. Donald would run a shuttle service for those who were without transport.

Mrs Gilgarry said to count her in. She had no intention of letting her beloved hotel in Lochaberdale be knocked down under any circumstances. "*Just let them try*!" she said, shaking her fist. Then without drawing breath she said to Alastair, "*Glad to see you looking so well. I thank you for your letter.*"

"*I thank you for yours,*" he replied in Gaelic.

Mrs Gilgarry was impressed. "*You'll be one of us soon enough,*" she predicted.

Alastair kissed her hand graciously, not quite sure what she had said, but not wishing to diminish his good standing with this redoubtable lady. He asked Mary afterwards to interpret her words. "Ah," he replied, once she had explained. "There's no arguing with that, I suppose!"

Michael and Mary worked happily together, playing their part in gathering and collating evidence. A deepening friendship had developed very rapidly between them since his return to Cairnmor. During that eventful week, as they were working on lists and tasks together in her cottage, he asked her to marry him.

"I know it's too soon after Adam. I know it's only been a couple of months since he went. I know we've only really known each other about three minutes but I love you and couldn't bear to lose you."

He looked pleadingly into her eyes. She looked back at him with tenderness and compassion; thinking, considering. She instinctively knew this man, she trusted him. He was decent, honest and caring with an incredible sense of humour. But above all she had come to care for him. It was a different feeling from that which she had felt for Adam, but it was better, calmer, deeper, *safer*.

Mary cast all doubts aside and jumped in with both feet. She smiled at him, his heart soared and she said, "Yes."

Overjoyed, he kissed her, hesitantly at first, then, sensing her responsiveness to him, with growing confidence. They agreed to keep their decision to themselves for a while, but that proved impossible, as everyone who saw them understood their radiance. Mourning convention was disregarded in Mary's case and their decision welcomed by everyone, even Adam's parents, who latterly had been all too aware of the trauma that Mary had endured because of their son's shameful behaviour and, as they were very fond of her, wished a better life for her. But it was especially welcomed by Gordon and Fiona, who above all other considerations, wanted their daughter to find happiness and contentment at last after everything she had suffered. Michael had already proved his good character to them by his actions, and they knew he would care and provide for Mary.

While all the evidence was being collected, Rupert and Lily inadvertently provided entertainment for the week at the hotel – at Rupert's suggestion, playing flute (Lily) and piano (Rupert); violin (Rupert) and piano (Lily); as well as piano duets, and improvising when they ran out of the limited supply of printed music that Rupert had brought with him from Canada, and Lily from home.

It was an unexpected joy for them both: for Rupert to have discovered such a talent, and for Lily to have found another musician who could understand her ability. So often, she had experienced a sense of frustration at not having someone who could immediately respond to her musicality – even Alex, who was not in practice so much these days.

The guests in the hotel dining room, as they filtered into the room before meals, were treated to impromptu concerts most days. Lily thought they should pay for tickets; Rupert said he had enough money!

260

This was something he was having to come to terms with – the inheritance his father had left him. The wily old man had repented, according to Alastair who had been his London solicitor during his final few years, and was genuinely sorry for the way he had treated Rupert and Mhairi. He had left Rupert everything as his way of atoning for his insensitivity and callousness.

However, Rupert viewed this very differently. It was an onerous burden to him and, if he looked at it cynically, the ultimate act of cruelty by his father. Charles Mathieson knew his son wasn't interested in the shipyard, knew he wanted nothing to do with it. Yet he had bequeathed it to him anyway, gambling that he, Rupert, would be unable just to walk away, knowing that his father had spent so many years building up what had become a famous and highly successful company.

Despite his reluctance to become involved, Rupert knew he owed him that much, to see that it remained prosperous and thriving. When they returned to the mainland, he would have to begin investigating possibilities. Thank goodness for the long summer recess: at least he had some time to consider the matter. But for now, he and Mhairi would enjoy their holiday on this beautiful island and look forward to the end of the week when their daughter would return from her honeymoon and they could really begin to get to know each other.

Katherine and Alex, arms entwined, walking barefoot along the pristine white-sanded beach early on the last evening of their romantic idyll, were surprised by the sight of Robbie's distinctive tan sails and blue-hulled boat in the distance. He had said he would collect them the next day, Saturday. They wondered if the weather was about to turn but the blue, cloudless skies belied that idea; or, if something was amiss.

"Is everything all right?" called out Alex when Robbie was within earshot.

"Aye, in a manner of speaking it is, yet it is not," he replied enigmatically, while Alex helped him beach his rowing boat. "However, I'm afraid I need to get ye back to Cairnmor. I'm sorry to have interrupted yere…" and here his blue eyes twinkled mischievously, "… holiday. I'll just sit on the beach here and wait whilst ye pack. Take yere time, there's no rush." And, as good as his word, he settled himself, smoking his pipe, contentedly surveying the horizon.

"This is all rather mysterious," said Katherine, as she put the remaining food from the pantry into water-tight tins, while Alex collected their luggage – they had already packed earlier, not being quite sure when Robbie would collect them on the Saturday – from the bedroom, checking to make sure that nothing remained.

Katherine dampened the fire in the range and then stripped the bed, putting the sheets and pillowcases in a bag to take with them, and the blankets and pillows in the cupboard for collection later.

It had been a wonderful week. They stood close together, their bodies exquisitely responsive to each other, saying farewell to the little cottage and the island that had been their first home as husband and wife.

Robbie helped them load everything onto the boat and after Katherine had got in, he and Alex pushed it back into the water, rowing with ease across the tiny wavelets to the fishing smack, lying peacefully at anchor in the azure sea.

Katherine looked back wistfully at the receding coastline as the boat set sail and Alex, sitting beside her, read her thoughts. They smiled at each other and he kissed her tenderly on the lips. There was no need for words.

When they reached Lochaberdale, Robbie told them to leave the luggage in the boat; they could come back and sort it out later. "She'll still be here. It'll all be safe. Now, away to the Great Hall both of ye, and I'll join ye shortly."

On the journey, he had said nothing of why they were coming home early. "Och, ye'll find out soon enough," was all he would say when they questioned him. They tried to thank the old fisherman, but he waved away their gratitude, saying, "We all do things for each other. Now away with ye, and let me make the boat secure."

The meeting had obviously been going on for some time, as they walked into the hall to an uproar of heated debate. All the seats were taken and people were standing around the perimeter.

Someone handed them a piece of paper, the contents of which they read in total disbelief, becoming immediately responsive to what was taking place around them. Father McPhee and Ross Muir were on the raised platform at the far end trying to bring some order to the proceedings.

"How can they drain the peat bogs?" asked one man. "What will we do for fuel?"

"If they extend the harbour, the southern shore will silt up. The fishermen tried it years ago and it didna' work," said another.

"What'll we do for food if they build on the machair?"

"Eat golf balls," quipped one bright spark, to general laughter and disconsolate mutterings of, "Aye, aye, that's all that'll be left of our fine land."

"Are the new Laird and his cronies completely mad?"

"Selfish."

"Stupid, most likely. They haven't a clue what they're talking about."

"Aye, imagine believing that grouse would survive here? One storm and all those delicate little birdies would be all blown away!" This comment raised ironic laughter, and murmurs of assent.

"But the tourists will bring money and wealth to Cairnmor," ventured one brave soul.

"Aye, wealth to line the Laird's pockets!" came the immediate retort.

"It'll create jobs for us," said his friend.

"And come the bad weather, the tourists'll be off to their comfy homes on the mainland and where will our jobs be then? Ye can't survive here on tourist trinkets in the winter."

"What about our homes and families? Where will we live if they take away our homes?" said one of the women.

"It's the clearances all over again, you mark my words," said Mrs Gilgarry. This was greeted with applause and nods of accord. "You just tell your employer to go and get stuffed, laddie!"

262

The hall fell silent as Ross stood up to speak. "I'm afraid I can't do that and carry any weight." The atmosphere was tense, expectant.

"Why not?"

"Because I've been given my notice." A feeling of sympathy went out towards this man who had for so many years been the intermediary between the Laird and his tenants.

"Ye've been a good and fair Factor. We thank ye."

"You're welcome."

"So, ye're with us now."

"Indeed I am." And a general buzz of conversation went round the room.

Katherine and Alex moved down to the front of the hall, where their families and close friends were seated. Mhairi was taking notes in shorthand, translating as she went, recording everything that each person said. She looked up and smiled with joy as Katherine and Alex approached them as unobtrusively as possible.

Alastair and Michael took Alex off to the side of the platform and quickly apprised him of their plans. He nodded in agreement and looked at Katherine who was talking to her mother and father, wondering how she would react. They had intended to spend another week on Cairnmor. "Then that is what we have to do," he said finally. He took a deep breath and sat down. It was back to work but with a real purpose, an urgent purpose.

Father McPhee raised his hand and there was immediate silence.

"There is a plan," he announced.

"Tell us, please."

"I'll ask our good friend Alastair Stewart to explain. For those of you who don't know him, Alastair has been living amongst us for the past three months or so. He's our Katherine's father-in-law and a solicitor from London. His son Alex is a barrister – that's an advocate to you and me – and so is his friend Michael."

Slightly shyly, after that introduction, Alastair took his place on the platform. "*Feasgar math* – good evening," he began, to loud applause and nods of appreciation. He continued in English while Mary stood at the side and interpreted.

"My friends, this is not going to be an easy task, but we shall do our best for you all. We have to object to these proposals. Your livelihoods, indeed, your very homes are at stake. Most of you have signed the petition that we brought round. If anyone hasn't, there are more copies on the table at the back of the hall. Please do sign, it could be very useful." He paused and drank some water, giving Mary a chance to catch up. "We have been gathering evidence on your behalf – the notes and statements that you provided me with when those two disagreeable men tried to coerce many of you into giving up your tenancy agreements; your verbal objections; the points raised at this meeting; the petition. We intend to go to the Land Court in Edinburgh and challenge these proposals."

"No offence, but advocates and solicitors cost a deal of money. We have verra little. How can we afford it?" someone called out. Others agreed while Mary interpreted their words into English for Alastair.

"Alex, Michael and myself will represent your interests where we are able. There will be no charge for our services. But if any costs are incurred, they will be covered." And Alastair sat down to heartfelt applause.

Alex shook his father's hand and Katherine kissed him on the cheek. "I guess that's next week sorted out, then," she observed drily, but not unhappily, to her gathered family.

"We shall all go," said Rupert. "Your mother is adamant that I am involved. Therefore I have no choice," he added kindly.

After that, there was more general discussion in the hall before the meeting adjourned and everyone retired to the side room for refreshments.

Initially, Katherine's mood remained suffused with the happiness of her honeymoon, but all too soon the reality of what they were about to face encroached upon her contentment as the seriousness of the situation made itself very clear.

CHAPTER 33

Glasgow/Edinburgh

The next week passed in a blur of activity. Michael headed off to Edinburgh to set the objection process in motion and to begin researching Scots Land Law. Meanwhile, Alastair took a very reluctant Lily home and then back to school on the Monday, much to her chagrin and disappointment, before heading back up north on the L.N.E.R. to Edinburgh, arriving exhausted at Waverley Station and meeting up with Michael at the Land Court in George Street.

Initially, Alex, Katherine, Rupert and Mhairi stayed in Glasgow and visited Mathieson's Shipyard. That first time was not an easy visit for either of Katherine's parents. They had left a long time ago and the circumstances of their departure and the preceding events came back to them vividly, despite their new life, despite the intervening twenty-seven years.

With their daughter now restored to them, they began to be reconciled to their past, to accept it in all its pain and difficulties, and gain a measure of objectivity. But when Rupert walked into Mathieson's that Monday morning, he felt the same dread, the same lowering of his spirits as he had experienced as a young man of seventeen.

What was he going to do with this enormous burden of responsibility which his father had bestowed upon him?

Alex introduced them to Laurence Hart, still acting as works manager in the absence of his superior. Laurence was delighted to meet Sir Charles Mathieson's son and invited him to sit in his father's chair at his father's desk. Rupert did so, trying to allay the irrational fear he had always felt in this room.

Mhairi stood by her husband's side, understanding his emotions, sharing the memories. However, she found that it was the good ones that she recalled – meeting Rupert, falling in love, and the moment when he appeared at the hospital, which signalled the beginning of their life together.

They had their daughter back, and had forged a successful life for themselves in Nova Scotia. The wrongs had been righted, but the pain of the past would take a little longer to heal.

Alex and Laurence, who had been deep in consultation, then turned to Rupert. Laurence cleared his throat and spoke. "I know it's very early days, but I, er, the Board were wondering what you intended to do with Mathieson's?"

What was he going to do? Rupert was silent before he replied, honestly and openly. "I'm not sure. What are my options?"

"Well, towards the end of his life, your father made the shipyard a limited company, making sure he retained the majority of the shares. So, there are a few other shareholders, a board of directors and a chairman. In effect, the Board oversee the direction the company goes in and have overall financial responsibility. Then there is the Managing Director, who sits on the Board and whose job it is to run the company and to present his plans. Your father became both Chairman and Managing Director, but during the last year of his life, he relinquished the latter and just acted as Chairman. The present MD wishes to retire, the Works Manager is on permanent sick leave, there is no Chairman and we're still fighting off this hostile takeover bid, so Mathieson's desperately needs strong leadership and a fairly quick decision."

Rupert liked this man. He had passion and enthusiasm and, from what Alex had told him, knowledge and expertise. It was a formidable combination.

"You really care about this company, don't you?" he observed.

"Yes sir, I do."

Rupert was thinking quickly. He was director of a music academy, therefore he had experience of running an organization. In effect, he was on home territory. But he knew nothing about the shipbuilding industry, or at least very little. He took a deep breath and turned to Laurence.

"There are many things to discuss but, theoretically, if I were to take on the role of Chairman, a very competent MD could run the company efficiently. It would be possible for me to live in Canada and return for Board meetings once or twice a year. Theoretically."

"Ye-es," said Laurence, with reservations.

"There are other possibilities," said Mhairi quietly.

Rupert looked at his wife. "Oh yes, I know there are," he replied thoughtfully and with reluctance.

"If you want someone to run the company," said Alex, "he's standing here in this room, right now. Laurence would make an excellent Managing Director."

Rupert regarded him shrewdly, looking for a moment exactly like his father. Then he nodded. "Yes, I believe he would."

And they all laughed at Laurence's dumbfounded expression.

"Would you like the job?" asked Rupert.

"I'd love it!" replied Laurence without hesitation.

"Then, subject to the Board's approval, the post is yours. I shall take over as Chairman temporarily, and I shall rely on you to guide me through the stormy sea of shipbuilding."

A little later, while the others were absorbed in conversation, Rupert turned to the portrait of his father.

"All right, you old bastard, you win," he said quietly. "I'll run your company just as you always wanted me to. For the moment," he added, with a penetrating look that was every bit as powerful as his father's.

Later, while the three men were in consultation with Mathieson's solicitors, Katherine and Mhairi took themselves off for a nostalgic walk around Govan in the vicinity of the shipyard.

"It's just as dirty, noisy and smelly as I remember when I was young," she said, proud to be out walking with her daughter.

"Yes, it's lost none of those things, that's for sure! I remember it well, too. You see, I lived not far from here when I was on teaching practice." She turned to her mother. "The school's just down the road."

"Not St Patrick's!"

"The very same."

"That was a tough assignment!"

266

"Er, yes, you could say that. A baptism of fire!"

"Where did you live?"

"Elder Street"

"No!" exclaimed Mhairi. "The old house where I grew up is in the next road, Howat Street."

The two women looked at each other in amazement.

"Incredible isn't it?" said Mhairi.

"I think it's wonderful," replied Katherine, "because it gives us such a common frame of reference which we wouldn't have had otherwise. And also with my studying at Edinburgh and Rupert going to school there." She hadn't quite reached the stage of calling him 'Dad' yet.

"I know exactly what you mean; it goes some little way towards making up for what we've missed. When I was a little girl, I used to love watching the ships go by from my bedroom window. If you stood at the far end of the street, it looked as though they were going across the road. They were huge, enormous. I loved visiting the shipyard with Pa. It was always so exciting, there was so much going on."

"I used to be fascinated by that too. And the gigantic cranes, like the one at Stobcross. I'd never seen anything like it! And it looked so funny when the steam engines would come out of one of the yards and travel along the road to the next yard using the tram tracks! I could hardly believe my eyes when I first saw that. There were so many things that made it a fascinating place to live; temporarily, that is," she added. "I wasn't quite so enamoured by the drunken brawls and violence though. Nor the squalor."

Mhairi agreed wholeheartedly and they continued on their way, reminiscing and retracing Mhairi's childhood haunts until it was time to return to Mathieson's and lunch in the staff canteen.

That afternoon, the family caught the tram to the Royal Lunatic Asylum. Dr Cameron greeted them with pleasure and surprise when Mhairi and Rupert were introduced. He saw the immediate resemblance between mother and daughter, and realized that Jock's reaction to Katherine had been very real, neither a mistake nor the ramblings of a senile old man.

They were shown into the same sitting room where Alex and Katherine had first met Jock. Once again he was there, sitting in his wheelchair, staring out of the window.

Mhairi's eyes filled with tears and her heart went out to this broken old man; the past forgiven, but not forgotten, and reconciled to the present.

She went over to him, and took both his hands in hers. "Hello, Pa," she said simply.

He turned to look at her; blank stare replaced gradually by open-mouthed recognition. "My Mhairi, my Mhairi!" he said, in a quavering voice. "You've come back, you've come back to your old Pa!" And the tears streamed down his cheeks.

"Yes, Pa," replied his daughter, her own emotion spilling over. "I've come back."

"Don't leave me again. Don't go away over the sea."

"Oh, Pa."

"Promise."

"I'll do what I can."

The old man seemed satisfied with this and held onto her hands and looked at her, saying over and over again, "I'm so sorry, I'm so sorry."

"It's all right, Pa, it's all right," she said, reassuring him and wiping his tears with her handkerchief.

They stayed together like this until the old man's words began to peter out and he became drowsy.

"We'll come back tomorrow," she said to Dr Cameron, looking at Rupert, who nodded in agreement, his own eyes full of tears. "If that's all right?"

"Of course it is. It will be just what he needs. Thank you. But be prepared that he may not know you tomorrow or you may have to repeat this process over again."

"I understand."

Mhairi and Rupert decided that they would remain in Glasgow for the present, meeting up with Katherine and Alex when they returned from Edinburgh – Mhairi to see her father, Rupert to meet with Laurence, and both of them to spend time in Cathcart, revisiting the places of their old lives.

Dr Cameron stated that it was probably better if they waited to see how Jock coped before springing a granddaughter on him. That might be one step too far for his limited faculties to understand.

So Katherine and Alex travelled to Edinburgh knowing that he, after consulting with Mathieson's solicitors, could represent himself and the islanders' interests in the Land Court, but that they would have to employ the services of an advocate if they had to take the matter to appeal in the Court of Sessions.

As an English barrister, Alex was not permitted to act as counsel in a higher Scottish court – unless he retrained as a Scottish advocate and was called to the Bar north of the border. He was reluctant to do this and it remained, for the moment at least, impractical. It might be something to consider in the future. In the meantime, they had to come up with a reason why he needed to represent himself in the Land Court.

"We could apply for the tenancy agreement on my croft to be put into your name," said Katherine, in a moment of inspiration.

"Brilliant! My guess is that it will be refused and I can then say that the due process of established law is not being followed, as the proposed changes to Transfer of Title have not yet been approved despite the application, and that I'm being deprived of my traditional and legal rights. Ha! Something else for them to swallow!"

They met up with Michael and Alastair and shared all they had learned. There was time to raise objections – but only just. It was as Alastair had feared – Sir Roger Caitiff had purposely left very little time for challenges to his proposals to be lodged. He had hoped to push through highly controversial changes unhindered.

They drafted their objections, completed the necessary forms and documents, and presented them to the Land Court office on the closing date itself. It would be at least a month before they heard the date of any hearing as the Land Court was required to contact the new Laird to gather information from his perspective before deciding whether the case should be resolved by a written decision, a hearing in the Divisional Court (in front of one court member and legal assessor) or the Full Court (in front of the chairman and two court members) depending upon the nature or scope of the dispute. So for now, at least, it was a waiting game.

They all returned to London; all, that is, except for Michael, who temporarily returned to Cairnmor to be with Mary, risking his career by doing so, as well as Rupert and Mhairi, whose stay in England was nearly over. Until that time, they remained in Glasgow to be near her father.

Jock was doing well; he seemed much happier since seeing his long-lost daughter and was content for her to visit whenever she could, having at last made his peace with her.

When she said goodbye to him on her last day, Mhairi explained that she was going on holiday for a little while but promised that she would come back. If he understood, no one knew, but he appeared to be reassured by her words and in her future correspondence with Dr Cameron, Mhairi was to learn that Jock was calm and doing well, given his condition. Reassured by this, she was able to resume her life with a clear conscience.

As for her husband, an extraordinary board meeting confirmed Rupert as Chairman (Acting) of Mathieson's Shipyard and Laurence as Managing Director.

Solicitors in Glasgow and London, under Alastair's supervision, began work on the probate, property and financial implications of Rupert's inheritance, a process that would take many months to complete. In fact, so much correspondence was to travel across the Atlantic that later, Rupert began to wonder whether his and Mhairi's future life lay back in Great Britain. They had dual citizenship, having retained their British nationality when they became Canadian subjects, so it was perfectly feasible. However, he remained reluctant to relinquish his beloved Music Academy.

When the time came for her parents to leave, Katherine travelled to Southampton with them to say farewell as they boarded *Queen Mary*. They planned to come over again to England as soon as they were able and extended an open invitation for her and Alex to come and stay with them. No one could predict the changes that might take place in the future, but for now, this was the way things had to be, difficult as it was for the three of them.

Katherine said a tearful goodbye to them, feeling that she had only just got to know them and now they were going again. It seemed to be the story of her life, meeting and then being parted from the people that she loved.

And so, having arrived back at Waterloo Station, she took a taxi to Cornwallis Gardens to begin her new life proper in London as Alex's wife. Although she missed Cairnmor intensely, she had to admit she enjoyed being in London, and she loved the house at Maybury where they spent their weekends, with the gentle Thames flowing along the bottom of the garden.

And the trees. The trees in full green leaf were a revelation to her, and she never tired of walking along the river bank with Alex or Alastair, or both of them, on a Saturday or Sunday afternoon.

The weather was glorious and on the whole, Katherine was happy in her new life.

When the date of the Land Court hearing came through, much against Sir John Pemberton's wishes, Alex, together with Katherine and Alastair, travelled up to Edinburgh, where they met Michael and Mary. The case was deemed of sufficient importance to merit a Full Court session.

They had prepared the ground as thoroughly as possible but Michael had some disturbing new evidence that the roads were already being marked out and the site of the golf course laid out with pegs and rope. Unfortunately, the sheep and cattle did not respect these new boundaries and spent their nights wandering around the machair, pulling down the unwelcome obstacles.

"How they got out from their enclosures is a complete mystery!" remarked Michael, feigning an expression of complete innocence. "The ropes kept ending up on the beach with the pegs still attached and in the morning, the animals were grazing peacefully on the meadow. The builders were puzzled by this, re-pegged everything and kept watch during the day, but saw nothing. The next morning, the ropes and pegs were to be found on the beach again. They gave up in the end and went away."

"Let me guess," said Katherine, keen to hear news of Cairnmor, "it was Gordon!"

"Quite right. But he had help," and Michael tried his best to look shamefaced, but failed miserably. Smiling, they all went into the courtroom.

Sir Roger Caitiff was not present but was represented by two Scottish solicitors. The Chairman welcomed everyone and the hearing began. The solicitors presented their case only adequately, but despite this, the Chairman seemed very impressed with the proposals and asked many questions, with the solicitors giving the false impression that the new Laird wanted to do everything in his power to help his new tenants and improve their lives on the island.

The Chairman said, "Yes, I once went to Cairnmor many, many years ago. A very backward place with poor crofters scratching a living from the land. Not much future there for them."

When Alex stood up to make his case, no matter how eloquently or persuasively he presented his argument, he knew he was on the losing side. In any other court, he would have had the judge eating out of the palm of his hand, but not here. There was no chance of success.

The Chairman wanted to know why an Englishman was speaking on behalf of the islanders.

"My wife is from Cairnmor," Alex replied. "She is the sitting tenant of the croft which belonged to her adoptive parents and wishes for the croft tenancy to be transferred into my name, in accordance with the law."

"Where is she living at present?"

Alex's heart sank. "In London, sir."

270

"With you?"

"Yes, with me."

"Do you have any intention of living on Cairnmor in the foreseeable future?"

"It is a possibility, but not in the foreseeable future."

Alex was kicking himself. They had slipped up. Taking a deep breath, he glanced at his father seated next to him. They exchanged the briefest of raised eyebrows. But, never despairing, Alex continued to present his case, laying out the islanders' objections clearly and precisely.

When he had finished, the Chairman consulted briefly with his two colleagues. Then he said:

"Do either of you have any questions for your opposing number?"

The solicitors of Sir Roger Caitiff said no, they were quite happy, but before Alex had a chance to give his reply, because this would be his opportunity to demolish the opposition's case, the Chairman thanked them and brought the proceedings to a close.

Alex was staggered and the two solicitors walked past him unable to resist a smirk in his direction. He felt humiliated, frustrated. This was not right, he had not been given the opportunity to question his opposite number. It was not correct procedure. Then it occurred to him. Maybe the Chairman had given him grounds for appeal.

Whether this was intentional or not Alex could not be sure. If the Opinion went against him, he could appeal on the grounds that he was not given a fair hearing and the point of law regarding Transfer of Title had not been resolved. The wily Chairman might have left that path open to him.

But why? The Chairman was taking a risk with his own reputation by not following proper procedure; on the other hand, he may have not wanted to be seen opposing a powerful landowner such as Sir Roger Caitiff, whose industrial empire also extended north of the border, even if he disagreed with what that landowner was trying to do.

Alex was still thinking about this when he saw the Chairman later as they were leaving. He was at the other end of a deserted corridor. The two men stood for a while looking at each other. Then the Chairman smiled the briefest of smiles and went on his way. Alex smiled back.

The written decision came back quickly. It was as Alex had suspected. They had lost the case but immediately they lodged an appeal, opting to take the matter to the Court of Session in Edinburgh, rather than ask for another hearing.

While they were waiting, Mary came to stay with Katherine and Alex in London and Katherine took great pleasure in showing her friend round. Mary was overwhelmed by the buildings, the noise, the constant *busyness* of the whole place. Never having had to make the adjustment to living in a large city, as she had never lived away from Cairnmor, she found the pace of life difficult to cope with. But she was happy to be with Michael and the four of them went to concerts and restaurants, while Katherine took Mary to galleries and museums.

When Alex and Michael once again stated that they would not be available for work over the next two weeks in order to attend the Court of Sessions hearing in

Edinburgh, Sir John Pemberton was not a happy man. He questioned their motives and asked how much money this would bring into Chambers. When they replied that there would be no income, as they were doing this for free, and, what was more, paying for the Scottish advocate and solicitor out of their own pockets, he could barely control his anger.

"You have constantly flouted my wishes, both of you," he fumed, pacing up and down the floor of his office, to where they had been summoned after informing the Head Clerk of their intentions, after which he had gone straight to Sir John with this information.

"You, Mr Granger, have taken extended leaves of absence from your work here. This fact, together with your flippant attitude, which I despise, calls into question your tenancy with Royal Court Chambers. I shall be monitoring your actions closely."

At least Alex and Michael now knew the reason why Michael had always hitherto been given all the worst cases.

"As for you, Mr Stewart, just be grateful that your brilliance in court outshines your stupidity away from it. If you are not prepared to take an interest in your future career, then neither shall I. Good day, gentlemen."

"I feel like a schoolboy having just been given a rollicking by the headmaster," said Michael as they left the office.

"Likewise, though I have to confess, I didn't get too many of those when I was at school."

"Creep," said Michael good-naturedly.

"Idiot," replied Alex affectionately.

"What time are we collecting the ladies?" asked Michael, changing tack.

"I told them both to be ready at four."

"What time did your Dad leave the day before yesterday?"

"He caught the ten a.m. from King's Cross. I hope he's managed to brief our counsel and his solicitor successfully. They come highly recommended but I wasn't overly impressed when I talked to both men on the telephone yesterday. Neither was Dad. They've had the paperwork for weeks but our advocate didn't seem to grasp the significance of the situation at all."

Alex's fears were well-founded. The advocate was good but not outstanding. He knew the facts but not how to manipulate them to the best advantage, and allowed his opposite number to outsmart him.

Alex sat in Courtroom Number One, amid the elegant and spacious surroundings of the Court of Sessions, in a constant state of frustration. He knew he could have done better; he knew if he had been on his feet, the case would have been won. The appeal was full of missed openings, missed opportunities, and Alex was afraid that once again, it was not going to go their way.

He was right. The opinion delivered by the three Scottish Lords of the Extra Division, Inner House, went against them as the Appellants.

Alex knew that the only course of action now available to them was to take the appeal to the highest court in the land – the House of Lords.

CHAPTER 34

London

Here at last, Alex was on home territory. As a barrister-at-law in England, he could now make sure to the best of his ability that the people of Cairnmor had the representation they deserved. He would be able to take on the case himself, working as a team with his father and Michael. There would be time for thorough and exhaustive preparation.

They had intended going to Cairnmor for a week after the hearing in Edinburgh, but Alex felt that they should return to London so that he could present the petition to the Appeal Committee at the House of Lords seeking leave to appeal as soon as possible. He wanted to make it as comprehensive as he could, checking that he had both an important principle and relevant points of law contained within it.

Mary needed to go home, so the following Saturday, Michael travelled with her as far as Oban and saw her onto the steamer, bidding her a reluctant farewell before returning to London, a painful parting that Katherine and Alex would have found only too familiar.

Several days of extensive preparation followed and the petition was delivered. Some weeks later, they heard that their petition had been allowed. They had, after this, expected to wait for up to a year for the hearing, but by a stroke of good fortune, the date was set for December.

"There must be some mistake!" exclaimed a very surprised Alex, one morning after breakfast. "To have a date given this quickly is unprecedented."

"Oh," replied Katherine, who had woken up feeling rather queasy that morning and was sitting with her feet up on the settee. "Perhaps they want to get through all their work by Christmas."

"Can you write to everyone and let them know."

"Everyone? What the whole world?"

"No, silly, Ross and John… on Cairnmor."

"I knew who you meant. I was just teasing." She moved position, adjusting her body to try and escape the discomfort. "I really do feel sick this morning. I must have eaten something last night when…" She stopped in mid-sentence. She and Alex looked at each other, the same thought occurring to both of them.

"You don't think…" began Alex.

"It could be…" replied Katherine.

"Doctor's today then. Don't forget, now," he said, smiling, excited.

"No, bossy boots."

And she waved him off to work, as she always did.

Katherine went to the doctor's surgery later that morning and he confirmed what she and Alex had been hoping was a possibility. She was pregnant and the doctor pronounced the mother-to-be in very good health but suggested she take it easy and come back for another appointment in a month's time.

Katherine could barely contain her excitement. She walked around Kensington Gardens for a while, thinking and planning and dreaming. She couldn't wait to tell Alex when he came home that evening.

Alastair was first to arrive and observed her discreetly over the top of the newspaper he was reading as he sat on the settee. She prowled around the room, sitting down, then standing up and going to the window, then sitting down again; tinkering on the piano, but not playing anything in particular. She looked pale, but her cheeks were flushed with an excitement she could barely conceal.

Alastair's mind went through numerous possibilities for her unusually restless behaviour but it was one in particular that made his heart beat faster; it was all he could do to stop himself from asking her. No, he decided, Alex must be the first to know, if, that is, he was correct in his assumption. They would tell him, Alastair, soon enough.

Now he could hardly contain himself. The newspaper lost its appeal and he got up and went into the kitchen, and asked Mrs Thringle to make them a pot of tea. This she did, slightly grumpily as she was in the middle of preparing dinner, and he took the tray of tea things back into the sitting room.

Katherine was perched on the window seat and she turned as Alastair came back into the room. He smiled at her, a wonderfully warm smile, standing motionless, regarding her.

In that moment, she knew that he knew. She returned his smile, no words were spoken but a feeling of utter delight pervaded the room and she became calmer and more settled, though nothing could still her beating heart, while she waited for her husband to appear.

Almost immediately, she saw him, and she was out of the door and down the stairs into the street as fast as she could safely manage. When she reached him, Alex knew that it was indeed as they had hoped and they hugged and kissed each other with sheer joy.

He dumped his bulging briefcase in the hall and they went upstairs immediately to tell Alastair, who shared fully in their happiness and excitement. And pride. Pride in his wonderful son and lovely daughter-in-law and pride in the fact that he was about to become a grandfather. It was a perfect end to the day.

Alex stayed awake for a long time after they had gone to bed that night. He kept looking at Katherine, sleeping peacefully beside him, the tiny life growing inside her.

His child. Their baby. A miracle. Girl or boy? He didn't mind, as long as Katherine and the child were both healthy and well.

Eventually, he fell asleep; a happy and contented man.

They gathered in the ornate splendour of the lobby inside the House of Lords, but nothing could prepare them for the effect of the lavish decoration inside the Chamber itself, where the centrepiece of the golden throne dominated the far end and the red benches and elaborate stained-glass windows and paintings contrasted richly with the wooden panelling.

It was truly awe-inspiring, from the decorated ceiling above, to the blue and gold patterned carpet below. It spoke of sumptuous grandeur, pomp and ceremony, wealth and power.

Alex stood with Alastair and Michael in the Lords' Lobby, waiting to enter. He was a junior barrister about to give the presentation of a lifetime. Silks were the order of the day in this illustrious setting, and he had yet to find out whom he was up against, as the King's Counsel appointed by Sir Roger Caitiff Associates had fallen sick at the last minute and his replacement had not yet appeared.

Unbidden, Alex's thoughts returned to early the previous day, when he and Michael had been summoned to Sir John Pemberton's office to be told in no uncertain terms that if they persisted in representing their clients in this appeal, they should consider looking for a new set of chambers. He would be quite happy to recommend a K.C., a close friend of his, as well as a junior barrister to take their places.

Alex and Michael had exchanged a glance of mutual understanding and Alex had replied, "In that case, after the appeal, when our current case load has been fulfilled, we shall indeed take your advice and look for a tenancy elsewhere." They thanked him for his time, and left the room.

Once they were outside in the corridor, Alex had remarked, "He's afraid of something."

Michael agreed and called him a very rude name, which fortunately no one heard.

At the back of the Lords' Chamber, sitting on the raised, raked wooden benches, Mhairi and Rupert, proud and delighted prospective grandparents, having come to stay for Christmas, had some news of their own to impart. After a lot of heart-searching and consideration, they had made the difficult decision that they were going to move back to England permanently, taking up residence in the Park Lane mansion.

It had proved impossible these past months to make a full contribution to the running of the shipyard from three thousand miles away. They felt they had worked hard for many years and deserved to be able to take on their new responsibility without additional stress. Besides, Rupert wanted to put his great wealth to good use.

Along with everything else, he had inherited his father's title and was now a Baronet with all the responsibilities that entailed. He could still support the excellent work carried out in the musical world in Nova Scotia as well as here in Great Britain, and he wanted to become something of a patron of the arts. But most importantly, they wanted to be near their daughter and her family and watch their grandchild grow up, something they had obviously missed with Katherine.

She was overjoyed, and felt they had made a good decision. "Now we can all be together. No more meetings and partings," she said, something that had become very important to her.

Next to her sat Mary, lovingly turning her wedding ring; for Michael and she were married, just. They had wanted a very quiet ceremony with only their families present and this they had achieved a week ago.

Katherine and Alex had understood, and were grateful as Katherine did not relish the prospect of the journey to Cairnmor in her present state of queasiness. She linked her arm through her best friend's. She was looking forward to having her here in London. They smiled at each other.

Lily, Gordon and Fiona looked on, overawed by the setting – overawed by the magnitude of the responsibility resting on Alex's shoulders. They pointed out the ceiling to Ross and Eve next to them, looking at the patterns within the gold squares that framed each design. John and Marion found it almost impossible to believe where they were.

Father McPhee chatted to Robbie, who wondered how their Lordships slept at night, remarking drily that, "Those benches don't look too comfortable and where are the blankets?" When Father McPhee told him not to be a daft beggar, Robbie regarded him with one of his rare smiles and an irrepressible twinkle in his eye, saying, "Well it is the *House* of Lords, isn't it? Och, do they not sleep here in their own house? Poor wee things!" and proceeded to adjust the cuffs of his new suit, his lips twitching.

Father McPhee nudged him and the two old friends laughed.

"Just a little joke," said the fisherman.

"A *very* little one!" rejoined the priest, indicating how small by putting his finger and his thumb virtually together.

Then, they were invited to stand. The proceedings were about to begin.

Michael waited in the background, his face pale. Alex stood there expectantly, every nerve tingling, his senses heightened. Alastair placed his hand on his son's shoulder: a very proud father, which Alex acknowledged with a slightly nervous smile, as much as he could manage.

Alex recalled Katherine's kiss on his cheek, telling him she loved him. He had to make this the best presentation of his life. It was the most important case of his career, but it was a personal one as well as professional.

Then the opposing solicitors and junior barristers came along the corridor into the lobby. They were late. There were five in all and they were followed by the replacement Silk. Alex couldn't quite see who it was, as his sight-line was blocked by a junior barrister. When this cleared, Alex gave a start.

His opposite number was Sir John Pemberton, K.C. He did not acknowledge Alex in any way as he arrived, nor as they were ushered into the Lords' Chamber and shown to their seats – the Appellants to the right and the Respondents to the left, facing down the Chamber towards the throne behind the wooden Bar, intricately carved and situated in the centre of the aisle.

Everyone stood as the five Law Lords entered the Chamber. They were informally dressed; no judicial robes were worn during appellate hearings, but the speaker was present, sitting on the Woolsack in the centre of the Chamber, and a clerk was at the large desk in front of the Bar.

As the Appellant, Alex was the first to present his case. He stood up and looked around him, drawing strength from the historical significance and beauty of his surroundings. A hushed, expectant atmosphere pervaded the Chamber. He took his time, preparing himself. Then Alex took a deep breath and began to speak, his words clear and his voice steady.

"Cairnmor is one of the Outer Isles, situated some eighty miles off the West Coast mainland of Scotland. It is a remote land, twenty-two miles in length and eight miles wide, a place of great beauty and undisturbed wilderness, a haven for wildlife, a land of white sandy beaches and inland fertile plains, a land where awe-inspiring mountains connect precipitously with the sea.

"It is a land that opens a path through history, encompassing the Vikings, the Celts, the Stuarts, the Clans and the Christian Church together with a vibrant Gaelic culture. It has a unique sense of community, forged through common purpose and the need to survive. It is subject to violent Atlantic storms, a land that can be isolated for weeks or even months at a time and where the islanders have to be self-reliant and self-sufficient.

"The principal economy is crofting. Tenants have the right to farm the enclosed land surrounding their croft or dwelling place, as well as common grazing rights on the machair, the fertile plain behind the coastal dunes. Each crofter also has a strip of land allocated to him on the machair upon which to grow arable crops and another on the peat bogs for fuel.

"There is no electricity and a Royal Mail steamer from the mainland brings in supplies and takes out produce and livestock once a week; provided, of course, the weather is favourable.

"It is a hard way of life: the islanders are dependent upon their own industry and skill. But it is a rewarding and settled life and moreover, it is of *their* choosing. It is a way of life evolved and handed down through countless generations, a way of life unchanged because it is successful. There is no doubt that the islanders would enjoy electricity and hot running water in their cottages. But these things are luxuries and not essential for survival. And survival is of the essence here.

"It is my intention, my Lords, in this presentation, to look at each of the relevant proposed changes in turn, within the context of legislation, citing case law and stating the objections of the people of Cairnmor, showing that the proposed changes are both impractical and unwelcome.

"The islanders know their land better than anyone; they know and understand the difficulties and hardships these changes will create. They are not changes for the better; they will not improve the crofters' lives. On the contrary, as I shall show, they will only serve to increase hardship and cause uncertainty.

"To build a Championship golf course and other amenities on the land known as the 'Machair'.

"The Land Settlement Act (Scotland) of 1919 was intended to provide land for men returning home after the Great War, where they could grow crops for food and have the right to graze their animals on common land. It was not intended in law that this land should be used to build professional-sized golf courses with all the associated buildings and amenities. This applies to the people of Cairnmor especially, with their reliance upon the land to grow crops in order to survive.

"The tenants are unanimous in their opposition to this scheme. It would deprive them of their legal right to graze their animals and reduce the amount of land available for them to grow food.

"To build a new hotel in South Lochaberdale and construct an access road to it.

"While the residents accept that a better road system on the island would benefit communication and safety, they feel there is no need for a new hotel to be built. The present hotel is a Victorian building of great charm and character and is a well-loved landmark in Lochaberdale. To demolish it in order to build a car park is tantamount to wanton destruction. I refer your Lordships to Wallace versus McCluskey Ltd (1924).

"The building of a new hotel in the proposed location would involve the demolition of a small crofting township, which contravenes the Land Settlement Act of 1922. The present tenants would lose their homes and their livelihoods.

"The harbour is to be extended to enclose the entire northern shore by Lochaberdale.

"At the end of the last century, this exact scheme was tried. In creating an extra 'arm' to the harbour, the tidal flow of the sea loch was altered and the southern shore began to silt up, thus preventing the free movement of larger, deep-keeled vessels in or out of the harbour. It took several years after the demolition and removal of the constructions for the balance to be restored. I refer your Lordships to Gilgarry and McBray versus Ling Fisheries Ltd (1904).

"The steamer is an essential lifeline for the islanders. Without easy access to the harbour their main supply, export and communication routes would be severely restricted.

"Peat bogs are to be drained and the land turned into moorland suitable for grouse shooting.

"There is sufficient moorland on Cairnmor without resorting to drainage of the peat bogs. Peat is the principal fuel on the island as there are very few trees to cut down for wood. It is too expensive to import coal from the mainland. If the peat bogs were drained, it would be a pointless and expensive exercise with very little gain but, most importantly, would leave the islanders without sufficient fuel for cooking, heating and essential repairs.

"I can find no case law to support this, nor precedents. But fuel is necessary for survival. In order to preserve supplies, only the amount needed is dug each year. The methods used, unchanged over hundreds of years, have ensured a lasting and adequate supply of fuel. To lessen this would undermine security of tenure.

"Any changes on the scale proposed by the new Laird would inflict insecurity and potential disaster on his tenants." Alex paused, expecting questions, but none were forthcoming.

278

The five Law Lords sat intent; not interrupting, but paying close attention. He continued.

"I now turn to matters of notice. One document only was sent to Cairnmor outlining the owner's intentions: a document received ten days before the expiry date for objections to be lodged with the Land Court. Given the remote location of the island, it would be very easy to assume that the new owner did not wish his tenants to offer any objection to his plans, given their controversial nature.

"No prior official notification has been given publicly or privately to any tenant *not* affected by these changes that their agreements would not be renewed or new ones issued. This is a new and disturbing development discovered quite by chance on application to the Land Court in Edinburgh for a Transfer of Title in an existing tenancy.

"Threats, attempted bribery and coercion also took place at the hands of two solicitors, acting as agents of Sir Roger Caitiff Associates, who came to Cairnmor in the spring of this year. Tenancy agreements were also physically removed from the possession of several tenants, without the tenants' permission. My Lords, sworn affidavits testifying to these actions are before you."

The senior Law Lord, Lord Applegate spoke. "This is disturbing evidence; very disturbing indeed. These events have not been given sufficient attention in the lower courts. It is my understanding that the affidavits were drawn up at the time of the agents' visit, is that correct?"

"Yes, my Lord."

"What were the rather unusual circumstances leading to a qualified solicitor," he referred to the papers in his hand, "Mr Alastair Stewart, of Stewart, Patterson and Faraday, being present at the time?"

"Pure chance, my Lord. My father, the solicitor in question, was recovering from pneumonia and had been resident on Cairnmor for some time in the care of my fiancée, now my wife, intending to return home once he was well enough.

"As the sitting tenant, the agents came to her cottage to perform their paid duty, unaware, until such time as he chose to reveal his identity, that the other person present in the room was a solicitor. You have his testimony before you.

"On discovering the extent of the attempted bribes and coercion throughout the island, my father made a point of recording each instance. He also recovered the illegally removed documents and returned them to their rightful owners."

The Law Lords were silent. It was clear they took a grave view of these events, but Lord Applegate's expression revealed a certain admiration for the way in which Alastair had dealt with these matters.

"Please continue, Mr Stewart."

"Thank you, my Lord. I beg leave of your Lordships, to introduce some further information which has only just come to light and was not possible to include in the original submissions."

The senior Law Lord gave his assent by inclining his head.

Alex continued. "Last week, the tenants affected by the changes were served with eviction notices rather than notification regarding non-renewal of tenancy agreements as had been originally stated by the new Laird. This clearly contravenes both the conditions of a secure tenancy not yet up for renewal, which these are, and the fact that the whole matter is on Appeal. I refer your Lordships to Douglas versus Glasgow City Council (1921) and Donaldson versus Willis and Garrard Ltd (1927).

"My colleague, Mr Granger, has just returned from Cairnmor bringing one of the letters with him, and has had sight of identical letters being served on other tenants. This letter is addressed to my wife under her maiden name."

"Is it possible to see this document?"

"It is, my Lord," and Michael passed Katherine's letter to the clerk at the large table, who took it to Lord Applegate. "Thank you, Mr Stewart, you may continue."

"Thank you, my Lord."

Alex then brought complex points of law into his presentation; citing relevant cases and precedents pertinent to the appeal. The Chamber was quiet, its occupants attentive; his eloquence conveying meaning and substance. With impeccable timing, he presented his conclusion:

"And so, my Lords, to sum up. The crofting way of life is an ancient one, a hard and precarious one. It takes a remarkable type of person to sustain it and make a success of it. The proposed changes would erode the freedom of both the individual and, in this case the community, to choose and sustain a unique way of life.

"Surely no landlord has the right to impose large scale alterations upon his tenants if collectively they oppose his wishes. It is better to work together to achieve mutually beneficial and compatible aims rather than displacement by heavy-handed tactics.

"The people of Cairnmor are not afraid of change; indeed change is welcome. But like common law, which is the foundation and guiding principle of justice in this country, it should be a gradual process, tried and tested and found to be substantive and sustainable, the precedent of sound practice protected by precedent in law. This is a fundamental principle which I hope your Lordships will appreciate and feel able to uphold in this, the highest Court of Appeal in the land."

"Thank you very much indeed," said Lord Applegate. "I have no questions at present." He conferred briefly with his colleagues, who also did not have anything to ask.

So Alex sat down. Michael gave him a subtle thumbs-up and Alastair winked at him. He relaxed for the time being and waited to hear the evidence given by Sir John Pemberton on behalf of the Respondents.

"My Lords," he said, coming to the Bar, his attitude pompous and over-confident. "I thank my friend for his statements. I shall keep mine as brief as possible, because I believe we have the law on our side and the matter should be easily disposed of."

Alex saw Lord Cameron's head come up, regarding the K.C. with a piercing look.

"The Island of Cairnmor is a poor, backward island of disparate communities who scratch a subsistence living from the soil. The standard of education is poor and statistically, the general population have a lower level of intelligence than the mainland average."

It was impossible not be aware of the collective intake of breath from the people on the visitors' benches behind Alex. It certainly did not go unnoticed by Lord Applegate. Notwithstanding this, the Silk continued.

"There are no roads to speak of; just stony tracks. There are no motor vehicles, apart from a post bus, so communication is slow and cumbersome. They are very behind the times. There is one doctor for the entire population and a heavy reliance on out-dated herbal and traditional remedies. Most of the crofters are illiterate and speak Gaelic, an old-fashioned and out-dated language."

"Has your client ever visited Cairnmor?"

"No, Lord Cameron."

"Why not?"

"He has not yet had that opportunity."

"I would have thought it very risky to purchase an island without first having seen it." He paused, then said, pondering the question: "It is obvious that we are being presented with two very different impressions of the same place. From whom did your client gain this information?"

"From the two solicitors appointed as agents who visited the island on his behalf."

"The two gentlemen who tried to coerce the tenants?"

Silence. There was nowhere to hide. Then, quietly, reluctantly, "Yes, my Lord. But they are no longer in my client's employ."

"I should hope not. And yet your client still relies on their testimony... Pray, continue."

"The changes that my client proposes will bring greater prosperity to the island through tourism and its associated trappings, better transport links and communication. My client intends to become a benefactor of the island, providing better schooling and building a hospital."

"I do not recall any of this in your submissions."

"No, Lord Cameron, these are new."

"Has the present owner of Cairnmor made any of this known in writing to the tenants?"

"Not as yet, my Lord."

"Ah, but he seems to have had the time to serve his tenants with notices of eviction. Am I alone in detecting the presence of a certain inconsistency?" The other Law Lords either shook their heads imperceptibly in agreement, or smiled. "No matter, please continue."

Sir John Pemberton forged on. "It is the right of any landlord to do with his land as he will." And the K.C. proceeded to quote numerous precedents and cases to reinforce his statement. "If landowners listened to their tenants' every objection, then nothing would be completed. Tenants are notorious for making a fuss..."

"Mine are very good, actually," interrupted Lord Cawthorn, exchanging a smile with his colleagues. "But, please, do continue."

"If a landlord cannot do with his own land as he wishes, then there is no point in owning land. All of the proposals my client suggests will improve the economy, provide jobs and bring prosperity to Cairnmor. He and his associates wish to transform the land into a place fit for the tourist trade. There is a need to expand

and diversify if the land is to be made to pay its way and make a profit. The land belongs to him and his associates. They are at liberty to do with it as they wish."

"But only within the law."

Sir John bowed his head graciously in acquiescence. "Of course, Lord Cameron." The Counsel allowed his words to hang in the air. Then he spoke again. "There is one further point I should like to make. I should like to draw your attention to the fact that my friend's wife and his colleague's wife are both from the island. There is a close personal connection and Mr Stewart should not be presenting this case. It represents a clear conflict of interest. I ask leave of your Lordships to postpone this hearing until other representation can be found for the Appellants."

None of the Law Lords made any movement to fulfil this request.

Then Lord Cameron said by way of dismissal, "*Tapadh leibh*, Sir John."

"I beg your pardon?" replied the Counsel, with a certain element of condescension in his voice.

"*Tapadh leibh*. It's Gaelic for 'Thank you'." Lord Cameron glanced at Alex, Alastair and Michael. He saw that they understood, and he smiled to himself.

"That will be all," said Lord Applegate, and Sir John sat down.

"Mr Stewart, representing the Appellants, please approach the Bar."

It was Alex's turn to give his Rebuttal.

"My Lords, the Isle of Cairnmor is not a backward illiterate community, as my learned friend suggests. The people of the island would take strong exception to that statement. Of a total population of approximately two thousand, fourteen hundred speak Gaelic as their only language, five hundred and fifty-two are bi-lingual, that is they speak both English and Gaelic, and the remainder are solely English speakers. These were tourists and others present at the time the census was conducted."

"When was this census carried out?" This was from the third Law Lord, Lord Campbell.

"In June of this year, my Lord."

"Who was responsible?"

"My father, Mr Alastair Stewart, my colleague, Mr Michael Granger, the Factor of Cairnmor, Mr Ross Muir and the Priest, Father Aidan McPhee, with the help of Mr Donald MacCreggan and his post bus." Alex could not help smiling. Nor could Lord Campbell.

"A tremendous undertaking."

"Yes, my Lord."

"Continue."

"The education system on the island is not a poor one. My wife has the equivalent of a first class honours degree from Edinburgh University and Mr Granger's youngest brother-in-law attends Frensham College in Edinburgh, where he has a full academic scholarship. Both are products of schooling on Cairnmor."

"Are they the exceptions rather than the rule?" This was from Lord Applegate.

"No, there have been others like them. It is true that the perception of a lower level of intelligence on Cairnmor exists. But this is not an accurate perception. It

282

is as a result of the education system imposed upon the Scots by law; a law that was brought into force in the aftermath of the Jacobite Rebellion. Gaelic is the mother tongue on the island but school lessons and tests still have to be conducted in English. Unless a child is quick to pick up English, or has parents who speak and write it, there follow subsequent difficulties in tests, with low scores generally being achieved. In recent years, there has been some recognition of the need for change and a few lessons are now given in Gaelic as well as English. However, exams and tests still have to be taken in English."

"I see. Thank you."

"My Lords, with regard to health care on the island, the doctor and herbalists work together in treating patients. The herbal remedies are potent and effective; my father knows this only too well, as his life-threatening pneumonia was cured by these so-called 'outdated' medicines.

"Diversification and expansion and a vision for the future are all very laudable, but only provided a landlord has the best interests of his tenants at heart. With the ownership of property, comes a high degree of responsibility. A landlord does not have the right to impose his wishes upon his tenants arbitrarily; indeed, laws that protect the tenant are there to prevent unscrupulous landlords from doing just that. No landlord has the right to ride roughshod over his tenants without due regard to these laws and he certainly does not have the right to begin making his changes while the due process of law is still taking place.

"Finally, with regard to the 'conflict of interest', a point which my learned friend has raised, there is none. I am here at the behest of the people of Cairnmor. I am representing their interests, expressing their concerns to the best of my ability in my professional capacity. It is true that my wife and my colleague's wife both come from Cairnmor. However, that fact, together with our shared familiarity and the extensive knowledge that my instructing solicitor also has of the island, gives us a unique understanding of our clients' wishes and enables me to represent them in a true and accurate manner."

"Thank you, Mr Stewart," and with those words from the Senior Law Lord, Lord Applegate, the proceedings were brought to a close.

A few weeks later, the Opinion of the Lords of Appeal for Judgment was heard at a full sitting in the House of Lords. Alex and Sir John Pemberton and their associates were ushered to the Bar, where they took their seats, waiting for the judgment to begin.

The atmosphere was tense, expectant. All the hopes and future security of the islanders' lives rested on these next few moments. The Clerk rose and faced the Lords present in the Chamber.

"My Lords, a Report from the Appeal Committee in the Appeal: The King on the application of Fraser, Muir and others against Sir Roger Caitiff and Associates. Lord Applegate."

The Senior Law Lord rose to his feet. His Opinion carried an enormous amount of weight. Alex and Michael waited with bated breath.

"My Lords, for the reasons contained in the speech I shall give, and which is available in print, I would uphold this Appeal."

Shivers of anticipation went up and down Alex's spine. The Senior Law Lord had given his judgment in their favour.

They listened to his speech with close attention. As well as the detail of his Opinion, it contained praise for the manner and thoroughness with which the Appellants had conducted their case.

Next it was the turn of Lord Cameron: "My Lords, for the reason that he gives, and with some additional reasons of my own which I shall give in my speech, I too uphold this Appeal."

Michael looked at Alex. Two down, three to go.

Lord Cawthorn: "… I, too, would uphold this Appeal."

It was the same with Lord Campbell. Now only Lord Salcombe remained. He stood and began to speak: "For the reasons that he gives, as well as a few brief reasons of my own…"

Alex sat there, every nerve tense.

"… I, too, would uphold this Appeal."

A unanimous result. All five Law Lords had upheld the Appeal. They had won! Alex and Michael could barely contain their delight. But they had to adhere to formalities, wait for the Opinion to be ratified by all the Law Lords, then bow, turn, and walk out of the House of Lords Chamber, smiling broadly at their gathered friends and family up on the visitors' benches.

Once outside in the Lobby they shook each other's hands vigorously. Nothing could diminish their delight nor the utter joy of the moment. It would always be the greatest highlight of their careers. And nothing could match the sheer ecstasy and relief when their friends and family joined them.

It was a moment they would remember for the rest of their lives.

EPILOGUE

London
December, 1937

The mansion in Park Lane was host to a very special celebration. After the heroes of the hour, Alex, Michael and Alastair had been congratulated and feted, all the guests separated into smaller groups, sitting or standing in the drawing room, while Thomas performed his duties as butler, delighted to see the house come to life again.

Lady Mathieson watched her son, overjoyed to see him, to be with him; and glad that his lovely wife, Mhairi, was happy for her to continue living in the mansion that had been her home for so long. Her husband had been an old fool for all his business acumen but it had all worked out in the end. Thank goodness she was still active enough to enjoy it all. Unexpectedly, she had a lovely granddaughter as well. And soon, she would even be a great-grandmama!

Alex and Michael stood talking together. After today their lives would take on a new direction. They had resigned their tenancy at Royal Court and had not yet applied for another elsewhere.

"What do you think you will do?" asked Michael.

"I'm not sure yet."

"Mary and I are going to settle on Cairnmor. It's going to be the crofting life for us."

"I think I'll suggest to Katherine that we join you – temporarily, at least," said Alex, who felt that a short sabbatical from work would not do him any harm. He would take the opportunity to do further study on Scots Law and qualify as an advocate in Scotland, thus enabling him to take on work both north and south of the border.

"She'll be delighted," replied Michael.

"I know she will."

"What are you two hatching?" asked Alastair, coming over to join them.

"We're talking about moving to Cairnmor," said Michael.

Alastair regarded his son closely. "Well, if you are, then you can count me in!"

"I was hoping you'd say that!" said Alex.

The two younger men moved away to talk to their wives. Alastair stood watching them; saw Katherine give Alex a hug of delight – although from her expression, he could see that she couldn't quite believe it – and Mary's face come alive with joy and relief. Then he moved over to the fireplace and propped himself up against the mantelpiece, looking into the flames as they flickered in the hearth.

His illness had taken a lot out of him and, apart from the recent Appeal in the House of Lords, he had found it increasingly difficult to regain the old enthusiasm he had once had for his solicitor's work.

If everything happened the way it seemed at the moment, he would continue to focus on Rupert's inheritance and once that was completed, he would sell his partnership, making enough money to live comfortably. His second-in-command, whom he had always regarded as an excellent solicitor, could become senior partner – he was ready to take on that responsibility and the firm would continue to thrive under his guidance.

When he was completely fit and well again, he would resume his sea-going activities with the Royal Naval Volunteer Reserve, rather than just the shore-based ones as at present, and look around to see what opportunity there was for useful employment using his skills and knowledge, for he was not a man who could be idle indefinitely, nor at his age was it right to be so.

Alastair put his hands in his pockets and in doing so, felt the hand-written note he had received that morning: a letter from Roberta. She had asked after him and the family, and had gone on to say that she had heard that Alex's wife was the daughter of a Baronet and that perhaps she had been too hasty in her judgement; that it was probably time for her to get to know her daughter-in-law.

What an unutterable snob his wife was, thought Alastair. He had been intending to show the letter to Alex, so that they could have a good laugh over it, but on reflection, he felt that perhaps it was better to preserve some dignity, at least in Alex's eyes, of the woman who had given him, Alastair, two of the most wonderful children for which any father could wish. For this he would always be grateful.

Reflectively, he tore the letter into tiny pieces and threw it onto the fire. He would acknowledge it politely in a few days. There was no hurry.

Rupert stood in the middle of the room, surveying the scene. Yes, it was indeed the right decision to move back to England. They would take up residence here while they were in London. No doubt much time would be spent in Scotland, at the shipyard and on Cairnmor, if their daughter had anything to do with it.

Lawyers north and south of the border were working to sort out the details of his inheritance. He had been to see the Director of the Royal College of Music with a view to taking up a part-time post as a professor of violin and composition, at some later unspecified date, with the opportunity also to conduct one of the student orchestras. Rupert did not need the money; but he did need the music. It would be an ideal arrangement to combine with his duties as Chairman of Mathieson's.

However, there was one thing that he had not spoken of as yet; one thing that only he and Mhairi knew and had decided upon. He called for attention and the murmur of conversation ceased, as all eyes turned expectantly towards Rupert. He put his arm round his wife, smiling at Katherine and Alex standing close by.

"This has been an amazing day for all of us. But there is one more thing to add; one more thing that will, I hope, make it perfect. As I was leaving the House of Lords today, one of the opposing barristers, on discovering I was one of the 'Cairnmor Crowd,' as we have been dubbed by the newspapers, approached me and said that as they are unable to carry out their intentions, his clients are putting Cairnmor up for sale. Therefore," and Rupert paused for effect… "therefore, I have decided to buy it myself – for Katherine, for all of us."

286

Everyone crowded round Rupert and Mhairi, shaking his hand, kissing her on the cheek, thanking them both – Robbie, John and Marion, Ross and Eve, Father McPhee.

However, their biggest reward came when Katherine embraced them and said, "Thank you, thank you so much for doing that. I can't quite believe it! Is it really true?"

"Yes, my dearest, it's true," said Mhairi, smiling up at her.

Katherine was overwhelmed. "You really are the most wonderful parents," she said, deeply moved by their generosity. "I'm so incredibly glad we found each other, so glad it was *you* who turned out to be my real mother and father. You didn't have to buy an island to make me to think that, but I'm so very glad you did!"

And with unashamed tears of joy, they hugged, the three of them, for a very long time.

Later, after supper, Rupert and Mhairi sat together in the drawing room, surveying their lovely daughter, her handsome, clever husband, and their friends.

The future looked exciting. There was so much to which they could all look forward; so many possibilities. Who could tell where these might lead?

Rupert held his beloved Mhairi close.

They had come home.

OTHER PUBLICATIONS FROM
ŌZARU BOOKS

Changing Times, Changing Tides
Sally Aviss

Book Two of the Cairnmor Trilogy

In the dense jungle of Malaya in 1942, Doctor Rachel Curtis stumbles across a mysterious, unidentifiable stranger, badly injured and close to death.

Four years earlier in 1938 in London, Katherine Stewart and her husband Alex come into conflict with their differing needs while Alex's father, Alastair, knows he must keep his deeper feelings hidden from the woman he loves; a woman to whom he must never reveal the full extent of that love.

Covering a broad canvas and meticulously researched, Changing Times, Changing Tides follows the interwoven journey of well-loved characters from The Call of Cairnmor, as well as introducing new personalities, in a unique combination of novel and history that tells a story of love, loss, friendship and heroism; absorbing the reader in the characters' lives as they are shaped and changed by the ebb and flow of events before, during and after the Second World War.

Currently in preparation

Reflections in an Oval Mirror
Memories of East Prussia, 1923-45
Anneli Jones

8th May 1945 – VE Day – was Anneliese Wiemer's twenty-second birthday. Although she did not know it then, it marked the end of her flight to the West, and the start of a new life in England.

These illustrated memoirs, based on a diary kept during the Third Reich and letters rediscovered many decades later, depict the momentous changes occurring in Europe against a backcloth of everyday farm life in East Prussia (now the north-western corner of Russia, sandwiched between Lithuania and Poland).

The political developments of the 1930s (including the Hitler Youth, 'Kristallnacht', political education, labour service, war service, and interrogation) are all the more poignant for being told from the viewpoint of a romantic young girl. In lighter moments she also describes student life in Vienna and Prague, and her friendship with Belgian and Soviet prisoners of war. Finally, however, the approach of the Red Army forces her to abandon her home and flee across the frozen countryside, encountering en route a cross-section of society ranging from a 'lady of the manor', worried about her family silver, to some concentration camp inmates

"couldn't put it down... delightful... very detailed descriptions of the farm and the arrival of war... interesting history and personal account" ('Rosie', amazon.com)

ISBN: 978-0-9559219-0-2

Travels in Taiwan
Exploring Ilha Formosa
Gary Heath

For many Westerners, Taiwan is either a source of cheap electronics or an ongoing political problem. It is seldom highlighted as a tourist destination, and even those that do visit rarely venture far beyond the well-trod paths of the major cities and resorts.

Yet true to its 16th century Portuguese name, the 'beautiful island' has some of the highest mountains in East Asia, many unique species of flora and fauna, and several distinct indigenous peoples (fourteen at the last count).

On six separate and arduous trips, Gary Heath deliberately headed for the areas neglected by other travel journalists, armed with several notebooks... and a copy of War and Peace for the days when typhoons confined him to his tent. The fascinating land he discovered is revealed here.

"offers a great deal of insight into Taiwanese society, history, culture, as well as its island's scenic geography... disturbing and revealing... a true, peripatetic, descriptive Odyssey undertaken by an adventurous and inquisitive Westerner on a very Oriental and remote island" (Charles Phillips, goodreads.com)

ISBN: 978-0-9559219-1-9 (Royal Octavo)

ISBN: 978-0-9559219-8-8 (Half Letter)

Turner's Margate Through Contemporary Eyes
The Viney Letters
Stephen Channing

Margate in the early 19th Century was an exciting town, where smugglers and 'preventive men' fought to outwit each other, while artists such as JMW Turner came to paint the glorious sunsets over the sea. One of the young men growing up in this environment decided to set out for Australia to make his fortune in the Bendigo gold rush.

Half a century later, having become a pillar of the community, he began writing a series of letters and articles for Keble's Gazette, a publication based in his home town. In these, he described Margate with great familiarity (and tremendous powers of recall), while at the same time introducing his English readers to the "latitudinarian democracy" of a new, "young Britain".

Viney's interests covered a huge range of topics, from Thanet folk customs such as Hoodening, through diatribes on the perils of assigning intelligence to dogs, to geological theories including suggestions for the removal of sandbanks off the English coast "in obedience to the sovereign will and intelligence of man".

His writing is clearly that of a well-educated man, albeit with certain Victorian prejudices about the colonies that may make those with modern sensibilities wince a little. Yet above all, it is interesting because of the light it throws on life in a British seaside town some 180 years ago.

This book also contains numerous contemporary illustrations.

"profusely illustrated... draws together a series of interesting articles and letters... recommended" (Margate Civic Society)

ISBN: 978-0-9559219-2-6

Sunflowers
– Le Soleil –
Shimako Murai

A play in one act
Translated from the Japanese by Ben Jones

Hiroshima is synonymous with the first hostile use of an atomic bomb. Many people think of this occurrence as one terrible event in the past, which is studied from history books.

Shimako Murai and other 'Women of Hiroshima' believe otherwise: for them, the bomb had after-effects which affected countless people for decades, effects that were all the more menacing for their unpredictability – and often, invisibility.

This is a tale of two such people: on the surface successful modern women, yet each bearing underneath hidden scars as horrific as the keloids that disfigured Hibakusha on the days following the bomb.

"a great story and a glimpse into the lives of the people who lived during the time of the war and how the bomb affected their lives, even after all these years" (Wendy Pierce, goodreads.com)

ISBN: 978-0-9559219-3-3

Ichigensan
– The Newcomer –
David Zoppetti

Translated from the Japanese by Takuma Sminkey

Ichigensan is a novel which can be enjoyed on many levels – as a delicate, sensual love story, as a depiction of the refined society in Japan's cultural capital Kyoto, and as an exploration of the themes of alienation and prejudice common to many environments, regardless of the boundaries of time and place.

Unusually, it shows Japan from the eyes of both an outsider and an 'internal' outcast, and even more unusually, it originally achieved this through sensuous prose carefully crafted by a non-native speaker of Japanese. The fact that this best-selling novella then won the Subaru Prize, one of Japan's top literary awards, and was also nominated for the Akutagawa Prize is a testament to its unique narrative power.

The story is by no means chained to Japan, however, and this new translation by Takuma Sminkey will allow readers world-wide to enjoy the multitude of sensations engendered by life and love in an alien culture.

"A beautiful love story" (Japan Times)

"Sophisticated... subtle... sensuous... delicate... memorable... vivid depictions" (Asahi Evening News)

"Striking... fascinating..." (Japan PEN Club)

"Refined and sensual" (Kyoto Shimbun)

"quiet, yet very compelling... subtle mixture of humour and sensuality...the insights that the novel gives about Japanese society are both intriguing and exotic" (Nicholas Greenman, amazon.com)

ISBN: 978-0-9559219-4-0

The Margate Tales
Stephen Channing

Chaucer's Canterbury Tales is without doubt one of the best ways of getting a feel for what the people of England in the Middle Ages were like. In the modern world, one might instead try to learn how different people behave and think from television or the internet.

However, to get a feel for what it was like to be in Margate as it gradually changed from a small fishing village into one of Britain's most popular holiday resorts, one needs to investigate contemporary sources such as newspaper reports and journals.

Stephen Channing has saved us this work, by trawling through thousands of such documents to select the most illuminating and entertaining accounts of Thanet in the 18th and early to mid 19th centuries. With content ranging from furious battles in the letters pages, to hilarious pastiches, witty poems and astonishing factual reports, illustrated with over 70 drawings from the time, The Margate Tales brings the society of the time to life, and as with Chaucer, demonstrates how in many areas, surprisingly little has changed.

"substantial and fascinating volume... meticulously researched... an absorbing read" (Margate Civic Society)

ISBN: 978-0-9559219-5-7

West of Arabia
A Journey Home
Gary Heath

Faced with the need to travel from Saudi Arabia to the UK, Gary Heath made the unusual decision to take the overland route. His three principles were to stay on the ground, avoid back-tracking, and do minimal sightseeing.

The ever-changing situation in the Middle East meant that the rules had to be bent on occasion, yet as he travelled across Eritrea, Sudan, Egypt, Libya, Tunisia and Morocco, he succeeded in beating his own path around the tourist traps, gaining unique insights into Arabic culture as he went.

Written just a few months before the Arab Spring of 2011, this book reveals many of the underlying tensions that were to explode onto the world stage just shortly afterwards, and has been updated to reflect the recent changes.

"just the right blend of historical background [and] personal experiences... this book is a must read" ('Denise', goodreads.com)

ISBN: 978-0-9559219-6-4

A Victorian Cyclist
Rambling through Kent in 1886
Stephen & Shirley Channing

Bicycles are so much a part of everyday life nowadays, it can be surprising to realize that for the late Victorians these "velocipedes" were a novelty disparaged as being unhealthy and unsafe – and that indeed tricycles were for a time seen as the format more likely to succeed.

Some people however adopted the newfangled devices with alacrity, embarking on adventurous tours throughout the countryside. One of them documented his 'rambles' around East Kent in such detail that it is still possible to follow his routes on modern cycles, and compare the fauna and flora (and pubs!) with those he vividly described.

In addition to providing today's cyclists with new historical routes to explore, and both naturalists and social historians with plenty of material for research, this fascinating book contains a special chapter on Lady Cyclists in the era before female emancipation, and an unintentionally humorous section instructing young gentlemen how to make their cycle and then ride it.

A Victorian Cyclist features over 200 illustrations, and is complemented by a fully updated website.

"Lovely... wonderfully written... terrific" (Everything Bicycles)

"Rare and insightful" (Kent on Sunday)

"Interesting... informative... detailed historical insights" (BikeBiz)

"Unique and fascinating book... quality is very good... of considerable interest" (Veteran-Cycle Club)

"Superb... illuminating... well detailed... The easy flowing prose, which has a cadence like cycling itself, carries the reader along as if freewheeling with a hind wind" (Forty Plus Cycling Club)

"a fascinating book with both vivid descriptions and a number of hitherto-unseen photos of the area" ('Pedalling Pensioner', amazon.co.uk)

ISBN: 978-0-9559219-7-1

Lightning Source UK Ltd.
Milton Keynes UK
UKOW04f2125140715

255186UK00003B/38/P